A KISS TO REMEMBER

"It was business that kept me away, Francesca," he told her. "Nothing else." Slater attempted to take her in his arms.

"Fine. Then let's go have our dinner." Her voice was curt and cold.

"Sweetheart…" Slater coaxed, with an engaging smile, turning on the charm as he pulled her into the circle of his arms. "I missed you today."

"I could tell by the way you hurried back to me," she retorted, trying not to look at him.

Despite her cool tone, Slater knew victory was close at hand. He lifted one hand and tilted her face up so she was forced to look at him. "Francesca…" He said her name softly as he slowly lowered his head to press a tender kiss to the corner of her mouth. "I really did miss you."

Delight tingled down every nerve in her body. Surrender was only a moment away. Looping her arms around his neck, she returned his flaming kiss full measure. "I missed you, too," she whispered when they finally ended the kiss.

"Do you still want to go to dinner?" he asked hoarsely, nuzzling at her throat.

"I'm hungry," Francesca answered softly. "But not for food."

Kiss Me FOREVER

BOBBI SMITH

LOVE SPELL NEW YORK CITY

This book is dedicated to Margie Roth, a friend from the very beginning, the gang at Reader's Haven—Bob, Joan, Janet, Alice and Debby, and to Ruth, Jerry, Steve and Ken at 4-Seasons.

Also, a special note of thanks to Dr. Alberto Soto, M.D. and Cathy Perrine, true pals, for help with research.

LOVE SPELL®

March 2005

Published by

Dorchester Publishing Co., Inc.
200 Madison Avenue
New York, NY 10016

ISBN 0-505-52599-2

The name "Love Spell" and its logo are trademarks of Dorchester Publishing Co., Inc.

Printed in the United States of America.

Visit us on the web at www.dorchesterpub.com.

Chapter One

Havana, Cuba—February, 1850

Francesca Marie Salazar MacKenzie was annoyed. *"No,"* she thought irritably, *"'annoyed' is much too mild a word for my current mood."*

She was angry.

It was already getting dark outside, and still, Slater, her husband of just three months, hadn't returned from his business meeting. In agitation, Francesca strode to the window of her hotel suite and pushed aside the heavy drape to get a good view of the street below. When she could see no sign of him, her cheeks flushed with high color and her dark eyes sparked with vexation.

"Where is he?!" the dark-haired, eighteen-year-old beauty fumed out loud to herself. "He should have been back hours ago!"

Francesca began to pace the room again, her fury with Slater growing with each passing minute. When he'd left early that afternoon, he'd promised his appointment would be over in plenty of time for them to dine together. She'd been so excited over the prospect of spending an intimate evening together that she'd worn her ebony hair down in a tumble of soft loose curls around her shoulders, just the way he liked it. Because she'd wanted the evening to be memorable, she'd even donned the low-cut, full-skirted teal gown that she knew was one of his favorites. She had important, wonderful news, and she'd hardly been able to wait for tonight, so she could get him alone and tell him. Now, though as the hours passed and he hadn't returned or sent word, her mood of eager anticipation had soured.

Aggravated, Francesca let the drape drop back and then turned away to go sit on the side of the bed. It was bad enough that she'd had to live in this hotel room since she'd eloped with the handsome, Louisiana plantation owner against her widowed father's expressed wishes. But lately, Slater seemed to be showing more and more disregard for her and her feelings, and that hurt Francesca for she loved him madly. She had willingly given up everything for him—her father, her friends, even her considerable inheritance, and his insensitivity troubled her.

Francesca argued with herself that it just wasn't like Slater to ignore her like this, that it had to be only because he was so busy with his business negotiations right now. Even as she defended her husband in her own mind, though, she was forced to admit that he had changed during these last few weeks. Lately, he'd been gone almost all day, every day, and some times into the night.

Slater had really never explained to her exactly

what it was he was doing. Francesca assumed it had something to do with his plantation and, so, had been completely supportive as a good wife should. He'd promised that just as soon as his work was finished, they would leave for his home in Louisiana, Highland Plantation.

Francesca was looking forward to traveling to Louisiana for she honestly believed their life together as man and wife wouldn't begin until they'd settled into a real home.

Angry though she was, thoughts of her broad-shouldered, dark-haired, green-eyed husband made Francesca smile. She'd known Slater for only a few weeks when she'd run away with him, but she'd never regretted her actions for a moment. Her father had been furious and had threatened to disinherit her, but his threats had fallen on deaf ears. She didn't care about the money. How could she, when she loved Slater more than life itself? In the short period of time they'd been together, he'd become her whole world. Her hand settled protectively over the slight swell of stomach. Soon she would have his child to complete their love.

Francesca sighed. While it was exhilarating to care so deeply for someone, it was also a little frightening. She just wished Slater would hurry up and finish whatever it was he had to do tonight, so he could hurry back to her. . . .

The sound of Slater's voice in the hall just outside the door brought Francesca quickly to her feet. *He was back! Finally!* Her heart leapt at the thought. *He was here!* All thoughts of being upset with him were gone as she rushed to the door to greet him. She paused for a second to wet her lips and straighten her skirts to make sure she looked her very best, then she threw the door open wide.

"Slater, I'm so . . ." The rest of what she was going to say caught in her throat as she found her husband standing in the hall, deep in conversation with the beautiful, sophisticated Anna Melena. The black-haired, black-eyed Anna was several years older than Francesca, and tonight she was wearing a very seductive gown with a bodice that was cut far lower than her own. Anna's cleavage was far more voluptuous than Francesca's, and it was all she could do not to look self-consciously down at her own bosom. Francesca knew that Anna was involved with Slater's negotiations. But business associate or not, she couldn't prevent the surge of jealousy that pounded through her.

"Good evening, Francesca," Anna greeted her, completely unaware of the other woman's feelings. For all that her appearance gave the impression that she was a sophisticate, Anna knew she was far from it. She thought Francesca the most stunning woman in Havana and, also, the luckiest for she had won Slater's heart and his undying love.

"Francesca . . . Hello, darling," Slater had been standing with his back to her, and he turned to give her a warm, loving smile. "I'm sorry I'm late, but there were things I had to deal with tonight."

"I see," she managed tersely.

"Anna, if you'll excuse me now?"

"Of course, Slater," Anna replied. "We'll speak again tomorrow. Good night, Francesca. I hope you two enjoy your dinner."

8

Anna's reply added to Francesca's irritation. *This woman even knew of her most private plans with her husband?*

"Thank you. I'm sure we will," she responded, her demeanor cool.

Anna cast Slater one last glance before turning away and moving off toward her own room at the far end of the hall. She had fallen in love with Slater the first time they'd met, and while she knew his faithfulness and loyalty to Francesca were part of the reason she felt as she did about him, there were times, like right now, when she wishd it was her bed he was coming to and not Francesca's.

For a moment, Francesca stood there watching Anna walk away. She could feel the heat of her temper rising. *So! Slater had been with Anna all this time, had he?* she steamed inwardly. *How dare he spend time with her while I'm sitting here waiting for him!* Her posture was rigid as she turned back inside the room and left her husband to follow.

Slater remained in the hall for a second to gather his wits. He had seen his bride's look of annoyance and knew explanations were in order. Though he longed to be able to tell her the truth about what he was doing, he couldn't. He'd chosen to keep his work as an undercover agent for the U.S. Government a secret from her for her own protection. He didn't want her involved in anything that might ultimately prove dangerous for her. His assignment in Cuba was to encourage the native-born Cuban people to revolt against the Spanish-controlled government, and since Francesca's father was a very influential government official, it was best that

9

he keep her out of it.

Sometimes, Slater found it hard to believe that they could have fallen in love so wildly and married so quickly. He was generally a cautious man, not given to emotional involvement, but there had been something so completely captivating and disarming about Francesca that he'd been lost almost from the first moment he'd seen her. He loved her with all his heart, and for that reason, he knew he had to make peace with her. He wouldn't be able to rest until he did. Slater followed her inside and closed the door.

"There honestly was a lot I had to take care of personally, tonight, Francesca," he offered again, a half-smile curving his lips as he moved toward her.

"Oh, I don't doubt you for a minute, and I'll just bet that Anna was a large part of it," she answered with disdain, her dark eyes flashing the fire of her wrath.

"It was business that kept me away, Francesca, nothing else," Slater told her, attempting to take her in his arms.

Francesca was not about to let him hold her, though, and she tried to move away. "Fine, then let's go have our dinner".

Slater was not about to let her get away from him in that frame of mind. He knew she was angry with him for being late, and justifiably so. He wanted to make it up to her. "Sweetheart . . ." he coaxed with an engaging smile, turning on the charm as he pulled her into the circle of his arms. "I missed you today."

"I could tell by the way you hurried back to me," she retorted, trying not to look at him. She knew she

10

was in danger of becoming soft putty in his hands if he smiled that certain smile at her and kissed her the way he always did when she was upset. She couldn't let that happen right now. She was furious at him for ignoring her as he had, and she wanted him to know it.

Despite her coolness, Slater knew victory was close at hand. He drew her even nearer until they were standing a mere breath apart, her breasts brushing sweetly against his chest, his hips fitting intimately to hers. He lifted one hand to her chin and tilted her face up so she was forced to look at him. His glittering emerald gaze met her troubled, dark brown eyes unflinchingly, for he had nothing to hide from her. Anna was someone he worked with, a friend, nothing more.

"Francesca . . ." he said her name softly as he slowly lowered his head to press a tender kiss to the corner of her mouth. "I really did miss you today."

Delight tingled down every nerve in her body, and surrender was only a moment away.

"Stop it!" she fumed, trying to push away from him. "I'm not forgiving you this easily!" She was fighting against not only his sweet seduction, but her own betraying senses as well. She tried to glare up at him defiantly, but when she saw the gentle laughter in his eyes, she knew it was a hopeless battle of wills.

"Ah, sweetheart, I do love you so . . ." Slater sought his wife's lips with unerring accuracy. With infinite care and tenderness, he kissed her softly, gently, urging her to give him freely that which he would not force from her.

It always amazed Slater that Francesca alone could

bring out this gentleness in him. He'd always considered himself a cooly logical man—a man who never let his emotions rule him. Yet where his young, beautiful wife was concerned, he would gladly do whatever was necessary to please her. He loved her utterly and irrevocably. She was his life.

Slater's sensitive handling of Francesca quickly devastated her defenses. His heart-stopping embrace swept all thoughts of resistance from her mind, and, as she'd feared, she found herself wondering distantly why she'd been upset with him in the first place. Looping her arms around his neck, she returned his flaming kiss in full measure and loved every minute of it.

"I missed you, too," she whispered in breathless wonder when they finally ended the kiss.

"Do you still want to go to dinner?" he asked hoarsely, nuzzling at her throat.

"I'm hungry . . . but not for food," Francesca answered softly, promising herself she would tell him the news about the baby just a little later.

"Good," Slater told her as he continued to trail heated kissed down the side of her neck. "Food is the furthest thing from my mind right now."

She arched backward as the touch of his lips sent shivers of delight coursing through her. She clung to his broad shoulders, reveling in his sensual ministrations. There was something about this man who was her husband that left her wanting him always, even when she knew she shouldn't.

At Francesca's invitation, Slater lifted his head to gaze down at her. He marvelled at the perfection of her beauty. She was lovely. Her creamy complexion was flawless. Her brown eyes were an expressive mirror of her soul, and her hair . . . God, how he loved her hair. The silken, ebony tresses just begged for him to run his hands through them. Without saying a word, he gently swung her up into his arms and carried her to the bed to lay her gently upon its wide softness.

"I love you . . . ," Slater said as he claimed her lips again in a devastating kiss. Following her down upon the bed, he began to caress her, cherishing every inch of her slim body. His need to be one with her grew. Their loving was always this way—explosive and wild. It seemed they only had to touch each other, and all else but melding together fled their minds.

Slater worked at the fastenings of her gown, freeing her round, creamy breasts to his ardent kisses. Francesca welcomed his touch eagerly, and she encouraged him with her own caresses and kisses. He was just about to finish stripping the barrier of her gown away when a loud knock sounded at the door. Slater froze in frustration, hoping whoever it was would go away. The pounding continued, though, and he scowled. His thunderous gaze met Francesca's wide, questioning one.

"Who could it be?" she whispered, not wanting to stop.

"I don't know, but maybe if we ignore them, they'll think we're not here . . . ," Slater answered. He cradled his wife close, unwilling to forfeit the glory of their embrace.

Whoever it was in the hall was persistent. It became obvious that they were not about to leave when they kept knocking loudly on the closed door. "MacKenzie . . ."

With a groan born of pure misery, Slater tore himself from his wife's loving arms. "I don't know who this is, but their timing is terrible."

Francesca gave him a teasing smile as she quickly pulled her gown back up and fastened it to cover her nakedness. "Go get rid of them and hurry back to me . . ."

He gave her a quick kiss. "Don't worry. I will." Straightening his own clothing, he brought his raging desires under control, then went to see who it was who was so determined to speak to him.

The three armed, burly men who'd been hired to kidnap Slater were ready and waiting when he opened the door. The moment they could, they barged into the hotel room and attacked him. Caught off-guard, Slater had little chance. He fought valiantly against his unknown assailants, but to no avail. He only had time to call out to Francesca once before they overpowered him.

"Slater!!" Francesca screamed, terrified as she watched the strangers brutally beating her husband. She threw herself from the bed and tried to help, but one of the thugs grabbed her by the shoulders and shoved her roughly aside. Francesca crashed backward against the wall. She hit her head forcefully, and her body was wracked with pain for an instant before blessed oblivion claimed her and she slumped to the floor.

The last thing Slater saw before he was clubbed into unconsciousness was his wife lying lifelessly on the floor across the room. It was an image he would carry with him forever.

* * *

At thirty-three, the rich, slickly good-looking, black-haired Armando Carlanta was a man to be reckoned with. His reputation as a man who got things done had earned him the notice of Cuba's chief administrator, the captain general. In a private meeting, the captain general had promised Armando a position of great authority in his government should he manage to prevent the discontented native-born creoles from rebelling against Spanish rule. Power-hungry as he was, Armando had no intention of failing in that duty.

Armando waited now in the privacy of his elegant home with his long-time friend and associate, Ricardo Salazar, for word of how his plot against the American spy, Slater MacKenzie, was progressing. He was completely confident of his own ultimate success, and he lifted his glass of fine wine in salute to his own cleverness.

"To my plan," Armando toasted, his snakelike, obsidian eyes glowing in anticipation of his triumph.

"Indeed," the silver-haired, fifty-year-old Ricardo concurred. "May it succeed in every way."

"It will," he replied as he sipped his wine.

"Good," the older man gloated. He smiled as he envisioned the troublesome MacKenzie being tortured. "I want him to suffer for what he's done."

"He will, have no doubt about it. Then, once we've learned all we can from him, I'm going to take great personal pleasure in making your daughter a widow," Armando told him, returning his savage smile. He had long intended, with Ricardo's blessing, to marry his daughter, Francesca, and he was not

15

about to let her elopement with MacKenzie stand in the way of that goal.

Armando still remembered when he'd first heard that Francesca had run off with the American. He'd been shocked, then furious. Ricardo, too, had been outraged by her open act of defiance. He'd discouraged her interest in the man from the very start for they'd been suspicious of his activities, but not yet certain that he was a secret agent. When she'd refused to stop seeing him, Ricardo had even threatened to disinherit her. His disapproval had meant nothing, though, and she'd eloped with MacKenzie in direct disobedience to his orders.

Shortly after her elopement, Armando and Ricardo had finally learned the truth of MacKenzie's identity—that he was an undercover agent for the U.S. government working in their country to try to stir up a rebellion against the current Spanish rule. They'd realized that if Cuba won its independence from Spain, it might be annexed by the United States and then they would lose everything. The hatred they felt for Slater MacKenzie grew, and they'd immediately started to plot his downfall.

Armando's plan was simple. He had hired several henchmen to kidnap MacKenzie, after which they would take him to his secluded estate in the country. Once they got him there, they would force him to reveal everything he knew about the revolutionaries he was secretly working with, then they would kill him.

"My only regret is that Francesca has to be involved in any of this," Ricardo said, frowning at the thought of his daughter. Though he had cut her out of his will upon her elopement, he still loved her. Once MacKenzie was out of the picture and she'd realized what a terrible mistake she'd made, he would welcome her back with open arms.

"I regret it, too, but it will ultimately be worth it. When my plan is carried to fruition, she'll be free of him," Armando pointed out. He wanted Francesca, and he knew it was only a matter of time until she would finally be his.

It angered Armando that he would not be Francesca's first lover. He had always treated her with the utmost respect, and for his courtesy he'd been rewarded by her running off with another man. Perhaps, he realized, he had been too kind to her. Perhaps, she was the type of woman who liked a more forceful man. If that was the case, he would be more than willing to accommodate, and he would greatly enjoy showing her just how forceful he could be.

"I can't believe we have come this far. In just a few more days this will all be settled."

"Yes, it will. Have you decided yet what you're going to tell Francesca?"

Ricardo's expression seemed innocent enough as he answered, but anyone who knew him could see the cunning mirrored in his eyes. "Why the truth, of course. It will be embellished somewhat," he said with a casual wave of his hand. "But when I get done explaining things to her, she'll despise MacKenzie and be begging me for forgiveness for marrying him in the first place." He shot Armando a knowing look. "I will, of course, forgive her."

"Be sure to keep my name out of it. I don't want her

to know my connection in all this."

"Don't worry, my friend. There is nothing I want more than a union between our two families. She'll know nothing of your involvement in bringing MacKenzie down."

"Good," Armando replied, satisfied that Francesca would fall into his arms like a ripe plum once she found out about her husband's lies and deceptions.

Ricardo glanced at his pocketwatch. "Shouldn't we be hearing something soon?"

"Any time now," he confirmed. He'd sent his men out to do his bidding several hours before, and he knew if things went according to the schedule they'd worked out, they would be reporting back to him at any moment.

When his servant Juan appeared in the doorway of the opulent parlor, it was almost as if he'd conjured him up. "Señor Armando?"

"Yes, Juan, what is it?"

"A man just drove up to the back of the house in a carriage. He says his name is Luis and that he needs to talk to you. He says it's important."

Armando and Ricardo exchanged satisfied glances, certain that everything was moving along without difficulty. "Send him in."

Juan disappeared for a moment, then returned, hustling the big, brawny, swarthy Luis ahead of him into the room. At his employer's direction, Juan quickly left, closing the parlor's double doors securely behind him to give them complete privacy.

"Luis . . . we hope you're bringing us good news," Armando said, anxious to hear his report of the evening's activities.

"There is good news, yes," Luis hedged, his discomfort obvious as he clutched his battered straw hat in his hands. He felt out of place in the richly furnished room and more than a little nervous about what he was about to report. "We got MacKenzie. The other two are taking him out to the country now. They should be there by midnight."

"Good. What about the woman?" Armando asked quickly, sensing he had more to relate.

Luis tensed at his query. "There was a problem with the girl . . ."

"With Francesca? Where is my daughter?" Ricardo demanded, angry and frightened.

"What kind of problem?" Armando's voice turned icy with anger, and his eyes narrowed dangerously as he regarded the now visibly shaking Luis. He'd given strict orders that she was not to be hurt in any way. There would be hell to pay if she'd come to any lasting harm.

"She foolishly tried to interfere. We didn't mean for it to happen, but she was accidentally injured."

"Where is she?!"

"Outside in the carriage . . ."

Both men were already on their feet, rushing from the room as he spoke. They hurried out the back of the house to where the vehicle was parked and threw the door wide to find Francesca lying pale and unconscious on the seat.

"Dear God!"

Chapter Two

Though her head was pounding and every inch of her body ached, Francesca fought to come fully awake. She had to get to Slater! She had to help him! The pain-free black well of unconsciousness beckoned her temptingly back into its folds, but she struggled against it. She couldn't give in to the comfort of forgetfulness! She had to be strong! Slater needed her!

With a superhuman force of will, Francesca overcame the physical agony that was besieging her and dragged herself back to reality. She opened her eyes. Her surroundings were so blurry and out of focus that she had to strain to try to figure out where she was. After a long, confusing moment her vision finally cleared, and she stared around herself in profound disbelief. It was daylight, and she was in her bedroom in her father's city house! *But why? How?* Again the memory of her husband's danger assailed her, and she pushed herself up quickly to a sitting position.

"Slater!?" Francesca cried his name. *She had to find him! She had to help him! Those men had been beating him. . . . She had seen the blood and knew he was hurt. . . .* She was just about to throw herself from the bed, when a wave of nausea swept over her, stifling her attempt. A moan of pure misery escaped her.

At Ricardo's direction, Teresa, Francesca's maid from when she'd lived at home, was keeping vigil in her room, and she had been ever since he'd brought her there two nights before. Teresa was standing at the window with her back to the bed staring out across the lush gardens when she heard Francesca cry out. Turning, Teresa found the young woman sitting up in bed, looking pale and shaken, her eyes wide with fear.

"Francesca! Thank heaven, you're better! Your father will be so relieved!" She was there beside her in a flash.

"Teresa?" Francesca was bewildered. "What am I doing here?"

"Let me get your father for you. I'm sure he can explain everything."

"But I've got to go find Slater!" She was nearly frantic as she tried to bring the nausea under control so she could get up. "Those men were hurting him, and I've got to help him . . ." She remembered the sickening sounds of their blows as they had beaten Slater into submission and the terrible sight of him bleeding.

"Please . . . please stay calm . . ." Teresa tried to soothe her. "Wait for your father to come. He will help you . . ."

21

"No . . . I can't wait! It's been too long already! I must go to my husband!" Francesca threw aside the blanket, but could do no more as another, more powerful surge of sickness stopped her cold. Sweat beaded her forehead and she found herself gritting her teeth against the terrible torment of her illness.

Seeing her distress, the maid pressed her back down upon the bed and then rushed from the room to call her employer.

"Señor Ricardo! Come quickly!" Teresa called as she charged down the steps of the Salazars' plush home in Havana.

Ricardo had been reading in the front parlor, but he came running at her call. "What is it?"

"It's Francesca! She's awake and trying to get up, but she's sick . . . too sick."

The moment Ricardo had been dreading ever since the night of the kidnapping was upon him. "Is she due for any more of the medication the doctor left for her?"

"No, not for another two hours."

"I'd better see to her myself, then." Ricardo frowned as he started upstairs to his daughter's room. The night of the kidnapping, he'd rushed her home and immediately summoned the doctor to examine her. Ricardo had been relieved to find that her condition had not been life-threatening. Once he'd been certain that she was not seriously injured and that she would make a full recovery, he'd made it clear to the doctor that he wanted his daughter confined to bed for several days so she could rest and get over the trauma she'd suffered. For a nominal fee, the healer had been convinced of the need and had given him a large enough supply of a potent sleeping potion to keep Francesca abed for the better part of a week.

To Ricardo's dismay, it now appeared that Francesca's will was strong enough to overcome even the effects of the medicine, and it annoyed him, just as it always had. She had never been a tractable child, and it was for that very reason that he'd wanted to keep her quiet in the first place. He had to give Armando time to take care of MacKenzie before he started dealing with her.

Ricardo hurried into her room to find her trying to sit up in bed again.

"My darling, you must rest. Doctor's orders," he told her as he went straight to her side and tried to hold her and calm her.

Francesca would have none of it, however. She pulled free of her father's smothering embrace. "Slater's in danger, Papa! I have to find him! I have to!" In her desperation to go to her husband's aid, she managed to swing her legs over the side of the bed and get to her feet, but she was instantly overcome by her own physical weakness. She felt dizzy, and she swayed unsteadily.

"Francesca . . . my darling child . . ." Ricardo quickly slipped his arm around her waist and helped her back into bed. "You must listen to me. You have to rest. You were injured. The doctor insisted that you stay in bed." He did not tell her that the faintness was really caused by the drug he was giving her. Instead, he quickly prepared another, stronger dose. "Here, drink this. It's what the doctor prescribed for you . . . It should help."

23

Francesca felt so bad and so weak that she took the medicine he offered her, then fell back limply on her pillow.

"But, Papa . . . What about Slater? He's in trouble . . . He needs me . . ." She turned dark, pleading eyes to her father.

Ricardo stalled in answering her, hoping the potion would hurry and do its trick. He tucked the light blanket lovingly around her as he murmured, "We'll talk more later, when you're stronger."

"But this can't wait . . . Slater . . ."

"Hush, now," he insisted, and when she complied without argument, he knew the medicine was beginning to work its charm. He sighed a sigh of great relief when her eyes drifted shut moments later.

Ricardo called for Teresa to return to the room to keep watch, then went back to his book. As he settled back in, he wondered how Armando was doing with his interrogation of MacKenzie.

Armando was furious as he stared at the beaten man tied to the chair before him. He had hated MacKenzie before today, but now he truly despised him.

For a full two days Armando had supervised the torture inflicted upon Slater by the guard Manuel as they'd tried to force the names of the islanders involved in the revolution from him. It outraged Armando that the American had not broken under the painful, degrading physical assault, and he realized now, in frustration, that he never would. His lack of success filled him with an even greater need to destroy this man. He wanted to see him completely shattered before he finally had him killed. This was a most personal vendetta, and he would be satisfied by nothing less than his humiliation and death.

"So you still refuse to give us the information we need?" Armando demanded haughtily.

"I can't tell you anything, if I don't know anything," Slater insisted through bloodied, swollen lips.

"MacKenzie, my associates and I are quite tired of your little game. We want the names, and we want them now," he said coldly.

"I don't know what you're talking about or why you're doing this. I just want to find out what happened to my wife! What have you done with her? Where is she?" The terrible image of Francesca lying unconscious on the floor was burned into his consciousness. Even with all the agony they'd been putting him through, she remained foremost in his thoughts. *Where was she? How was she? What had they done to her? Awful visions of her, helplessly in the power of these cruel, amoral men haunted him. Had they raped her? Tortured her? They had been kissing and touching . . . so close to making love and now . . . ?* Not knowing Francesca's fate tormented Slater almost as much as the physical pain Manuel and Carlanta had dealt him.

At Slater's mention of Francesca, Armando believed he'd finally found his one weakness. Though he'd really wanted to keep any mention of her out of this, he decided to use her against him. Armando smiled savagely. "Ah, yes. Your lovely wife . . . It's quite a pity about her."

"What are you talking about?" Slater demanded, tensing as he sensed a note of perverse pleasure in the other man's voice.

"Why, I'm talking about your wife's foolishness. Her attempt to come to your rescue proved disastrous for her. She's dead, MacKenzie, and it's all because of you."

Unbearable pain shot through Slater. *Carlanta couldn't be telling the truth! Francesca couldn't be dead!* "You're lying!"

"No, I'm not," he said coldly, with utter indifference. "Things like this happen when you involve yourself in business that is not your own."

"Francesca's not dead!" Slater argued, not wanting to believe it. *I would have felt it if she was dead!* he told himself. *I would have known!*

"Don't doubt it for a moment, my friend," Armando snarled with hateful glee, "and you'll soon be joining her if you don't give me the information I need."

"No . . ." Slater's response was a groan as he tried to come to grips with the torturous news. Francesca had to be all right. . . . She had to be. . . .

Armando erupted at his continued refusal to talk. With vicious intent, he back-handed Slater with all his might, relieving some of his pentup frustration. He took some enjoyment in inflicting the pain himself. He was tired of this man's stubborness. He was weary of playing stupid games. "Talk, Mac-Kenzie!"

The pain of Armando's forceful blow was nothing next to the agony in Slater's heart. Memories of Francesca besieged him—memories of the joy they'd shared at their wedding, memories of her kiss and touch, and finally the terrible memory of her valiant attempt to help him. Trapped as he was in his own private hell, nothing Armando could do to him could be any worse. His tormentor's continued spiel of threats echoed around him, but Slater didn't hear them. All physical awareness left him, and a remoteness of spirit overcame him. He withdrew into himself to a place where nothing could touch him . . . not bodily torture . . . not emotional agony . . . nothing. Francesca was dead. Nothing mattered. His own death would be a release.

Slater's lack of response to his brutality made Armando even more angry. This man had thwarted him at every turn! He'd taken the woman he'd considered his own, and even now, he'd resisted torture that would have destroyed any other man. Armando wanted to see him crawl. Giving in to his white-hot fury, he brushed Manuela aside and began to beat Slater with methodical, diabolical glee. The fact that Slater still didn't react only urged him to be even more violent. He didn't stop until Manuel spoke up.

"He's unconscious, Señor . . ."

"Throw some water on him!" he ordered, caught up in his bloodlust.

Manuel did as he was told, but it still didn't rouse him. The guard shrugged helplessly as he looked at his boss. "It's gonna be a while before he comes back around."

Armando was slowly regaining control of his frustration. He knew he could kill Slater right then and there, but he decided against it. "All right, I leave him to you, but keep a close watch. I don't want to chance his escaping."

"Yes, sir," he replied respectfully, though he wondered how his boss could worry about this man going anywhere in the condition he was in. He was nearly dead now.

Francesca awoke to find herself alone in her room. She felt cold and oddly disconnected from her body. Not wanting to try to move, she lay perfectly still as she tried to recall what had happened. She had a vague remembrance of having talked to her father, but she wasn't sure if that had been earlier today or some time ago. Her thoughts were fuzzy and disconnected for a moment until the electrifying memory of Slater being in trouble jolted her.

Francesca sat up, and, though that same sickly feeling gripped her again, this time she refused to bow to it. Mustering what little strength she had, she rose from the bed and made her way to the wardrobe where her dressing gowns were kept. She grabbed one blindly, then pulled the rose satin garment on over the gown she was wearing. *Slater . . . Dear God, she had to find Slater. . . .*

Her undying love for her husband driving her on, Francesca crossed the room to the door. She was going to find her father and beg him, if she had to, to help her save Slater. Exhaustion claimed her by the time she reached the door, and she was forced to pause there, leaning against it, to catch her breath. When a little of her energy returned, she headed the rest of the way downstairs to seek help.

The door to her father's study was closed, but Francesca didn't bother to knock. She opened it without hesitation and walked in.

"Francesca!" Ricardo exclaimed, coming to his feet. It had been three days since she'd last been coherent, and though he'd deliberately reduced the amount of her medication that morning, he hadn't expected her to be up and about so soon. "What are you doing out of bed? You're ill."

"I don't care about me, Papa! Slater's in trouble! You have to help me!" Francesca pleaded as she went to him. Her face was pale and gaunt from the ordeal she'd just been through, and her brown eyes were wide and imploring with her very real concern.

"Francesca, darling," Ricardo hurried around his desk to help her to a chair. "Please, sit down."

"I don't want to sit down. I want to . . ."

"I know what you want, Francesca," he replied in a stern voice that warned her he would brook no argument, "but you must sit down and listen to me first."

It was a command she knew she had to obey. It wasn't often that her father spoke to her in such a manner, but she'd always known he was very serious when he did.

"What is it? What's wrong?" she asked in a strained whisper after she was seated before his desk.

"I have a lot to tell you. There's so much you don't know . . ." He let his words hang meaningfully as he returned to his own seat.

"I don't understand . . ."

"I know you don't."

"But Slater . . ." She tried to turn the conversation

back to her frantic worry about her husband.

"Yes, Slater," he cut her off harshly. "How I wish you'd listened to me from the very beginning."

"Papa, you're not going to bring that up now . . . not when I need your help so desperately?" she protested, not wanting another lecture on loving the wrong man.

"I want you to know the truth, Francesca. It's time I told you everything."

"What do you mean 'everything'?" A knot of fear formed in her stomach, and her expression grew even more worried and anxious.

"You'll listen to what I have to say?"

She nodded, not quite sure of what was to follow and more than a little frightened of what it might turn out to be.

"Your 'husband,'" he said the word distastefully, "is an American spy. He was sent here by his country to stir up the Creoles in revolution against our government."

Francesca stared at her father in disbelief. "No, that's not true. Slater's a plantation owner from Louisiana. He's here on business."

"He's here on business, all right—his government's business!"

"You're wrong!" she argued.

"Oh?" Ricardo gave her a challenging look. "Did MacKenzie ever tell you exactly what he was doing here in Havana? If he only had plantation business to tend to, why are you still here, living in a hotel room three months after your wedding?"

"Slater had some important negotiations to complete, and he told me that once they were done we'd go to Louisiana," she defended.

"I can tell by your expression that you still doubt me." Ricardo made a great show of unlocking his center desk drawer and taking out an envelope that contained the final, damning piece of proof against Slater. "Here, Francesca." He walked around the desk to hand her the letter, then leaned back against the desk to watch her as she read the evidence. "If you won't believe me, then believe your husband's own written word. This message was intercepted by one of our own men as it was being sent back to the States."

Francesca lifted a troubled gaze to her father's as she took the letter with a trembling hand. She glanced at the note, not wanting any of this to be true, but she immediately recognized her husband's handwriting. While that surprised her, it was the contents of the message that left her in shock.

My work here is nearly complete. My contacts have been most helpful. The woman, as you know, has played a great role, but there will be no continuing involvement there on my part. Disregard anything you might have heard to the contrary.

MacKenzie

When Francesca looked up at her father again, her expression was one of complete confusion and pain.

"This is why I warned you away from him, why I tried to convince you not to see him or have anything to do with him. Early on, I suspected he was involved in something illegal, but I wasn't positive of his identity. I couldn't reveal anything until I was sure.

31

But by the time we intercepted this letter and knew who he really was, it was too late, you were already married to him."

"Slater's really an American agent?" she repeated still stunned by the revelation and what it meant to their marriage.

"Yes, and he's determined to see our government overthrown and our way of life destroyed," her father concluded coldly.

"No . . ."

"I'm sorry, darling. I didn't want you to find out this way, but after all that's happened, I had to tell you. He will stop at nothing to topple our rule here. He only used you to further his cause. Having you for his wife gave him the legitimacy he needed to move about in our society. He never loved you. He took advantage of your innocence and naiveté. Perhaps now, you understand why I objected so fiercely to your interest in him."

Her father's words were like lashes from a whip, tearing at her heart with brutal intensity. She realized miserably that he'd been right about Slater all along. Proud woman that she was, though, Francesca refused to let him see the depth of her heartbreak. When she looked up at her father, her face was a stony mask.

"Where is Slater now? I want to speak to him." Her voice was void of emotion.

"I'm afraid that's impossible," Ricardo lied smoothly, fully prepared for this reaction from her. "You see, after our government officials detained him and questioned him, he was released, and he immediately left the country."

"He what?!"

"MacKenzie sailed for New Orleans several days ago." He paused to let his announcement sink in.

At the news, so bluntly delivered, Francesca's heart was completely broken. Her effort to remain in control faltered and her composure, so hard fought for, slipped.

"He's gone . . ." The words were strangled in her throat as she struggled to understand everything her father had just told her. *Slater had left her. . . . He had gone from her life without a word. . . . Slater, who'd said he loved her . . . Slater, who'd sworn undying devotion . . . Slater, for whom she'd given up everything . . . She'd been played for a fool.*

"Yes, I'm afraid so. He made no inquiry as to your whereabouts and left no message, Francesca. I'm sorry."

Her heart cried out that it couldn't be true. But when her gaze dropped to her lap and the note she still clutched in her hand, she knew there could be no denying it. Slater had lied to her about everything. Their life together had been nothing but a farce, and now he was gone.

Mortification filled Francesca as she thought of how she had given herself so completely to Slater. She had given him her heart, her body, and her soul, and while he'd seemed the ardent lover, it had all been an elaborate deception on his part. Everything he'd ever told her, every promise of love and unending devotion, had been a lie.

Ricardo saw her stricken expression and wanted to reassure her a little. "You know you are not to blame for any of this, don't you? MacKenzie was a very calculating man, and he took advantage of you. You were unlearned in the ways of such men. You knew nothing about the way they manipulate people to their own ends." *And you still are,* he added to himself gladly, hoping she never found out what really happened.

Francesca didn't answer right away. She just rose with all the dignity she could and said softly, "If you'll excuse me now . . . I think I'll go back to my room."

"Of course, my dear. If you need anything . . ."

"I'll be all right. I just need to be alone for a while, that's all. I need to think things through . . ."

With that she was gone, unknowingly leaving a very triumphant, very happy father behind.

It was much later that night that Francesca sat alone by the window in her room, staring with sightless eyes out across the moonlit grounds. It was warm, and a gentle breeze stirred the curtains. Generally, she would take great delight in such a sweet evening, but tonight the pain she was feeling was so great she was completely unaware of the beauty before her.

Tears traced silent, crystalline paths down her cheeks, and in a fit of fury Francesca dashed them away, resentful of the weakness they represented. The strength of her emotions angered her. After all she'd learned that day, she was furious to find that she still cared about Slater.

Her hand dropped to the slight roundness of her

stomach. Slater's child nestled there, growing beneath her heart. What was she going to do? How was she going to live?

A part of her argued that her father might have been wrong . . . that Slater really did love her and that this was all some kind of terrible mistake. But her more logical side presented the proof of the note over and over again, refusing to offer her any solace as it replayed the words in her mind:

> *The woman, as you know, has played a great role, but there will be no continuing involvement there on my part. Disregard anything you might have heard to the contrary.*

Francesca shivered as she tried to fit the Slater in the note to the man who'd held her in his arms and made passionate love to her . . . to the man who had created this new life she harbored safely deep within her. Had Slater's love really been just an act?

A sob tore from her throat as she gave in, at long last, to the turbulent emotions that threatened to destroy her very sanity. Turning away from the window, she threw herself across her bed and buried her face against her pillow to muffle the sounds of her cries. She did not want her father to know of her heartbreak.

When the tears were finally spent, Francesca rose from the bed and moved to her washstand to bathe her flushed, tear-stained face with cool water. Glancing up at her reflection in the mirror, she was shocked by the look of desperation on her face. Something hardened inside her as she realized how truly vulnerable and innocent she'd been before. There in the cold, lonely darkness of her room, she vowed solemnly never to allow herself to be hurt this way again. She was going to leave Havana and go to her father's country estate. She would have her baby there, and she would stay in the country and raise her child alone.

Returning to her bed, Francesca sought the blessed release of sleep. After long hours of restlessness, slumber finally did come, but as she drifted off, her last, fading thought was of Slater and the ecstasy that had been hers when she'd been in his embrace.

Chapter Three

Highland Plantation in Louisiana
Fifteen months later

Francesca's arms were silken tethers binding Slater to her as their naked bodies twined together in a sinuous dance of love. Slater was a willing slave to his wife's passion, and he surrendered freely to her ardent lead. Their lips met, and the boldness of her flaming kiss seared his senses. Heated excitement pulsed through him, and he began to move against her with rhythmic intent, letting her know just how much he wanted to be one with her . . . how much he wanted to bury himself deep within her hot sweetness.

Francesca shifted their positions, then, pressing Slater down upon the bed beneath her. She was fully aware of the fire of his need, and she gave a soft, triumphant laugh as she moved over him. Her breasts were a soft, velvet crush against his muscled chest, and her hips nestled tantalizingly against his.

"I want you," she whispered.

Slater gazed up at his wife adoringly, the deep, abiding love he felt for her clearly revealed in the depths of his green eyes. He had fallen in love with Francesca the first moment he'd seen her and that love had only grown with time. Raven-haired beauty that she was, she could have had her pick of men, and he'd been thrilled when she'd returned his devotion full-measure. Though they'd been married only a short while, Francesca had come to be his whole world . . . his reason for being . . . his life. Slater never wanted to be without her. He needed her always. Only when they were one, did he feel that she was completely his and that he would never lose her.

"I want you too," he murmured after a long breathless moment, the force of what he was feeling, making his voice a husky rasp. "And I always will."

Slater framed her face with gentle hands and drew her to him for a heart-stopping kiss.

"Then love me . . . ," Francesca pleaded.

The power of her words and her kiss set Slater's blood to racing and shattered the fragile control he'd had over himself. His need for her was all-consuming, and he could wait no longer to possess her.

Taking charge of their lovemaking, he rolled over, bringing her with him and pinning her beneath him on the wide softness of the bed. Famished for a full taste of her love, he kissed her hungrily. His hands began a restless foray over her slender curves, seeking out those places most sensitive to his touch. Slater skillfully roused Francesca's passion to a fever pitch, until she was crying out to him to put an end to the exquisite agony he'd created deep within her.

"I love you," he swore as he drew back to look down at her once more. His heartbeat quickened at the sight of her love-flushed cheeks and passion-glazed eyes. His gaze held hers as he positioned himself between her thighs and with a single possessive thrust, he entered her.

Slater was enveloped in pure ecstasy as the heat of her body sheathed him. This was his Francesca . . . his love. With her utmost pleasure in mind, he began to caress her again, drawing her with him to abandonment and beyond. They soared together, higher and higher, reaching for the pinnacle where they knew the climax of their excitement would burst upon them and leave them radiant with rapture.

"Francesca . . . I love you," Slater groaned hoarsely. "Ah, Francesca . . ."

Slater MacKenzie came awake with a start, the sound of his own voice waking him. He sat up and stared around himself in the darkness of his bedroom, his expression wild-eyed and disbelieving. Slowly, agonizingly, he realized the truth. It had been *the dream* again . . . the mirage his dying heart conjured up so he could be with Francesca. But Francesca had never really been there. He was alone . . . so very alone.

Slater drew a ragged breath as he raked an unsteady hand through his sleep-tousled hair. Sweat beaded his brow. His whole body was tense and he was shaking almost uncontrollably. He felt as if someone had stuck a knife in his gut and savagely twisted it.

Slater cursed violently and nearly threw himself from the bed. Only then did he realize he was still fully clothed. He wondered how long it had been since he'd stumbled up here to his solitary bed and sought rest. Minutes? Hours? Silently, he berated himself for having drunk so much whiskey before retiring. *How could he have forgotten that his sodden mind always played such vicious tricks on him?*

Stalking to the window, Slater stared out across Highland's lush grounds and rich, productive fields. He had everything a man could want—money, power and prestige—and yet, in reality, he had nothing. None of it mattered. He knew he would trade everything he owned in a minute for the chance to be with Francesca again . . . to hold her in his arms once more and to tell her that he loved her.

Ah Francesca . . . he reflected in pure agony. *How am I supposed to live without you?* Slater's shoulders slumped. He felt weary, defeated. He was a strong man; a man used to taking charge and being in command; a man accustomed to winning, but this was one situation where no matter how hard he tried he couldn't win. No one could conquer death . . . and as much as it hurt him to admit it, Francesca was dead.

Slater turned away from the window, finding no beauty in the starry sky or the moon-silvered countryside. The view seemed cold . . . empty . . . almost lifeless, much like he felt about his own existence right then. There had been a time not too long ago when he'd thought his future happiness had been assured, but he didn't feel that way anymore.

Memories of the terrible time surged forth and refused to be denied. Slater's hands clenched into fists of rage as he remembered all that had happened in Cuba . . . Francesca's death and his own months of imprisonment. Even now, he broke into a cold sweat as he recalled the endless, hopeless weeks of torture he'd suffered at the hands of Armando Carlanta and his right-hand man, Manuel. Only a timely rescue initiated by Anna, who'd summoned his lifelong friend, Nick Kane from Louisiana, to help, had saved him from certain death.

Though he'd been seriously injured and very weak at the time of the rescue, Slater hadn't wanted to return to Louisiana with Nick. He'd wanted to stay, to find out what had happened to Francesca and to make Carlanta pay for what he'd done. His friends had discouraged him, though, reminding him of just how very powerful Carlanta was. It had been a terrible decision for Slater to make, but he'd known his friends had been right.

Since returning to Highland, Slater's tortured body had healed, but not his tortured heart. The pain of losing Francesca was always with him. Sometimes, it was a deep, black despair welling up around him, like now, and other times, it was a subtle, aching sorrow. Always, though, the pain and grief were there.

As Slater stood alone in the middle of his night-shrouded room, he realized he would never be able to deal with Francesca's death until he'd gone back to Cuba and faced the demons that possessed him. Only then, if he survived, would he be able to find some measure of inner peace. Slater lay back down on the cold sheets to wait for dawn, but even as he closed his eyes, he knew he would not sleep.

"You're what?" Nick Kane, a tall, lean, dark-haired man, demanded angrily the next afternoon as he faced his friend Slater across the width of the study at Highland. He had ridden over to Slater's home to invite him to a barbeque he and his wife, Jordan, were giving in two weeks and had discovered that Slater was packing in preparation for a trip to Cuba.

"I'm going back to Cuba just as soon as I get everything arranged," Slater repeated, not flinching in the face of his friend's outrage.

"For God's sake, why? You've quit your job with the government. Why put yourself in that jeopardy again?"

"I have to go." Slater's voice was quiet, but firm.

"Slater—" Nick began, but Slater cut him off.

"Nick, I've waited too long already. I have to know the truth. I have to find out what happened to Francesca."

Nick fell grimly silent for a long moment as he accepted the inevitable. He could see the raw pain in Slater's expression, and he realized the time had finally come. Stubborn Scotsman that Slater was, when he had made his mind about something there was never any stopping him.

"I've always known I wouldn't be able to hold you here forever," Nick admitted with regret. As much as Slater's determination to return to Cuba worried Nick, he also understood. He loved Jordan more than life itself, and if anything ever happened to her, he would be driven to do the same thing. "But is finding out what happened to Francesca going to be enough to satisfy you? What about Carlanta?"

Slater's expression hardened at the mention of the other man's name, but his voice remained carefully disinterested. "What about him?"

"He's not going to like your coming back, you know."

"I'm not working for the government anymore. Why should he care?"

Nick gave a harsh laugh. "In case you've forgotten, you weren't supposed to escape from that quaint little prison he'd arranged for you on his plantation."

"I haven't forgotten." Slater said flatly.

Nick knew then that there was more on Slater's mind than just finding Francesca's grave. "Do you want me to come with you?"

"No. This is something I have to do on my own . . . alone," he answered with grim determination.

"You'll watch yourself around Carlanta?"

"He'll never catch me unaware again, Nick. You can count on that."

"I hope so," Nick told him with a smile to lighten their mood. "I certainly don't want to have to come down and rescue you again."

"You won't. Not this time."

Adrian Strecker was on the young side of forty. His height was medium, his weight average. His dark blonde hair was kept carefully trimmed, and he wore a close-cut beard now merely because it suited him to do so. There was nothing particularly outstanding or menacing about him, and he was glad. He blended in well with the populace and could pass through crowds without detection.

Those who knew Adrian, however, understood

43

what a dangerous man he really was. His bright blue eyes gleamed with a shrewd, cold intelligence, and his photographic memory was legendary among his peers. He had worked his way up through the ranks of government service, and, after having proven his worth time and again, he'd been put in charge of the covert work that needed to be done in Cuba.

The job itself was of a very delicate, political nature, and as such, not widely known. The United States—the South in particular—was eager to bring Cuba into the Union as another slave state, and it was working toward the goal by sending men to the island to incite a rebellion against the Spanish ruling class by the native-born people.

There was good news and bad news, however, to Adrian's achievement in working toward that goal. The good news was that they were making progress in encouraging the educated and landed classes to speak up against governmental abuses. The bad news was that after a year and a half of working without incident, two of his agents had just recently disappeared.

Slater MacKenzie's kidnapping and near murder early the year before had taught Adrian a lesson he'd never forget. When Adrian had learned of Slater's disappearance, he'd followed procedure and gone to his superiors to get permission to set up a rescue mission to save him. His efforts, and the comments he'd delivered to his bosses when they'd turned him down, had earned him a severe rebuke and weeks in the brig. By the time he'd been released, Slater, luckily, had managed to escape on his own.

Adrian now made it a point to warn his men before

they accepted their assignments that they were on their own if anything happened to them. He told them point blank that the government would do nothing to help them. Of course, what the government didn't know, couldn't hurt it, and it was for that reason now, that he was riding for Highland Plantation to pay his ex-best agent, Slater MacKenzie, a call.

Raleigh, the tall, dignified, gray-haired man who'd been the butler at Highland for over twenty years, knocked softly on the door to Slater's suite of rooms. "Mr. Slater?"

"Yes, Raleigh, come on in," Slater invited, turning away from his packing to face his servant.

"There's a gentleman downstairs, sir, who says it's very important he speak with you," he announced.

"Who is he?"

"He says his name is Strecker, sir, Adrian Strecker."

At the mention of the name, Slater went completely still. His easygoing manner instantly vanished. "Strecker . . ." Slater repeated the name out loud making it sound as if it were the most vile curse in the English language.

Startled by his reaction, Raleigh waited in silence, not sure quite what to expect next.

"Tell him, I'll be down in a few minutes," Slater finally directed, a muscle working in his jaw as he fought to contain the rage that filled him.

"Yes, sir." Raleigh hastened from the room, closing the door behind him.

It took all of Slater's self-control not to put his fist

through a wall. *Strecker! What the hell was he doing here?* He'd thought the cold-hearted bastard was out of his life forever. *Why had he come back now? What did he want?*

Slater took the time to bring his temper back in line, then left the room to meet with the man who'd once been his boss, and his friend—the man he hadn't seen in over a year, the man he'd hoped to never see again. When Slater descended the wide staircase that led to the main hall, he appeared coolly composed. No hint of his anger showed on his strong, handsome features.

Adrian had been shown into the parlor by the servant, and, after refusing an offer of refreshments, he'd been left alone. He was not a man used to waiting on others, but today he knew he had no other choice. This was important.

A man of boundless energy, Adrian paced the richly appointed room in restless agitation. He finally stopped by the floor-to-ceiling windows to gaze out across the lush gardens that surrounded the massive, Grecian style house. At the sound of footsteps in the hall, he turned to face the doorway and the man, who by rights, he knew probably hated his guts.

"Adrian," Slater said his name in a curt greeting as he entered the room.

"Good to see you again," Adrian responded, and he meant it. He hadn't seen him since Slater had insisted they meet shortly after his escape from Cuba. It had been a brief, curt encounter during which Slater had turned in his resignation. He had still been in pretty bad shape at the time, and it had deepened

Adrian's anger over what had happened.

Looking at him now, though, Adrian was relieved to see that none of Slater's physical injuries had been permanent. Outwardly, he looked the same, but they both knew he wasn't. Too much had happened. He'd been through hell and had lived to tell about it. Slater had made it plain when he'd quit that he'd wanted nothing more to do with Adrian and his operations, and though Adrian didn't blame him, he hoped he could change his mind.

"What do you want?" Slater didn't bother with any pleasantries. He knew this was no social call.

"I need your help," he answered with equal directness, not offended by Slater's bluntness. If anything, he was pleased that he showed any interest at all. It wouldn't have surprised him in the least if Slater had refused to even see him today.

"Forget it," he responded quickly, not bothering to ask him to elaborate.

"You know I wouldn't have come to you unless it was important." Adrian refused to accept his first rebuff. "You're the only one who can help me with this."

"And just where were you when I needed *your* help?" Slater countered caustically.

"Look, Slater, I know how you must feel and—"

"You don't know anything about how I feel," Slater cut him off harshly. "So why don't you just get the hell out of here and leave me alone?"

For a moment, Adrian almost considered it, but the thought of the agents in danger stopped him. He had failed his men once. He would not fail them again. Slater was the best. He needed him. "I'm not asking for me. It's Tebeau and Favre."

Slater's eyes locked with Adrian's. "What about them?" he ventured cautiously.

"They're missing."

Slater swore violently as Adrian quickly and precisely gave him the few facts he knew about their disappearances.

"It's a serious breach for us. There are tentative plans for an invasion near the end of summer by some Cuban expatriates. If the security has been compromised, it will have to be called off," Adrian concluded.

"Did Tebeau and Favre know the details?"

"Yes, and if they reveal any of it, a lot of lives will be lost . . ." Adrian let the sentence drop. "There's not much I can do officially. As far as the government is concerned, Tebeau and Favre never existed. I haven't even bothered to notify my superiors this time."

"What do you mean 'this time?'" Slater asked.

Adrian had never told Slater what had happened behind the scenes when he'd been held captive in Cuba. He hadn't wanted to defend himself, for he hadn't suffered unduly during his weeks of solitary confinement. Slater was the one who had suffered. Now, though, as desperate as he was, Adrian was ready to use whatever measures he could to convince Slater to help.

"When you were reported missing, I asked for permission to go in and rescue you. I was denied, and when I questioned their leadership ability, they got a little angry."

"Oh?"

"I was thrown in jail so I wouldn't take matters in my own hands. By the time I was released, you were already free. I thank God for that, but ultimately the responsibility for what happened rested with me. I vowed then and there that it would never happen again. Somehow I'm going to get Tebeau and Favre out of there."

The two men studied each other from across the room. Slater's green eyes bored into Adrian's blue ones. He could see that his ex-boss was telling the truth, and he realized that he'd judged him too severely. When he'd been held by Carlanta, he hadn't understood why someone from the organization hadn't come for him. Now, he knew why. There had been no one to come.

"How long ago did Tebeau disappear?" Slater asked as his thoughts raced ahead. His plans for his return to Cuba had already been set in motion, but Adrian didn't know that. It occurred to him that Adrian's need of him just might prove highly beneficial to his own cause. He would search for the agents and at the same time use Adrian's intricate network of contacts to seek the answers—and the justice—he personally needed.

Adrian gave an inward sigh of relief at Slater's question and hurried on to give him the rest of the information he had. "You'll do it then? You're back in?"

"If I go, I go as a rogue. I'm not back in the organization. I'll find Tebeau and Favre, and if they're still alive, I'll get them out."

"I can't ask for more than that. Use Rafael Ramirez for your initial contact. Your cover about having business dealings with him is still intact. He'll help you while you're in Havana."

"All right." Slater nodded, remembering the work he'd done with Ramirez during the months he'd been on the island. The sophisticated Cuban intellectual was a man of deep thought and great pride, who added legitimacy to the Creole cause.

"Slater . . ."

"What?"

"Be careful. Carlanta has increased his power since you were there last. We know he's a ruthless bastard, and your life is going to be on the line again. Stay out of his way if you possibly can."

"I know, I'll be careful."

They said their good-byes, and Slater watched from the gallery as Adrian rode off. He hadn't told him that he planned to do everything in his power to get in Carlanta's way and stay in his way until he'd destroyed him. He also hadn't told him that he didn't expect to come back alive.

Chapter Four

Rafael Ramirez was a tall, whipcord lean man just over thirty years old. His aristocratic, darkly handsome good looks coupled with his great wealth and distinguished family background made him a favorite with the single ladies, all of whom longed to get him to the altar. Playboy that he was, Rafe was wise to their ultimate goal. Having decided early in his life that he was in no hurry to tie himself down to just one woman, he made it a practice never to get too deeply involved. He enjoyed the women he courted, but he pledged his devotion to no one.

While most of society focused their attention on Rafe's amorous pursuits, there was another side to the man. He was not merely a mindless, wealthy Don Juan aimlessly chasing after hedonistic pleasures. He was also one of Cuba's leading intellectuals. He had studied at universities both at home and abroad, and during the course of those studies, he'd become firmly convinced that the Cuban people were entitled to the same freedoms enjoyed by the Americans and the French. Their revolutions had put the power back in the hands of the people, and he was committed to the belief that his people deserved no less.

Rafe was never one to react hotheadedly, but the abuses of the Spanish-controlled government against the native-born Cubans had driven him to take action. He had secretly joined the revolutionary movement and was using his position in the upper echelons of society to gather information for them. Rafe had also become the main liaison between the rebels and the American government, and for that reason, he was now riding toward the prearranged rendezvous spot where he would meet with Anna Melena, his contact with the rebels. He was pleased to find that the young woman was already there waiting for him when he rode up to the secluded grove of trees.

"Anna, I'm glad you came," Rafe said as he swung down from his horse and went to greet her.

"Your note said it was important," Anna answered quickly. In the nearly year and a half since Slater had been forced to flee the island, she had matured into an even more lovely woman. But the revolution was her life now, her one all-consuming passion, and when she wasn't in the city, she made it a practice to keep her attractiveness hidden beneath loose-fitting peasant's garb. If she couldn't have Slater, then she didn't want anyone.

"It is. Word came from Strecker late yesterday."

"And?" At the mention of the American, a rush of excitement surged through her. She tried to fight it down, telling herself that just because there was news from Slater's boss, didn't mean it had anything to do with Slater. But no matter how hard she tried to deny it, her hope that Slater was returning, was still there—as it had always been, ever since he'd left. She loved Slater MacKenzie as she had never loved another man, and she knew she always would.

"And Slater's coming back. Strecker somehow managed to talk him into it."

Anna could scarcely believe her ears. Slater was coming back! He was actually returning! Memories of that last night on the beach when they'd said good-bye returned, and she remembered how kind and wonderful he'd been. Her heart began to pound fiercely in her breast at the thought of being reunited with him. Maybe by now, things had changed with him. Maybe by now enough time had passed, and he'd been able to forget Francesca. . . . "When?" was all she could manage.

"He's arriving on the Gulf Stream the day after tomorrow, and I want you to be there with me to meet him. Hopefully, he'll bring us some news of how the plans for the invasion are faring."

"I hope so, too. We need to find out what's going on." With the rebel movement once again foremost in her mind, she turned her thoughts away from Slater and back to their current situation. "What exactly do you want me to do?"

"Go back and tell the others in your camp the news, then come here and stay with me. You don't need to worry about your reputation. You can have a whole wing of the house to yourself, and I will provide a chaperone if you want one."

"I'm not worried about my reputation. I trust you," she replied. She was surprised when Rafe gave a hardy laugh out loud.

"You are one of a very few ladies who do," he chuckled.

"You've never been anything but a gentleman with me, Rafe."

"And I'll continue to respect and defend your honor," he replied with gallant good humor. He had long admired Anna and the dangerous work she did for their cause. "How soon do you think you can get back?"

"I'll ride straight to our encampment in the hills right now. I have a few things to take care of there, but with luck, I should be able to make it back here by some time early tomorrow."

"I'll be watching for you. Do you have other clothing? Something suitable for socializing?"

"Yes. I'll bring my things with me." She was pleased that he'd asked, for it meant she'd be staying at Rafe's home with Slater for a least a little while.

Anna was nervous and more than a little excited as she waited on the dock with Rafe in his elegant, open-air carriage. Though she knew their situation was a serious one, she couldn't stop her spirits from soaring. *Slater was coming! He would be there any minute!*

Anna had fallen in love with Slater MacKenzie the first day she'd met him almost two years before when he'd first come to Cuba to work covertly with the revolutionaries. Slater, however, had thought of her only as a good friend, and her heart had been broken when he'd fallen in love with and married the rich and beautiful Francesca Salazar. Loving him as she did, though, when Francesca had been killed and

Slater had been kidnapped and tortured by the powerful Armando Carlanta, Anna had come to his rescue. She'd worked feverishly and at great danger to herself to set him free. Slater had been forced to run from the island to save himself, but not before he'd thanked her for saving him. He'd given her access to the hidden cache of money he'd left behind. With the money, she'd been able to care for her elderly parents and devote even more of her time to the cause.

Since Slater had been gone, Anna had prayed endlessly for him to return. She loved him and wanted to see him again. She needed to be sure that he'd survived the horrors of his captivity and to know that he was fine.

Now, at long last, the moment Anna had longed for was upon her. She clasped her hands tightly in her lap to quell their trembling as, heart in throat, she visually searched the deck of the Gulf Stream for him.

"Do you see him yet, Rafe?" she asked.

"No, no sign of him yet," he replied, his dark gaze fixed upon the ship, too.

Anna sighed anxiously. She remembered all too clearly how beautiful Francesca had been. So she'd chosen her gown with great care, wanting to look her very best for her reunion with Slater today. The dress was demure yet fashionable, and it set off her stunning figure to perfection. She hoped Slater would notice.

The Gulf Stream started to lower its gangplank, and Anna straightened beside Rafe, straining to catch a glimpse of the man she loved with all her heart.

"There he is," Rafe pointed out when he finally caught sight of Slater on deck, and he quickly jumped down from the carriage. "Wait here, I'll go get him."

"All right," Anna answered, unable to drag her gaze away from the sight of Slater descending to the dock. He looked the same . . . so tall and handsome and powerful. Her pulse quickened as he drew ever nearer. She wanted to follow Rafe to his side—to race to Slater, throw her arms around him and kiss him passionately. She wanted to tell him how much she loved him, how much she'd missed him and how very glad she was that he was back. Instead, Anna forced herself to act the well-bred lady. She remained where she was, waiting.

Slater was halfway down the ramp before he caught sight of Rafe making his way across the crowded dock to meet him. Adrian had sent him word before he'd left New Orleans that Rafe would meet him in Havana, and he was pleased. Although they had only known each other for a few months when he'd been in Cuba the year before, Slater considered him a good, trustworthy friend. He was glad they were going to be working together again.

"Rafe!" he called out. He set his bags aside as they came together and embraced like brothers long parted, clapping each other on the back. "It's good to see you again!"

"It's good to see you, too! I've missed you," Rafe told him as he paid one of the young boys hovering nearby to carry Slater's bags to the carriage. "I'm glad you're here. You look well."

"I am," Slater answered quickly.

"Good, then let's get out of here, shall we?"

"Fine, let's go." He knew the faster he got away from the waterfront, the better. News traveled

56

quickly, and he didn't want to make it too easy for Carlanta to find out he was back.

Following the boy who'd taken his luggage, Slater and Rafe moved through the crowds toward where the vehicle was parked.

"Another friend of yours came along to meet you," Rafe gestured to where Anna was waiting.

Slater glanced in the direction he'd indicated, and his expression immediately changed from puzzlement to thrilled recognition. It was Anna, and she was looking as beautiful as ever.

"Anna . . ." He said her name as he came up to the side of the carriage.

"Hello, Slater," Anna answered softly. She wanted to vault out of the carriage and into his arms. She wanted to grab him and never let him go. Instead, she dazzled him with a smile.

His emerald gaze swept over her appreciatively. "You look wonderful."

"Thank you." She beamed. "So do you."

He gave a small, self-deprecating laugh as he climbed in the carriage ahead of Rafe and sat down beside her. "I'm sure I do compared to the last time you saw me."

"It was pretty bad, was it?" Rafe entered the conversation after he'd directed the loading of the luggage and gave the youth a tip for his efforts.

"Let's just say that if I ever get the chance to return the favor to our friend Carlanta and the man who works for him named Manuel, I'll do it without a second thought."

Both Anna and Rafe heard and understood the controlled savagery in his tone. Rafe climbed into the carriage to join them and settled in the opposite seat.

He then directed the driver to take them home.

"I've heard of this Manuel," Rafe offered. "His full name is Manuel Garcia, and according to talk, he's one mean bastard."

"The talk's too easy on him."

"So, how are you now?" Anna interrupted, not wanting to think about that horrible time. "I've worried about you . . ." She put her small hand over Slater's big one as she gazed up at him. Her wide, dark eyes roved over his features, seeing some small scars from the beatings he'd suffered, but no lasting damage.

"There was no need. Thanks to you and Nick, I got home safely."

"But . . . ," she began.

"I've recovered completely," Slater told her a bit more sharply than he'd intended, and he looked away from her probing gaze.

"I'm glad." Anna heard the harshness in his tone and quickly changed the subject. "How is Nick?" she asked, thinking of his friend from Louisiana who'd helped her with the rescue attempt when no one else could.

"Nick is fine. He got married shortly after we returned to New Orleans."

"That's wonderful." Anna knew the woman who'd captured Dominic Kane must have been someone very special.

"They're very happy. Jordan's been good for him," he concluded. He glanced up at the passing scenery and grew increasingly tense. Memories of the last time he'd been in Havana tore at him with jagged claws, and he forced them from his mind. This was not the time to remember. Later, when the time came to face down Carlanta for Francesca's death, he would allow his wrath full rein.

Anna sensed the change in him, and realized how painful returning had to be for him. She, too, fell quiet. Slater would need time to deal with his own memories, and she would be there to help him in any way she could.

As Slater settled in at Rafael's home, a messenger from Armando was already being sent to the Salazar home in the city.

"I have a message for Señor Ricardo Salazar," the messenger announced when the servant answered his knock at the door.

"I will take it," Ricardo's servant answered.

"No, Señor Carlanta said I had to deliver it to Señor Salazar personally and wait for a reply."

"All right, come in." The servant directed him to stay in the foyer while he went to speak to Ricardo. He was back within minutes to guide the messenger into the parlor.

"I'm Ricardo Salazar," Ricardo announced. "I understand you have a letter for me?"

"Si, señor." He handed over the missive to the distinguished looking man, then stood quietly to await his response.

Ricardo ripped open the envelope and as he began to read the contents of the letter, a string of vile curses erupted from him. "Where is Carlanta now?" he demanded.

"He's at home. Do you have a message you'd like me to take back to him?"

"No. I must speak to him, myself. I will ride back

with you."

"Sí."

Ricardo crumpled the note and stuffed it into his pocket as he strode from the room. He called out to the servants to have his horse brought around, and within minutes he was riding full speed for Armando's with the messenger struggling to keep up. When Ricardo reached Armando's home, he was quickly admitted to the house and taken straight into the study where his host awaited him.

"I had a feeling you'd come," Armando told him, his expression almost amused.

"How could I not?" he demanded in irritation. "Are you sure about this?"

"Yes, I'm sure. He arrived just a short time ago," Armando told him brusquely, annoyed that Ricardo would question him. "One of the men I employ to keep watch at the docks verified that he got off the Gulf Stream and was met by Rafael Ramirez and a woman we haven't been able to identify."

"Ramirez . . ." Armando said his name slowly, pondering his connection in all this. "You don't suppose he's involved in the rebellion, do you? He's got as much to lose as we do."

"We've had him checked out thoroughly, and you can rest assured that he's not involved in any of it," Ricardo told him. "No, I think he and MacKenzie are just business associates, just as we discovered the last time the American was here."

"Then MacKenzie's using Ramirez?"

"I wouldn't doubt it for a minute, although I'm sure Ramirez is unaware of it. The only business MacKenzie came back here for is his government business. He's planning something." His expression turned thoughtful, then diabolical.

"Thank God, Francesca's at the country house. We've got to keep them apart."

"Do you really think it would matter? She despises him."

"And I want it to stay that way. I don't want them together."

"You don't have to worry, Ricardo. I have already put plans into action that will finish what I'd originally started with him."

Ricardo looked relieved. "You're going to have MacKenzie killed?"

"As quickly and as quietly as possible before he even has the chance to cause any new trouble."

"Good. I'll be waiting to hear from you that he's dead."

Armando nodded. "I'll send word as soon as it's been taken care of. Until then, rest easy. My men are watching his every move."

"I am counting on it, Armando. I don't want him anywhere near my daughter."

"Neither do I."

It was much later that evening, after Slater had settled into his quarters at Rafe's house and the three of them had shared the evening meal, that they gathered in Rafe's parlor to talk and enjoy a few after-dinner drinks.

"What did Strecker advise?" Rafe ventured.

"Nothing as yet. I've got to find the agents first, then he'll decide. But I'm not really here for him."

"What? He sent word that you . . ."

Slater held up a hand to stop him. "I agreed to

come down here and try to get Tebeau and Favre out, but I am not working for Strecker or the government. I'm here for another reason."

Anna and Rafe both watched him expectantly as he paused before finally broaching his true reason for returning.

"I'm here to find Francesca."

"But . . . but she's dead . . ." Anna blurted out in confused surprise. It hurt her to think that he still cared so deeply for the other woman even after all this time.

Slater looked up at them, the truth of his feelings showing clearly in his pain-filled expression. "I know."

"Then . . . ?" Anna could see the misery mirrored in his eyes and she understood the hurt and agony he was still feeling.

"I need to find out exactly what happened. I have to visit her grave . . . to see the physical proof that she's really gone from me. Do you know where she was buried?"

"No," she answered. "I never heard any more about her at all. I only know what you know—that she died the night you were taken from the hotel."

"No public notice was ever made of her funeral or burial, so her father must have kept it very private. I would imagine her grave is probably in the family cemetery somewhere on his plantation," Rafe offered.

"Wherever she is, I'm going to find her." His statement was fierce, and his emerald gaze glowed with feverish intent.

"But Slater, she's dead. It's time you let it go," he encouraged. Understanding him as only another man could, Rafe feared that Slater might feel compelled to take action against Carlanta in a quest for revenge after he'd proven to himself that Francesca had indeed perished, and he didn't want his friend to take the risk. Carlanta was much too powerful now.

"I can't. Not yet."

"Don't you think that if she were still alive, she would have found you?"

"I have to see her grave. Maybe then I'll finally be able to accept that she's really dead."

It was after midnight when they retired. The drinks Slater had shared with Anna and Rafe had not relaxed him. Instead, they had loosened the floodgates of his memory. Fully clothed, he lay on his back upon the bed now with his arms folded beneath his head, his mind overflowing with images of Francesca and memories of the few short months of happiness they'd shared.

Slater had not thought that his returning to Havana would affect him so profoundly, but it had. It was almost as if Francesca was alive and he could feel her presence near him. It seemed as if he only had to reach out for her and she would be there, warm and willing, in his arms. With a groan of despair, he rolled over and tried to sleep.

Chapter Five

Though it was past two in the morning, Anna was still awake. Her every thought was focused on Slater. She'd witnessed the great depth of the bitterness in him earlier that evening, and it hurt her to know he was in such pain. Anna loved him, and her love was strong. She longed to ease his agony, to help him forget the past and start a new life. More than anything, she wanted to erase the memories of his long-dead wife and replace them with new, loving ones of her.

Lying there in the darkness of her own bedroom, Anna envisioned herself in Slater's arms. Heat pulsed through her body as she imagined his lovemaking. She actually ached physically to be with him. She tried to put the sensuous images out of her mind, but they remained, taunting her.

When she could stand the fantasy no more, Anna rose from her bed in restless agitation. Her body was on fire. She wanted Slater more than she'd ever wanted anyone or anything in her entire life. Anna stood in the middle of the room caught in a duel between the desire that was tearing her apart and the fear that he would reject her. Since she had never been reticent about going after something she wanted, she made her decision. She would go to him and deal with the consequences of her actions later.

After donning her dressing gown, Anna paused before the full-length mirror to make sure she looked her best. Her hair was a sleek, soft tumble about her shoulders. Her cheeks were tinted with the flush of excitement she was feeling, and her eyes shone with the hope that her love would be fulfilled. The robe was a seductive wrap, clinging enticingly to her very feminine curves, and she hoped it would tempt Slater. Satisfied, she wet her lips in a gesture of nervous anticipation then slipped quietly from the room.

Slater had given up all hope of sleep. A burning, driving energy filled him. He wanted to begin his quest to find the truth about Francesca now. He didn't want to waste another moment. Pacing his darkened room like a caged jungle cat on the prowl, Slater could hardly wait for first light.

Slater strode to the nightstand to get his half-filled glass of whiskey. Rafe had had his room stocked with a decanter of his best, and Slater had taken full advantage of his thoughtful generosity. He tossed down the fiery contents in one swallow, then resumed his pacing.

A soft knock at his door startled Slater, and he hurried to answer it. He expected it to be Rafe, and he wondered what could be troubling him at this time of the night. When he opened the door, he went abruptly still.

Time seemed suspended as he stared down at the figure of the lithe, young woman standing in the shadows of the hallway before him. She was clad only in a very revealing dressing gown, and for just that fraction of an instant, he could have sworn it was Francesca. His heart contracted in his chest, and his breathing became labored. He was reaching for her, almost ready to snatch her up in his arms to make sure she was real, when she spoke and the illusion was shattered.

"Slater . . ." Anna said his name in a husky voice.

With the sound of her voice came recognition, and Slater was jarred painfully back to reality. The lightness that had gripped his soul for that brief moment in time suddenly turned leaden. He felt like a fool, and he was glad there were no lamps lighted so his discomfort couldn't be seen.

"Anna? Is something wrong?" Shaken by his own weakness, he didn't understand the reason for her being there.

Slater sounded so formal that the fantasy she'd harbored that he would give her a passionate welcome was dashed. "I wanted to talk to you for a minute," she offered a little awkwardly.

Slater stepped back to allow her to enter, and she did so quickly, closing the door behind her.

"What is it? Does Rafe have a problem?"

"No. This has nothing to do with Rafe. It only has to do with me . . ." Anna knew her move was bold, but she didn't care. She cast her fate to the wind and brazenly moved closer to Slater. In an intimate gesture, she rested both hands against his chest then

66

rose up on tiptoes to lean against him fully and kiss him on the mouth.

The scent of Anna's perfume was heady. The touch of her lips was stirring, and the feel of her body pressed to his definitely inviting. For a moment, Slater allowed himself to enjoy her nearness. It felt good to have a sweet and willing woman in his arms. Had Slater been less of a man of honor, he might have taken advantage of what she was offering, for her generous curves were tempting. But Anna was his friend. He respected her and cared about her. He would not use her just as a vessel to slake his physical needs. She deserved more than that, and right now he couldn't give her more. Reaching up to grasp her forearms, he put her from him.

"Anna . . . no . . ."

"But Slater . . . We'd be good together, I know it. Just give us a chance . . ."

Slater gazed down at her. She was very beautiful, and he knew if he allowed himself to make love to her, they probably would be good together. But he could make no commitment to Anna with his heart, and one without the other would be pointless. He released her and walked away to light the lamp on the nightstand. "It wouldn't work."

Anna couldn't fathom why he was turning her away, when all she wanted to do was love him. "I love you, Slater. Let me show you how much . . . ," she pleaded.

He faced her in the muted golden glow of the low-burning lamp. His emerald gaze was intense as it met and held hers. "Anna . . . I really care about you. You know that, and it's for that very reason that I won't use you."

"But you wouldn't be using me, not if I came to you because I wanted to. I can make you forget Francesca, I know I can!"

Slater's expression was melancholy as he shook his head to discourage her from saying anything more. "In a way, I almost wish that were true, Anna."

"But it is true . . ." She clung to a last shred of hope that somehow she could convince him of the futility of loving a ghost.

"No. There's no future for you in loving me, Anna."

The finality in his words struck her open, tender heart like a blow. Embarrassed, her cheeks flamed with color. "I see," she choked. She knew she had made a complete fool out of herself, and she felt both crushed and cheap.

Slater saw how humiliated she was. He longed to take her in his arms and try to explain further, but he didn't. As appealing as she was, he knew he couldn't risk any more physical contact with her. So instead, he tried once more to explain, wanting to be conciliatory. "I can't let anything get in the way of what I have to do here, Anna. I need to keep a clear head. I don't want any emotional ties. Not now . . ."

At his words, a glimmer of hope survived within her breast. *He'd said 'not now' . . . Maybe that meant that one day he'd get over Francesca . . . that someday he would be ready to love again.* Her spirits rose a little as her determination not to give up on winning his love returned. One day he would forget Francesca and when he did, she would be there waiting to love him.

"I understand," she said at last, wanting to ease the tenseness from the conversation and their relationship. If she couldn't have his love, she would settle for whatever he offered just to be near him.

"I hope you do. Our friendship means a lot to me."

"It does to me, too."

"We've been through a lot together, and it's good to know I have you with me again. I count on you, Anna, and I may need your help one day soon."

"Why? Are you planning something more than just finding Francesca's grave and rescuing the two agents?" Anna questioned, suddenly suspicious.

"You know me too well." His look turned ferocious.

"So, you're not going to accept Francesca's death and just let it go, are you? You're going after Carlanta . . ."

He nodded tightly. "He's the one ultimately responsible for what happened to Francesca and me, and I'm going to do whatever I have to to bring him down."

"He's dangerous."

"I know, but then so am I." His words were deadly.

"Have you made any plans? Can I help?"

"No. This is something I have to do alone. I plan on talking with her father tomorrow."

"But Ricardo hated you for marrying Francesca," Anna cautioned. "It'll only be worse between you now that she's dead."

"I would hope, as her father, that he'd be interested in helping me find the man who killed her."

"You could end up walking into a trap. Salazar and Carlanta are close."

69

He shrugged off her warnings. "This is something I have to do, Anna. If I don't, I'll never be any good for myself, let alone for any one else."

"Just be careful, please." It pained her to admit it, but she did understand his need for revenge.

"I will."

Her throat was tight as she went to him and pressed a soft kiss to his cheek. "Good night, Slater."

"Good night, Anna. I'll see you in the morning." He watched her go, his mood strangely bittersweet. He hadn't wanted to hurt her, but he knew it was for the best that they keep their relationship strictly one of friendship. Francesca had been the one love of his life, and there would never be another who could take her place.

The baby's cry was soft, yet Francesca, who'd been having trouble sleeping, heard it. She threw aside the covers and rose from her bed to go to her son, who was in his crib in the connecting nursery. After lighting a lamp on a nearby table, she bent over his crib.

"Michael . . ." Francesca smiled serenely as she whispered his name.

The cherubic nine-month-old was pleased to see her, and he gurgled with delight.

"You should be sleeping . . . ," she whispered, scooping him up in her arms and carrying him back to her room with her. "What are you doing awake this time of night, young man?" Francesca scolded lovingly as she curled up on the wide comfort of her bed with him. "Couldn't you rest either?"

She knew, of course, that the conversation was foolish for Michael couldn't answer her, but it didn't matter. He was the one person in the world she could be completely honest with. She cuddled him near and pressed a kiss to the top of his head.

"I've been thinking too much tonight," she confided a bit sadly.

"Remembering too much . . ."

A sigh wracked Francesca as Slater slipped into her thoughts. Right after he'd deserted her, she fed upon her hatred for him to keep from thinking about him, and she'd succeeded for a little while. But after the birth of his son, all the heartrending memories of his love and betrayal had returned. It always left her depressed when her wayward thoughts conjured images of what their life could have been like if Slater had really been a Louisiana planter in Cuba on business. In her mind's eye, she invariably pictured them as a loving family. She imagined Slater taking pride in watching his son grow. She daydreamed of the love they would have shared and the future they would have had together. Annoyed, Francesca jerked her thoughts back to reality . . . to the present.

"You know, Michael, Armando wants to marry me, and he says he wants to be your father. Would you like that?"

As if on cue, Michael set up a fuss, and Francesca couldn't help but give a quiet laugh at his perception.

"For some reason, I have the same reaction every time I think about it." She calmed her son with soft-spoken words and warm, gentle caresses. "I think perhaps we'll stall him a while. That won't make your grandfather happy, you know. He likes Armando

71

a lot, although I wish I knew why. There's something about the man that leaves me very uncomfortable. I mean, when he kisses me . . ." She paused as she thought about Armando's hot, wet, demanding kisses. Though she didn't want to dislike them particularly, she found his kisses repulsive compared to Slater's. "Well, it's just not the same . . ."

Suddenly realizing the direction her thoughts were taking, Francesca scolded herself. "Why do I do that, Michael? Why do I always compare everyone to your father?" She gazed down at him, seeing his startling resemblance to Slater in everything from his beginning growth of downy, dark brown curls to his vivid, intelligent green eyes. Tears burned her eyes, and she didn't even bother to fight them back. He was so much like his father . . . so much . . .

Michael continued to regard her steadily, openly. His expression seemed to denote that he understood exactly what she was saying, but she knew that couldn't be.

"Slater MacKenzie was not a nice man, even though he did make a beautiful baby," she told Michael.

Michael scowled at her as if he disapproved of her comment and was about ready to set up a squawk about it.

Francesca quickly corrected, "All right, he made *handsome* babies, but I still think you're beautiful, and I'm your mother."

Michael yawned and rubbed his eyes with chubby fists before closing them in sudden weariness.

Francesca fell silent to encourage him to rest. She let her thoughts drift as she nestled her warm, sleepy bundle of love to her breast. She vowed to herself as she lay there with him that even if Michael looked like Slater, she was going to do everything in her power to make sure he didn't turn out like him.

A great feeling of melancholy now overwhelmed her as she remembered how stupid she'd been during those first long months after Slater had left. There had been a small, secret part of her that had held out hope that her father had been wrong, but as time had passed and Slater had not returned, it had died a painful death. She'd allowed her father to take charge of the divorce and the annulment for her then, and relief had been the only emotion she'd felt when he'd shown her the papers, completed and signed a month after she'd given birth to Michael.

Francesca had asked her father at that time if Slater had been informed of his son's existence. Her father had assured her that he had, but that he'd wanted nothing more to do with either her or the child. The news had crushed Francesca for Slater had once told her that he'd hoped they would have a son so he could name him Michael after his father who'd died many years before. The undeniable revelation that Slater was honestly gone from her life, smothered the last faintly glowing ember of hope she'd carried hidden deep in her heart.

In the time since Michael had been born, Francesca had matured far beyond her years. She felt more confident, more independent, more capable of taking care of herself now. She'd also made up her mind that she would never allow herself to be used by a man again.

It seemed to Francesca now, though, that both her

father and Armando, subtle though they were, were pressuring her to make a commitment long before she felt she was ready. True, the divorce was final, but that didn't mean she was prepared to marry again so soon. She had a son to raise. Michael was her life now, and she had to consider his future in every decision she made.

In the morning Slater left Rafe's home as soon as he could and headed straight for Ricardo Salazar's office in the main government building. He was not looking forward to meeting with the man again, but he knew it had to be done. The last time they'd spoken had been right before he and Francesca had eloped. They had gone to him, at her insistence, to ask his blessing on their wedding. He'd tersely refused and had warned Francesca that if she'd married Slater he would have nothing further to do with her. Her father's unreasonable stand had saddened Francesca, but had not deterred her. She had gone on with the wedding. She'd told Slater later that she'd never regretted her choice for a moment. It was that memory that gave him the strength to face Ricardo now. The way Slater figured it, they would both be on the same side. He wanted to find the man who'd killed her, and he assumed her father would, too.

"Señor Salazar, please," he announced to Federico, the clerk, in Salazar's outer office.

"Who shall I tell him is calling?"

"Slater MacKenzie."

The man hurried to knock on the door to Ricardo's

office and, when told to do so, he opened it and went in.

"What is it?" Ricardo demanded irritably. He'd been tense and disquieted since learning MacKenzie was back, and he was waiting anxiously for word from Armando that the trouble-making American had been eliminated once and for all.

"There's a gentleman here to see you, sir—a Señor MacKenzie."

Ricardo went rigid, then forced himself to relax and answer in a calm voice. "Send him in."

Ricardo remained seated at his desk, his facade of control carefully in place. It wouldn't do for any of his nervousness to show, not now, not in front of MacKenzie.

A moment later Slater was ushered into the office. The coldness and hatred that existed between Slater and Ricardo was an almost tangible thing as they faced each other across the width of the room.

"MacKenzie," Ricardo acknowledged him tersely. "I suppose you have a good reason for coming here."

"I want to know where Francesca is," Slater stated, his eyes locking with the other man's.

Ricardo almost panicked. How had MacKenzie found out that Francesca was alive? A flicker of fearful caution showed in his eyes.

"Why?" he countered sharply, trying to bluff his way through and not give anything away.

"I'm her husband," he declared, wondering what the quick flash of fear he'd seen in Ricardo's gaze was about.

"That's a misfortune of which I'm only too well aware," he said with cold sarcasm. "But what pos-

75

sible reason could you have for coming back here and wanting to know where she is after all this time?"

"She was my wife. I have a right to know where she's buried."

"Buried' . . . *he'd said "buried."* Relief washed through Ricardo. MacKenzie didn't know! In command and confident once again, he went on the attack. "You have no rights where my Francesca is concerned! No rights at all!"

"I'm going to see that those responsible for her death pay." Slater's expression turned savage.

Ricardo took the opportunity to torment Slater about her 'death.' "Then look in the mirror, MacKenzie, if you want to know who was responsible. You were—no one else!"

"You're a cold bastard, Salazar. Carlanta was the one behind it all. Don't you even care?"

"I told you and Francesca both that I washed my hands of her when she married you. Do you think I lied? Once she became your wife, she was no longer my daughter."

"How can you turn your back on your own flesh and blood this way? Francesca was your only child. Your nourished her and you raised her. How can you not want to see those responsible for her death brought to justice?"

"Get out of my office, now!" He charged to his feet threateningly.

"Obviously, I loved her more in the short time we had together, than you did in her whole life," Slater said condemningly. "Well, you may have forsaken her, but I haven't. I'm going to find her grave, Salazar, with or without your help, and then I'm going to find the ones who killed her." He strode from the room an angry man.

Ricardo loathed Slater so much that had he had a pistol close at hand he would have used it on him right then and there. Instead, he kept rein on the murderous urge and waited until Slater had gone. When he had, Ricardo sat down and wrote out a terse note. He summoned Federico to him.

"I want you to take this message to Carlanta right away."

Since no public notice had ever been made of Francesca's burial, Slater felt certain that Rafe had been right—that she'd been buried privately on her father's estate. As he left Salazar's office, he had only one goal in mind—to go to the Salazar country home and find her. In his heart, he knew he'd waited too long already.

Slater headed toward Rafe's house intending to let Rafe and Anna know where he was going, then make the long ride to the Salazar estate. His thoughts were dark and vengeful, and his soul was filled with solemn determination.

"MacKenzie actually came here?" Armando was surprised at the American's daring.

"He did, less than half an hour ago. I thought you were going to take care of this?" Ricardo challenged.

"I am, Ricardo, have patience. These things take time."

"It had better not take too much time. He's trying

to locate Francesca's grave, of all things. I don't want them to run into each other. He thinks she's dead, and I want to keep it that way. I want him eliminated, and I want it done now!"

Armando fixed Ricardo with a cold glare, wondering at his audacity in issuing orders to him. "I have a man following him," he explained levelly. "But the time and place have to be right if we want to prevent an incident."

"To hell with the time and the place! With our positions of authority, we can cover up anything. Just do it!"

"You're getting reckless in your old age, Ricardo," Armando chided.

"Where my daughter is concerned, I'm entitled to be a bit reckless. I have her back now. I don't want to lose her."

"And you won't. You may rest assured on that."

"I'm counting on your dealing with this quickly, Armando," he pressed, fearful.

"We won't have to concern ourselves with Mr. Slater MacKenzie much longer."

A short time later, Sanchez, the man Armando had hired to keep track of Slater, got word from his boss of what he was to do. As he maintained his watch at the Ramirez house waiting for MacKenzie to reappear, he pulled out his sidearm and checked to see that it was fully loaded.

Chapter Six

Slater approached the Salazar estate cautiously, skirting off the main road to avoid any possible confrontations. During their whirlwind courtship, he had come here several time with Francesca, and so he was somewhat familiar with the lay of the land. He cut across some fields, then reined his mount in on a rise overlooking the sprawling house with its red tile roof and lush gardens.

Slater watched the pastoral scene below for a moment, wanting to make sure it was safe, then urged his horse down a side path that led through a tangle of vegetation toward the rear of the estate. The Salazar family cemetery was located about a mile from the house in a secluded grove of trees. His hands tightened on the reins as he drew near the place that would end his search and his agony. Soon, he would have his proof and he would no longer be able to deny what had happened to Francesca.

Slater reached the graveyard and reined in. He just sat there for a moment on horseback, staring around himself. A slightly rusty, wrought iron fence enclosed the cemetery and lent it a sad, neglected look. When he couldn't stand it any longer, he finally gathered enough nerve to dismount and face the truth he'd sought for so long. After looping his reins over the fence, Slater opened the gate and went forth to seek his answers.

Slater's steps were slow, almost reluctant, as he approached the row of tombstones. His chest was tight, his hands unsteady, his stomach in knots. He felt a coldness descend upon him as he stopped before the first stone. He felt as if he were dying a thousand deaths. He wondered a little crazily if it wasn't easier to suffer the uncertainty of never seeing Francesca's grave, than to actually see it and know for certain that she was gone from him forever.

The torment he'd suffered while back at Highland burned in him, though, and Slater knew he had to find his answer. He forced his gaze up so he could read the inscription on the tombstone:

Gisela Salazar, born 1801, died 1846, beloved wife of Ricardo and mother of Francesca.

Slater was totally surprised to find that the grave wasn't Francesca's. For some reason, he'd expected hers to be the one nearest the gate. Relief filled him, although he knew it wouldn't last.

Frowning a little, Slater moved on with slow steps to the next tombstone. Again his heart beat erratically and his breath caught in his throat. His hands were fists at his sides as he fought his own inner fears. He felt cold with dread. It was almost over. He knew it. The torture of not knowing was almost finished. Yet Slater knew that when this particular torment had ended, his misery would begin all over again.

Preparing himself for the worst, Slater read the next stone. He fully expected to see his wife's name engraved there. He stared in shock at Francesca's grandfather's name where it appeared on the marker.

Slater wasn't sure whether to celebrate or worry. He moved on, his expectation growing worse with each succeeding tombstone. Tension radiated from him as he moved down the line of markers and found no trace of his beloved Francesca anywhere.

Where was she?

As Slater approached the very last stone, he was sure in his heart that it had to be hers. He girded himself. This would be it. The end of his search would be here. Slater looked up to read the inscription only to find to his surprise that it belonged to Francesca's grandmother.

The revelation that Francesca had not been buried in her family's plot left Slater deeply troubled. *Had Salazar despised his daughter so much for marrying him that he'd refused to let her be buried here, with her own relatives? Had her father really washed his hands of her so completely that he let her be interred in some pauper's graveyard somewhere? Was she lying there now, in an unmarked grave, totally alone?* The thought haunted him. His heart wrenched. It had been terrible enough imagining her being put to rest here with her family, but to think that she might be buried somewhere else where he might never find her, nearly destroyed him. *How could Salazar have been so cruel? Francesca was his only child. . . .*

Slater was standing there lost deep in thought when the first shot was fired. He heard the crack of the gun's report at the same time the bullet grazed him, and he dove automatically for cover. A barrage of gunfire followed, pinning him down where he crouched behind the stand of headstones.

Slater drew his own sidearm and returned the shots in the general direction from where it had come, but he had no clear target. After a moment, it grew quiet, and he ceased his fire to wait his cowardly assailant's next move.

It was then that Slater first noticed the pain in his head, and he reached up tentatively to touch the side of his head near his temple. He stared in amazement when he withdrew his hand and found it covered in blood. Rage tore through Slater, and he began to shake with the fury of a man pushed to his limits. With a snarl of anger, he rose, gun still in hand, ready to do mortal combat. But all was quiet. His attacker had already fled.

Swearing in frustration, Slater ran to his horse and mounted up. He was certain that the shots had been heard at the house, and he wanted to be gone before anyone came to investigate. He put his heels to his mount's flanks and galloped away from the cemetery, his need to find Francesca growing even more powerful.

"Someone took a shot at you while you were in the graveyard?" Rafe echoed Slater's words in horror as he stood across the bedroom from him watching him gingerly doctoring his head wound later that day.

Slater gave a terse nod. "I should have been expecting it. I was lucky to get that far without them taking a potshot at me."

"That was no potshot, another inch and . . ."

"He missed. I'm alive, and I fully intend to stay that way." He shrugged off his concern. "Right now, all I care about is finding Francesca. The rest I'll handle later."

His words left no doubt in Rafe's mind that he would, indeed, handle it later.

"Then why don't you come with me Saturday night? Carlanta's widowed sister, Rosa Valequez, is giving a ball. I try not to socialize with this group too often, but maybe this time I should accept her gracious invitation. All the 'right' people will be there."

"The 'right' people, eh?" Slater was applying antiseptic to his wound, but he smiled in spite of the sting. "I wouldn't miss it."

"I'll send a note to Rosa right away asking if it's all right for me to bring along two extra guests."

None of Marita Valequez's sophisticated society friends would have understood what the young, well-educated, eighteen-year-old beauty was doing at the home of Pedro Santana. Pedro was a kind, portly, Creole gentleman of some fifty-odd years, who had been a close friend of her dead father, Antonio. After her father's death when she was ten, Pedro had stayed in contact with her. He had talked with her often, and as she'd matured, they'd broadened their discussions to cover politics and the need for reform on the island. It was through his teachings that she'd learned of the need for changes in the Spanish-ruled government.

"Pedro, I'm so glad you're home," she greeted him as his servant ushered her in to join him in the sitting room.

"Ah, Marita!" Pedro smiled a warm welcome as she came in. He loved her as much as he loved his own twenty-year old son, Estevan, and he rose to give her a warm hug. "Come sit with me. I've missed you," he invited.

"I've missed you, too," Marita admitted. She loved Pedro almost like a second father, and at his encouragement, she'd dared to become involved with the revolutionaries. Because of her closeness to her Uncle Armando, she had assumed the secret identity of La Fantasma—the spirit. As such, she supplied Pedro with information she learned by associating with her uncle's friends and by listening carefully whenever she was out at any social functions.

"Have you any news?"

"There's been no mention of the missing Americans at all, but at a party I attended last weekend, I heard talk that some troops might be transferred out of Havana to the hill country to search for our stronghold." Marita was one of very few peninsulars who supported the idea of an independent Cuba. Because her beliefs were so strong, she had to be very careful whenever a social discussion came up about it. She usually affected the air that she couldn't care less about such things, while, in reality, she listened avidly for information that might help the freedom fighters. Marita was certain that no one suspected she was an ardent supporter of the rebels, and she wanted it to stay that way. Should the truth of her loyalty ever become known, she might find herself in great danger.

"It troubles me about the Americans. As evil as your uncle is, I'm afraid they're as good as dead."

"I hope you're wrong."

"Carlanta's an outrageous man. He deals with others by his own set of private rules. He means to remain in power, no matter what the cost in lives."

"Then we must make sure he doesn't," Marita told Pedro. The dedication she felt to her countrymen was more powerful than her blood relation to her mother's brother. She knew Pedro's description of Armando was completely accurate. She'd heard Armando's views on those who opposed Spanish rule, and she knew he would do whatever was necessary to preserve the current system under which he prospered.

"With your help, we just might be able to do it," Pedro encouraged.

"My mother's giving a big party on Saturday night," Marita went on. "I'll be listening."

Pedro nodded. "I'll pass your news about the troop movements on to the others, and I thank you, La Fantasma."

"I'll let you know as soon as I hear anything else, Pedro.

"Vaya con Dios, little one."

Marita left his house unnoticed and headed for the dress shop where she had an appointment for a fitting.

Marita swept into Señora Gomez's shop, eager to see the progress the dressmaker had made on the gown she was to wear Saturday night. They had selected the pattern from a magazine of the latest styles from the continent, and she could hardly wait to try it on. Off-the-shoulder in style, the rose silk creation was fitted through the waist with dramatically flaring skirts. The color was her best, and she was looking forward to wearing it at her mother's party.

"Ah, señorita! I'm so glad you are here," the short, heavyset señora exclaimed as she bustled forth to greet her. "I've been waiting all morning to see you in this."

She led the way to back of the shop, directed Marita to the dressing room and then brought her the nearly completed garment to try on. After helping her disrobe, she lifted the ball gown over Marita's head to assist her in putting it on. Then, the señora stepped back to survey her handiwork.

"Magnifico!" she proclaimed happily.

"It's lovely," Marita breathed as she stared at herself in the full-length mirror. "It's turned out better than I ever imagined! You're a miracle worker."

The seamstress laughed in delight. "No, you're the miracle worker, Marita. The gown was just a pretty dress until you put it on. You're going to have the men falling at your feet on Saturday."

Marita gave a carefree laugh as she twirled about to get a look at the back. "I think I just might enjoy that. When will you be finished with it?"

"Friday. We can have the final fitting then."

"Fine, I'll be here."

Dressed once again, Marita thanked the señora for her help and started from the store. She was looking back over her shoulder saying good-bye as she opened the door, when she almost walked point-blank into the solid wall of a man's very wide, very powerful chest.

"Excuse me . . . ," she said quickly, a bit flustered as she glanced up to see who it was. "Why, Rafael . . ." Her look of surprise turned to pure pleasure on discovering it was none other than Rafael Ramirez.

"Marita, it's wonderful to see you," Rafe told her, and he meant it. Marita Valequez was one very beautiful woman.

His voice was deep and velvety, and a quiver of excitement raced through Marita at his nearness. She shook off the mesmerizing feeling, refusing to fall prey to what many of the women called his fatal charm. "What brings you to Señora Gomez's shop?" she asked, intrigued at finding him there. She had just spoken when she noticed the pretty young woman standing slightly behind him. For some unknown reason, Marita felt a sting of resentfulness at her presence.

"Let me introduce my cousin Anna to you. Marita, this is Anna Melena. Anna, Marita Valequez." Rafael drew the other woman around to make the introductions.

A strange relief filled Marita for she remembered, then, her mother had mentioned that very morning that Rafe had accepted her invitation to the party and would be bringing his cousin and another houseguest with him.

"It's wonderful to meet you, Anna. I understand you'll be joining us on Saturday?"

"Yes, we're all looking forward to it," Anna assured her, thinking Marita one of the prettiest women she'd ever seen.

They said quick good-byes then, and as Marita left, Rafael dominated her thoughts. She told herself it was ridiculous to even give him a second thought.

Handsome and intelligent though he was, he was still a peninsular just like her uncle. There was no point in thinking about him in a romantic way at all for he would certainly think her a scandalous traitor for supporting the rebels. Putting Rafe effectively from her mind, Marita climbed into her carriage with the driver's assistance and directed him to take her home.

After holding the door for Marita to leave and Anna to enter, Rafe watched in silent admiration as Marita made her way to her waiting carriage. The gentle sway of her hips and the trim curve of her waist held his attention, and he was hard put to remind himself of just why he was there in the first place. Sternly, he told himself that while Marita was a very lovely woman, his interest was just a purely normal male reaction, and that it stopped there. She was, after all, Carlanta's niece. Enough said. Still, Marita hovered at the edge of his thoughts as he turned his attention back to the matters at hand—that being, finding Anna a gown suitable to wear to the Valequez party.

Anna was ecstatic as she wandered among the tables piled high with every kind of fabric and trim. She'd never been in a shop like Señora Gomez's before, and she touched the expensive silks and satins with something akin to awe.

"My cousin's in need of a gown, señora," Rafe announced to the shop's owner.

"Something fancy?" the señora questioned.

"Most definitely, it's for her to wear to the Valequez party Saturday night," Rafe explained.

"Then it must be perfect."

"Indeed."

"I understand this party is going to be the event of the season. It seems everyone who's anyone will be attending."

"I wouldn't doubt it for a minute." Rafe and Anna exchanged a look that only they understood.

"Since our time is limited, let me show you the gowns I have already made up. Perhaps one of them will please you."

"Anna, I leave you in the señora's capable hands. I'll be back in say . . . an hour?"

"That should give us plenty of time," the seamstress agreed. "Do you have a certain amount you want to spend?"

"I trust my cousin's judgment completely. Select the one you like the best, Anna, and don't concern yourself with the cost."

"Are you sure, Rafe?"

"Positive," he answered, giving her a warm, encouraging smile. He knew she must be feeling much like a child in a candy shop, and he wanted her to enjoy herself.

Half an hour later, Anna was modeling a pale gold gown that fit almost perfectly. The neckline was just low enough to be daring without being tasteless or shocking, and the fitted waist showed off her slender figure to best advantage. She felt and looked like a princess. *Maybe this would help her win Slater's heart. Maybe now, I'll be beautiful enough to wipe Francesca from his thoughts once and for all.* In a flash of a daydream, she fancied herself being squired around the dance floor in Slater's arms as he had eyes only for her. She smiled dreamily to herself at the thought.

"What do you think?" Señora Gomez asked as she

scurried around Anna with her measuring tape and cushion of pins. "With a tuck here and a seam taken in there . . . Do you think this one will do?"

"Oh, it'll more than do," Anna told her, her dark eyes sparkling with excitement as she planned to make her daydream come true. "I'll take it."

"I want you to come back to the city with me," Ricardo announced to his daughter as he dined with her at their country estate that evening. After learning that Armando's first attempt to kill Mac-Kenzie had failed, he'd left the city in a panic, determined to keep a very close watch over his daughter until the man was out of the way.

"You know how I feel about going back to Havana," Francesca resisted. She had not been back since that fateful night with Slater. She'd passed her entire pregnancy here on their plantation and was perfectly happy to remain right where she was.

"I know, but Rosa is giving a party, and Armando asked specifically that I bring you."

"But father . . ." The mention of Armando was certainly not an incentive for her to attend the party.

"I won't take no for an answer," he replied sternly. "It's time you got out. I've already told Teresa to prepare your things. We'll be leaving first thing in the morning."

"What about Michael?"

"I'm sure he will be fine here without you for just a few days. It will do you good to relax and enjoy yourself for a while."

Francesca was tempted to argue, but realized that perhaps he was right. Maybe it was time she began to socialize again. Not that she was looking for any romantic attachment, but there was no reason why she shouldn't go to town and see some of her old friends. "All right. I'll be ready."

"Good girl." Ricardo gloated, knowing that he would be able to relax more if he kept her in his sight, and that Armando would be pleased.

When she returned to her room later, Teresa was already there packing her clothes.

"Doña Francesca, is there a particular gown you want to take along for the ball?"

"Let me see," she answered thoughtfully, going to her wardrobe to look through the vast array of rainbow-hued dresses. Since Michael's birth her figure had changed. She was definitely fuller through the bosom now, and she wondered which one, if any, would fit.

Francesca's gaze fell upon her very favorite gown. It was a stunning creation of emerald satin that did wonderful things for her. She knew she looked ravishing in it. She'd worn it the night she'd first met Slater . . .

Annoyed, Francesca pushed the unbidden thought of her ex-husband from her mind. What did it matter that she'd had it on that particular evening? It was still her prettiest dress. She would wear it again, she decided assertively, and this time, she would create new and even better memories while she had it on.

"This one," she declared, and she handed the gown to the maid.

Chapter Seven

The tension within Slater grew with each passing day as he waited for the coming of the party that weekend. He was looking forward to seeing Carlanta again, and this time facing him as his equal. The temptation to shoot the vicious government official on sight was great, but Slater knew he couldn't do it. There were other, more important things he had to accomplish first; and besides, he wanted Carlanta to suffer for a while. Killing him straight out would be much too easy on him.

Having donned his dark suit, fancy waistcoat, snowy white shirt, and fashionable narrow tie for the evening's festivities, Slater waited with the equally elegantly clad Rafe in his study for Anna to join them. His mood was strained as he took the tumbler of whiskey Rafe proffered.

"This should help a little," Rafe remarked, sipping his rum.

"It will," Slater agreed, drinking of his favorite potent brew.

"My 'cousin' Anna should be down any minute, and then we can be on our way," he said with a grin.

"Your 'cousin'?" Slater cast him a quixotic look.

"It was the most expedient way I could think of to explain why I was buying her a gown."

"That's a good idea. We have to protect her."

Anna had come down the steps quietly for she wanted to surprise Slater and Rafe. When she heard Slater's words, her heart sang. Though it was no declaration of love, his concern proved that he cared for her at least a little bit. She hoped with time that caring might change to something more. Smiling brightly, Anna stepped forth from the hallway into the study.

"Well, *dear cousin*, I'm dressed and ready to go," Anna announced.

Both men looked up at her declaration and stared at her, impressed. She looked more beautiful than either one of them could have imagined.

Their sudden silence unnerved her a bit, and she went on quickly, "Thank you for the necklace and earrings, Rafe." She touched the expensive jewels reverently. "I'll be sure to take good care of them. They're so beautiful . . ."

"I'm sure you will, Anna. They barely do you justice." He'd loaned her some of the priceless jewelry he'd inherited when his mother had passed away many years before.

"You look wonderful," Slater told her earnestly. He'd always thought her attractive, but tonight she looked lovely. Gold proved definitely to be her color for it brought out the warm tone of her complexion and the bright sparkle in her eyes.

"Indeed, you do," Rafe agreed. "Señora Gomez is as talented as they say she is. The gown is perfect on you."

"Thank you." She flushed with pleasure at their praise, relaxing a bit. She knew they were the kind of men who wouldn't lie just to make someone else feel good. For that reason, their compliments meant even more to her. "Shall we go?"

Slater and Rafe downed the balance of their drinks and moved to accompany her outside to where the carriage awaited them.

"I'm sure I must have the two best-looking escorts in all of Havana," she told them proudly.

They handed her into the vehicle then climbed in themselves. Rafe took the opposite seat, while Slater sat down beside her.

Anna was silently thrilled by Slater's attentiveness. He looked unbelievably handsome tonight, and she was excited at the thought of being with him at this fancy ball. Anna knew she couldn't let too much of her emotions show, though. She would never forgive herself if she made a fool out of herself over him again. Slater had told her the way it was with him, and she knew she would have to bide her time until he came to terms with his life.

The carriage lurched slightly as it pulled away from the house to begin the trek to the Valequez home. They remained mostly quiet during the ride. Thoughts of Francesca and of what he would discover about her death tonight occupied Slater. Anna was silent as she anticipated with joy, pretending for this one evening that she was Slater's woman. And Rafe was pondering the political situation and wondering what news he might learn

94

tonight that he could pass along. In the back of his mind, though, too, was the pleasant thought that Marita would be there and the memory of how wonderful she'd looked the other day when they'd run into each other at the dressmaker's shop.

The Valequez home was a stone mansion of near palatial proportions. Bright lights shone from its every window, and the lilting strains of a waltz drifted lightly thought the night.

Rosa Valequez, a matronly forty-year-old woman with silver-frosted dark hair and dancing black eyes, stood in the wide, two-story foyer of her magnificent home welcoming her newly arriving guests with open pleasure. She always enjoyed entertaining, and she regretted now having waited so long to have this party.

Rosa had already been wealthy in her own right when she'd married the very rich Creole, Antonio Valequez, some twenty years before. Their marriage had been made in heaven, but had ended tragically after twelve years when he'd been killed in a riding accident. Widowed and alone, she'd devoted herself to raising her only daughter, Marita, to become a woman he would have been proud to claim.

Rosa also had a very close relationship with her younger brother, Armando Carlanta. She took great pride in his accomplishments, seeing only the good in him and never the bed. He'd confided to her recently that he planned to marry Francesca, and at first she'd been overjoyed for she'd felt it was time he settled down. When she'd had time to think about it, though, she'd had to ask him how a union with

Francesca was possible when she'd already married the American the year before. Armando had told her that Francesca's marriage had been a terrible mistake and that her father had intervened and had seen to it that it had been rectified.

Though Rosa would have preferred her brother to marry someone without any taint of scandal to her reputation, she knew better than to question Armando's decision. It was obvious that he wanted Francesca to be his bride, and Rosa knew that whatever her brother wanted, he got. When she'd received word from Armando that Francesca would be attending her ball tonight accompanied by her father, she'd been delighted. She was looking forward to seeing Armando together with the woman he loved.

As Ricardo Salazar came through the door right now with Francesca on his arm, she welcomed him with open enthusiasm. "Ricardo! Welcome!"

"Good evening, Rosa. You look marvelous tonight," Ricardo complimented their hostess.

"Thank you. Francesca! How very good it is to see you again!" Rosa greeted the young woman at her father's side. She hadn't seen Francesca in quite a while, but she could understand now why her brother was so determined to marry her. She was positively breathtaking in her low-cut emerald gown.

"Thank you, Rosa. It's been a long time," Francesca responded with a bright smile to her cordial welcome. She felt her mood suddenly improve, and realized that her father had been right, it had been too long since she'd been out socially. She put all thoughts of her embarrassing, ill-fated marriage from her and, with a determined lift of her chin, decided to enjoy herself to the fullest tonight.

"Armando is already here. He's been waiting for you," Rosa confided to Francesca happily.

Francesca managed to maintain her smile, though she wasn't all that thrilled with the thought of being in Armando's company all evening. He could be more than overpowering when he chose to be, and she'd hoped to avoid him for at least a little while. That hope ended as quickly as it had come when he emerged from the ballroom and walked straight toward her.

Armando's black-eyed gaze was fixed on Francesca with an intensity that left her very uncomfortable.

"Francesca . . . my darling, I'm so glad you came." He boldly moved to kiss her to establish his possession of her. She was by far the most gorgeous woman at the party, and he wanted her all to himself.

Francesca's instincts were quick and accurate, though, and she presented him with her cheek, thereby avoiding the full kiss on the lips he'd intended. "Armando, it's good to see you, too."

He linked her arm possessively though his, not allowing her any chance of escape while he greeted Ricardo. Then, turning his attention back to her, he asked, "Shall we join the others?"

"I'd like that, Armando," Francesca responded, trying to convince herself that she really was going to have a good time tonight. He was, after all, a handsome man and certainly more than attentive to her needs.

"Good." He whisked her off into the ballroom.

* * *

"They make a very handsome couple, don't you think, Ricardo?" Rosa sighed as they watched Francesca and Armando disappear into the ballroom.

"Very," Ricardo replied in whole-hearted approval. "Perhaps soon we'll have cause to celebrate where they're concerned."

"I hope so," she agreed.

More guest began to arrive then, and Rosa was forced to turn her attention away from her brother. Ricardo was very pleased with how things were progressing, and he moved off in search of refreshment.

In the ballroom, Morena Calderon stood with Nita Gonzalez and Catalina La Paz. Morena was a good-natured, outgoing girl, who wanted nothing more than to marry and raise a family. Her weight problem, however, had hampered her efforts in snaring a husband. Nita was much Morena's opposite. Short and thin to the point of being scrawny, her tongue was acerbic, and she exercised little ability to curb it. The last of the trio of friends, Catalina, was neither bright nor dull-witted. With her average looks and easily led personality she fit in comfortably with the other two. Standing at the sidelines of the dance floor, they watched the couples dancing by with more than a little envy. It was Nita who spotted Francesca first as she entered the ballroom with Armando.

"I don't believe it!" she exclaimed in a whisper, grabbing Catalina's arm in her excitement.

"Don't believe what?" Catalina asked, always a

little behind the sharper Nita.

"Look who just walked through the door with Armando!" She gave Morena a nudge with her elbow as she shifted her position. She didn't want to look like she was gawking, but she had to get a better look at what was going on.

The other two girls turned to look, and both were astonished to see Francesca on the rich bachelor's arm.

"It's Francesca!" Morena's delight was undisguised.

"I know, and after everything that's happened . . ." Nita felt duty-bound to bring up the unsavory side of things. "You'd think she'd worry about what people were going to say."

"Nita, be quiet. Francesca's our friend." Morena was annoyed by her attitude. Before Francesca had made the unfortunate mistake of running off with that dreadful, but very handsome American, she'd been one of their dearest friends.

"Well, it's true," Nita maintained.

"I don't care if it's true or not," she corrected. "We'll not speak of it again. She's been through enough, without our adding to it."

"You're right, Morena. I like Francesca, and I've missed her," Catalina finally spoke up.

"I like her, too. But if she'd only used a little common sense none of this would have happened to her in the first place."

Morena gave Nita a pained look. "Are you saying you would have been able to resist that man? We only met him the one time, but he certainly made an impression on me," she confessed.

"If he'd asked me to run away with him, I'd have

gone in a minute!" Catalina told them, remembering the tall, good-looking man who'd swept Francesca off her feet.

"It certainly wasn't the logical thing for Francesca to do, but then when is love ever logical?" Morena concluded.

"Well, I think what happened proves it wasn't love on his part." Nita's expression was set in disapproving lines.

"Whatever happened is over. She's obviously beginning a new life for herself, and, as her friends, we should be completely supportive."

"You're right," Catalina agreed.

"Come on, let's go say hello."

Nita reluctantly went along.

As Armando led Francesca into the crowded ballroom, she found she was more than a little nervous. It had been nearly two years since she'd seen most of these people, and she wasn't sure what kind of welcome she would receive. She knew her elopement had been all the talk, and she was certain, since bad news traveled twice as fast as good news, that most were aware of the dismal outcome of her rash action. She grew tense, and Armando sensed it.

"You needn't worry, you know," he said softly, leaning toward her in an action that implied intimacy. "You're under my protection now."

Though his declaration rankled her, Francesca soon discovered he was right for she was quickly surrounded by Morena, Nita, and Catalina.

"Francesca! I can't believe you're actually here!" Morena told her as she hurried across the ballroom to hug her.

"Morena! It is so good to see you." Francesca was happy to see her friend, too. "I was hoping you'd be here tonight . . . and Catalina and Nita, too!" she greeted the two other women who approached.

"We've missed you," Catalina said as she, too, hugged Francesca in welcome.

"Have you been well?" Nita asked.

"I'm fine," Francesca replied without going into any detail. She wanted to start fresh tonight, not rehash the past.

"It's good to have you back." Morena turned her good-humored, brown-eyed gaze on Armando. "I'm so glad you brought her."

"So am I," he answered proudly.

The music began again, making it impossible to talk with any ease.

Since he was eager to have Francesca in his arms and all to himself, Armando invited, "Let's dance."

"Of course," Francesca acquiesced gracefully. Then she said to Morena and the others, "We'll talk more later?"

"Fine," they answered as they watched Armando guide Francesca out onto the dance floor.

"I wish Armando would look at me the way he looks at her," Catalina sighed to her companions.

"I know. With his power and influence, he's quite a catch. Francesca's almost like a cat, you know? She keeps landing on her feet," Nita remarked.

Hearing the touch of snideness in her voice, Morena scolded quietly. "Mind your tongue. Francesca's been through a lot. Let's wish her happiness, now. It's the least we can do."

"You're right." The would-be gossip was suitably

chastened; and after one last glance at the gracefully dancing couple they moved off toward the refreshment table to see what there was good to eat.

"You look positively breathtaking this evening," Armando told Francesca once he'd managed to get her away from the gaggle of homely young women. It seemed an eternity since he'd last held her in his arms, and he meant to take advantage of every moment they had together this evening.

"Thank you. I have to admit, it is nice to be here," Francesca answered, enjoying the gentle rhythm of the music and the excitement of being out among people her own age again.

"You should have come back to the city sooner." Armando lowered his voice to give it intimacy. He let his gaze linger on the creamy swell of her breasts above the low-cut bodice of her gown.

"You know that wasn't possible before." She thought of Michael and the time she'd needed to get her life back together.

"You're right, of course," he said solicitously. "And there's no reason for us to concern ourselves with anything but the present. We're together now. That's all that matters."

Francesca's benign smile belied the uneasiness she was feeling. She'd agreed to come to this party, nothing more! But the hot familiarity of his hand at her waist and the smugness of his expression told her he thought differently. Francesca was relieved when the music ended, and she could move out of his embrace.

"Would you care for some refreshment?" he offered solicitously.

"I'd love something to drink."

They made their way toward the festively decorated refreshment table where a sumptuous array of foods and punches awaited them. Armando had just handed her a cup of the potent concoction when Marita sought them out.

"Francesca, I'm so glad Uncle Armando convinced you to come."

"I wouldn't have missed it," she told her, sipping of the heady wine punch. "Your mother gives fabulous parties."

"I'll tell her you said so. She'll be pleased."

"You're looking particularly lovely tonight, Marita. Are you expecting a special gentleman?" Armando inquired.

"All the young gentlemen of Havana are special," Marita deferred lightheartedly, not willing to admit to her uncle, or anyone, for that matter, that for some reason she'd been thinking about Rafael Ramirez all day and could hardly wait to see him again.

"Always the coqueta. Will you ever settle down?" he teased.

"Will you?" she countered his question with a question.

"Time will tell," Armando responded, focusing his attention on Francesca.

His intense regard bothered Francesca, and she quickly downed the rest of her punch, hoping it would give her the fortitude she was going to need for the rest of the evening to come. Armando immediately saw that her cup was refilled and served his

103

niece some too. They spoke of inconsequential things for a few moments until several of Armando's business acquaintances joined them and drew him into a business conversation.

Francesca was glad to have his attention diverted away from her for a while, and she chatted easily with Marita as they both enjoyed their punch. Marita tried to listen in on her uncle's conversation while she and Francesca talked, but she was thwarted when Armando excused himself.

"Francesca, darling, I must speak to my associates alone for a few minutes," he apologized.

"Of course," she said with great understanding, actually pleased at the idea.

"I'll be in the study, should you need me. Marita, I'll speak with you later." He moved off with his companions.

Marita was irritated that he was going into the study to talk, but there was nothing she could do about it without drawing undue attention to her interest.

"Would you like to go upstairs and freshen up?" she asked Francesca, knowing there was no point in staying there any longer.

"I'd like that."

They made their way to the wide front staircase that led to the spacious second floor where a special room had been set aside just for the ladies. They were so engrossed in their conversation that they didn't notice the front door opening or Rosa going forth to greet the new group of late arrivals.

Chapter Eight

Ablaze with lights and alive with the sound of music and revelry, the Valequez mansion was an impressive sight. Excitement quivered through Anna as she realized that tonight she was actually one of the guests there. For a moment she almost allowed herself to believe that tonight was real, but her hard-earned maturity convinced her of the fallacy of such a dream. It was enough that she was going to have this evening with Slater. She didn't dare grasp for more for she knew greed always bred disaster.

When their carriage drew to a stop, both Slater and Rafe climbed down first. Slater remained to assist Anna in her descent, while Rafe went to give instructions to the driver. That done, they started inside.

Slater played his role as Anna's escort with accomplished ease, and to all outward appearances, they seemed the perfect couple. She looked sophisticated and worldly. He looked dashing and debonair. Eyes turned when they made their entrance, and more than a few of the bachelors who were in attendance wondered at Anna's identity.

Slater's nerves of steel, developed from his years as an agent served him well now. No one suspected that his carefully composed expression and cavalier manners were a deception. Beneath his highly polished, civilized veneer, his heart was savage. His gaze was watchful and alert as he readied himself to face, for the first time since his imprisonment and torture, his most hated foe.

They entered the foyer. Slater with Anna on his arm followed Rafe's lead. As they moved forward to meet their hostess, some movement on the stairs caught Slater's attention. Wary, expecting trouble, he looked up, but all he caught was a quick glimpse of the backs of two women as they disappeared down the upstairs hall.

Slater relaxed a bit as he realized his foolishness in reacting so suspiciously, but then, another emotion came into play as he realized that one of the women had been wearing a dress the exact same color as the gown Francesca had worn the first time they'd met. Slater tried to put the memory from him, but he knew he would never be able to forget that night and how absolutely ravishing Francesca had been. He'd known immediately that he'd wanted her for his own.

The ache within Slater expanded until his chest was tight. He gave himself a fierce mental shake as he drew a steadying breath. He wondered if the time would ever come when he would stop thinking about her and looking for her . . . stop expecting to hear her laugh at any moment . . . stop expecting to see her bright, sunny smile.

"Slater?" Anna had sensed that there was something troubling him, and her expression was concerned as she gazed up at him.

He flashed her a disarming smile to discourage any questions, then turned his full attention back to Rafe who was ready to make the introductions. He drew Anna long with him.

Anna didn't believe his display of casual unconcern for a minute, but she let it pass, knowing there was nothing else she could do.

Rafe, meanwhile, was caught up in the effusive welcome Rosa was bestowing on them.

"Rafael, I'm so pleased you could come and bring your guests with you tonight." Rosa beamed up at him. She thought him an especially attractive man and knew he would be a good match for Marita. She just wished that she could convince her headstrong daughter to start looking seriously for a husband.

"Thank you, Rosa. We appreciate your thoughtful invitation." There was no doubt in his mind about that. "Let me introduce my cousin, Anna Melena. Anna, this is Rosa Valequez, our hostess."

"It's so nice to meet you," Rosa welcomed Anna, thinking her one of the most striking women she'd ever seen.

Anna returned her greeting.

"And this is my good friend, Slater MacKenzie. Slater, I'd like you to meet, Rosa Valequez."

"Welcome." Rosa's eyes widened ever so slightly at the mention of Slater's name. She wondered if Francesca was aware that he was there tonight and knew she'd better tell her brother as quickly as possible, just in case she didn't.

Slater noticed the spark of recognition in her gaze.

"It's a pleasure to meet you, Señora Valequez."

"Rosa, please. Enjoy yourselves tonight. Many of your friends have already arrived, Rafael." Rosa suddenly wanted to move them along into the ballroom so she could go find Armando. Feeling as her brother did about Francesca, Rosa knew he would want to protect her from embarrassment.

When Rafael, Slater, and Anna headed into the ballroom, Rosa rushed down the hall toward the study. The door was closed, but she didn't care. This was important. She knocked with loud insistence and waited until she heard him call out to her.

"It's me, Rosa," she answered impatiently.

Armando was annoyed by the interruption. His discussion was important. He was scowling his disapproval when he opened the door. "Yes? What is it?"

"I must speak with you," she said with hushed urgency, her eyes dark mirrors of worry.

"I'm busy right now . . ."

"I know that, but this is important," Rosa insisted.

Seeing the earnestness in her expression and knowing she wouldn't have bothered him unless it was truly necessary, he held the door wide for her to enter. "Gentlemen, it seems something unexpected has come up, and my sister is in need of my counsel."

"We understand, don't worry. We can finish our talk at another time," the two men said amicably. They left the room to give Armando and Rosa the privacy they needed.

"Armando," Rosa began, going to him to touch his arm as soon as he'd closed the door. "Is Ricardo near?"

"Ricardo? Why do you want him?"

"This concerns Ricardo, as well as you."

"What does?" he asked exasperated.

"Rafael Ramirez just arrived," Rosa explained quickly.

"Yes, so?" He shrugged as if his being there was supremely unimportant.

"He's brought Slater MacKenzie with him."

Armando's eyes immediately narrowed to dangerous slits, and he went completely still as he stared down at his sister. "MacKenzie is here?" he repeated in disbelief.

His sister nodded. "He just arrived. He's escorting Rafael's cousin, Anna."

"Has he seen Francesca yet?"

"No. She's still upstairs with Marita. That's why I came to get you right away. I don't know all the details about Francesca's past, and I don't want to know. I just thought this might prove to be very awkward for her if she were caught unawares."

"You did the right thing," he praised her.

"Shall I go tell her?"

"No . . . leave that to me," Armando insisted, his mind filled with evil designs. He had no doubt that Francesca would be able to handle seeing MacKenzie again, for there was certainly no love lost on her part where he was concerned. But MacKenzie . . . now there was something else. The American thought his wife was dead. What was he going to think if he came face-to-face with her in the middle of a crowded ballroom and discovered she was there with him? Armando smiled broadly at the amusing prospect.

"You find this funny?"

"Hardly, sweet sister," he replied as his thoughts raced over the myriad of possibilities before him.

"Will you do me a favor?"

"You need to ask?"

"I want you to go upstairs and stall Francesca and Marita, but don't tell them anything."

"All right. I'll go now."

"On your way, have one of the servants find Ricardo and send him to me."

Rosa nodded her agreement, but there was no need for she almost ran into a white-faced, wild-eyed Ricardo as she left the room.

"Ricardo . . . ?" She stopped abruptly to stare up at his pale features.

"I'm sorry, Rosa. Is Armando in here?" he asked hurriedly.

"Yes . . . and he wants to speak with you."

Ricardo brushed past her without another word. "He's here!" He nearly shouted after he'd slammed the door behind him.

"Yes, I know," Armando replied calmly. "He's here as Ramirez's guest."

"We should have known he'd do something as outrageous as this!"

Armando dropped into the chair behind the desk and sat back. He looked almost relaxed, and his unconcerned manner annoyed the older man.

"Don't you even care that he's shown up?"

"Naturally, I care. I'm sure there's nothing our friend MacKenzie would like better to do than put a bullet in me. But I'm not concerned." He waved away any worry.

"Then you're a damned fool!"

Ricardo's charge angered Armando. "No, you're the fool if you let this American get to you. We are in

110

control here, not MacKenzie."

"But . . ."

He held up a hand to silence him. "First, you must speak to Francesca. She'll be angry, I'm sure."

"And then?"

Armando leaned forward, resting his elbows on the desktop as he steepled his fingers thoughtfully before him. His expression was savage, almost barbarous. "And then we go on as if nothing's happened. Francesca came here to enjoy herself, and I intend to see that she does."

"I don't understand. How will she be able to enjoy herself with him around?"

"I tried to break MacKenzie before, but nothing worked . . . not even my telling him that Francesca was dead. But hating me as much as I'm sure he does now, when he sees his 'dead' wife in my arms, laughing, and having a wonderful time . . . It should be very effective, don't you thin?"

Ricardo's distress eased a little, but he still had serious concerns. "But what if she and MacKenzie talk? What if she finds out that the divorce never took place? What if she finds out he doesn't know anything about Michael?"

"How will she find out? After what she thinks MacKenzie's done to her and their son, I'm sure she'd rather shoot him than talk to him."

"That's true. His 'rejection' of the baby was really the killing blow for her." He managed a small, cunning smile.

Armando chuckled evilly, equally pleased. "I knew I was going to enjoy myself tonight, but I had no idea how much."

Ricardo was glad that Armando was in control of the situation. "This should truly be a memorable evening."

They exchanged confident looks.

"Go find your daughter. She's upstairs with Rosa and Marita. Tell her what's happened and tell her that I'll be waiting to help her."

Armando watched the older man leave, then leaned back in the chair once again feeling particularly triumphant. He'd been unable to defeat Mac-Kenzie before, but tonight everything was different. Tonight, he would win.

Francesca and her father were alone in the ladies' sitting room, and she was staring at him, stricken. Her mind was spinning. Her heart was throbbing painfully in her breast. *This couldn't be happening . . . not now!*

"I don't believe you," she whispered, struggling to control the frenzy of conflicting emotions that were playing havoc with her sanity.

"What reason would I have to lie to you? He came in with Rafael Ramirez and a woman named Anna."

At the mention of Anna's name, a spark of fire burned in Francesca's eyes. *Slater was here and he was with Anna . . . Hadn't she somehow always known there was more to their relationship than just 'business'?* Tears of pain and frustration threatened, but she refused to give in to them. Slater meant less than nothing to her. Anything she'd felt for him was in the past. It was over.

"I came up here to tell you myself privately, because I wasn't quite sure how you wanted to handle this. We can leave now if you'd like. You don't even have to see the man or speak to him."

"Leave?" Francesca lifted her head with pride. She wouldn't give Slater the satisfaction of thinking she'd run from him. "Why would I want to do that? I came here to enjoy myself, and I intend to do it."

"Armando said to tell you that he'll be waiting for you downstairs."

For the first time that night, Francesca was glad for Armando's presence. "Tell him I'll be down in a few minutes."

"I will." Ricardo went to her and pressed a fatherly kiss on her cheek. He then left her alone.

When her father had gone, the pride that had sustained Francesca in his presence drained away. She slumped down on the seat at the dressing table and tried to regain control of herself. *Slater was back!* The thought echoed through her mind as she sat there numb and unmoving. For so long she'd prayed for this moment, but eventually, those prayers had died, unanswered. She'd been forced to accept the truth—that Slater didn't love her and that he never had. His rejection could have broken her, but her pride had saved her, giving her the will to go on. She'd kept her head held high and had continued with her life, making Michael the center of her existence.

Francesca thought it was miserably unfair that Slater had decided to come back now, just when things were going so well. Knowing that he was a man who never acted without an ulterior motive, she couldn't help but wonder why he had returned.

Francesca lifted her gaze to study herself in the mirror. She had changed a lot since she'd last seen

Slater, but except for the new fullness of her bosom, a quick glance wouldn't reveal the difference. Her eyes were still the same, except now, instead of shining with the innocence of youth, they mirrored the knowledge of a woman. Her smile appeared the same, but it had lost is spontaneity. It was given far less freely now, and usually only to Michael.

Francesca was glad that outwardly she looked the same. She didn't want the scars on her heart to show. She didn't want Slater to know how he'd nearly broken her or how, if it hadn't been for Michael, she wouldn't have cared about living. She was glad, too, in a perverse way, that she'd decided to wear her hair up in a coronet of braids tonight, since Slater had always preferred her hair down. She would show him that he meant nothing to her. She would show him that his leaving hadn't mattered to her at all.

Francesca drew a deep, steadying breath and tried to calm her racing heart. What did she care that they were finally going to meet again? She hated Slater, didn't she? Her hands were strangely cold, and she rubbed them together to warm them. She wasn't about to give Slater any indication that his being there affected her. Slater was lower than the lowest in her estimation, and she wanted this confrontation over and done with. She had her own life to lead.

Drawing upon her anger, Francesca lifted her chin stubbornly. It wasn't going to be easy, but that didn't surprise her. When had anything been easy lately? The self-confidence she'd achieved during the months since Michael's birth gave her the strength to stand and walk regally for the door—her shoulders back, her head held high. By the time the evening ended, she would have Slater MacKenzie convinced that his leaving had been the best thing that had ever happened to her.

Francesca paused to smooth her skirts before going out into the hallway, and she smiled, more pleased than ever now with her choice of a gown. She'd show Slater MacKenzie that she hadn't believed all his undying declarations of love. She'd prove to him that he hadn't been the only one acting during their marriage. It had all been just a charade—on both their parts. Opening the door, she stepped out into the hall, heading off on her collision course with destiny.

The lilting music of the waltz filled the ballroom, swirling romantically around the couples who were moving gracefully about the dance floor. Slater was dancing with Anna, and he almost would have enjoyed the moment had he not been filled with poignant memories of Francesca. His mind and heart kept playing tricks on him. Each melody the musicians played seem to remind him of his wife and of something that had happened to them during the short time they'd been together. Sometimes a woman's laugh would sound so much like Francesca's that he was compelled to glance around. He knew he was being foolish, but for some unknown reason, tonight, he couldn't stop.

It troubled Slater to be so vulnerable. The rawness of his emotions left him uneasy for they were far too close to the surface to suit him. Tonight was the night when he would face Carlanta for the first time and, hopefully, find out the complete truth about Francesca. He couldn't afford to let his emotions rule. He had to be cool-headed and in complete control.

"You're an excellent dancer, Slater," Anna spoke up, interrupting his thoughts.

"You make it easy," he replied with a smile, glad to be distracted.

Anna was in ecstasy as they continued to practically float around the room. For years, she had fantasized about what it would be like to dance with Slater, and as wonderful as her dreams had been, they hadn't even come close to the reality. She had never known a more breathtaking moment. Anna wished it could go on forever, but unfortunately, the melody came to an end.

"That was wonderful. Thank you."

"My pleasure," he answered. Taking her arm, he escorted her to the side of the room.

The feel of Slater's muscled arm pressed to the side of her breast sent shivers of awareness through Anna. She knew this was all playacting on his part, but she couldn't help but wish that he felt the same way about her as she did about him.

Rafe sought them out after delivering the eligible young maiden he'd just danced with safely back to her mama.

"Have you run into Carlanta yet?" Rafe asked, his piercing gaze sweeping the crowded room for some sign of their mutual adversary.

"Not yet, but I know he's here somewhere. I can feel it."

As they were speaking, Rafe glanced out through the double doors that led to the foyer and spotted Ricardo descending the staircase.

"Well, well, well, look who else is in attendance

tonight." Rafe pointed Francesca's father out to his companions.

Slater scowled blackly at the sight of Ricardo. "I think I'll get a drink. Would you like anything?"

Rafe declined, but Anna requested a cup of punch. "I'll be right back."

Slater had just walked away when Marita left a group of her own friends and made her way across the room to join Rafe and Anna.

"Good evening, Anna. It's good to see you again. You look lovely tonight," she greeted the woman she thought was Rafael's cousin.

"Hello, Marita. You look beautiful, too," she returned the compliment.

"Thank you. The señora is a fine seamstress."

"Indeed, she is."

Marita turned her attention to Rafe, then. "Rafael Ramirez, we haven't had a chance to speak all evening," she teased with a pretty pout.

"That's because every time I tried, you were surrounded by a crowd of ardent admirers, and I couldn't even get close to you," he told her gallantly.

"And you wouldn't want to join a group of my admirers?" Marita asked archly, pretending to be hurt, though the light of her good nature shone in her eyes.

"Why stand among the crowd and be lost in a sea of faces? I wait until I can take the day, then I act." As his eyes met hers, he realized again just how beautiful she was. He wondered distractedly how it was that he'd known her so long and never fully appreciated her loveliness before. From her mane of raven curls to the sweet curve of her waist, she was a walking dream, a goddess of loveliness. He knew then why so many of Havana's men made fools out of themselves over her. She was irresistible.

"I look forward to the battle," Marita replied, gazing up at Rafe in wonder, her heart fluttering a bit over the intensity of his declaration. For a moment, she almost believed he might be serious, but then she remembered his reputation as the most notorious bachelor in all of Havana. She was sure he was well-practiced at delivering such romantic lines.

The awareness of the power of his attraction for her left Rafe confused and distracted. Suddenly, all that was important was that he hold Marita in his arms. Giving in to his demanding need, he held out his hand to her and invited, "Would you care to dance?"

"Have you taken the day, my handsome caballero?" She put her hand in his and felt excitement skitter through her at just that simple touch. She almost withdrew, but knew that would look ridiculous. What harm could there be in simply putting her hand in his?

"You tell me," he answered in a deep voice as he swept her out onto the dance floor. By the time the dance had ended, Rafe was so entranced that he found he'd made a date to have luncheon with her the following day.

Chapter Nine

Ricardo's mood was ebullient as he hurried from the foyer to seek out Armando where he still waited in Rosa's study.

"Francesca's deeply disturbed, but only because she hates him so much," he confided.

"Good, good." Armando smiled. "Did she say how long she'd be before she came downstairs?"

"Just a few minutes."

"I'd better go out and wait for her. I don't want her to face MacKenzie alone this first time. It's important we orchestrate this just right. I want MacKenzie to know from the start that Francesca's mine."

As Francesca walked down the hall toward the staircase and the moment of confrontation with Slater, her resolve to face him without flinching grew even more fierce. She stopped at the top of the stairs to glance down and see who was in the foyer, and it was then that she saw Armando waiting for her. She

119

smiled broadly at him, thinking how kind it was that he was going to help her through these next difficult hours. She began her descent with elegant dignity, her chin up, her back straight, her gaze focused solely on Armando.

Francesca refused to think about the way her heart was pounding. She concentrated only on the fact that Slater was there somewhere. She hoped his eyes were upon her now for she wanted him to find out just how little he meant to her.

Slater had gotten himself a tumbler of whiskey and returned to Anna's side, bringing her the drink she'd wanted. They were standing together observing the dancers, when for some unknown reason Slater felt compelled to look toward the foyer.

From where he stood there with Anna on the far side of the ballroom, Slater could see a full sweep of the staircase from about halfway down. As he watched, he caught sight of the bottom hem of a woman's dress as the woman wearing it came down the stairs. The gown was full-skirted and emerald in color, and he realized it was probably the same woman he'd gotten a glimpse of earlier when they'd first arrived.

In spite of his determination to try to put Francesca from his mind, seeing the dress again brought thoughts of her back to Slater with a vengeance. He wanted to look away. He knew he was torturing himself. He knew it couldn't be Francesca coming down the steps. She was lost to him forever. She was dead. Still, he stared, frozen in place, mesmerized by the unknown, as yet unseen, woman making her slow, steady, almost sensuous descent.

Without even being aware of it, Slater took a stiff drink from his tumbler of whiskey and finished more than half of it in the one swallow. Even as he drank, though, his eyes never left the woman who was moving step-by-step more fully into his view.

Francesca . . . Francesca . . . Francesca . . . Her name thundered through his mind and heart.

Slater knew it was ridiculous to feel this way. What did it matter if this stranger was wearing a gown that resembled the one Francesca had worn the night they'd first met? Though he argued logically with himself that there was no point in staring, his arguments did nothing to convince his aching, lonely soul. He was held enthralled by the fantasy that maybe . . . just maybe . . .

"Slater? What is it?" Anna touched his arm as she spoke, jarring him. She'd watched his expression change from one of polite interest in his surroundings to one of fierce intensity, and she wondered if he'd finally seen Carlanta.

"It's nothing . . ." Slater tore his gaze away from the mystery woman to turn to Anna. He was frowning as he tried to clear Francesca from his thoughts. It couldn't be her. "For a moment there, I was just thinking . . ."

"Thinking what?" He sounded so confused and troubled that she had no idea what was on his mind.

Slater lifted his gaze toward the foyer once again, doubting himself and his wild imaginings. This time, though, when he glanced in the woman's direction, his eyes widened in disbelief. *Francesca . . .*

121

The woman looked like Francesca.

Slater couldn't move or speak for a moment. He was held spellbound by what he believed was a mirage. This couldn't be Francesca. It had to be just some woman who resembled her. The woman was stepping off the bottom step now, smiling brightly as if she hadn't a care in the world. He knew she wasn't his wife, and yet . . . Her hair was the same color as his Francesca's, but Francesca had usually worn hers down and this woman had done hers up. Their eyes were remarkably alike, though, and so were their features. Slater was standing rigidly as he mentally compared the emerald-clad temptress whose curvaceous figure was only slightly more lush than his wife's had been.

Francesca . . . he silently called her name. His mind told him it wasn't her. His heart cried out that it could be no one else.

Without taking his eyes off of her, Slater reached out blindly to set his glass on a small table that was close by, then started across the wide, crowded dance floor in her direction. He had to find out who she was . . . He had to know . . .

Anna had seen the tenseness in him and when she'd looked up in the direction he'd been staring, she gasped out loud. Her mind shrieked that it couldn't be Francesca, but the vision standing in the foyer told her otherwise. By the time Anna realized why Slater had gone so quiet, he had already moved off without a word. She didn't hesitate to follow him.

Slater was a driven man as he shouldered his way through the dancing couples, his eyes fixed on his goal. He fully expected to emerge from the crowd and discover that he was wrong, but knowing that didn't stop him. He had to get closer to the woman who looked so much like Francesca. He just wanted to be near her for a little while.

Moving ever onward, muttering apologies as he went, Slater kept his regard riveted on the scene in the foyer. He was halfway across the dance floor heading for the door that led to the entryway, getting closer and closer, when he realized the truth. This was no dream . . . no fantasy . . . no figment of his overactive imagination. The lovely woman there in the hall wearing the emerald gown *was* Francesca.

Logical questions of 'how' and 'why' pounded at him; but, at that particular moment, Slater was so filled with joy that none of it mattered. All that mattered was that Francesca was alive and well. He didn't care about anything except seeing her, speaking to her again, and holding her in his arms once more. It had been so long, and he'd missed her so desperately.

"Francesca . . . " her name was almost a soft groan on his lips as he picked up his pace again.

What happened next, though, struck Slater like a violent, physical blow. Francesca was making her way across the foyer as he drew near. He was just about to call out loudly to her, when she walked straight into the arms of the waiting Armando Carlanta and kissed him full on the mouth! Francesca was the woman he loved beyond reason . . . the woman he would gladly have given his own life for. Yet she was here, alive and well when he'd thought her dead, and obviously very much in love with the man who'd tried to kill him not so long ago.

Slater stopped, then took an involuntary step backward as if recoiling from some unseen attack. His hands clenched into fists of rage at his sides. *Carlanta and Francesca?!* He felt cold, then hot, then cold again as the shock of his discovery reverberated through him. The emotional blow was almost too much for him to bear, and momentarily, he moved away from the sight that almost physically sickened him . . . Francesca in Carlanta's arms . . .

Their loving embrace wrenched at his vitals and left him grasping for some kind of understanding. Slowly, what must have been the horrible truth became clear to him. Their marriage—the union he'd thought would last a lifetime—had been nothing but a farce . . . a travesty . . . a cruel and bitter joke played on him. He had been the only one who'd loved. The entire time they had been together, Francesca must have just been helping Carlanta and her father with their plot against him. All his mourning, all his despair had been for a dream that had never really existed. The Francesca Salazar he'd married had been no more than a common whore . . . bargaining her body to aid her lover and her father in their quest for power.

A hatred unlike anything he'd ever felt before gripped Slater. Ice encased his heart, freezing the hopes and dreams he'd harbored just moments before. All that was over now. He knew the truth, and the truth was pure hell.

Anna reached his side and quickly, without making a scene, grabbed his arm. "Slater, wait. Stop and think before you act!" she said. Having witnessed the whole thing, she was afraid he might try to kill Carlanta right here and now and in doing so put himself at risk.

He looked down at Anna, seeing her, but not seeing her. Anna found his expression so strangely composed, his eyes so frigidly intense, that she felt a chill of fear.

"I have no intention of doing anything untoward," he assured her with deadly calm. "I just intend to greet the wife I haven't seen in over a year."

Anna kept her hold on his arm. "I'll go with you."

Looking much like a very happy, loving couple, they walked forward to face Francesca together.

When Francesca had reached the bottom of the stairs, she hadn't hesitated for a moment, but had gone straight to Armando. For the first time ever in their relationship, she was the one who was aggressive. She kissed him. It wasn't a passionate kiss, but one that gave the impression that their relationship was one of intimacy, devotion, and tenderness. Armando reveled in the power her demonstrative move gave him. He felt he'd won, at last.

"Thank you. You'll never know how much I appreciate your kindness," she said softly, then stepped back.

"But I haven't done anything," Armando answered with false humility. In truth, he wanted to hear more of her heartfelt appreciation. It warmed him, and somehow made all his earlier plotting against MacKenzie worthwhile.

"Oh, yes, you have," Francesca contradicted, giving him a tender smile. "It would be far more difficult to face this without you here at my side."

"I'm glad I can help. You know I care about you, Francesca." He lifted one of her hands to his lips and kissed the back of it with all the ardor a gentleman was allowed. His black eyes met her dark-eyed gaze as he did so.

In spite of the fact that Francesca was tremendously grateful to him for helping her right then, the touch of his lips on her hand still left her feeling uncomfortable. "Shall we join the party?" she suggested, eager to put an end to this sudden intimacy that had unwittingly blossomed between them.

"Are you sure you want to?" He was more than willing to leave with her now. In fact, there was probably nothing he would have liked better than to get her alone.

"I'm positive." She was firm in her determination.

"There might be talk."

She managed a small shrug. "They'll talk anyway. I'm sure they did before, and those who know him are probably talking now."

"MacKenzie might try to cause trouble."

"How? He can't hurt me now. I don't love him anymore."

Armando was thrilled at her confession, but he didn't betray it to Francesca. "As you wish, then. Let's go in and join the others."

Francesca allowed him to take her arm, and they turned, ready to return to the party and do battle. As they did, they came face-to-face with Slater and Anna just as they walked into the foyer.

Several other couples were passing through the

entryway at just that moment, and their intrusive presence made it impossible for anyone to say anything right away. Slater was glad for the reprieve for he found himself rendered momentarily mute. Francesca looked so lovely that it was painful for him. His gaze drifted over her, settling fleetingly on her mouth while he remembered tasting of its sweetness, then shifting lower to her breasts where they swelled so temptingly above the low-cut bodice of her gown.

A hot flare of desire rushed through Slater as the now-forbidden memory of the last time they'd been together surged into his thoughts. But as he remembered the wonder of being in her arms making love to her that night, he also remembered what else had happened. He recalled how he'd been beaten and dragged from the room on Carlanta's orders, and he had no doubt now that it had been with Francesca's full knowledge and involvement. It was ugly, but it was the truth. His own wife had worked with Armando to set him up. All these months he'd been mourning her, she'd been alive and well, and, from the looks of things, bedding Armando the whole time.

It was the biggest battle Slater had ever waged, trying to keep from revealing his feelings of anger and confusion. Endless questions beleaguered him. How could he have been so wrong about Francesca? He had loved her. He had made her his wife. Slater had always considered himself to be an excellent judge of character. How could Francesca have been so conniving and deceitful, and he'd never known? Perhaps it was true what they said about only fools falling in love. There certainly could be no denying it, when he had all the answers to all his questions standing right there before him.

Every fiber of his being was still aware of Francesca's presence, but Slater fought it down, as he did his near violent hatred of Carlanta. His nerves were stretched taut, but he managed to keep his expression reflecting only a mild interest in the both of them.

"Francesca," he said her name easily, as if she were just a passing acquaintance he hadn't seen in a while. "How good it is to see you again. You're looking so *well*." He wanted to add *'for a dead woman,'* but he managed to restrain himself.

"Hello, Slater," Francesca returned with a calm she certainly wasn't feeling. Slater was here! He was actually standing there only a few feet from her . . . with Anna on his arm.

Francesca's heart was pounding as if it would burst. She had longed for this moment; yet now that it was here, she wondered how she was ever going to go through with it. She didn't know if she was a good enough actress to pretend she felt nothing for Slater, when even after all this time she'd been unable to forget the glory of his kiss or the wonder of making love to him. He had promised her so much, and she'd been foolish enough to believe him. That misplaced trust had nearly turned her life to ashes. Slater had lied to her. He'd married her for his own selfish reasons, then used her and deserted her just when she'd needed him most. Francesca swallowed tightly as she pushed the errant thoughts from her mind. She would play the game, and this time, she would win.

"It's so nice to see you, too. You've met Armando, haven't you?" She turned an adoring gaze on Carlanta as he stood proudly at her side.

"We've met," Slater replied simply, though it was a credit to his incredible self-control that he didn't physically attack the arrogant Cuban official at that very moment. It was bad enough that Francesca—the wife he'd been told was dead—was greeting him as casually as if they'd only been apart for a few days. But to find her on the arm of the one man he despised above all others was almost more than Slater could bear. This was Carlanta—the man who'd tortured him and would have killed him had he not managed to escape. For just a fraction of an instant, Slater wondered if his tenuous control over his more savage emotions would hold. Bloodlust filled him. He wanted to take them both by the throat. He wanted to kill. . . .

"It certainly is a pleasure to run into you again, MacKenzie," Armando announced with a wide smile. His obsidian eyes were shining with vicious triumph, though he could detect no ounce of defeat in Slater.

"Yes, I'd been hoping to have another meeting with you, too. When we met before, I was restrained by circumstances beyond my control. This time, however, I feel no such constraints." His tone was conversational, but the message, and challenge, was there.

Armando's smile broadened. "I'm looking forward to renewing our acquaintance."

Slater gave a slight inclination of his head as he turned his attention back to Francesca. "I'm sure you remember Anna."

"Oh, of course. How have you been?" Francesca was amazed that she could sound so cordial, when all she really felt like doing was clawing the other woman's eyes out.

"I've been fine." Anna deliberately moved a little closer to Slater to subtly imply just what kind of relationship theirs was. She had always known Slater was good at what he did as an agent, but the sang-froid he was displaying right now during what had to be one of the most difficult times of his life, left her admiring him even more. The slight tensing of his arm beneath her fingers was the only indication he gave that seeing Francesca again had upset him.

"Obviously," Francesca drawled, glancing between them.

Anna gave her a confident smile as she added cuttingly, "It seems you've been fine, too."

Francesca missed her insinuation completely. "Life has been very good to me lately." She gave Armando a look that spoke volumes.

Anna felt Slater go rigid at her side, and the jealousy she'd felt for Francesca now turned to a burning hatred. Anna didn't know why the other woman had lied to Slater about her own death or why she was here tonight with Carlanta, and she didn't care. She only knew that Francesca had deliberately hurt Slater and that alone was enough to make her despise her forever. Anna cast Slater a sidelong glance, hoping to catch his eye and give him a reassuring smile, but to her heartache, she found his attention was completely on his wife.

"*Whatever* it is you're doing, certainly agrees with you." Slater's gaze slid over her with open familiarity before moving to Armando and back.

Francesca knew what he was thinking, and she was determined to match him in this challenge of wits. She gave a little nonchalant shrug as she eyed the beauteous Anna clinging so possessively to his arm. "You, too. You're looking well, and obviously Cuba's entire female population is glad you're back."

"Indeed, we are," Anna put in with a Cheshire grin.

Had Francesca been a cat, her hackles would have been up. "Have you had any more narrow escapes since we last saw each other, Slater?" She was referring to his escape from their marriage.

Slater's green eyes glinted dangerously at her words. He thought she was talking about his escape from Carlanta, and it infuriated him that she could speak so casually of his torturous imprisonment. He suddenly wanted to punish her for what he'd suffered. "Why don't we discuss it while we dance, *my love?* I'm sure Anna won't mind if I leave her alone for a moment, and surely, Armando can live without you for that long." He turned a daring gaze on his enemy.

Armando started to protest, but Francesca spoke up before he could say anything. She was going to handle this herself.

"I'd be delighted," Francesca answered before Armando could protest. She sounded sweetly indifferent, but she was really seething. She wasn't "his" anything, let alone "his love," and she knew she never had been. She wanted to tell him to take his precious Anna and leave. She wanted to tell him that she hated him and never wanted to lay eyes on him again. Instead, she excused herself from Armando with a casual, "I'll be back."

"Of course, my dear," he replied with courtly graciousness as he handed her over to Slater.

Chapter Ten

The music had just ended, concluding a very enjoyable sojourn on the dance floor for Rafael and Marita when she was stolen away by one of her ardent suitors. Rafe realized with some surprise that he was reluctant to let her go, but there was little he could do. The other young man already had his hand at her waist and was guiding her away from him.

Masking his disappointment and wondering about it at the same time, Rafe decided to seek out the company of the men where they'd gathered to drink, smoke cigars, and play cards in one of the other sitting rooms. He was just starting from the ballroom, when he looked up. What he saw before him caused him to come to an abrupt halt. He stared openly, unable to believe his own eyes. There, in the open doorway was Slater—with Francesca on his arm!

"Madre de Dios!" he muttered to himself, quickly trying to grasp what had come to pass. He caught a glimpse of Anna entering the ballroom through the other door at the far end of the room, and he hurried toward her as the musicians began to play a waltz.

Anna saw Rafe coming and waited for him there in a quiet, nearly empty corner of the room. "You saw?" she asked in a low voice when he reached her side.

"Yes! But how? She's supposed to be dead!"

"It was lies, all lies," Anna told him in a strangely strangled voice.

She sounded so different that Rafe glanced down at her. What he saw startled him a bit. He'd always thought of Anna as a strong woman. Her bravery in fighting for their cause was well-known. But seeing her now with her eyes shimmering with unshed tears and her bottom lip quivering slightly as she fought for control of her emotions, showed him what a truly vulnerable female she really was—where Slater was concerned. It was more than plain to him that she loved him deeply, and his heart ached for her.

"Anna, what happened?"

She quickly explained how Slater had seen Francesca from across the room and how he had rushed to her. "I couldn't believe it, Rafael! Francesca is his wife, and yet she had the nerve to stand there before him with Carlanta as her escort!"

"How did Slater handle it?" Rafe was concerned that his friend might be planning to do something dangerous.

"He seemed all right, but this is such a shock . . . I mean just an hour ago we thought she was dead . . . He came to Cuba to find her grave . . . and here she was alive and with Armando the whole time!"

"I don't understand any of this." Rafe shook his

head slowly as he tried to put it all together, but none of it made sense. Where had Francesca been hiding all this time, and why?

"I always knew Francesca was no good," Anna was saying. "She thought her money and position made her special and privileged, but she's really worse than the lowest whore working the docks! At least they're honest about what they do!" She paused and glanced over at Rafe, the pain in her heart showing in her dark eyes. "How could she have done this to Slater? If she really loved him, how could she have let him be hurt that way?"

"I don't know," he answered grimly. "But if I know Slater, I'm sure he plans to find out."

Slater and Francesca had just begun to dance to the strains of a lilting, romantic waltz, when Rafe saw Armando enter the ballroom and stand off to the side. Rafe got Anna's attention, then nodded in Carlanta's direction. They both looked on in silence. Rafe was tense for he expected trouble at any moment, while Anna was faced with a terrible, heartbreaking reality she didn't want to acknowledge.

Feeling more than confident about the way things were going, Ricardo had begun to drink and celebrate with several of his friends near the refreshment table. However, when he caught sight of his daughter dancing with Slater, he nearly choked on his liquor. Without looking too much the fool, he searched out Armando and nearly dragged him out of the ballroom.

"What the hell is she doing dancing with him?!"

he demanded tautly.

"MacKenzie asked her and she accepted," Armando told him, sounding as if it were of little importance.

"What do you mean, *'He asked and she accepted'*? Don't you realize . . . ?"

"Ricardo, my friend, have you lost your faith in me already?" he challenged him with a sardonic lift of one brow.

Ricardo shut up, but the nervousness he was feeling did not abate as he let his gaze follow Francesca around the room.

Morena, Nita, and Catalina were standing together again, looking much like the wallflowers they were. Though the party was a good one with excellent food and drink, of which Morena had had more than her share, the evening was proving a complete disaster for them where romance was concerned. As troubling as that was though, the excitement being acted out before them right now, made it seem insignificant. It didn't matter to any of the three that they hadn't been asked to dance for the past half hour, for they were too caught up in the intrigue that was swirling about them.

"Oh, my God! Can you believe it?" Nita remarked to her friends, keeping one eye on Francesca and Slater dancing together as she leaned toward them to whisper in a scandalized tone.

"It's him and they're actually dancing together!" Catalina exclaimed.

"I just can't believe he's here. The last rumor I heard was that he'd left the country," Morena told

136

them, unable to look away from the couple.

"I wonder why he came back?" Nita pondered out loud.

"He came back because he really loves Francesca and couldn't live without her," Catalina put in, ever the hopeless romantic. "Just look at the way they're moving together and the way they're looking at each other . . . It's like they're one person—in spirit and mind and body. They were meant to be together." Her eyes were glued to Francesca and Slater as they swirled about the floor in graceful, sensuous rhythm with the music.

"Hardly," the sarcastic, mean-spirited Nita decried.

"Where's Armando?" Morena looked around suddenly realizing that Francesca's escort for the evening was nowhere to be seen.

"I don't know, but wherever he is, he's probably not too happy about this."

"Who cares about Armando?" Catalina sighed happily. "Just look at them . . ."

All three women fixed their gazes on the dancing couple, whose movements seemed fluid and perfectly atuned.

"They do seem happy . . . ," Morena admitted, and Catalina's dreamy expression never faltered as she nodded in agreement.

When Francesca had gone into Slater's arms, she'd been determined to act like she was dancing with any other man. She'd believed that she only had to get through the next few minutes without faltering and then she would never have to see Slater or suffer his touch again.

Hers was a noble goal, but the moment Slater's hand settled with familiar dominance at her slender waist and they began to move to the seductive rhythm together, Francesca's self-control wavered dangerously. She didn't want to feel it, but it was there—the sweet, drugged sensation that always came from being held by him, and it left her feeling furiously helpless to combat it.

Memories of other nights and other waltzes overwhelmed her. A shiver trembled through her, and she hoped against hope that Slater hadn't noticed. She didn't want him to realize how upsetting it was to her to be in his arms.

Slater felt her tremble and smiled grimly to himself. He assumed Francesca was shaking because she was scared, and he was glad. Knowing she was worried about what he was going to do next, gave him a powerful advantage, and he planned to make full use of it.

In an unexpected move, Slater swirled her expertly around, drawing her closer to him as he did so. Francesca followed his lead without missing a step, but tried to resist the pressure he was exerting to bring her near. She realized finally that her struggle against him was useless, and she surrendered gracefully.

"Even from the very beginning, we've always danced well together, haven't we, Francesca?" he inquired in a conversational tone.

"It's the only thing we did do well together," she retorted.

"Oh, I don't know . . ." Slater drawled, giving her a maddening grin. "I can think of a few other things . . ."

"Why, you . . ." She stiffened, embarrassed.

"You know, Francesca, some people say that if a couple dances together well their lovemaking is sure to be just as good. Tell me, is Carlanta a good dancer?"

Francesca went rigid in anger and humiliation at his implied insult. "Damn you, Slater MacKenzie! You think you have all the answers to everything, don't you?"

"I know more now than I ever wanted to know, *sweet wife.*" His emerald gaze turned icy as he struggled to maintain the fragile hold he had over himself. He lifted his head to look around and noticed that they were very near the open doors that led out into the center patio. Needing to get out of the ballroom and away from prying eyes, he waltzed Francesca toward the exit.

Francesca was unaware of his plan as she glared up at him, her cheeks flushed with fury. "You know nothing, and you have no right to call me that! Not anymore, not when our marriage was based on nothing but lies."

"And you know all about that, don't you?" He felt the rein on his temper slipping, and in the blink of an eye, he whisked her outside into the cool, enveloping darkness of the night. The moment they were out of sight of the people of the ballroom, he stopped dancing and took her by the wrist to draw her farther away from the house.

"What do you think you're doing?!" she de-

139

manded, trying to dig in her heels, but his pull was relentless.

"Why, I'm taking you outside for a walk in the moonlight. What did you think I was doing?"

"Let me go!" She tried to yank free, but his hold, while not painful, was firm. "I have nothing more to say to you."

"No, but I'll bet you always had plenty to say to Carlanta, didn't you?"

"I don't know what you're talking about. Let go of my arm! I want to go back inside."

"Do you think for one moment that I care what you want?" Slater's anger was ruling him now. It didn't matter to him that they were at a party where almost anyone could come upon them or that within minutes Carlanta would discover they'd disappeared from the ballroom and start looking for them. He took her along with him away from the lights of the house to a secluded corner of the patio that was lush with fragrant blossoming foliage.

"Of course not, you never did! You never cared about anything . . ." She finally managed to jerk her arm away from him. She stood there then, her temper fiery, her passions running high.

"That's where you're wrong, Francesca. I care about a lot of things . . ." Slater said softly, threateningly, as he loomed over her, his face stark and almost terrifying in the night-shadowed darkness. He brought one hand up, snaring her chin and holding her immobile as his mouth came down upon hers in a powerful, punishing kiss.

Francesca gasped and tried to twist away. "Why don't you just go away and leave me alone?!"

"Oh, no. This time I'm not going anywhere . . ."

Squirming, she kept up her fight for freedom, but he grabbed her wrists with his other hand and held her easily. His mouth moved over hers again with dominating insistence, evoking feelings deep inside her she'd thought long dead.

Francesca wanted to get away, but there was no escaping this exquisite torture. For a moment, she let herself relax and enjoy the wonder of his flaming kiss. She'd wanted this for so long, ached for this . . . Yet, before she could surrender to the bliss of his embrace, Francesca remembered the truth. He'd walked out on her and left her to bear his child alone. He'd written that note, and he'd proven it to be true when he'd told her father he wanted nothing more to do with he when he'd agreed to the divorce! She didn't know what Slater thought he was doing, but she wished he'd go away and never come back.

Francesca began to fight again in earnest, but try as she might, she could not get away from him. It frightened her to know that her struggles were futile against his overpowering strength.

Suddenly then, Armando's call pierced the night. "Francesca? Are you out here?"

Slater abruptly ended the kiss as his enemy's voice intruded on the moment. He released her and stepped away. She swayed unsteadily for a moment before him.

Slater's expression was forbidding as he stared down at her in the moonlight. Francesca looked so lovely that he almost reached out to touch her again. Only his iron will, now back in command, stopped him. He wondered how she could look so completely innocent, when he knew she was just the opposite. When he spoke, his words were harsh and rasping.

"Good night, Francesca. Enjoy your lover—and the bed you've made for yourself."

Before Francesca could say a word, Slater was gone, leaving her there alone and suddenly very confused.

Armando and Ricardo had returned to the ballroom to discover that both Slater and Francesca were missing. Armando hadn't minded her dancing with MacKenzie, but he didn't trust the American one bit. Knowing they could only have gone out on the patio, he told Ricardo to wait there, then strode across the room with a casualness of purpose that belied his concern and went outside. As he stepped out into the cool night air, he called out to her. There was no immediate answer, but a few seconds later Slater appeared and strode past him on his way back in.

"Carlanta," was all Slater said as he moved back into the house.

Armando noticed that his expression seemed somewhat smug, and he grew worried. He hurried off into the darkness to look for Francesca.

After Slater had stalked off, Francesca had found to her dismay that she was shaking. Desperate to pull herself together before she had to go back inside and face her father and Armando, she'd made her way to the bench near the fountain and sank down weakly upon it. It angered her that Slater's mere kiss could threaten her composure this way. He'd abandoned her and their son! She hated him, for heaven's sake!

Yet, she'd almost forsaken her pride when he'd kissed her. She was lost so deep in her troubled thoughts that she didn't even hear Armando coming toward her.

"Francesca? Are you all right?" he inquired, relieved to find her sitting there in the moonlight.

"Oh, Armando . . . Yes, I'm fine."

"Are you sure?"

"Why wouldn't I be?"

"MacKenzie . . . he didn't . . ."

"No, everything went very well. Quite like I'd hoped it would, in fact. After tonight, I don't think I'll ever have to see him again."

"Would you like to talk about it?" It was obvious that MacKenzie hadn't told her his version of what had happened when he'd disappeared, yet he was still anxious to know what had been said between them.

"There's nothing really to talk about," Francesca told him as she stood up, still feeling too upset by her own reaction to Slater to want to discuss it. She gave Armando a convincing smile as she took his arm. "Let's go back inside, shall we?"

Slater was barely able to maintain a civilized manner as he reentered the house. He knew he had to leave as quickly as he could or risk doing something he might later regret. He found it hard to believe that Francesca could face him down so cooly after all she'd done; but then, he realized that he shouldn't have been surprised. She'd more than proven herself to be an accomplished actress in the way she'd made a fool of him during their "marriage."

Slater's jaw tightened as he imagined Carlanta and Francesca together. He wondered if the Cuban had seen to his torture and then gone back to a waiting and willing Francesca. The thought fueled his already powerful need for vengeance.

Anna and Rafe had been watching for Slater, and when they saw him, they immediately went to him.

"Slater . . . ?" Rafe's tone reflected his concern about his friend.

"I think it's time I take my leave," he told them without preamble. "I'll see you back at the house."

"I'll go with you," Anna offered, not wanting him to be alone right now.

"Suit yourself." Slater didn't care about anything right then except getting away from the sight of Francesca and her lover.

"Take my carriage and then send it back for me. I'll meet you at the house later." Rafe knew his friend was deeply troubled and he wanted to help, but there were other matters he had to attend to first.

"Thanks."

Slater turned to go with Anna on his arm, but as he did, he happened to see Ricardo standing directly across the room from him. Their gazes met, and Slater went completely still as he stared at the older man. Francesca's father had known the truth all along and had deliberately withheld it from him during their confrontation earlier that week. His hatred of the man now ran deeper than ever.

Having seen Slater return without Francesca, Ricardo's confidence was restored. He met Slater's regard and smiled at him in triumph. He was tempted to lift his glass in salute as a final insult, but as the younger man continued to stare at him without blinking, a terrible chill ran down his backbone. He was greatly relieved when the woman at Slater's side urged him away. He didn't breathe a complete sigh of relief until the American had gone from the mansion.

Slater and Anna made the trip back to Rafe's house in silence. Slater's thoughts were chaotic as he tried to put together all the pieces of the puzzle that was Francesca into something that made sense. He had loved her more than he'd ever loved anyone in his entire life. Her 'death' had come close to destroying him, and it was that recognition of his own weakness that tore at him the most.

Slater had always prided himself on being a good judge of character, and the revelations about Francesca had shocked him. He didn't understand how he could have missed the truth about her. Had he been like so many others he'd known through the years— so blinded by lust for a woman that his good judgment had been cast aside?

Slater dug through the memories of their time together, trying to find his mistakes so he wouldn't make them again. But as he reviewed his days and nights with Francesca, he could find no flaw in her act, no clue to her real plan. She had come to him a virgin, and he had initiated her into the rites of love on their wedding night. With the remembrance of her lovemaking and vows of lifelong devotion came the image of her kissing Carlanta at the ball, and Slater's frustration and fury increased tenfold. He thought of Francesca giving herself to his arch enemy, and then he thought of all the nights he'd lain in his solitary bed, aching for the wife he believed dead.

Slater wanted to hit out at someone, to throw something, to shout his outrage, but he couldn't. He knew he had to use his anger as he'd taught himself to do many years ago. Anger unrestrained was destructive, but anger channeled could be a very useful tool, and he needed all the help he could get right now.

Anna was aware that Slater had to have time to think things out, and so she remained quiet, waiting for him to initiate the conversation. When they reached the house, he helped her down from the carriage and then, always the gentleman, escorted her inside. They were in Rafe's sitting room, and Slater had already down a half-full tumber of whiskey and was refilling his glass before he finally spoke.

"I'd hoped to find out the truth about Francesca tonight, but I never imagined it would be anything like this," he said rather sardonically.

Anna came to stand beside him. She could sense his pain and wished there was something more she could do for him. Her touch was gentle as she lay her hand upon his arm. "It was a shock."

"Do you realize that until just a few hours ago, I was still mourning her? That I was desperate to find her grave?" He paused, his expression turning ugly. "Now, I wish I had." His words were filled with bitterness as he lifted hard, glittering eyes to hers.

"I know . . . ," she sympathized.

"I can't believe I actually thought I loved her."

"You loved what you thought she was, Slater.

146

How were you supposed to know she was a liar and a cheat?''

Slater looked away, his confidence still shaken, as he tossed off the rest of his whiskey. "I haven't stayed alive in this business this long by making mistakes about people.''

"But Francesca's very good at what she does. It's obvious now that she was trained by a master. Carlanta must have taught her everything she knows.''

"I don't doubt that for a minute," he sneered, stalking over to the floor-to-ceiling casement windows to stare out into the darkness. His soul felt as black as the night.

"It wasn't just you, Slater," Anna tried to encourage him. "She had us all fooled. Not a one of us suspected she was trying to set you up. Even after you escaped, there was no reason for us to doubt the story of her death. No one knew a thing.''

"But now *I know*," he ground out harshly as he turned back to face her.

"What are you going to do?" Anna asked, almost holding her breath as she waited for his answer.

"I haven't decided yet, but I will," he promised, and she knew he would.

Chapter Eleven

It was near midnight when Rafe finally thanked Rosa and departed. While the evening had been illuminating in many aspects, he still felt a little frustrated as he headed home. He'd hoped to dance with Marita once more, but every time he'd seen her, she'd been surrounded by a crowd of admirers seeking to gain her favor.

Rafe tempered his disappointment by reminding himself that he had made a date with her for the following day. But as he thought about his impulsive invitation, he wondered why he'd done it. Logically, he knew he had no business trying to develop a relationship with Armando's niece, especially after discovering Francesca's treachery. But all the logic in the world couldn't dismiss the memory of how perfectly Marita had seemed to fit in his arms and how good it had felt to hold her close.

Rafe wondered idly what it would be like to kiss her, but when he felt a stirring of interest deep within him, he forced the thought from his mind. He had more important things to think about than Marita Valequez's kiss.

Although she'd never let her discontent show, Francesca had passed a miserable evening. Armando had remained by her side the entire time, never allowing her even a moment to herself. It wasn't that she hadn't appreciated the help he'd given her when Slater had been there, but she'd found his continued possessiveness after he'd gone very annoying. She was her own woman now, not some sweet, young innocent who did whatever a man told her. Her mood had grown more tense as time had passed, and as the long party had finally begun to draw to a close she'd felt like celebrating its end.

"Francesca, my dear, I have to speak with your father for a few minutes. Will you be all right by yourself?" Armando had inquired, knowing Ricardo had been anxiously awaiting the chance to talk to him about their plans.

"Of course, you go right ahead." Though she'd managed to act disappointed that he was leaving her, inwardly she'd been almost rejoicing.

"This shouldn't take too long. I'll be back as quickly as I can," he'd told her, then had moved off to find her father.

When Armando had gone, Francesca had breathed a sigh of relief. At the beginning of the party, she'd thought spending the entire evening with him would be difficult, but then Slater's showing up had turned what had been just a tedious situation into a nightmare.

The stress of the evening had taken its toll on her, and she was now totally exhausted. All she wanted to do was to go home. She wanted to leave the party and Havana with its painful memories and return to her baby. Only when she was holding Michael in her arms again would she feel safe. He was her anchor in the storm of her life, and she needed him desperately right now. Anxious to leave, yet stuck because her father was with Armando, Francesca wandered to the refreshment table to join Rosa and some of her friends where they were partaking of the cool punch and watching the few remaining dancing couples.

Marita was frustrated. She'd tried all night to position herself in such a way as to pick up information for La Fantasma, but her efforts had proved useless. There had been very little in the way of political conversation tonight. The highlight of her evening had been her one dance with Rafael. Even now, just thinking of it quickened her heartbeat. She sighed. Rafael Ramirez was a special man, and she was thrilled that they would be seeing each other the next day, but she doubted he would ever understand her desire to help the native-born Cuban people achieve equality. Maybe someday things would be different.

Needing a breath of fresh air away from the young men who pursued her so doggedly, Marita slipped from the ballroom and disappeared into the shadows of the patio. There were several couples strolling in the moonlight, sharing forbidden kisses, and she diverted her gaze to allow them privacy. She was heading for her favorite wrought iron bench that was secluded in a distant corner when she passed by the window of her mother's study. The sound of her uncle and Ricardo Salazar in hushed conversation inside brought her up short, and she paused there in the cover of the night shadows to listen.

"We're going to have to do something! You know he's not going to give up easily," Ricardo was insisting.

"He's not going to give up at all. That's why we'll have to separate Tebeau and Favre and keep them on the move until he's out of our way," her uncle explained.

Marita recognized the names as those of the missing agents and grew excited. She needed to know where the two men were now being held and where they were going to take them. Breathlessly, she waited for her uncle to say more. She wondered, too, as she waited, who the 'he' was they were talking about.

"Are you going to have Manuel take care of it?"

"Don't I always? He's very good at these things. Had I given him free rein the last time, we wouldn't be having this difficulty now."

More was said, but their voices grew muffled. Eventually Marita heard the door open and in the silence that followed she realized that they'd left the room. She wasn't sure what stroke of luck had brought her to walk past the study window at that particular moment, but she was excited over her good fortune. She could hardly wait to get word to her friends.

Armando and her father emerged from the study to

find Francesca still there at the refreshment table with Rosa.

"Would you like to share one last dance?" Armando put Francesca on the spot, although he certainly didn't see it that way.

With no way out of it, Francesca accepted his invitation and was led out onto the dance floor.

"You've made this one of the most enjoyable evenings I've had in ages," Armando told her in a deep, suggestive voice. "Perhaps we can arrange to spend more time together now that you've decided to free yourself from your self-imposed exile."

"That would be nice," she answered without heated enthusiasm. "But I do have Michael to consider. I really should get back to him. He's young and he needs me there with him."

"Perhaps there are others who need you as well," he insinuated without declaring himself.

"Ah, but not as much as my son," she softened her words of rejection with a smile.

When the dance finally ended, Armando took her back to her father, who was waiting for her to depart.

"I trust I'll see you again soon?" He gave her hand a warm, familiar squeeze.

"I'd like that," she replied, supressing the feeling of uneasiness that came with his touch.

"Good night, Armando. I'm sure we'll speak in the next day or so," Ricardo told him.

"I'll be looking forward to it."

There was a double meaning to their words, but Francesca didn't know it.

Ricardo ushered Francesca into their waiting carriage, and they started on the trip back to their own spacious home. He was eager to find out exactly what had happened with MacKenzie, and he broached the subject as soon as they'd settled in.

"I'm sorry you experienced such unpleasantness tonight."

"So am I," she answered heavily, her weariness overwhelming her now that the evening was finally over.

"When I encouraged you to attend, I had no idea MacKenzie was back in the country and certainly no idea that he would show up tonight."

"I know. I don't think anyone knew."

"You seem unhappy, my darling. Is there anything I can do to help you with this?"

"No, Papa. It's something I just have to deal with myself."

"Did MacKenzie say anything to upset you?"

"Just seeing him was upsetting enough, although I have to admit it made me furious when he called me his 'wife.' How can he even think of me that way after all that's happened?"

Ricardo felt a shiver of fear. "MacKenzie's a very dangerous man, Francesca. He played you for a fool once before, and I don't want him near you ever again. God only knows what he might try to involve you in, even after you've already suffered so much because of him. Perhaps tomorrow you should return to the country."

"I do miss Michael already," she admitted.

"Then go back to him. I've always known what was best for you, haven't I? Trust me in this," he encouraged her.

"I'll go home tomorrow." Francesca was very

pleased that his suggestion agreed with her own heart's desire. Once she was away from Havana she wouldn't have to worry about dealing with either Slater or Armando. She'd be free of them both.

"Good girl. You won't regret this, I promise."

It was much later, long after the moon had set, that Francesca lay curled up in her bed. She had taken a nice hot bath upon returning to their home, and now in the stillness of the predawn hours she allowed herself to reflect on what had transpired between her and Slater on the patio.

In some ways, during their few minutes alone, it had almost been as if nothing had changed between them. When they'd been married, Slater had always been able to bend her to his will with just a touch and a kiss, and to her horror, it had almost happened again tonight. Francesca remembered his lips on hers, so masterful and demanding, and even as determined as she'd been not to feel anything, she had. Heat had rushed through her, and with that heat had come the sweet, burning memory of what it was like to be his completely—in every sense of the word. She was thankful now that she'd had enough sense to keep on fighting and not give in to him. Her pride was all she had left, and she wouldn't, no couldn't, forfeit that, too, and survive.

At the same time Francesca was remembering their encounter, Slater was thinking of her too. Anna had long since retired, and now he sat with Rafe alone, sharing a drink and their thoughts.

"I couldn't believe it when I saw you two standing

together in the ballroom doorway. What on God's earth did she have to say for herself?" Rafe asked.

"What could she say?" Slater returned sarcastically. "Just seeing her with Carlanta and watching her kiss him the way she did, told me the whole story. She's obviously been in with them from the start."

"How did you manage to stay in control?"

"I don't know," he answered, his eyes shadowed in pain. "Years of practice, I guess."

They were quiet for a second.

"What are you going to do now?"

"I'm going to find the agents. That's what Strecker wants."

"What about what you want?'

Slater smiled a particularly nasty smile at his friend. "Don't worry about me. I'm going to take care of Tebeau and Favre and get what I'm after at the same time."

Rafe frowned, wondering at his statement. "Just what is it you're after, Slater?"

"Revenge, Rafe. Just revenge."

Rafe saw the wildness in his gaze and heard the coldness in his voice and knew there would be no discouraging him.

Marita was nervous. The guests had all departed, and it was late—already past two in the morning, but her mother was still up and moving around the house. Marita knew she was supervising the servants as they put the house back to rights again, but she'd hoped they would have been done by now. She was worried about the news she'd overheard from her

155

uncle, and she was anxious to pass it along to Pedro.

Marita strode to the window to look out across the grounds. It was very dark and quiet outside, so she knew she wouldn't have any difficulty once she was out of the house. It was just that getting out of the house was causing her so much trouble. She flopped down on her bed in agitation to wait it out, fearful that even as she did the agents were already being moved.

Nearly a half an hour passed before Marita could make her escape. Dressed in dark peasant's clothing, she slipped away and hurried along the deserted streets to the Santana home. It was a long trek, but she knew it was worth any risk. Her knock at Pedro's back door was answered quickly, and the sleepy servant, an older woman she'd met before, recognized her immediately and brought her inside to safety.

"I need to speak to Pedro," she said urgently.

"Sí. Wait here. I'll get him."

Within minutes, Pedro was there. Just awakened from a sound sleep, he looked rumpled in his hastily thrown-on clothing and very worried. "What is it? Has something happened?"

"I must talk to you . . . privately."

Without another word, Pedro led the way to the front sitting room and closed the door behind them. "Has there been trouble?"

"No, not yet, but I heard my uncle talking with Ricardo Salazar tonight at my mother's party."

"And?" Pedro's eyes lit up at the thought. He knew how much power and influence the two men wielded in the government, and he hoped she'd brought news they could use.

"And the missing agents are to be separated and moved."

"Did he say when or where?"

"No," she admitted in frustration. "I was hoping to learn more, but that was all that I was able to hear."

"They must be nervous about something if they're going to risk moving the Americans," he said thoughtfully.

"For what it's worth, I heard them talking about someone being back and how he wasn't going to give up. Whatever that means," Marita offered, hoping it would help.

Pedro had a good idea what Armando's conversation was about, but he didn't try to explain it to Marita. He firmly believed the less she knew about what was going on, the better. She was safer that way. "You've done well," Pedro praised her.

"I hope it helps."

"It does. Your father would have been proud of your dedication, child." He pressed a kiss to her forehead. "But now you must return home before anyone finds you're gone. We wouldn't want anyone to start asking questions."

She smiled faintly. "You're right. I doubt Uncle Armando or even my mother would be very understanding about this."

"I'll have one of my servants accompany you to make sure you get home safe."

"No. That's not necessary. It's late and there's no one about. Even if I do run into anyone, dressed as I am, they won't pay any attention."

"You're sure?"

"Positive. I'll come to you again, just as soon as I can learn anything more."

"You needn't wait that long. You know I always enjoy your visits." He walked with her back to the door. "Besides, Estevan is gone now, and it is lonely here."

"Where is he?"

"He's gone into the mountains to work with the others." His voice was heavy with worry for his only offspring.

"You sound concerned."

"These are dangerous times, and he's young and has a hot temper. He's growing impatient with our ways. He thinks he can change the world overnight."

"He knows better than to do anything rash."

"I hope so, but sometimes the young are too much in a hurry to be cautious."

"Estevan's smart. He won't do anything stupid." She tried to reassure him. "He is your son, you know."

Her words brought a smile to his lips. "Ah, Marita, you have always known how to warm my heart." He gave her a hug then held the door for her.

"Good night, Pedro."

"Good night, little one." He watched as she disappeared into the night. When she'd gone out of sight, he closed the door and returned to his bedroom.

Though Pedro did lie back down, he did not sleep. His thoughts were filled with the news Marita had brought. He found it most encouraging that Carlanta and Salazar were moving the agents. In their positions with the government, Pedro realized it was an unusual occurrence for them to feel threatened in any way. Considering their actions, he felt reasonably certain that the rumor he'd heard among the rebels about the Americans sending help was probably true.

Determined to find out if help had arrived, Pedro decided to relay Marita's information to the rebel camp himself. He was already mounted up and riding out as dawn lightened the eastern horizon.

Estevan Santana, a broad-shouldered, darkly handsome young man of some twenty years, stood on the crest of the hill, keeping watch over the trail below. He'd been guarding the entrance to the secluded, mountainous camp since the cool hours of early morning, and he was glad now that his time was almost over for it had grown hot as the day had aged. He was just about to glance away when a movement on the road drew his attention. Silently signaling Carlos, the other lookout, he drew a bead with his rifle and waited for the rider to get close enough to identify.

"What is it?" Carlos asked quietly as he hurried to join him.

"Someone's coming, and he's moving fast," Estevan told him. "There." He pointed down the trail.

Carlos nodded, and the two men remained silent as they watched and waited. Word was out that there might be trouble some time soon, and so they were being extra cautious. They were tense as the rider drew closer, and it wasn't until Estevan recognized his father that they both took a heavy breath and relaxed their deadly stance. Estevan put his gun away as he stood up.

"Hola!" he called out to his father as he waved both arms over his head to let him know the way was clear and safe.

Pedro heard his call and, spotting Estevan at the lookout point, returned his greeting. He'd known to watch for the guards, and now that they'd recognized him, he urged his mount to an even quicker pace and rode straight on in to the encampment.

The rebel hideout was perfectly situated high up in the forested hill country. Because of the looseness of their organization, the camp itself consisted of nothing more than several groupings of huts made of palm fronds and bark, spread out over a large area. The men of the camp were sitting around the cook fires with their weapons close by their sides within easy reach. They observed Pedro closely as he rode past them. When they recognized who he was, their look of distrust vanished. They began to call out to him in welcome, for he was considered one of their own.

"Where's Martinez?" Pedro asked as he reined in and dismounted. "I must speak to him at once."

"He's in his hut," one of the men answered, gesturing toward a building across the clearing as he took his reins from him.

Pedro thanked him, and, leaving his exhausted horse in his care, he rushed off to seek out the man who was the leader of the group.

"Martinez?"

"Sí?" Martinez answered to his call. The fifty-year

160

old rebel leader, was a leanly built man, of average height with sharp, black eyes, silver-streaked black hair, and a thick, heavy, black mustache. He emerged from the dirt-floored dwelling that served as his home to find his long-time friend awaiting him. "Pedro! It's good to see you!"

"It's good to see you, too," he answered. "We have to talk. La Fantasma had brought me news."

Martinez took him inside. "I hope it's good. Since the Americans disappeared, we've lost heart. There can be no further plans made for the invasion until we know what, if anything, has been revealed to the government."

"That's why I'm here." He went on to quickly explain that La Fantasma had said the agents were to be separated and moved.

"They must be afraid of something if they would dare to move them."

"Or someone," he pointed out. "La Fantasma said they mentioned that 'he' was back and 'he' wasn't going to give up."

A light of understanding shone in his eyes. "Ah, of course . . . It must be MacKenzie."

"MacKenzie?" Pedro had not heard this name before.

"He's an American who worked with us some time ago. He, too, was kidnapped by them, and from what I understand, he suffered badly at their hands. Luckily, though, he escaped and returned to the States."

"Why do you think he's the one making Carlanta and Salazar so nervous?"

"I received word not long ago that he was coming

back, and since he knows the island and both men very well . . . I'm sure he must be the cause of their fear."

"But why would this MacKenzie deliberately put himself in danger again? He's not even Cuban . . ."

"I don't question good fortune. Maybe he believes in what we're trying to do or maybe it's something else. Whatever it is, I don't care as long as we have his help. You see, he's good, very good."

"If he's so good, then how did they catch him?"

A flare of anger shone in his eyes. "He was betrayed."

"By whom?"

"We never knew for certain. Perhaps we will find out now that he's back."

"What are you going to do?"

"First, I'm going to tell the others your news and have them pass it along. Someone just might see the agents being moved, and if they do, we might be able to help them."

"And then?"

"Then, I will wait to hear from MacKenzie. If he's here, he will be joining us soon."

Pedro followed his friend outside and waited while he spoke with the necessary men.

When Martinez came back, he asked, "Will you be staying on tonight?"

"Yes, I've missed Estevan and want to visit with him for a while. It's good to see he's doing well."

"He's a true patriot," he praised Pedro's son. "He's a bit zealous at times, but that will become tempered after a while."

"It's a problem with youth. They always want to

take action first and think later."

"Yes, but without youth on our side, what chance do we old men have of winning our independence? We must harness their aggressiveness and team it with our experience, so we can forge a new nation together."

"You make it sound so simple, my friend."

"I wish it were that simple," he said wearily, his enthusiasm fading as they moved back inside to sit down again. "I sometimes worry, though, that this could drag on for years. The injustices are many and our native-born people are outraged, but I don't know that they are willing to band together to do what must be done to throw out the Spanish."

"We can't give up. The time is coming when we will be free of Carlanta and men of his kind."

"I hope so."

"Father?" Estevan's time on guard duty was over, and he'd come looking for his father as soon as his replacement had arrived.

"Come in, Estevan," Martinez called out to the young man. "We were just talking about you."

Estevan smiled cautiously as he joined them. "You were saying good things, I hope."

"Of course. Your father has brought us promising news. Carlanta's planning to move Tebeau and Favre to a new location soon, and I think it's because Slater MacKenzie's back."

Neither of the older men noticed the slight change in Estevan's expression upon hearing that MacKenzie was back. Out of necessity, he'd become quite adept at disguising his emotions.

"Good, maybe now we'll be able to take some

action," Estevan said calmly, not revealing any of the sudden fury within him.

"That's what we're hoping. From the sound of things, the move is going to take place quickly, so we should know something in the next day or two."

Chapter Twelve

Armando and Manuel sat across the desk from each other in Armando's office early the next morning. Armando appeared studious as he considered all his options. When he finally looked up at the expectant Manuel, his smile was cunning.

"I have an idea. We know the troublemaking revolutionaries have people watching all over the island for the agents, but they are looking for men. I think perhaps our 'guests' should be disguised during the move. Do you suppose two elderly women being driven around town would be considered anything unusual?"

Manuel's expression showed appreciation for his boss's ingenuity. "I think two old women could move about much more freely than two young men. I'll take care of it. But what about MacKenzie? Do you have a plan?"

Amando's mood soured. "Had that fool, Sanchez, done what he was told to do at the cemetery the other day, none of this would be necessary. As it is, I'm forced to try again."

"Then you're planning on killing him outright?" He was a bit disappointed.

"The fastest, most efficient way possible," he concluded. "Why? Did you want to renew your acquaintance?"

Manuel's smile was feral. "I would have enjoyed finishing what I started last year."

"I understand completely, and I sympathize. I'd like more than anything to get my hands on him again, but there's no time. We have to act, and act quickly. Just take care of what I've given you and know that, hopefully, after today MacKenzie will no longer be a problem for us."

"I'll let you know as soon as the move has been completed."

"I'll be waiting to hear."

"Good luck with MacKenzie."

"It's not luck. It's a matter of timing. I have everything I need right here." He opened his desk drawer and lifted out a vial of liquid.

"What is it?"

"One of the most deadly poisons around. Should MacKenzie be unfortunate enough to take even a small dose, he'll be dead before he hits the floor."

"But how are you going to get him to drink it?"

"The American only drinks whiskey. He's staying with Ramirez, and since I have a connection in the Ramirez household . . ." He shrugged. "Money can influence a lot of people to do a lot of things they normally wouldn't do, my friend."

"Aren't you afraid someone else could get his whiskey?"

"No. Ramirez's drink is rum. This will work."

"Good." Manuel nodded his understanding and left to take care of his own business.

Armando waited until he'd gone, then sent for Jorge, the servant he employed in his stables. A man of about twenty-five years of age appeared in his office a while later. He was intimidated as he faced his boss, though his eyes reflected a certain weasel-like intelligence.

"Jorge, it is my understanding that you are familiar with a certain young woman employed by the Ramirez household . . ."

"Sí, Señor Carlanta. My fiancée, Calida, is a maid there," he answered quickly, confused as to why he would even ask.

"How would you like to earn enough money to marry her right away and move from Havana to your own farm?"

"Sí. I would like that very much! What is it you need me to do?" Jorge agreed avidly. He waited eagerly to hear what his employer had in mind.

"This job I have for you is special, and it will require Calida's help."

"That is no problem. She will do whatever I tell her to do," he announced with dominating male pride.

"Good. That's what I wanted to hear. Now, here is what has to be done . . ."

Jorge listened carefully to the instructions. His eyes widened in fear. "But, señor . . . ," he began to protest.

Armando had no patience with cowardice. He told him what he would be paid and then put the situation to him bluntly "Do you want the money or not?"

When Jorge was told the amount he would be paid for his efforts, he quickly accepted without a second thought. Morality be damned. He had his future to take care of. "I will do it."

"Fine. You will be responsible to see that your woman does as I've instructed, then both of you return here and I will pay you. But I warn you, Jorge, do not try to cross me in any way."

The ice in his voice left no doubt in the young man's mind of what would happen to him should he betray him. "Don't worry, Señor. I will do exactly as you say."

It was morning, and Slater was restless. He had not slept all night for his mind had been racing, feverishly searching for the perfect way to exact his vengeance against Francesca and Carlanta. Over and over through the night he'd envisioned them together—first, as they'd looked in the foyer at the party and then as he imagined they looked in bed together making passionate love. Obsessed with getting even with her for her treachery, several schemes had occurred to him, but none of them had been good enough. He needed to free the agents and destroy Francesca and her lover at the same time. He had to find a way, and he knew, somehow, he would. A knock at his bedroom door drew him away from his dark, brooding thoughts.

"What is it?"

"Rafe and I are downstairs about to have breakfast,

and we wondered if you'd like to join us?" Anna inquired through the closed door. She'd been concerned about him all night, and she wanted to make sure he was all right.

The last thing Slater felt like doing was eating or socializing. He wanted time alone to think and plan. He wanted to find Francesca and get his hands around her pretty throat. He knew his thoughts were self-defeating, though, and he agreed to Anna's invitation. "I'll be down in a few minutes."

"I'll tell Rafe."

A short time later after he'd washed, shaved, and changed clothes, Slater joined his friends in the dining room.

"Good morning, Slater. Did you get any rest?" Rafe asked as he came into the room. He'd wondered if he would be able to sleep after the shock he'd suffered.

"Not much," he told them honestly. "I had a lot to think about."

"Are you feeling all right?"

"I'm fine." He brushed aside the query.

"Have you decided what you want to do yet?" Anna asked.

"I need to get up to the rebel camp and talk to Martinez. I have to find out what they know before I can make any plans."

"I have some things I have to take care of here in town today, but I can leave first thing tomorrow. Is that soon enough for you or do you want to go ahead with Anna now?"

"I can wait." There was something else he knew he had to do before he left Havana.

"After what happened at the graveyard, why don't we leave early, before sunup? That way we can be sure there's no one following us."

"That sounds like a good idea. I'm sure last night didn't change anything as far as they're concerned."

"I'm sure it didn't either." Slater smiled grimly. "They still want me dead."

"Well, we'll just have to make sure that doesn't happen."

"It won't."

"I'll be gone for most of the day, but I'll be back in time for dinner." Rafe rose from the table and excused himself to leave for his business meeting.

After Rafe had gone, Slater rejected any efforts at making small talk with Anna. She eventually drifted away from the table to see about her own interests, and Slater finally moved off to Rafe's study to sit in solitude and think.

Manuel enjoyed his work, and he was smiling widely now as he entered the windowless storeroom where the two American troublemakers were being held, bound and gagged. "You have done a good job, Rodolfo, far better than your predecessors."

"Thank you, Manuel," the guard replied, pleased that his diligence was appreciated. He'd heard the story of what had happened to the two men who'd been guarding the captive who'd escaped from Manuel the year before, and he'd had no desire to meet their same fate. He knew how dangerous and deadly his boss really was, and he was determined not to give him any reason to be angry with him.

"I will need your help even more so now."

"What can I do?"

Manuel took the guard back outside and closed the door again, so Tebeau and Favre couldn't hear his plan. "There is a chance that there might be trouble, so Carlanta wants us to separate these two and move them to new locations. I know there are those who will talk to the rebels if they see anything out of the ordinary, so Carlanta wants us to use these."

Rodolfo watched as Manuel opened the bag he'd brought with him and took out some old peasant women's clothing and two scarves.

"We will dress them in these, cover their heads with the scarves and then move them later tonight after dark."

"It will work," the guard agreed, impressed.

"All right, this is where we will take them." He began to outline Armando's plan to keep the agents hidden.

Rosa looked surprised and then completely pleased as she stared at her daughter. "Rafael Ramirez is coming here for luncheon?"

"Yes, Mama, and I was wondering . . . is there anyone you need to go visit this afternoon?" Marita knew she wasn't being particularly subtle, but subtlety had never worked on her mother. For some unknown reason, she wanted desperately to have some time alone with Rafael, and to do that she had to get rid of her mother.

"Marita! I'm shocked! How could you even suggest such a thing? You are a beautiful young woman of marriageable age. A gentleman would be totally shocked to find you without a chaperone! Don't even think such things!"

"Yes, Mama," she replied dutifully, though it annoyed her greatly to do so. Rafael Ramirez was Havana's most sought after bachelor. Every woman wanted him. Ever since they'd danced last night at the party, Marita had wanted desperately to spend more time with him, but she had never gotten the chance. Now, today, he was coming her to her house and she was going to have her mother sitting with them during every minute of his visit. She almost wanted to scream.

"Have you decided what to serve for the meal?"

"That's why I came to talk to you. I thought you might be able to help me think of something exciting."

"Indeed, I can," Rosa told her excitedly. "Rafael is quite the handsome one. We'll have Cook fix him something special that he will never forget. Oh, you two would be so wonderful together . . . And Marita . . . he is so rich!"

"Mama!" Marita was embarrassed to hear her going on that way.

"Come on, come on. We must hurry. He'll be here in just a few hours."

For some strange reason, Rafe was feeling anxious. He didn't understand it. He was Rafael Ramirez. He had dined with more women than he cared to remember, and yet the thought of luncheon with

Marita rendered him nearly boyish in his anticipation.

Rafe did not think it was humorous. He told himself over and over again that Marita was closely related to Carlanta and that he shouldn't get too involved. Even so, he couldn't deny that he could hardly wait to see her again and it had barely been twelve hours.

The phenomenon bothered Rafe, especially because he couldn't seem to concentrate on his work. He was a man used to being in complete command. He'd expected to get a lot done during his business meeting that morning, but he'd constantly been distracted. By the time the meeting was concluded, he was running very late.

Rafe felt like an idiot as he rushed to the Valequez home. Yet, no matter how ridiculous he felt, he didn't slow down.

Rosa had been keeping watch for him, and as high as her hopes were that there might be a match between these two, she found her spirits wilting as the appointed hour of his arrival came and went.

"Rafael isn't here yet?" Marita asked as she came downstairs after styling her hair down so it fell around her shoulders in a cascade of curls and changing into her favorite pale yellow daygown.

Rosa looked up from where she kept her vigil. "No . . . not yet," she sighed.

Marita was about to become concerned when she heard a horse outside. "That must be him, Mama . . ."

Her mother brushed the drape back a little and a big smile creased her face. "It is." She patted her daughter's cheek as she walked past her to answer the door. There would be no servant greeting Rafael. She would do it herself. This was one man she didn't want to get away.

Rafe regretted his lateness, but hoped Marita would understand, especially since he'd stopped on the way through the town marketplace and bought flowers for both her and Rosa. He knocked and was glad when the door opened almost immediately.

"Rafael! It's wonderful to see you. Please, come in." Rosa was effusive in her greeting as she held the door wide for him.

"Good afternoon, Rosa. It's good to see you again."

"Thank you. Marita is expecting you." She ushered him inside as Marita emerged from the parlor.

"Hello, Rafael," she said softly.

Rafe looked up, and for a moment he couldn't say anything. Last night Marita had worn a gown that was sophisticated and very exciting, but today, in this simple, yet elegant daygown, he thought her just as lovely. "Hello, Marita. You look very pretty today." He knew it was silly when he said it, but he couldn't help himself. "I brought these for both of you . . ." He offered Rosa her bouquet and then crossed the few steps that separated them to hand Marita hers.

"Thank you, Rafael," Rosa said.

He didn't hear her, though, for he was too busy gazing at Marita.

Marita, too, felt she'd been momentarily stuck dumb. Rafael looked so handsome standing there before her that she could only smile up at him

174

stupidly. From his dark hair, his sparkling eyes, and his ready smile, to his broad shoulders, trim waist, and easy male grace, she thought him the most attractive man she'd ever known, and she realized that that was probably why he had such success with women. Finally, reminding herself of just who she was dealing with here, she managed to get out a few words. "They're beautiful. That was very thoughtful of you."

"I'm glad you like them."

"Here, Marita, give me yours and I'll put them in a vase," Rosa offered. She remembered very well the sensual tension that had existed between her and her own beloved husband all those years ago before they'd married, and she could have sworn the same awareness now existed between Marita and Rafael. She couldn't have been more excited. "Why don't you two go on into the dining room? I'll tell Cook we're ready to eat."

They barely noticed when she'd bustled off to the back of the house, grinning from ear to ear.

Marita led the way into the dining room. Rafe followed her, and he found he couldn't take his eyes off the smooth sway of her hips as she walked. There was something so very feminine about that gentle motion that he didn't want to look away. Rafe had never been so mesmerized by a woman before, and he frowned slightly as he forced his gaze away from her.

Usually when a woman appealed to Rafe, she was the type who knew exactly what he wanted and how to give it to him. He would go after her with one goal and one goal only in mind, and that goal definitely wasn't marriage. But Marita was different. For all that the men of Havana were hotly pursuing her, he knew Rosa was far too diligent in her chaperoning to have allowed anything scandalous to ever take place with her daughter. Marita's honor had been carefully protected. She was the type of woman a man would marry, and his attraction to her puzzled him for he knew it would never lead to anything.

"Did you enjoy yourself last night?" Marita asked as she turned to face him.

"Definitely. Your mother's parties are legendary, you know. It was quite an exciting evening."

"I'm glad you thought so, Rafael," Rosa said as she came into the room carrying a huge crystal vase filled with his fresh blossoms, and she placed it in the center of the table so they could enjoy them while they dined. "I think most everyone had a good time. The meal is ready, if you'd like to eat . . ."

They dined on a light, but sumptuous fare, graced by a fine white wine. Rosa's presence kept the conversation from drifting to anything but the most mundane of topics.

Rafe found himself chafing under the restraint. He couldn't remember the last time he'd suffered a chaperone, and he knew with certainty that he never wanted to go through this again. But just when he'd decided that he was being an idiot for putting himself through all this, his gaze met Marita's across the table. Sparks of hot, molten desire erupted through him. He suddenly wanted to get up and leave and take Marita with him. He wanted to whisk her away for an afternoon ride—just the two of them. He wanted to . . .

"Isn't that true, Rafael?" Rosa was asking.

Rafe had no idea what the question had been. He glanced over at Marita's mother and said apologetically, "I'm sorry, Rosa, but I was so enthralled by your daughter's beauty that I completely missed what you were saying."

Rosa thought his answer was perfectly wonderful. She gave him a warm smile. "It doesn't matter. I was just babbling on."

"Señora Rosa?" the maid appeared in the doorway of the dining room.

"Yes, Juanna, what is it?"

"There is a problem that only you can help us with . . . ," the young girl told her.

Rosa turned back to Rafael and Marita. "If you will excuse me, I must see what's wrong. If I don't see you again before you leave, Rafael, it was a delight sharing your company for lunch."

Rafe got up from his chair as Rosa stood to leave. "I thank you for having me."

"Any time, my dear boy, any time." Rosa followed Juanna from the room, leaving Marita and Rafael alone. When she got out of earshot, she gave the maid a friendly pat on her shoulder. "Well done, Juanna. I think I'll go upstairs and rest for a while."

"Yes, señora."

In the dining room, Rafe remained standing. "I think perhaps it's time I go . . ."

Marita wanted him to stay, but she knew it wasn't possible. She started around the table to show him out. "I'm glad you came."

"So am I," he found himself replying as he watched her draw near. He was obsessed with the idea of kissing her, and he had been ever since last night.

He kept wondering what it would be like to taste the sweetness of her . . .

Then, suddenly, she was there before him and they were alone and Rafe couldn't help himself. He reached out to her and she came to him without a word, almost as if she'd wanted this too. Rafe drew her near and kissed her. What had been meant to be a tentative, soft exploration exploded into a passionate exchange that surprised them both.

Marita had been kissed before, but compared to Rafael's embrace, the one's who'd kissed her previously had been inexperienced little boys. Rafael was a man. Enthralled by his masterful persuasive kiss, she melted against the hard width of his chest and allowed him to lead her wherever he wanted to.

Rafe had never known that one simple kiss could wreak such havoc on his senses. When Marita leaned ever so lightly against him, he was jolted by the strength of his reaction to her. Desire, sudden and potent, pounded through him and centered low in his body. It was an elemental reaction, a primitive response, an essential, instinctive recognition, and it was more powerful than anything he'd ever experienced before. It surprised Rafe so much that he broke off the kiss and put her from him.

"I'd better go," he said quickly, not sure what else to say.

"Oh . . . ," Marita returned simply, gazing up at him in wonder. Her cheeks were slightly flushed and her lips were slightly swollen from his kiss. She couldn't imagine what secret power Rafael had over her, but he did. His kiss was more wonderful than any she'd ever known, and just being near him had been heavenly.

Unable to stop himself, he put one arm around her shoulders and brought her close for one last, quick, sweet exchange. When he discovered it was just as exciting as their last kiss, he ended it and stepped away. "I'll speak to you again soon."

"All right . . ."

He started for the door, and she called out to him, wanting to say more, but not quite knowing what.

"Rafael?"

"Yes?"

"Thank you for the flowers . . ."

Rafe strode from the house, his mood troubled. He couldn't care for her. She was Carlanta's niece, and any relationship with her would only lead to complications he didn't need. But even as Rafe argued with himself that there could be no future for them, he kept wondering how quickly he could get back from the rebel camp so he could make arrangements to see her again.

Chapter Thirteen

Armando was feeling quite confident as he was admitted to the Salazar home in Havana. He had spoken with Ricardo in his office and upon learning that Francesca was returning to the country today, he'd decided to pay her an unexpected call.

"I'll tell Doña Francesca that you're here," the maid who'd answered the door told him after directing him to wait in the front sitting room.

"Gracias." Armando crossed the room to where a portrait of Francesca hung, and he paused there to admire it. She had been lovely when the painting had been made several years before, but now she was even more stunning. Francesca was a showpiece of a woman, someone any man would be proud to have at his side, and he meant to make her his.

Francesca had been in the midst of packing for her trip home when the maid informed her that Armando had arrived. She would have loved some way to avoid him, but realized it was impossible. She hoped there wasn't some kind of difficulty, for Michael was foremost on her mind, and she longed to be with him.

Francesca regretted that she didn't have time to change before seeing Armando. She preferred to play the sophisticate whenever she was with him for it gave her a sense of control; but today, planning for the hours in the carriage, she'd donned only a simple daygown and had left her hair free to fall about her shoulders. Girding herself, she went out to see Armando, her attitude slightly apprehensive.

"Armando? Is there something wrong?"

The sound of her voice behind him caused Armando to turn abruptly away from her portrait. She had been gorgeous in the picture, but now wearing only a simple daygown, she looked even more desirable. There was something about the plainness of the dress that enhanced rather than detracted from her beauty.

"Now that I've seen you," he began in flattering tones, "how could anything be wrong?" He strode toward her to take her hand and lift it to his lips. "You were a vision last night, but today, you look even more lovely."

"Thank you." Though it was a warm day, Francesca shivered at the touch of his lips. She would have pulled her hand away from him, but he gave her no opportunity as he tucked it around his arm and drew her with him to the sofa.

"I've been worried about you," he told her in earnest as they sat down together.

"Me? Why?" She was surprised by this.

181

"I was concerned that seeing MacKenzie last night might have upset you more than you were willing to admit."

"There's no reason for you to worry. It was a shock, but I'm fine. After we left you last night, my father suggested that I return to the country, and I think it's a good idea. I'll be leaving within the half hour."

"Yes, we spoke earlier this morning, and he said that you'd be going. You see, that's why I came. I wanted to see you one more time before you left."

"That's nice." Though she told herself that she should be thrilled at being the focus of his attentions, Francesca wished he'd managed to restrain himself. She knew there were many women who would have joyfully traded places with her, but it didn't help. She just wanted to be left alone . . . to go home to Michael and stay there.

Armando didn't notice that her response was less than rapturous. He was too wrapped up in his own desire for her to even think or care about what her feelings were.

"I'm going to miss you, Francesca," he said ardently as he slipped an arm around her shoulders to pull her close.

Armando's mouth found hers before she could argue or try to slip away, and she found herself trapped in his embrace. She accepted his kiss without protest, but felt smothered by his closeness. The kiss was nothing like Slater's, she realized distantly. There was none of the fire she felt when she was in Slater's arms. Armando's touch left her cold and unmoved. When Francesca recognized the direction of her thoughts, she became annoyed with herself.

Why was it Slater somehow always managed to slither into her thoughts at the most inopportune times?

Armando mistook Francesca's acquiescence for a sign that she was enjoying his touch. Knowing that they wouldn't be interrupted, he decided to press her further. Boldly, his hand sought her breast.

"Don't!" Francesca surprised him completely when she jerked forcefully away and stood up. "You really should go now . . ."

"But you must know how much I want you," he told her, his voice husky with desire, "and how long I've waited."

She moved away from him toward the door, hoping to encourage him to get up. "I have packing I must finish."

"Ah, Francesca, my precious, you know you can't run from me forever." Armando rose and followed her, enjoying the chase. His gaze went over her features, noting the flushed cheeks and sparkling eyes. It never occurred to him that she might be irritated by his advances, he thought she was as excited as he was. "I'll come to see you just as soon as I can get away, and perhaps then we can talk about our future."

She wanted to tell him that she had no intention of spending her future with him; but instead, just to get rid of him, she smiled sweetly in response as she accompanied him to the door. "I'll be looking forward to your visit."

Armando slipped his arm around her slender waist as they reached the door and opened it. Then, just before heading down the walk, he maneuvered himself to the advantage again, holding her close and kissing her. He enjoyed the feel of her breasts against his chest and the way she struggled a little in surprise, trying to get free. Armando liked being dominant. He released her reluctantly.

"I'll meet you as soon as I can get away," Armando vowed, feeling quite smug and vastly superior to most of the human race. He was confident as he rode away that as soon as MacKenzie was dead, Francesca would be his bride. Then he would have it all, the powerful position in government he wanted and the woman he lusted after. He was so entranced by his dreams of glory that he did not notice the man watching from across the street.

As Slater had watched Armando kiss Francesca, his hands had clenched into fists of rage. Though his fury was white-hot, he was glad that he'd come. In a moment of weakness while he'd been sitting alone in Rafe's study that morning, drinking and thinking about the night before, he'd decided to try to see his lovely wife and talk to her once again. He'd thought confronting her in the light of day might change something between them, but arriving as he had just in time to see Francesca passionately embrace Carlanta only reaffirmed what he'd discovered at the party. Her betrayal of everything they'd shared— their love, their vows, their desire for one another— was real.

Slater turned away in disgust, his face set like a mask of stone. He mounted up and rode for the Del Rio Cantina near the dock area. It was the saloon where he had first met Anna and some of the others involved in the revolutionary movement. Slater knew he should be careful as he rode the streets of Havana. He knew he should keep careful watch and protect his own back, but right then, he didn't care. He just wanted to find a place where he could be alone.

At night, the Del Rio was a wild place, vibrating with loud music and crowded with drunks and curvaceous barmaids. During the day, however, it was mostly deserted, and Slater was glad. After getting a bottle of whiskey and a glass from the bartender, he made his way to a secluded table in the rear where he could drink undisturbed. He felt he deserved a few stiff drinks after finding out that Carlanta had probably just shared his wife's bed. Slater had downed his whiskey and quickly poured another.

The trip back to the country estate had never seemed so long to Francesca before. She sat alone in the carriage, longing for the seemingly endless miles to pass so she could be back in the safety of her haven with Michael. She missed him dreadfully and could hardly wait to hold him in her arms again and snuggle him close.

A yawn threatened, and Francesca wondered just how much longer she could stay awake. She'd gotten little sleep last night for her thoughts had been in a tormented jumble. Every time she'd started to drift off, Slater's image appeared in her mind and jarred her back to miserable wakefulness.

Francesca was the kind of person who handled a crisis better after a good night's rest. Sleep had a way of putting everything into perspective for her. But when slumber had proved impossible the night before, the light of the new day had just made everything seem worse, and then Armando had shown up at the house. She gave a weary shake of her head, just glad that she was away from it all now.

Wedging herself in the corner of the carriage, Francesca let her eyes drift shut. She hoped that she might be able to nap a little, and, indeed, she did, for the next bump she felt was the one that came when the driver turned into the main drive that led up to the house. Glad to find that the ordeal of the trip was over, she sat up straight and watched eagerly for some sign of her son. As soon as the driver had drawn the vehicle to a halt before the entrance, she climbed out by herself.

"Maria!" she cried, rushing indoors to find her child.

"Doña Francesca, what is it? Why are you back so soon?" Adela, the housekeeper, asked as she came running at the sound of her call.

"Adela, where are Maria and Michael?" Francesca asked, eager to hold her baby.

"She is helping with the chores, and he's taking his nap," the older woman told her, her dark eyes twinkling with understanding now that she knew there was no emergency. "So you missed your son, did you?"

Francesca was already on her way to Michael's bedroom to look in on him, but she glanced back over her shoulder to give Adela a big smile, feeling suddenly much better than she had. "I should never have gone away and left him!"

Hurrying on, Francesca reached his room. After

opening the door carefully so as not to wake him, she paused in the doorway to watch him sleep. He looked beautiful lying there in his crib, and tears stung her eyes as she realized again just how precious he was to her. She wanted to cradle him to her heart and never let him go, but she contented herself with just studying him in repose. He was hers . . . all hers.

Francesca's sweet expression turned grim as Slater slipped unbidden into her thoughts. She was still angry over seeing him again, and she hated him immensely for all the cruel things he'd done. But as she stared at her child, she knew there was one thing she would never regret about their relationship.

Michael's eyes opened as if he'd sensed her presence, and he gave a happy little gurgle as he saw her. Unable to resist any longer, Francesca crossed the room and gathered him up in her arms for a warm hug and big kiss.

"I love you, Michael, forever and ever . . ."

Calida was nervous. Señor Ramirez had left his home early that morning, and she had seen the American ride away from the house. That left only Doña Anna and the other servants to worry about, and she was worried. She looked around carefully to make sure no one was watching before she slipped quietly from the kitchen.

One of the kitchen cats followed her, and though she tried to shoo him back into his own domain, the feline refused to budge. Fearful of making too much noise and being found out, she gave it up and allowed the cat the run of the house. There were other things more important for her to concern herself with.

Calida carefully checked to make sure Doña Anna was in her room and then hurried through the house and into the study. Safely alone for the moment, Calida dipped into her pocket and pulled out the vial Jorge had given her earlier that day. His instructions had been simple—*Pour this into the bottle of whiskey from which the American drinks*. Things couldn't have worked out more easily for her, for Señor MacKenzie had already been drinking that day and had left the bottle sitting open on top of the desk. In the flash of a moment's deadly deception, she poured the poison into Slater's whiskey.

Keeping her composure, Calida tucked the telltale vial back into her pocket. She left the house without tellng anyone she was going. It was much later that day before anyone needed her and started looking for her. By then, she was already far away, celebrating their new wealth with Jorge.

It was late that afternoon when Slater finally returned to Rafe's home. The pain he refused to acknowledge gnawed at him like a living thing, and his mood was tense and ugly. His resolve was fierce. Just weeks ago he'd thought he had no reason for living without Francesca. Now, however, she was his reason for going on, and for that, at least, he could thank her. He felt almost like a madman, so intense was his need to wreak his vengeance against her.

Anna hadn't discovered that Slater had gone out alone until long after he'd departed. As the hours had

188

passed, she'd worried continually for she'd been fearful of another incident like the one that had almost claimed his life at the Salazar graveyard. She was sitting in the front sitting room petting the cat Calida had tried to catch earlier, when she heard him return. Anna hurried to see him, leaving the cat to trail behind after her out of curiosity.

"Slater, I'm so glad you're back. Where were you?" she asked as she met him in the hall.

"What's it to you?" Slater returned harshly, his expression reflecting the bitterness that filled him.

Anna could tell he'd been drinking, but even so, his unusual brusqueness hurt. "I care about you, Slater. You know that. I was afraid that something might have happened to you," she explained softly, sensing his mood and wanting to help ease it if she could.

Her gentleness struck a soft chord deep within Slater, and for a moment, he softened. Turning to Anna, his gaze met hers, and he saw mirrored in the depths of her dark eyes all the love and devotion she felt for him. Once, not too long ago, Francesca had looked up at him in exactly the same way. At his treacherous wife's intrusion into thoughts, the gentleness was ripped away from him, and he hardened his heart and soul again.

"It's stupid to care that much about anyone, Anna," he sneered sarcastically as he walked on into Rafe's study. He was glad to see that his bottle of whiskey was right where he'd left it, and he headed straight for it. Another drink sounded real good.

"You went to see *her* again, didn't you?" Anna demanded hotly, following after him. "Wasn't last night enough? Why did you set yourself up to be hurt that way again?"

"What the hell difference does it make to you?" Slater challenged viciously. His movements were marked by anger as he strode to the desk and picked up the bottle of liquor. His glass was still there from before, and he splashed a healthy amount into it before slamming the bottle back down on the desktop "What I do or don't do is none of your damn business!"

His callous, heartless remarks were the final straw. Anna's temper exploded. Furious, she stood before him, her hands on her hips, her eyes shooting fire. "How dare you talk to me that way? You have no right!"

He tried to act as if what she had to say was unimportant, but she refused to let him ignore her.

"You seem to have forgotten, Slater MacKenzie, that if it hadn't been for me, you'd be dead right now! I'm the one who wrote to Nick and helped rescue you! I'm the one who smuggled you off the island. I'm the one who took all the risks for you! Don't you dare confuse me with the two-faced, lying, little rich bitch who's betrayed you at every turn!"

Ignoring her, Slater started to lift the glass to his lips to take a drink. Anna was so angry and hurt that when he went to take a drink, she swung out at him and knocked the crystalline tumbler from his hand. They were both stunned when her action sent the glass crashing to the floor.

"Maybe now I have your full attention?!" she demanded.

Her action so infuriated Slater that he grabbed her

by her forearms and hauled her up against him. "Just who the hell do you think you are?" he snarled.

Though his hands were tight upon her flesh, Anna showed no fear as she met his emerald glare. "I'm your friend, Slater," she offered, though it tore at her heart to say it. She wanted to be so much more, but he wouldn't allow it. "A friend who loves you and cares about you."

They stood like that for a moment, glowering at each other, testing their relationship to the very limits. An awareness of Anna's soft curves and warmth seeped into Slater, dulling his anger. He was reminded of just how attractive Anna really was and of how much he liked her. She was all fire and spirit. She was intelligent and brave. He was tempted again to taste of her love, but he held himself back. He owed her too much to do it. Friends didn't use their friends.

With careful control, Slater let his hands drop away from Anna, and he started to step back, breaking off all contact with her. It was then that they both heard it—the soft, strangled cry of a small animal in distress, coming from across the room.

"What was that?" Anna asked looking around in puzzlement.

"It came from over here . . ." Slater led the way to the far side of the desk.

Their expressions turned horrified as they stared down at the floor in disbelief. There, lying limply near the spilled whiskey, was the cat.

"Slater . . ." Anna dropped down on her knees, refusing to believe what she was seeing. With shaking hands, she reached out to pick up the cat and see what was wrong, to see if it was hurt and if she

191

could help it. As she tried to lift it, she realized with painful clarity that it was dead. She lifted frightened eyes to Slater as she let it drop back to the floor. "It's dead . . ."

"Dead?" The truth came to him in a crashing blow as he stared down at the dead cat and the spilled contents of the glass he had been about to drink from. The color drained from his face and his expression turned from one of horrified confusion to deadly understanding. "It was the whiskey," he seethed. "It was the damned whiskey!"

Anna stood up, grabbing his arm as she did to turn him to her. Her face was pale and her eyes were wide with terror. "Dear God . . .," she whispered nearly frantic. "It must have been poisoned . . . And it was meant for you . . ." She choked on the words, but she knew they were true.

"I know," Slater answered slowly. His anger with Francesca and Carlanta had been a fearsome thing before the death of the cat, and now it had deepened. He realized his would-be murderers had gone so far as to breach the sanctity of Rafe's home in their quest to kill him. For all their devious, desperate means, though, they'd failed again. He was very much alive, and he knew now that nothing, absolutely nothing was going to stop him. Two could play their game.

Anna finally shook herself from the stunned moment of inactivity that had claimed her. "You drank from that bottle earlier, right?"

"Yes."

"Then whoever poisoned it, did it while you were gone . . ." Anna rushed to the door of the study and called out for the servants to come running.

"Sí, Doña Anna! What is it?" Lola, the woman who ran Rafe's household, got there first.

"Who came into the study today after Señor Slater left?"

"Why, no one that I know of," she answered nervously, wondering what the problem was. "Is there something wrong?" She looked between Slater and Anna.

"Yes, there's something wrong! Look!" Anna was angry as she pulled the maid over to see the dead cat.

Lola let out a little cry of terror at the sight. "But how? Why?"

"Someone poisoned this bottle of whiskey while I was gone," Slater explained, picking up the bottle from the desk. "Did anyone come to the house for a visit while I was away?"

"No, señor," she denied.

Anna and Slater exchanged troubled looks, then Anna asked, "What about the servants? Did you know where they were all the time today?"

"No, Doña Anna. I give them jobs to do, and they do them. I only have to make sure the work is done."

"Are they all still here?" Slater followed up. "I'd like to talk with them, if I could."

"I will check." Lola left the room, but returned a short time later with the group of servants. "There is one girl missing," she offered right away. "Her name is Calida. She was here this morning, but no one has seen her since about noon."

Slater asked a few pertinent questions of the others, but quickly realized they knew nothing. All had been working with a partner for most of the day. Only the missing girl had had enough time alone to do her lethal deed.

Two of the servants started cleaning up the mess made by the thrown glass of whiskey. Slater and Anna watched in silence as the feline was carried from the room. Slater realized that the experience had been a very sobering one, and his taste for whiskey had suddenly disappeared. When the servants had finally finished and had gone, Slater glanced over at Anna. He could tell she was still shaken by the whole thing, too.

"Anna . . ." He spoke tenderly to her.

"Yes?" She was reliving just how close Slater had come to death, and her answer was strangled in her throat. Tears threatened, but she fought them back.

"Anna . . . I'm sorry."

"For what?"

"I was wrong. If you hadn't cared enough about me to get angry with me, I'd be dead right now."

Anna stared up at Slater, thinking him the most handsome man in the world, loving him and wanting him. She was desperate to go to him and hold him and reassure herself that he was fine, but she held herself back. She knew better than to try. He didn't love her as she loved him. "I told you before, Slater. I'm your friend."

"And I'm yours, Anna. Never forget that."

Chapter Fourteen

Rafe had been as outraged as Slater and Anna when he'd returned home and discovered the diabolical plot that had gone on under his own roof. Though he'd had little doubt about who was responsible, he'd done some further checking on the missing Calida. It had come as no great surprise to him when he'd discovered that her boyfriend, Jorge, had been employed by Carlanta and had disappeared too. That had been the final proof positive for him.

The outrage Rafe felt toward Carlanta and the corrupt government he represented grew fearsome. The man was evil, and it was obvious he would stop at nothing to achieve his goals.

Marita slipped into Rafe's thoughts then, and the good feelings he'd had about her earlier in the day were tempered. She was Carlanta's blood relative, and they were a very close-knit family. As much as he'd enjoyed her company that afternoon, he realized now that he would never be able to trust her, never. Even as he admitted that to himself, though, he recalled the sweetness of her kiss and how wonderful she'd felt when he'd held her close. Sleep proved next to impossible for him that night.

They made plans to ride out several hours before dawn and Rafe was dressed and ready long before the others. They kept careful watch as they left town, and they were pleased to find that no one followed them. By the time the sun came up, they'd been riding for quite a while, and they made good progress the rest of the morning. It was just before noon when they started up the winding path on the last leg of the journey through the hills.

It was then, after making most of the trip in silence, that Slater revealed the plan he'd devised to seek his revenge.

"I've got an idea of how we can get Tebeau and Favre back quickly and quietly," Slater told them as they rode single file up the trail toward the rebel camp.

"How?" Rafe asked. "Martinez has already tried just about everything."

"It's simple, really. We'll just make a trade." His tone was conversational, leaving the others to wonder at his train of thought.

"A trade?" Anna repeated. "But we don't have anything he wants."

"Not yet, but we will," Slater said with certainty.

"What have you got in mind?" Rafe trusted Slater and wanted to know more of what he'd come up with.

"Two agents would be a small price to pay to get your lover back, wouldn't it?"

"You can't be serious . . ." Anna was shocked.

"I'm dead serious. All I have to do is catch Francesca when she's by herself. I know the floor plans of both the Salazars' country home and their house in town, so it shouldn't be too difficult."

"But she's your wife . . . ," Rafe said slowly.

Slater gave him a measured look. "She forfeited that claim when she crawled into bed with Carlanta. I'll bring her back here to the camp, but I'll keep her blindfolded so she won't know where we are. We can keep her here under guard until a swap can be arranged."

"Don't you think you're being foolhardy? They've already tried to kill you twice. Do you really think they're just going to let you ride in and take her?" Anna forced the issue.

"It would be dangerous." Rafe cautioned.

"And you don't think it's dangerous for Tebeau and Favre right now?" he countered sharply, remembering the endless days and nights of torture he'd endured at the hands of Manuel and Carlanta. "I don't care about the danger. I'm more than willing to take the risk. That's why I came back. I told Strecker I would do what I could, and I will. Francesca has played a part in all their plans, and it's only right that she reaps some of the rewards."

His companions heard the steely quality to his voice and knew there would be no discouraging him.

"MacKenzie! I'm glad you're here! I've been expecting you! Rafe . . . Anna . . . It's good to have you back," Martinez welcomed them when they rode into the encampment a short time later.

"Hello, Martinez." Slater dismounted and went to shake hands with him. "It's been a long time."

"Too long," he told him earnestly. "Come, come in and sit down with me. We'll have something to drink and eat. The trip from Havana is always a long and tiring one." He led them into his hut so they could relax for a while.

From across the clearing, Estevan looked on. He was thrilled to see that Anna had returned, but his excitement quickly changed to jealousy at the sight of the American who'd accompanied her.

Estevan loved Anna. He had for some time now, and it was difficult for him to control his temper as he watched her with the other man. He had thought them well rid of MacKenzie all those months ago when he'd been taken by Carlanta; yet here he was, back again, and it seemed Anna's feelings for him hadn't changed at all.

"Give it up, amigo," Carlos advised Estevan, giving him a jab in the ribs to draw his attention away from Anna.

"I can't give it up. I love her," he declared in undertones to his friend.

"It doesn't matter that you love her. What matters is that she loves him," he pointed out with simple logic.

"But that could change."

"You think so?" he scoffed. "If that was going to happen, it would have happened by now. She doesn't love you. She loves only the American—and the revolution."

198

"We will see." Carlos's words made Estevan mad, even though he knew Carlos was speaking the truth. His love for Anna had been unrequited from the start, but like any hot-blooded, young man, he still believed he could make her love him.

"Come on, we have no time for this. There is work to be done."

Estevan went off with him reluctantly, hoping he would get a chance to talk with Anna later.

"We need you here, Slater MacKenzie," Martinez was telling him in earnest as they sat with Anna and Rafe in his hut discussing the current situation. "Why, just your returning to Cuba has already been of help to us."

"It has? How?" Slater was surprised.

"One of our men heard from La Fantasma . . ."

"La Fantasma?" Slater and Rafe asked.

"La Fantasma's an informer," Anna explained. "No one knows who she is, but she's good."

"And very reliable," Martinez added the admiration he felt for the mysterious woman evident in his voice. "She sends us news that usually helps a great deal, and yesterday word came that Carlanta was concerned about your being back in Cuba and was going to move the agents to a new hiding place."

"Did you find out when or where?"

"No," he replied in frustration. "But knowing Carlanta, I have to think he did it quickly—if not yesterday, then early today. I sent word out across the island right after I found out, but we've heard nothing back. I'm afraid we missed the move."

"How much longer do you want to wait to see if you hear something?" Slater asked.

"Why? Do you have another idea?"

Slater nodded. "Carlanta likes to play rough, and I intend to oblige him this time."

"How?" Martinez couldn't imagine what he had in mind.

"A barter. I intend to trade him something he wants for the two missing men."

"But we have nothing . . ."

"We will have," he told him confidently and then went on to outline what he planned to do.

"You say the man wants your wife, and you're willing to give her to him?" Martinez was shocked.

"The marriage between Francesca and me is a mere technicality, and I intend to put an end to it just as soon as I can. Carlanta's more than welcome to her."

"It's outrageous," Martinez said slowly with a disbelieving shake of his head. "But it sounds like it will work. How will you manage to get her?"

"I have my ways. Don't worry about that."

"I trust you. You know that. Is there anything we can do to help?"

"I need to know her exact location. Can you have your men check for me? Yesterday she was still in the city, but that could have changed by now."

"That will be easy."

"Good. Then, once I've captured her, I'll bring her here—blindfolded, of course. Do you have a hut I can use?"

"That won't be a problem, there's plenty of room."

"Good. We'll also need to keep her under guard. I don't trust her at all."

"There are always men around who can watch. When do you want to do it?"

"Just as soon as possible. The faster Tebeau and Favre are freed, the better. It's been too long already."

"What do you mean everything is quiet at the Ramirez household?" Armando stood behind the desk at his office, staring with angry eyes at the man who'd brought him the news.

Sanchez was surprised by his boss's volatile reaction to his news. "Ramirez is out of town. He had business in Cardenas, and both MacKenzie and the woman have gone with him. There was no one at the house, but the servants."

"I don't believe this . . . ," Armando swore under his breath. His plan to poison MacKenzie had been flawless, but it had obviously gone wrong just as the assassination attempt at the graveyard had failed. Armando didn't like being wrong once, let alone twice. Failure didn't sit well with him, and he was not going to let MacKenzie get away. "All right. Never mind. You can go."

When Sanchez had gone, Armando sat down at his desk and pulled out a piece of paper. He had just gotten a good start writing a note to Ricardo telling him what he was going to do next when there was a soft, single knock at his office door. Before he had a chance to respond, it opened unexpectedly. Armando was annoyed by the intrusion, and he instinctively crumpled the sheet of paper in his hand as he looked up. Though he was irritated by the interruption, he hid his displeasure as soon as he saw that it was

Marita at the door.

"Uncle Armando . . . your assistant said it would be all right if I just came on in," Marita told him with a sweet smile. She'd noticed his furtive movement with the paper, and her curiosity was piqued.

"Of course, my dear. It's always a pleasure to see you." He rose, dropping the wadded note into the small trash basket he kept by his desk, and went to kiss her in welcome. "To what do I owe the honor of this visit?"

"I was going shopping, and Mother wanted me to stop by and ask you . . ." She was about to say more, when Armando's assistant came rushing into the room.

"I'm sorry to interrupt, señor, but there's a problem . . ."

"Can't you handle it?" he asked in exasperation.

"No, it's something you will have to take care of personally."

"Marita, do you mind waiting for me for just a moment? I'm sure this won't take long." He was apologetic.

"Not at all."

"Make yourself comfortable. I'll be right back." With that Armando followed his assistant from the room. He closed the door behind them.

Marita waited only until the door was closed before she grabbed the rumpled sheet from the trash and spread it out to read it.

The plan did not go as expected. We'll have to rely on our contact within the rebel group to . . .

Marita stared at the note in frightened disbelief. There was a traitor in their midst! The heat of terror flushed through her, followed by a deep, abiding, bone-chilling cold. Pedro might be hurt, maybe even killed, along with Estevan and all the others! Her heart pounded fiercely as the icy dread possessed her.

Crumpling the note back up, Marita threw it in the trash again. The last thing she needed was for Armando to discover that she'd been digging through his trashcan. Her hands were cold and trembling as she quickly sorted through the papers on top of his desk, looking for another clue to the identity of the traitor. She tried the desk drawers too. One was locked, but the others were open and held nothing important.

At the sound of voices outside the office, Marita moved away from his desk to pull herself together before her uncle returned. There was no way she could let him think that something had disturbed her. When he came back in, she graced him with a wide, charming smile.

"Did everything turn out all right?"

"Yes, it's all resolved. Now, Marita, what can I do for you?"

"You can come to dinner tonight. Mother and I were hoping you could join us."

"You're invitation is appreciated more than you can know, but I'm afraid I can't get away tonight. Tell your mother I thank her, though, and I'll be in touch with her soon."

"Of course," Marita accepted his refusal gracefully, letting her expression reflect disappointment.

"But it would have been nice."

"I know, but sometimes there are business dealings that I can't put off." He escorted her to the door of his office, thinking she was a most charming young woman. Not only was she pretty, but she had a good figure and was suitably docile where a man's world was concerned. He was sure she would make some lucky man a good, submissive wife.

"I understand, and I'll tell Mother."

Leaving his office building, Marita climbed into her carriage and directed the driver to take her straight to Pedro's home. Once there, she rushed inside anxious to tell him about the devastating contents of her uncle's note. It upset her tremendously to find that Pedro was not yet back from his trip. Troubled about what to do next, she returned to the waiting carriage and headed for home.

Marita debated the few choices she had as the carriage moved along the bustling streets of Havana. She could sit tight, wait for Pedro's return and pray that the traitor, whoever he was, didn't take any action during that time, or she could take the risk and go to the rebel camp herself. It was a five hour ride in daylight, and it would go much slower in the dark. Once she got there, she knew she would be safe, for even if Pedro had already gone, Estevan would still be there. The only trouble was, Marita wasn't sure how she could make the trip there and back without being missed.

Her dilemma was real, but as the carriage stopped before her home, Marita realized she could do no less than journey to the camp herself. If she stayed safely at home and something happened, the guilt would weigh upon her forever. Part of supporting the revolution meant being willing to put your life on the line. She would do it.

"Mother?" she called out as she went inside, ready to begin her deception.

"Yes, Marita?" I'm right here." Rosa appeared from the back of the house and came forth to see her. "Did you speak with your uncle?"

"Yes, I did, but he sends his apologies. He has work to do tonight that can't be put off."

"That's too bad. I was looking forward to seeing him. I suppose we'll just have to spend a nice, quiet evening together."

"I'm sorry, Mother, but I'm not feeling too well. Would you mind terribly if I just go upstairs and lie down?"

Rosa noticed then for the first time that Marita did look a little pale and asked, "What's wrong, darling?"

"I'm not sure," Marita lied. "But my head hurts and my stomach feels uneasy."

Rosa touched her forehead, concerned, but could discern no fever. "Well, maybe it's a good thing Armando isn't coming to dinner." Rosa patted her cheek affectionately. "You go on to your room, and I'll bring you up something soothing to drink. Maybe that will help."

"Thank you, Mother." Step number one had been taken care of—convincing her mother that she was ill. Marita felt reasonably confident that she'd been believable. Now, all she had to do was convince her mother that she wanted to sleep undisturbed all night and that she didn't need to be checking on her every other hour . . .

Marita stripped off her dress and donned her nightgown. In the few minutes she had before her mother appeared, she dug through her armoire to find the peasant clothes she always wore when she went out at night. They were hidden in the back, right where she'd left them, and she pulled them out and stuffed them under the bed so she could get to them easily when the time came. As soon as darkness descended, Marita knew she would have to be out the window and on her way. There wouldn't be a minute to waste. Satisfied that she'd done all she could for now, Marita climbed in bed and pulled the covers up to her chin to wait for her mother.

"Here you are, dear," Rosa said as she came into the room a short time later. She was carrying a steaming cup of her own special herb tea that she was sure cured just about any female complaint. "This should help."

Marita almost grimaced and groaned out loud. She hadn't thought about that. She hadn't thought that her mother would bring her the infamous *herb tea* . . .

Marita sat up and took the brew from her mother, knowing to refuse would only arouse her suspicions. The healing concoction was as bitter and nasty as ever, but Marita paid the price. She made that ultimate sacrifice, albeit a tad reluctantly, for the cause. She paused halfway through downing the noxious brew to take a breath.

"Marita, you know you have to drink it all for it to do any good," Rosa reminded, keeping an eagle eye on her. Even though Marita was grown now, Rosa still remembered the days when her daughter used to find creative ways to avoid taking the medicine.

"I know," she replied, trying to keep her lip from curling in disgust as she stared down at the vile potion. She wondered if anyone who was healthy had ever gotten deathly ill from taking this stuff. She hoped not. There was a lot she had to do tonight.

"Come on," her mother continued to coax her as she smoothed out the covers on the bed, tucking her in to make her more comfortable.

"All right." Marita felt like she eight years old again as she surrendered to the inevitable. She drained it all, and the last swallow was almost impossible to get down.

"That's a good girl." Rosa praised her. She took the cup and smiled as she watched her daughter snuggle down. "Rest now, and we'll see if you aren't feeling a little better soon."

Marita did as she was told, giving her mother a tentative, half-hearted smile as she started from the room. The smile was not faked. Her stomach was suddenly feeling terribly strange. "Thanks."

"I'll be back in a little while."

The minutes passed like hours as Marita waited for the day to end and for her stomach to settle. Rosa checked back on her several times during the rest of the afternoon, but did not try to force another tisane on her, to her great relief. As dusk finally claimed the land, Marita was feeling herself and more than ready to embark on her mission. Rosa came just at dark to offer her some dinner.

"I really don't want anything," Marita declined,

even though she was now starving for she hadn't eaten a thing since breakfast. "I just feel really tired. I think I'll go to sleep for the night. Maybe if I get a full twelve hours of rest, I'll be better tomorrow."

"All right, sweetheart." Rosa pressed a loving kiss on her forehead, and she was pleased to find her daughter was still cool. "You sleep for now, and I'll see you in the morning."

She left the room quietly, certain that Marita must really be feeling badly, because, even though she didn't have a fever, it was not like her to languish in bed.

Chapter Fifteen

Marita waited only long enough to make sure her mother was out of earshot before she jumped out of bed and changed into the nondescript, boy's peasant clothing. She then plumped up her pillow and rumpled up the blankets to make it look like she was still lying there. That done, she opened the shutters on her window and sized up the branch of the massive tree that loomed nearby. As a child, she'd climbed the tree often. Her mother had never approved of her boyish ways and in her effort to turn her into a lady had punished her several times. Marita was glad as she looked down at the ground below that she still retained some of her youthful nerve. She put on the straw hat that finished off her disguise and after jamming her hair up underneath it, she started out the window. Grasping the branch, she began her dangerous descent.

When Marita's feet finally made contact with the ground, she drew a shaky breath and sent up a silent prayer of thanks for her deliverance. At a run, she made her way to the stables and, after saddling her horse, she led it out and away from the house before mounting up. She put her heels to the mare's flanks and rode from the city at as fast a pace as she could without drawing attention to herself.

The trip to the hidden encampment was long and arduous for Marita. She was thankful that the moon was bright for the way grew tricky near the end. It was just after midnight when she finally reached the narrow trail that led the last few miles through the hills to the hideout, and her mount was decidedly weary. She slowed down and took the path cautiously for she knew there were guards posted who might be tempted to shoot first and ask questions later should they feel the need. A short time later, when the armed, dark-clad man stepped out from his hiding place in the overgrowth of vegetation to challenge her, she was not alarmed.

"Who are you and why are you on this road tonight?" the man demanded as he snared her reins and stopped her advance. He kept his gun trained on her as he awaited her answer.

"I'm La Fantasma," she answered. "I have come because I must speak to Pedro Santana."

The guard had heard of how the mysterious La Fantasma helped them, but he had never seen her before. He peered up at her in the darkness, trying to get a good look at her face. Still apprehensive that she might not be who she said she was, he kept hold of her reins and called out to the other guard, "Alfredo! Get Estevan! We will wait here for Estevan."

"You are a cautious man. That's good." she complimented him.

In just a few minutes, Estevan appeared out of the gloom. He recognized her immediately.

"La Fantasma!" he welcomed her openly, knowing not to use her given name.

"Hello, Estevan, it's good to see you again." Marita dismounted and went to him.

"What brings you here? Has there been trouble since you last spoke with my father?" He knew she wouldn't have dared make the journey to the camp unless something was terribly wrong.

"Yes. I have some vital, new information. It's important I speak with your father at once!" she told him. "Can you take me to him right now?"

Estevan could tell she was upset, and he knew what he had to tell her would only upset her more. "I wish I could, but he's not here," he explained quickly. "He left this afternoon."

"But he wasn't at home, I went there first . . ."

"No, he was going to stop and visit our relatives who live west of town before he returned to the city. Why don't we go up to camp? You and your horse can rest, and we can talk. Maybe I can help you."

"All right, but I can't stay long. I've got to get back home before dawn," Marita agreed as they walked the final distance to the campsite.

"You're going to ride back tonight?" He was incredulous.

"I have to. My mother thinks I'm sick and asleep in my bed."

"I hope you make it."

"So do I. I don't even want to consider the alternative. It wouldn't be an easy thing to explain . . . my being gone all night."

211

"I understand."

The camp was quiet. Few people were stirring. Estevan took her to his hut and told her to wait there while he went to get her something to drink and then take care of her horse. He was back within minutes.

"What is it that was so important you felt you had to travel all the way here tonight?" he asked when he'd joined her in the hut. He'd brought a cup of steaming coffee for her to help her stay awake on the ride back to town and some leftover cold meat from their dinner and a thick slice of bread.

"I came across some information in my uncle's office, and according to what I found out, there's a traitor here in your camp."

"What?" Estevan felt a surge of panic at her words.

"It's true."

"Did you find out a name?" he asked nervously.

"No. No name was mentioned."

Estevan couldn't let it show, but a wave of almost dizzy relief swept through him. "Then how can you be so sure?"

"I saw it in a letter he tried to destroy when I walked in on him unexpectedly. He doesn't know I read it, but I did. That's why I had to come here to let you know. Can you get Martinez so I can tell him?"

"He left camp for the night." Estevan's lie came out in a rush. "But he's supposed to be back in the morning, and I'll make sure to tell him first thing."

"Thanks." Marita was appreciative. She made short order of eating the food and drinking the strong coffee he'd brought her, then rose to go. "I have to leave. It's much too late already."

"I'll get your horse for you."

While Estevan was gone, Marita wandered outside the hut. She was standing in the shadows, just idly looking around when she first caught sight of him. She froze and stared in fascination at the tall, handsome figure of Rafael Ramirez where he stood near the main campfire talking to another man she didn't recognize.

Marita's heart gave a wild lurch. Rafael?! Here?! What was he doing here?! A thousand, deeply troubling questions exploded in her mind. He was a wealthy, educated man. He was a member of the peninsular class just like her uncle! Was he the traitor? Could he be the traitor? Marita's mind screamed that it had to be him, for why else would he be there? Her heart cried out that it couldn't. Her senses were rent asunder by angry confusion and doubt.

In all her life, Marita had never been more grateful for her ability to blend in with the scenery. Hidden as she was by the quiet cloak of night, no one could see her distress. She could observe without being observed. She only wished she could hear what was being said between Rafe and the stranger, but they were too far away.

Marita considered rushing to find Estevan and blurting out her suspicions about Rafael to him, but she realized that could ultimately prove to be dangerous. She was, after all, Carlanta's niece. If the truth of her own identity was to become known, who would believe her? She might even end up being accused of being the betrayer, herself. Marita knew that until she had solid proof of Rafael's guilt, there would be no point in making any accusations.

For some unknown reason, Rafe looked up right in her direction just then. Marita felt as if he saw and recognized her even with her disguise, and she grew nervous. She backed farther into the darkness so she would be completely out of his line of vision.

Marita vowed to herself then and there that she was going to find out the truth about Rafael. As much as the prospect hurt her, if Rafael did prove to be the one who was working with her uncle, she knew she was going to have to expose him.

Estevan returned with her horse then, and Marita swung up into the saddle ready to begin the trek back.

"You'll be careful?"

"Don't worry. Everything will be fine as long as I make it home before daylight."

"I'll tell Martinez your news tomorrow, and if anything comes of it, I'll let you know."

Having known Estevan since her childhood, Marita didn't doubt or mistrust him for a moment. "Good. When I hear something more, I'll be in touch."

After one quick look back in Rafael's direction, Marita put her knees to her horse's sides and urged it on, into the darkness. She had miles to go and very little time.

When Estevan walked back into camp, Rafe called out to him.

"Yes?" the younger man asked as he went to see what Rafe wanted.

"Who was that you were just talking to?" Rafe inquired, curious. He didn't understand exactly why, but there had been something vaguely familiar about the unidentified boy.

"Just one of the young boys who helps us out once in a while, why?" he returned, taking great care not to identify Marita by either her real name or by La Fantasma. He didn't want anyone asking questions about why La Fantasma had been in camp. She'd confided her news to him, and he was going to make sure that no one else ever heard it.

Rafe gave a dismissing shake of his head. "He just looked familiar to me for some reason, but I guess I was wrong."

Rosa had passed the evening quietly, reading and doing needlework. Several times she'd been tempted to go upstairs and check on Marita, but she waited, thinking sleep might really be the best thing for her. When at last it was near midnight and she was ready to retire, she stopped by her daughter's room just to take a quick peek at her and make sure she was resting well.

Rosa noticed immediately that the shutters were open on the window and thought that Marita must have gotten too warm during the course of the evening. Worried that she might be developing a fever, Rosa crossed to the bed, intending not to wake her, but just to feel her forehead and see if she was feverish.

There was no other word than shocked to describe the way Rosa felt when she gently drew the covers back and discovered that her daughter was missing. Her heart actually seemed to skip a beat, and it was all she could do not to cry out in alarm. Terrible scenarios rushed through her mind . . . had her daughter been kidnapped? Had some awful person stolen her from her bedroom?

Rushing to the dresser, Rosa lit the lamp there and turned it up to full light to get a better look around. It was clear to her then, as she stared about the neat, undisturbed room that the bed had deliberately been made up to look like Marita was still lying in it, asleep. Common sense told her that a kidnapper wouldn't have gone to such lengths. The thought that followed, though, did nothing at all to reassure her. Wherever her daughter had gone, she'd gone because she wanted to, and that worried Rosa almost as much. Whatever her daughter was doing, it was something she couldn't do in daylight.

The temptation to rouse the household was great, but she refrained. The fewer people who knew about Marita's blatant indiscretion, the better. She left the room and summoned her most reliable servant to her, then sent him off to get Armando. She needed her brother's counsel on this for she wasn't quite sure what to do. Armando would know the best way to handle this, and she trusted his advice implicitly.

Almost an hour passed before Armando arrived. The servant had been unable to tell him what the nature of the emergency was at Rosa's house, and so, after hurriedly throwing on his clothing, he had ridden there at breakneck speed. He found his sister waiting for him in the foyer, looking distraught.

"What is it, Rosa? What's happened?" He knew it had to be something drastic for her to send for him in the middle of the night this way.

"Come with me . . ." She dismissed the servant who'd accompanied him back, then led the way

216

upstairs to Marita's room.

"Has something happened to Marita?" Armando asked as they started inside his niece's bedroom.

"You tell me," Rosa replied, waiting until he'd followed her into the room and then shutting the door firmly behind them. "Look." She pointed toward the bed.

"She's gone?" He gave her a puzzled look. "Where?"

"That's what I'd like to know. She told me she wasn't feeling well this afternoon, so she came up here to lie down. I checked on her several times, the last time being just before dark, and it was then that she told me she thought a good night's *uninterrupted* sleep might help. I didn't catch the significance then, but now I do."

"She didn't want you to check on her again, and with good reason," Armando said.

"Where could she have gone?" Rosa was stricken. She'd tried to raise Marita right, but she'd always been a headstrong and willful child.

"I don't know. But why don't we wait here until she returns and then ask her?"

"You think she's coming back?"

"She'll be back. She has no reason to stay away, does she?"

Rosa shook her head no. "We were getting along fine."

"What about men? Was there anyone in particular that she might be running away with?"

"She did see Rafael Ramirez yesterday, but I didn't think it was anything serious."

"Well, let's just wait and see."

"You don't mind staying with me?"

"Of course not. I wouldn't leave you here to face this alone. It's obvious she needs a man's guiding influence, someone to take a firm hand with her, and I intend to do just that. This kind of behavior is not acceptable. She cannot be allowed to soil her reputation and the Carlanta family name this way."

"Thank you, Armando. You have always been such a great help to me."

Rosa sat at Marita's dressing table, while Armando got another chair from the guest room down the hall. When they'd both gotten comfortable, Rosa turned down the lamp, and they sat in the darkness to await Marita's return.

For the entire ride back to Havana, Marita had been besieged by disconcerting thoughts about Rafael. Was he the attentive man who'd treated her so wonderfully when they'd been together and whose kiss had seared her very soul? Or was he a scoundrel working with her uncle to smash any attempts the rebels might make for freedom?

Thinking that Rafael was really the former and was keeping his support of the rebels a secret made her spirits soar. She had always found him attractive, but if he shared her same love and concern for the future of their country . . . Even as she let her mind wander, she realized that the alternative about Rafael was a far more real possibility. It left her angry and suspicious to think that he was so unprincipled as to make himself welcome in the rebel camp and then betray them to their enemies. She knew she would have to find out the truth about him as quickly as she could.

Marita reached the edge of the city just at dawn, and though her mount was nearing collapse, she could take no time to rest. With every passing moment the sun was edging higher above the horizon.

Never one to panic unnecessarily, Marita now found herself nearly crazy with the fear that she would be discovered. She had to get home, and fast! She couldn't be found out! What would she say? What would she do? She put the frightening thought from her and concentrated only on getting back to the house.

Marita finally made it back without incident. She was thrilled to find that there was no one moving about. She counted her blessings, telling herself that the hour was still early, and her luck seemed to be holding. She quickly saw to her horse, then darted for the tree and made the climb to safety.

The window to Marita's bedroom faced to the west, so her room was still darkly shadowed when she slipped inside. She felt safe at last as she turned away, yanking the hat from her head and letting her hair tumble freely down her back. She was just about to start shedding her disguise when she realized, to her horror, she was not alone. Jolted by the discovery, her eyes widened in alarm as she found herself standing before her mother and her uncle, her hat in hand.

"Mother . . . ," she gasped her name in surprise. A terrible, nauseating, sinking sensation pulsed through her and settled like an iron weight in the pit of her stomach. Her breathing became shallow and strained, and all the color drained out of her face as she began to tremble. She was caught—well and good. There was no way out. *What was she going to do?*

"I don't believe what I'm seeing." Armando's voice was hard and condemning as he turned up the lamp. He stood and approached her, his manner threatening. His expression was harsh as he stared at his niece. He walked around her, studying her clothing as if she were a slave at auction. "You are a Carlanta, or have you forgotten?! Have you given any thought at all to the consequences of your actions? Only common *putas* act as you have acted!"

"Uncle Armando . . ." Marita stumbled nervously over her words, desperately searching for some way to soothe his anger, but she knew there was nothing she could say or do to change things.

"Marita, how could you have disgraced us this way?" Rosa went to her daughter, her feelings a confusing mix of anger and mother's love. "Why are you dressed this way . . . like a boy? What have you been doing? Where have you been? We've been waiting most of the night, and we've been so worried . . ."

"Yes, young lady, just *where have* you been?"

The moment Marita had feared the most had come to pass, just like a nightmare. She couldn't confess the truth. God only knows what her uncle would do if he found out she was involved with the rebels. He might kill her outright or worse beat everything she knew out of her. Marita knew she had to come up with a story that was believable. Something that they wouldn't doubt, but what?

"Well? We're waiting," he demanded.

The answer she flung back at her mother and uncle startled her almost as much as it startled them.

"I've been with Rafael." It was out before she knew it, and she flushed painfully when she realized what she'd done.

"You spent the night with Rafael Ramirez?!" Rosa and Armando repeated in stunned unison.

Marita nodded. She told herself it wasn't *really* a lie. She had been with Rafael. He just didn't know it. So what if she'd embroidered the truth a little? He'd never have to find out.

"You went to Ramirez looking like that?" Armando disparaged, giving her clothing a scathing look. He then sneered, "I didn't know Rafael's tastes ran to boys."

"It doesn't!" Marita replied, jarred by his ugly accusation.

"Then why these clothes?"

"Because it makes it easier for me to leave the house at night without being bothered by anyone," she answered honestly.

"You have no idea what you've done, do you?" Armando challenged.

"I'm sorry."

"Do you think an apology rights this? What about our family's honor and pride? I'm afraid you're much too trusting and naive, Marita. The damage to your reputation is irreparable."

"What do you mean?" Icy fingers of dread seized her. Guilt assailed her over the lie.

Armando saw the guilt in Marita's expression and had no doubt about her culpability. He chose to ignore her question as he turned to his sister. "Don't worry about a thing, Rosa. I'll handle it."

"Handle what?" Marita repeated, growing more scared by the minute. She looked questioningly from her mother to her uncle, but they offered her no answers.

"Marita, you stay in this room," Armando dictated.

"But . . ." She grabbed his arm to stop him, afraid of what he meant to do. "Uncle Armando . . ."

His black gaze bored into hers. "Take your hand off me, Marita. You are very lucky that I haven't beaten you within an inch of your life for the dishonor you've brought upon our family."

Marita let her hand drop away as if she'd touched an open flame.

"You will remain here, locked in your room, and you will not communicate with anyone until I send for you. I do not want to see you or hear your voice. Is that clear?"

All she could do was whisper a quiet yes.

Rosa and Armando left the room, and Marita's already flagging spirits were completely demoralized when she heard her uncle lock the door.

Chapter Sixteen

Rafe would have liked to have remained in camp for another few days, but he knew it was important that he not be gone from the city for too long. He couldn't give any of the people he was associated with in Havana a reason to suspect his activities.

Rafe had passed a restless night, not falling asleep until well after midnight and then waking again long before dawn. By the time the sky began to lighten, he was already prepared to ride out. Slater was standing with him, and their mood was restrained.

Rafe faced his friend, his tone serious as he spoke, "Be very careful with what you've planned. You're taking a big chance."

"Don't worry. The element of surprise will be working for me this time," Slater told him. For the first time in months, he was feeling completely in control. He knew exactly what he had to do, and he was going to do it as soon as word came of Francesca's whereabouts.

"I'll be expecting to hear something from you."

"I'll send word before I leave the island," Slater promised.

They clasped hands, then Rafe vaulted easily into the saddle. Their good-byes said, Rafe rode for Havana, blithely unaware of the tumult that would soon envelope him.

Armando was angry, but in spite of his anger, he could still see some good coming out of Marita's immoral activities. At least, he reasoned dispassionately, she had chosen her lover well. Ramirez was not only well-respected around town, his wealth was unquestionable and his status assured. All those things combined to give Armando the upper hand in his dealings with him. With the leverage of his honor and station in life, he was sure he could bring about a resolution to the problem very quickly. He hoped force would not be necessary, although he had not completely ruled it out as a way of convincing Ramirez to do the right thing by Marita.

Armando was late arriving at his office that morning, and almost immediately called his assistant, Federico, in to him.

"I want you to take this note to the home of Rafael Ramirez and wait for a reply."

"I'll go right now."

"Be sure the message is delivered directly to Rafael and no one else. Understand?"

"Sí, Señor Carlanta."

*   *   *

Rafe had only been back home for about an hour when the servant came to him to tell him that a messenger had arrived with a letter from Armando Carlanta. Cautiously intrigued, he went forth to meet with Federico.

"Señor Ramirez, I have this letter for you." He presented him with the missive that had been entrusted to him.

"Thank you," he dismissed him after taking the envelope.

"I was told to wait for your answer," Federico explained apologetically.

"I see. Well, then, come with me into my office while I have a look," Rafe invited, leading the way. He sat down behind his desk and waved the young man into a chair before him, then turned his full attention to Armando's letter.

Rafael—
It is important that I meet with you at once to discuss a matter of great importance to the both of us. Please let me know the time that will be most convenient for you.
                                        Armando Carlanta

Rafe stared down at the note, puzzled. As much as he despised the amoral bastard, he couldn't imagine anything they had in common, let alone a reason that would require a meeting between them. Rafe knew a refusal to meet with Carlanta would only cause trouble, so he jotted down his answer at the bottom of the letter, telling him that he would meet him at 7 p.m. that evening here at his own house. Rafe suspected the underhanded official might be trying to set him up, and he didn't want to give him any advantage.

"Here you are, Federico," he said as he sealed the note in another envelope and handed it back to him.

"Gracias, Señor Ramirez."

Armando arrived at Rafe's door at precisely seven o'clock. The servant admitted him and escorted him into the sitting room to wait for Rafe. Armando made himself comfortable in the luxuriously furnished room, taking note of the expensive decorations and oil paintings that adorned the walls. He enjoyed being surrounded by rich things and friends . . . and relatives. Very soon, Ramirez would be his nephew by law, and he found the prospect pleasing as well as promising.

As he waited for Rafe to appear, Armando's thoughts turned to MacKenzie. The American was nowhere to be seen, and he wondered if he was still a guest at Ramirez's house. He hoped not, for it would be far better for Rafael not to be associated with him any longer.

"Armando . . ." Rafe said his name as he came into the room. "It's good to see you again."

Armando rose stiffly from where he'd been sitting to acknowledge him. "I hope you are still feeling that way after we've spoken."

"I'm afraid I don't understand." He frowned, subtly tensing. *Had Carlanta found out about his involvement with the revolutionaries? Or worse yet, did he know of his connection to Strecker and the*

Americans? Rafe knew he would have to bluff his way through until he could find out exactly what he was leading up to. He remained composed as he listened.

"Think about it, my friend," he said smoothly, yet with unyielding, icy undertones. "I'm sure you know exactly why I'm here—last night, for instance."

Rafe looked his enemy straight in the eye. It took a Herculean effort on his part to make sure no emotion showed. "What about last night?"

"Your display of innocence is remarkably convincing, but I already know the truth. Marita has told me."

"Marita?" Rafe really was surprised by the mention of Marita, and it showed. What could Marita have possibly told her uncle about the two of them last night when he hadn't even seen her!

Armando misread Rafe's perplexed expression for one of guilt, and he continued pressing his point, "Yes, Rafael. We are very aware of the fact that you two spent the night together."

Rafe stared at him dumbstruck. "Marita told you *that?*"

"There's no point in your trying to deny it." He refused to believe the other man's act of surprise at the news. "Rosa and I know everything."

"You do?"

"Yes, and my question to you is a simple one. Precisely, what do you intend to do about it?" Armando glared at him, tension emanating from him as he sensed that Rafe just might balk.

"Do about what? Nothing happened!" Rafe protested, his mind racing as he tried to figure out just what Marita had done, and why.

Armando drew in a sharp breath and went rigid at the implied insult to his family honor. He had always had the highest regard for Rafael and had thought him the perfect gentleman. "Are you calling my niece a liar?! Whether anything happened between you or not, is irrelevant. What matters is that her honor has been compromised."

Rafe couldn't believe this was happening. He could tell Armando was dead serious about what he was saying, and he realized that even if he told the truth as he knew it to be and denied Marita's claim, they would still end up on a field of honor. His choices were few—death, dishonor, or a marriage to Marita. Rafe lifted his gaze to meet Carlanta's, his expression stony.

"I would be honored if you would give your blessing to a marriage between Marita and myself," he bit out.

Armando smiled, glad that his judgment of Rafael's honor and character hadn't been wrong. "Of course, and I welcome you into the family. I will tell Rosa immediately so the plans can be made."

"Fine."

"It will be best, I think, if we do this as quickly and as quietly as possible. The less scandal, the better, if you know what I mean."

"I do." *He was going to marry Carlanta's niece!* The thought reverberated through him with chilling intensity.

"I will be in touch after Rosa and I have spoken with the priest to let you know what's being done. Also, it might be a good thing if you do not see your bride again until the actual time of the ceremony."

"All right." Rafe was willing to agree to anything just to get Carlanta out of his house so he could have time to think.

Armando started for the door, accompanied by Rafe, but paused before leaving. He put a hand on Rafe's shoulder in a gesture that indicated closeness. "Since we will soon be family, I think it's important that I give you one other piece of advice about something . . ."

Rafe could not imagine another thing this man could say to him today that could possibly make things any worse. "Oh?"

"The American, MacKenzie . . ."

"Yes, what about him?" He asked expectantly.

"I know that you have regular business dealings with the man, but he is not held in high regard by our government. In fact, your continued association with him is not at all advisable. You would do well to sever all ties with the man."

Armando's statement confirmed what Rafe had long suspected—that the government had checked into his private dealings with Slater. He was glad now that he had taken such care to make sure everything seemed legal and above board. It was good to know that he had passed their intense scrutiny and was now considered trustworthy by them. It gave him additional power to use in his work for the rebellion.

"I find MacKenzie a likeable sort. Our business connection goes back several years. Why is he held in such disfavor?" He took the opportunity to probe just to see how much Armando would tell him right now.

"We know for a fact that he has certain ties to those who are trying to encourage Creoles to fight for independence from Spain," he confided.

"I had no idea..." Rafe sounded sufficiently startled to be convincing.

"I'm sure you didn't. It's not widely known on the island, and that's why I thought it best to warn you about him. If I were you, I'd end my association with him as soon as possible. You never can tell when trouble may start, and I wouldn't want you or Marita to be innocently caught up in something that could become very ugly."

"I thank you for your counsel."

"We are family, now." Armando told him as he departed. He strode from the mansion, feeling very good about what had just transpired. He knew his own power would increase dramatically now that Ramirez's fortune was practically at his disposal.

Rafe closed the door after Armando had gone from sight, then stormed into his study and poured himself a glass of tequila. He couldn't believe what had just happened. He was going to be married! And to Marita! Whether he wanted it or not! The thought left him fuming. He didn't want to get married. It wasn't even something he'd seriously considered yet. He was still young.

For a moment, Rafe permitted himself to think about his newly acquired fiancée, and the memory of how wonderful she'd felt in his arms, and how exciting her kiss had been slipped warmly into his thoughts. As quickly as the memory came, he dashed it away.

This was no love match that was being arranged.

230

Marita wasn't marrying him because she loved him. This whole thing was based on a lie. Marita had lied to her uncle and mother. She'd been with someone else last night, and yet she sought to lay the blame at his door. Rafe couldn't imagine why she'd felt the need to drag him into it. She wasn't a fortune hunter. She had no desperate need for his money. Yet even as he questioned her motive, a part of him couldn't help but wonder who she'd really been with.

Rafe's fury at being trapped into marriage this way faded a little after his second drink. He began to think more coldly then, and more logically. It occurred to him that he could take advantage of his upcoming "union." Certainly, he would be closer to Armando now, and possibly even held within his confidence. Faintly, too, he admitted to himself that he had no objection to sharing his bed with the lovely Marita. Obviously from her behavior, she had had lovers before so there would be none of the wedding night shyness usually expected of virgin brides. He would just have to make sure never to trust her for he knew the truth about her now.

It was midafternoon when the men Martinez had sent to town to check on Francesca's whereabouts the day before, returned. They had ridden hard and fast with the news that she had left the city to go to the country. Pleased with their efforts, he thanked them, and then summoned Slater to his hut so he could tell him what they'd learned. Slater appeared moments later with Anna at his side.

"My men have done well. Your wife has left

Havana and is now at the Salazar country estate."

"Good. This makes everything far more simple," Slater told the rebel leader, his eyes gleaming in anticipation of the night to come.

"When do you plan to go?"

"I'll leave right away. Enough time has been wasted already."

"How many men do you want to ride with you?"

"None. I'll go alone. It will be better that way. A lone rider will draw less attention."

"I'm riding with you, Slater," Anna insisted, refusing to be left behind. "You'll need at least one person to watch your back."

He wanted to argue, but he knew she was right. As tempermental as Francesca was, she might prove to be more than a handful, and he might need help. "All right. Anna can go, but that's it, just the two of us."

She was pleased that he'd agreed. She'd been afraid that he would refuse her offer of help, and she'd be forced to remain behind, worrying.

"The one thing we will need is an extra horse."

Martinez nodded his approval. "Take what you need from the camp. Is there anything else I can do for you?"

"No, that should do it."

"How soon do you think you'll make it back?"

"It will just depend on how things work. If I can get in and out of there quickly, without detection, we should make it back by tomorrow."

"We'll be watching for you. Vaya con Dios."

Slater and Anna hurried to pack up the few things they needed, and they rode out of camp less than an hour later.

* * *

Francesca wondered at her own strange mood as she wandered through the house. Since she'd returned from the city yesterday, she'd spent every waking minute with Michael. Now that he was taking his afternoon nap, she was free to relax, but the trouble was, she couldn't. Every time she sat down to rest, her thoughts turned back to Slater and their encounter at the party.

Slater had looked so handsome . . . even handsomer than she'd remembered him, and that disturbed her. The element of leashed violence she'd felt in him had disturbed her too. During all their time together, she'd never known him to be anything but gentle and kind. Now, though, she realized that that had all been a part of his carefully cultivated act of innocence. An innocence that was all a sham. There had been nothing gentle or kind about the endless lies he'd told her, about the note her father had showed her, or in his eyes and words when they'd been on the patio together.

It annoyed Francesca that she couldn't completely banish Slater from her mind. She berated herself angrily for allowing him that kind of power over her. She knew what kind of man he was. No passionate kisses or sweet words would change her heart toward him. He had nearly destroyed her with his duplicity, once. She would never give him another chance.

Francesca left the coolness of the house and moved out onto the tiled patio. The day was warm, and the splashing fountain sparkled in the afternoon sun. She paused there to enjoy the sunshine and the heady fragrance of sweet blossoms that graced the profusion of flowering plants growing there. It was always calming for her to spend time here, and she lingered by the noisy fountain until Maria's call drew her attention.

"Doña Francesca? There is someone here to see you," Maria called to her. "And he's a very handsome man . . ."

For some reason, at her words, Francesca felt a chill run down her spine. She turned slowly, fearing she would find herself facing Slater, but when she turned, she found only Maria holding Michael.

"It's Michael. He just woke up and wanted his mother," the servant told her, giving her a big smile.

Francesca went limp as all the fear washed away. She returned her smile with open happiness and hurried to take her son. Hugging him close, she pressed a kiss on his cheek. "Gracias, Maria."

"He's your joy, isn't he?" Maria asked, watching the adoring mother cradle her child.

"He's my whole life," she admitted. "I don't know how I ever existed before I had him or what I would do now if I lost him."

"Well, you don't have to worry about that. Nothing's going to happen to Michael."

"I hope you're right, Maria." Francesca didn't understand the sudden sense of forboding that possessed her, and she held her son even closer to her breast. "I hope you're right."

The night was dark. Only a sliver of a moon shone

in the black, vast emptiness of the night sky. The stars were out, but to Slater they seemed cold and distant. It was a hunter's night—a night to move about without being seen—a night to stalk—a night to be a predator.

And Slater felt exactly like a predator as he moved away on foot from the place where he'd left Anna and the horses. They had made it onto Salazar land to the point overlooking the house without anyone seeing them, and he prayed his luck would hold for a little while longer.

Anna stood near where she'd tied the horses, watching Slater disappear into the darkness. She ached with worry for him, but she couldn't speak of it. She knew he would never approve. She had to satisfy herself with only his friendship, even though she was dying inside.

When his tall, dark-clad figure had gone from sight, Anna turned back to the horses. She had to keep them quiet while she waited and listened. Slater had told her to stay there until he returned or, if she heard gunshots, to run and never look back. Anna had already made up her mind that she wouldn't interfere unless she heard gunfire. Despite his direct orders to the contrary, there was no way she would ride off and leave him to the Salazars. Friends stood by friends, and she would never desert him—not under any circumstances.

Anna settled in by the three mounts, her senses alert, her rifle, loaded and ready, in hand. She wasn't particularly thrilled with the idea of having Francesca around, but if Slater could use her to free the missing agents, it would be worth it. As she sat in the pitch blackness, Anna offered a prayer that everything went right for Slater.

"Doña Francesca, can I get you anything else?" Maria asked as she turned back her bed and lit the lamp on the bedside table.

"No, Maria, thanks," Francesca answered from where she sat in her rocking chair with her son. She had already donned her nightgown and brushed out her long, dark hair so it hung loosely about her shoulders in a veil of silken ebony. The earlier sense of foreboding that had nagged at her that afternoon had gone, and she felt wonderfully content.

"Would you like me to put Michael down so you can go to sleep?"

"No, he's being really good, so I think I'll sit up with him for just a little while longer," she told her. "You can go on to bed if you like."

"All right, then. Good night."

"Night."

The maid left, closing the door quietly behind her as she went, leaving Francesca and Michael alone.

Francesca nestled Michael to the softness of her breast as she kept up her soothing, rocking pace. There was something very intimate in rocking him to sleep in her arms, and she loved every minute of it. A lullaby of mother's love swelled in her heart, and she hummed it softly as she caressed his downy cap of dark curls.

At the sound of her song, Michael sighed as only contented babies can and let his eyes drift slowly shut. He was safe, and protected, and warm, and loved. His life was perfect.

They were the picture of maternal bliss. They looked beautiful. They looked like Madonna and Child in the glowing golden lamplight.

Slater approached the hacienda on silent tread. If there were guards posted, he didn't run into them. With utmost caution, he skirted the outbuildings and made his way toward the back of the house where he knew her bedroom was located. Had the lights been out, he'd intended to sneak in and surprise her either in bed or when she came to bed. But, as it was, her bedroom lamp had been lighted, so he assumed Francesca was already there, preparing to lie down for the night.

Slater didn't know what he expected when he crept closer to the window to get a look. He had considered that she might not be alone. He had thought that one of the servants might be with her or worse yet, Carlanta, but never had he imagined finding her as he did right now. He froze, unable to move, as he stared at the scene before him.

Francesca—his wife—was sitting in a rocking chair with a baby in her arms, and from the way she was cradling it and singing to it, he knew immediately that she was the young child's mother!

Chapter Seventeen

Concealed by the night, Slater was able to observe without being observed. He continued to watch Francesca through the open window as she held the child cradled in her arms and softly sang to it. A part of Slater ached to think that this was what their married life could have been like. They would have been living happily at Highland now, and the baby could have been theirs . . .

The vicious ugliness of the situation wouldn't let Slater continue with the dream, though. Heated emotions raged within him as he realized that the baby had no doubt been fathered by Carlanta. It infuriated him to think of how quickly his precious wife must have sought Carlanta's bed after having arranged his kidnapping. For what must have been the hundredth time since the party, he cursed his lack of judgment in having fallen so foolishly in love with her and, even worse, for having taken her as his wife.

Slater's wrath was nearly uncontrollable, but he knew he couldn't let it rule him. When men allowed violent emotions dictate their actions they made mistakes, and he was not about to make a mistake now that he was this close to achieving his goal.

With pure force of will, Slater struck all emotion from him. His thinking once again unimpaired by his distracting, volatile feelings, he realized that the baby was a bonus he could use to his own advantage. Carlanta might have tried to play games if he only took Francesca for a hostage; but if he were holding the child, Carlanta would have to negotiate. Not anticipating trouble, but wanting to be prepared, Slater drew his gun. Boldly, he stepped forward through the open floor-to-ceiling window and into the light of Francesca's bedroom.

"Hello, Francesca." Slater spoke with just enough menace to jar his wife from her reverie.

"Slater . . . !" She whispered his name in a strangled voice as she was startled from her contentment. Slater's tall, broad-shouldered, dark-clad figure loomed larger than life before her. He looked mean . . . threatening . . . and her heart was suddenly pounding full force as she stared at him and the gun he held at ready in his hand. "What are you doing here?"

"Now, is that any way to greet me?" he drawled sarcastically, his intense, green-eyed gaze locked on her and the baby. "Especially after I rode all the way out here to see you?"

"What do you want?" she demanded, sounding more in command than she really was. "Take whatever it is and go!"

"That's exactly what I intend to do." Slater was enjoying the sense of power the situation was giving him. Very calmly, he moved to the door and locked it, never taking his eyes off Francesca. He then closed and locked the connecting door that led to Michael's room.

She watched his moves and grew more and more frightened with each passing moment. She wanted to run. She wanted to cry out for help, but she honestly doubted whether anyone would be able to hear her. Her room was situated far from the servants' quarters and since her father was living in the city right now, she was quite alone. "Get out or I swear I'll scream!" Francesca threatened, clutching Michael even tighter.

"If you do, it'll be the last sound you'll ever make," Slater responded coldly. With that he lifted the gun and pointed it directly at the baby. "I suggest you put the baby on the bed and get dressed."

"Why?" Her eyes widened with terror. She couldn't imagine what he wanted.

"We can play your little question and answer game later, Francesca. Right now, move."

"But . . ."

"Move!" he repeated, this time more angrily.

Francesca was frantic. She considered trying something, but the savage look in Slater's eyes stopped her cold. Had she just been afraid for herself, she might have gone ahead and tried, but she had Michael to worry about now. Resignedly, she moved swiftly to do as she was told. She lay Michael down near the center of her bed to make sure he wouldn't roll off, and then grabbed up the dress and under-things she'd discarded earlier and headed toward the dressing room to put them on, but Slater's terse call stopped her.

"Oh, no, you don't. If you think I trust you out of my sight, you're wrong. You get dressed out here. I want you where I can see you all the time."

Infuriated, but helpless, Francesca shot him a black look, but did as she was told. The humiliation was great as she stood before him. Her movements were angry as she sorted through her undergarments trying to decide what she could put on without removing her nightgown. Finally, she struggled to pull on her underpants.

Slater stood across the room, his arms folded comfortably across his chest as he watched her efforts. He would have thought it humorously entertaining if he hadn't been in such a hurry. "In case you've forgotten, I have seen you naked before, Francesca. You've got nothing to hide from me."

"Oh . . . you!" Her face flamed with frustration and embarrassment.

"Yes?" he returned.

Francesca was so angry that she was shaking. "I hate you!" she seethed.

"It seems our feelings for one another are mutual then," he replied with bitter amusement. "Now get dressed and be quick about it!"

Slater's gaze seemed indifferent as it rested upon her. The truth of it was, though, that when she threw off the cumbersome nightgown and began to dress in earnest, a strong surge of desire stirred in him. Her legs were long and slender, and he remembered how velvety they'd felt when they'd been clasped about his waist during the throes of their passionate love-making.

A heat rose in Slater's body. He denied it and shifted his position slightly. Still, he continued to watch her. Her waist seemed just as tiny as before, even though she'd been through childbirth, and he was sure it could easily have been spanned by his two hands. Beneath the muslin of the undergarment she'd already donned, the plane of her stomach was still flat, and there was no sign that any of her silken flesh had been marred by having carried the child to term.

Slater almost allowed his gaze to drop lower to the enticing apex of her thighs, but brought himself up short. He lifted his gaze, only to discover that that was an equally bad mistake. Though she was rushing to don her chemise and cover herself, her bosom was still bared, and his regard lingered there with scorching intensity.

Where before he'd thought Francesca well-proportioned, now he thought her figure absolutely glorious. Her breasts had filled out. They were lush and full, and the pink crests, taut now in their exposure, seemed to beg for the touch of his lips and hands. It was all Slater could do not to throw his wife on the bed and slake his growing passion deep within her sweet, tempting body.

Francesca happened to accidentally look up at Slater right then, and she recognized all too clearly the look of hunger on his face. She trembled at the thought that he wanted her. She remembered clearly the power his lovemaking had over her, and she felt desire bud within her. Angered by her body's betrayal, she turned away from him and hurried to finish covering herself.

"Suddenly shy, my love?" Slater drawled sardonically as he strode closer to her. "I'm sure you aren't this bashful with Carlanta, are you?" Acting very cocksure of himself, he lifted one lock of her ebony hair from her shoulder and rubbed the silken tresses between his fingers.

Until he'd spoken, Francesca had managed to control her upset, but his nasty, degrading remark pushed her over the edge. Her temper erupted. Though she was standing there wearing only her underthings, she didn't care. She spun around and swung at Slater with all the strength she could muster. Francesca wanted more than anything to slap the smug, knowing look from his face.

For some reason, Slater had felt driven to remind himself, and her, of her betrayal with the other man. He was ready for her reaction when she tried to slap him. His reflexes were lightning fast, and he snared her wrist with ease, stopping her assault before it started. His smile was savage as he glared down at her.

"That wasn't smart, Francesca. That wasn't smart at all. Considering how precarious your situation is, I would think you'd want to be nice to me . . ."

"You can go to hell!" she snapped, trying to wrestle free of his grip.

"I've been there, Francesca," he answered brittely. He shoved her away from him almost violently, as if it suddenly somehow pained him to touch her. "Get dressed." His order was succinct. He moved to stand between her and the baby, just in case she took a notion to try to grab the child and run.

Francesca wasn't sure if she was more furious or frightened as she hastened to pull on the rest of her clothes under his steady, seemingly emotionless stare. It was unnerving to say the least, and she was relieved when she finally buttoned the last button on the bodice of her dress. "All right. I'm done. Now what do you want?"

"Get what you need for the baby and let's go," he directed dispassionately.

"Go? Where?"

"That, my dear, is none of your business. Just get moving." He waved her toward the bed with the gun and stood back to watch as she hurriedly gathered the baby's bottle, blanket, and an extra diaper. "Get a big towel of some kind, too. We'll need it."

Francesca stuffed the few baby items into a pillowcase to carry them, and then turned to Michael. She was busy wrapping him in the blanket when Slater came up behind her and grabbed her. Not knowing what he was doing, she was about to scream when he gave her a fearsome jerk backward against the hard wall of his chest.

"Be quiet or I swear I'll tie your hands behind you, and you won't be able to hold the baby."

Slater's words were breathed so cynically in her ear that they sent shivers of terror down her spine. His hands were like steel bands on her upper arms, and Francesca knew he was serious.

"All right. I'll be quiet." She went quietly, offering him no resistance.

"Good. This is just to make sure you don't do anything foolish as we leave the house." He quickly and efficiently gagged her with a bandanna he'd brought along. "Now, let's go, but if you give me any trouble . . . any trouble at all, I'll leave the child wherever we are, and you'll never see it again. Do you understand?"

Francesca nodded, horrified by the thought of Michael being abandoned in the midst of the

244

wilderness. She wondered how any father could be so cold-blooded where his offspring was concerned. it hurt her that he hadn't paid even cursory attention to his own son. Even the fiercest animals in the wild cared more for their young than Slater did.

Slater said nothing more, but waited while she'd picked up the sleepy baby. He took a note out of his pocket and dropped it on the bed where it would be easily seen. Then grabbing up the pillowcase she'd packed, he turned out her lamp before pushing her slightly ahead of him out of the room the same way he'd come in.

"This way," he ordered in a low voice when they were outside. He took her wrist to pull her with him.

Francesca knew better than to resist. Without protest, she allowed him to drag her along. All that mattered what that she protect Michael and keep him safe from harm.

Slater's pace was quick, but wearing a dress as she was hampered Francesca's movements. Determined not to give him any reason to get angrier, she hiked up her skirts to give herself more freedom so she could keep up with him.

Francesca was amazed at how quiet Michael was being, and she thanked heaven for that one small favor. As vicious as Slater's mood was, she wasn't sure how he would have reacted had Michael cried.

Anna had been watching for him from her hiding place, and she called out in a hushed voice to direct him to where she waited.

"Slater! Here!" She appeared at the top of the low rise, already mounted and leading the other two horses behind her.

"Thanks, Anna."

Francesca stared in amazement at the woman she'd considered her rival. Anna was wearing men's clothing, and in fact, could have passed for a man, had Francesca not known her. She was stunned. Slater and Anna definitely had been 'business associates,' but it had been the business of the rebellion that they'd been working on together. Francesca wondered what other secrets this woman held.

Slater took the baby from Francesca. "We've had to bring a baby along. I'll need you to hold it for the ride back."

Francesca bit back a sob as she watched Slater offer her son to the other woman.

"A baby?" Anna was shocked.

"Oh, yes. My wife became a mother during my absence."

His words were spoken with such venom that Anna said nothing more as she took the infant from him.

Slater dug in the pillowcase and pulled out the towel. "I think you can use it for the baby on the ride back."

"All right." Anna knew the way peasants carried their children and she quickly fashioned a carrier that bound the child safely against her breasts for the trip. She was surprised that Francesca's baby was being so good-natured, for infants usually cried when they were taken from their mothers. Anna tried to get a good look at his face, but the night was dark, and it was difficult to make out what he looked like.

While Anna was taking care of the baby, Slater got the short rope he'd brought with him and tied Francesca's hands together in front of her. Her eyes widened at his efforts, and she tried to fight against his bondage, but he held her firmly.

"This is just a little extra insurance, Francesca. I want to make sure you don't try to take off on me." He smiled at her obvious fury as she sputtered angrily behind the gag. Without another word, he lifted her into the saddle of the extra horse. Her skirts were awkward, but Francesca tucked them under her as best she could. He grabbed up the reins to her horse and his own as he turned to Anna.

"I'll go first and lead her horse behind me." Slater told her. "Are you ready?"

"Let's ride." Good horsewoman that she was, Anna had no trouble managing the baby and her own mount. She waited until Slater had started off, then followed after him. She made sure to keep a careful watch behind them for any signs of trouble.

They rode at a subdued, measured pace. Behind them, the hacienda remained dark and quiet. All were asleep, unaware that Francesca and her son had been spirited away against their will in the middle of the night.

Francesca was livid. She glared at Slater's back as they rode through the night, and she wished with all her heart that looks had the power to kill. She wanted to scream at Slater that he was the most vile man who had ever walked the face of the earth! That he had no right to do this to her, no right at all. The gag, however, combined with the fear that he just might follow through on his threat to leave Michael prevented her from even attempting to vent her fury.

As the miles and the hours passed, Francesca slowly managed to bring her raging temper under control. She tried to think more logically and tried to figure out just what it was Slater hoped to accomplish by kidnapping her like this. Certainly, he hadn't taken her with him because he wanted her. Francesca knew that for a fact that that could not be the case. Slater didn't want her. He never had, and he never would. She had to assume that his actions had something to do with the political intrigue he was involved in and with her father's activities. The thought frightened her, for who knew what kind of deadly, vicious game Slater was playing?

Fearful for her son's life as well as her own, Francesca resolved that no matter how difficult things became, she would do whatever she had to to survive. She vowed, too, that should the opportunity arise for her to escape from Slater with Michael, she would.

Slater kept up the ground-eating, steady pace until just after dawn. He'd kept them well off the main roads to avoid trouble. When he was satisfied that they'd traveled far enough from the Salazar property, he finally reined in in a small, secluded clearing near a stream to let the horses rest and drink. Slater dismounted first and went to help Francesca down.

Francesca couldn't believe that Slater wanted to assist her. Proud as she was, she didn't want him anywhere near her, let alone his help. She knew she could get down by herself! She just wanted him to go away. But try as she might to avoid his hands, Slater was too quick and too strong for her.

"Damn it, Francesca!" Slater swore, irritated because she wouldn't give in gracefully to his attempt to help her descend. He finally managed to grasp her firmly by the waist and then he started to drag her bodily from the saddle.

Francesca realized it was useless to continue to try to evade his touch, so she looked him brazenly in the eye as she turned toward him. She allowed his help, her eyes spitting fury as she glowered at him.

Slater was swearing under his breath at the aggravation she was causing him. He was surprised when she suddenly gave in. As he was helping her down, she braced her bound hands on his shoulder as best she could and ended up sliding down the length of his body as he held her at the waist.

Suddenly, everything changed. Slater glanced down at Francesca and lost track of all his thoughts. Never before had she looked so magnificent to him.

Her eyes were flashing with the turbulence of her emotions, and her cheeks were flushed with high color. The thick, silken veil of her hair had always been his weakness; and now, unbound as it was, it fell about her shoulders in a riotous tumble of curls that he found nearly irresistible. Her breasts were crushed against his chest igniting unwelcome fires of desire within him. Though he despised Francesca, the temptation to taste of her lovemaking was a powerful one right then.

"Slater."

Anna's call distracted him, penetrating the haze of sensuality that had momentarily enfolded him and rendered him nearly dim-witted. Slater looked over in Anna's direction, glad for the chance to regain his equilibrium.

"The baby's sleeping. Can you take it from me so I can get down?"

Almost casually, as if Francesca mattered very little to him, he released her and walked away.

Though Francesca had been mad over his manhandling of her, she'd been stunned by the explosion of desire that had rocked her when she'd found herself at the mercy of his touch. Watching Slater go to Anna and take their son from her, she refused to identify the emotion that seared her soul as jealousy.

It hurt Francesca that Slater didn't even bother to look at his own son as he held him. All Slater did was hold him long enough for Anna to dismount and then hand him back to her. They spoke a few words Francesca couldn't hear, and then he stalked away by himself. The pain in Francesca's heart over Slater's complete and final rejection of his own flesh and blood was excruciating. She wondered why she had expected more.

Anna felt as if she'd won a major victory as Slater walked away. She was thrilled that he wasn't being fooled by Francesca anymore. She felt confident as she walked over to the other woman and, as Slater had instructed, untied and ungagged her.

"Slater said we were too far away for anyone to hear you now, so it won't matter if you scream or not," Anna informed her casually, handing Michael to her just as he began to stir and come awake.

Francesca took her sleepy child back eagerly and felt a surge of maternal love unlike anything she'd ever experienced before. Slater might not want his son, but she did. She would make sure Michael knew he was loved every second of every day and every night. Wandering a short distance away from Anna, Francesca sat down on a grassy spot beneath a spreading tree and quickly tended to her small son's needs.

Slater's manner was tense and his expression

thunderous when he returned to join Anna some time later.

"Is something wrong?" Anna asked. She had no idea what could have caused the mood change in him since things seemed to be going very well.

"No," he replied tightly. He could no more explain to Anna what he was feeling than he could explain it to himself. It troubled him deeply that he could still desire Francesca, even after knowing the truth. She had set him up to be tortured and murdered. She had bedded his worst enemy, and the finally paralyzing blow of discovering that she'd given birth to the other man's child while still bearing his name. "Have the horses drunk their fill?"

"Yes."

"Then let's go. The sooner we're safely back in camp, the happier I'll be."

"Are you going to tie her up and gag her?" Anna nodded in Francesca's direction.

"As long as you've got the baby, I don't think she's going anywhere, but I'll tie her hands again just in case. We'll stop before we reach the last turnoff so I can blindfold her. I don't want to take any chances that she might be able to identify the area once she's been released back to Carlanta and her father."

Slater ordered Francesca to give Anna the child once more, and then with complete detachment he put her back on her horse. They headed on their way again, glad to be on the last leg of their journey into camp.

Because their pace had been so slow, it was near noon when they finally reached the cutoff to the encampment. Michael had begun to fuss and though

251

Anna had tried to calm him, he would not be quieted. When Slater reined in unexpectedly, Francesca feared he was going to make good on his threat to leave Michael behind.

"Please . . . give me my baby . . . ," Francesca begged as Slater maneuvered his horse around. "I can calm him down. He's my son . . ."

Her son . . . At her words, Slater saw the worry in her eyes and realized the direction of her thoughts. His mouth thinned into a firm line. He couldn't believe that she thought him that much of a monster that he would hurt a baby. Not that he cared about the child. He didn't. The baby was Carlanta's, and that alone was enough to insure that he held no great affection for it, but he was not the kind of man who would wreak his vengeance on an innocent.

"Your son is fine right where he is, Francesca. Turn your back, you're going to need a blindfold from here on in," he directed, disgusted with her for thinking him capable of such an act.

Her relief was great at finding out he only wanted to put a blindfold on her. She turned in the saddle as he'd said to and waited while he tied the strip of cloth around her eyes. Then they were riding again, heading into the hill country on the final part of their trek to the rebel encampment.

"Martinez! They're coming!"

The cry went up from the guards, and the rebel leader rushed out to greet Slater and Anna on their return. He was pleased to see that they had Francesca with them, but the sight of the baby with them gave him pause.

"Congratulations, Slater. It looks like things went according to your plan," he told him as he welcomed him back into camp.

"Everything went perfectly," Slater agreed, dismounting and going to shake his hand.

"Were you followed?"

"No. I got in and out of the hacienda without anyone knowing. I'm sure we got at least four hours headstart before they even found out they were missing."

"Why did you bring the child along? Whose is it?" Martinez inquired as he saw Anna climb down from her horse with the baby in her arms.

"It's Francesca's son. I thought we could use him for extra insurance against Carlanta and her father . . . and to keep her in line in case she tries to give us any trouble."

"Wise decision," he agreed. "I have a hut ready for your use."

"Good. I'll need a constant guard outside it until the exchange is made."

"That's no problem. It can easily be arranged."

"Fine. If everything from here on goes as well as last night, Tebeau and Favre will soon be freed."

"And our plans for the revolution will be able to continue . . ."

Chapter Eighteen

Slater returned to Francesca's side and helped her down from the horse. She remained standing passively before him while he untied her wrists and removed her blindfold.

"Where's my son?" she demanded anxiously the moment she was free.

Anna quickly appeared by her side and handed Michael to her. "Here he is."

"Thank you," she said stiffly, resenting having to be grateful to the other woman.

Martinez, meanwhile, found Estevan and directed, "Take the woman with Señor MacKenzie to the hut nearest mine. Then stay and guard the door. She's not to be allowed to leave unless MacKenzie is with her. Understand?"

"Sí." Estevan agreed and hastened to do as he was told. He found Francesca standing with the baby near the horses. "Your hut is there." He gestured toward one of the small, native structures near the center of the camp.

With her head held high, Francesca turned on Slater and shot him one last look. "I'm going to see that you pay for this, Slater MacKenzie."

"No, Francesca, your father and Carlanta are the ones who are going to pay," he answered her with a mocking smile.

Maintaining her dignity, she refused to rise to his bait. She moved off in the direction Estevan had indicated, and she never looked back.

"This is where you'll be staying for now," Estevan explained as they reached the dirt-floored native hut that was constructed from the bark and leaves of the royal palm trees.

"Thank you," she tried to dismiss him, but Estevan had no intention of leaving her alone.

"I'll be right outside if you need anything, señora."

Francesca wanted to scream at him that she was not a "señora," but she knew better than to even try to explain. She went inside the small, windowless structure and stared around herself in misery. The building was cramped and dark. The only furniture was a makeshift table, two very rickety chairs and a low-slung, narrow bed barely wide enough for one. As prisons went, she realized this one probably wasn't all that bad. At least she wouldn't be tied up anymore, and that was a relief. When she turned back around, Francesca discovered that there was a flap of heavy material tied back over the doorway, and she let it drop down to afford herself some privacy.

Cut off from prying eyes, Francesca finally let her guard down. She sank down on the side of the hard bed. Her shoulders were slumped in defeat, and her eyes were hot and burning. She was bone-weary from being up all night and hungry, too, but it was the humiliation of being at Slater's mercy that caused her the most distress. The only comfort she had right then was Michael. He was her reason for living. He was her reason to go on.

Francesca lay Michael down beside her, and she was amazed when he curled up quietly. She knew then that he was as exhausted as she was, and she hoped he'd take a nap so she would have a few minutes to get her thoughts together.

"Sweet dreams, sweetheart," Francesca whispered, and she pressed a soft kiss to his cheek. She leaned back and tried to get comfortable bracing herself against the side of the hut as she waited to see what was going to happen next.

Outside, Estevan stood guard, making sure MacKenzie's "guest" didn't escape. As he remained faithfully on duty, he kept one eye on Anna as she continued to speak with Martinez and the American. Though she was dressed like a young peasant boy, he still thought her the most beautiful woman in the world. He'd loved her from afar for what seemed like a lifetime, and he prayed that one day soon she'd realize the way he felt about her. Estevan just wished that MacKenzie would go back to his own country and stay there.

When Estevan saw Martinez move off and Slater and Anna start his way, he drew himself up to full height. He was anxious for the chance to speak to her and knew he had to take advantage of every opportunity. As they drew near, though, he accidentally over heard a part of their conversation, his eagerness turned to jealous anger.

"You can sleep in with me if you want to, Slater," Anna was offering. She would have liked to think that their sleeping in the same hut might lead to something, but she knew better. The suggestion was made openly as a convenience for Slater, but she also had an ulterior motive. Anna wanted to keep him away from Francesca as much as she could. Francesca was a gorgeous woman, and since Slater had been susceptible to her charms once, Anna didn't want to give the other woman another opportunity to betray him.

"No, I'll sleep in the same hut as Francesca," Slater declined her invitation. "Until the time of exchange, I intend to keep a close, personal watch on her."

"If you change your mind, you don't have to ask. There's room." Though Anna had expected him to refuse, she was disappointed by his answer. Her hope of keeping them apart was dashed. Every night, until the swap was made for the missing agents, Slater would be sleeping near his wife . . . the woman he'd once adored.

Jealousy ate at Estevan, and he was hurt and in agony as he'd waited for MacKenzie's reply to Anna's offer. Only when he turned her down, did his pain east a bit. As wonderful as Anna was, he didn't understand how MacKenzie could, but for his own sake he was glad that he had.

Estevan managed to keep a calm expression as Slater approached and nodded a greeting to him. When Slater went inside to speak to Francesca,

Estevan hurried after Anna.

"Anna . . . I'm glad you made it safely back."

Anna had been heading for her own hut, and she was surprised by his initiating a conversation. She thought Estevan a nice enough young man from a good family in town. Beyond that she knew only what she'd heard from the others in camp—that he was an ardent patriot, who was eager for Cuba to become independent. "So am I. It was frightening for a while."

"Were you in danger?" he asked.

"No, but we could have been very easily. Luckily, Slater knew exactly what he was doing," she told him proudly.

Slater . . . Slater . . . Slater . . . Estevan couldn't stand the man! Did he never do anything wrong? He wished just once that Anna would say his own name the same way she said MacKenzie's and look at him the same way she looked at Slater. He was beginning to wonder if that day would ever come!

"It was a daring thing to do, riding into Salazar's place like that. I just can't believe that he's really willing to trade his own wife for the other agents. She's an attractive woman." Estevan knew the details of Slater's plan from talk in camp.

It was bad enough for Anna that Slater had announced that he was going to share the hut with Francesca, but for Estevan to sing her praises was more than she could bear right then. "You men are all alike! Francesca may be pretty on the outside," she snapped, "but inside, she's a betraying bitch who's getting exactly what she deserves!"

Estevan was surprised by her vehemence. "What did she do?"

"Slater was kidnapped and tortured by Carlanta the last time he was here working with us, and she's the one who was responsible. She turned her own husband over to them to be killed. If J hadn't arranged for his escape, he'd be dead."

"It's a good thing you got him out." The guilt he'd long borne over his actions regarding MacKenzie bore down on Estevan heavily right then. He was tempted to confess the truth to Anna, but feared she'd hate him forever if she found out. Estevan knew for a fact that MacKenzie's wife wasn't the one who'd betrayed her husband. In his jealousy to get the American out of Anna's life, Estevan, himself, had sent information about MacKenzie's activities to Carlanta all those months ago. At the time he'd had no idea that they would torture him, he'd thought the government officials would only throw him out of Cuba. The results of his jealous plotting had horrified him. He hadn't wanted MacKenzie dead or hurt, he'd just wanted him gone.

"Slater's a good man. He deserves better than her."

Estevan heard the touch of wistfulness in her voice and wondered miserably if she would ever think of him that way. "Is he going to stay on here or go back with the others once they're freed?"

"I'm sure he'll be going back," she sighed. "Why do you ask?" She was curious as to what his sudden interest in Slater was.

"We need more men like him," he answered quickly, not wanting her to suspect that he had a far more personal reason for inquiring. He was buoyed by her reply, but her obvious disappointment in the fact that MacKenzie would be leaving made him realize that he still had a very long way to go if he was ever going to win her heart.

"I know. We could use a thousand like him, especially if General Lopez goes ahead with his plan to invade."

"Has there been any further word about it?"

"No, and there won't be until this situation is finally cleared up. It's been so many weeks now, God only knows what Tebeau and Favre have told Carlanta."

"How did Carlanta even know they were involved?" Estevan had played no part in their disappearances. He'd been as shocked as the others when the two agents had been kidnapped together during a secret meeting in one of their hotel rooms.

"Pure luck, from the way I understand it. It seems one of the hotel maids had overheard them talking one day and had reported it to Carlanta for a sizable sum. He'd started having them followed and then pounced when he could catch them both together."

"Well, if MacKenzie's plan works, they'll soon be free again."

"I hope so. So much depends on this invasion . . . Everything we've worked for will be ruined if General Lopez's plan has to be called off."

"We'll have our independence soon," he promised her, his eyes aglow with the fervor of his faith. "You'll see."

Anna gave him a warm smile. "I wish I shared your enthusiasm."

"You do. You're just tired right now," Estevan said it with more personal, intimate intensity than he'd meant to reveal.

She regarded him curiously for a moment, looking at him almost as if she were seeing him for the first time. He was a handsome young man, and from the tone of their conversation, it was obvious that he was very dedicated to their fight for freedom. "You're right," she finally agreed. "It has been a long night. I think I'd better get some sleep."

"If you need anything, let me know."

"Thanks, Estevan," she replied wearily as she wandered off toward her own hut.

Slater stepped into the hut to face his wife and found her sitting on the bed near her sleeping son.

"Are the accommodations to your taste?" he asked sarcastically, stung again by her obvious attachment to the child.

Francesca's expression was hostile. "Why did you bring us here, Slater? What's the point in all this?"

"The point is, my darling, you're going to help me rectify a certain damaging situation."

"I'm not going to help you rectify anything!"

"You really have no choice in the matter," he continued. "Consider it just a little payback for the last time."

"I have no idea what you're talking about."

"Right," he replied drolly, not believing a word she said no matter how innocent a look she managed to affect. "I'll be sending a note to your father in a little while. Would you like to include a message of any kind to him?"

She scowled at him. "Yes, tell him to shoot you on sight!"

"My, my," Slater taunted. "You have turned into a blood-thirsty little wench, haven't you? Or perhaps you were this way all along and I just never realized it."

"You never realized a lot of things."

"So you keep telling me, but let me assure you of one thing, my sweet bride, I may not have known what was going on when we were first married, but I know everything now."

"I'm not your 'sweet' anything. Remember that!" she countered hotly, keeping her voice down so as not to disturb Michael.

"My dear Francesca, until I hand you back over to your father, you are completely in my power. You will be whatever I tell you to be, and you will do whatever I tell you to do."

"Like hell I will!" she snarled. "You stay away from me and my son. Do whatever it is you came back here to do and then go away and leave us alone! I don't know why you came back anyway. Wouldn't it have been easier just to stay away?"

"Ah, but why would I want to make things easy for you, Francesca?" Slater enjoyed pressing her this way. It was high time she suffered a little for all the pain she'd caused him. He moved even closer to her to touch her cheek.

"Get away from me!" Francesca jerked her head away from the fiery caress of his hand.

"You look so sweet, and so innocent, and so pure of heart," he chuckled, sounding terribly evil to her.

"It's amazing how deceiving looks can be, isn't it?" He was talking more to himself than to her.

"Oh, you couldn't be more right about that!" She thought about all the lies he'd told her and how she'd believed him to be who he'd said he was. Gathering her wits, she forced down her temper and tried to appear calm. "Tell me something, Slater. There must be a reason you're here. What did you come back for? What is it you're really after?"

She looked up at him with an expression that seemed so open and honest that Slater had a difficult time keeping himself from throttling her. His heart hardened as he leveled a frigid, green-eyed gaze upon her. He wouldn't tell her that his mourning for her had driven him back to Cuba . . . that he had missed her so badly he had barely been able to get out of bed in the mornings and face the empty, pointless days of his life without her . . . that he had loved her with all his heart and soul and that now he was ruined to love and trust for the rest of his life. No, he couldn't tell her any of that for that would give her power over him . . . then she would know how truly and how deeply he had loved her . . . in the beginning. A slow, cruel smile curved his handsome mouth. Then he answered her. "That, my dear, you will find out when the time comes."

Francesca had been watching him closely and had seen a flicker of some strange emotion in his eyes just before he spoke. Almost as quickly as it had come, though, it was gone. Slater shuttered his expression.

Francesca was frozen with fear. She had no idea what was behind all this or what he was going to do next. She watched in silence as Slater strode from the hut, and she heard him call out an order to Estevan to resume his guarding of her. She listened until Slater's footsteps had faded, and only then, when she was sure he was gone, did she realize just how nervous she'd been in his presence.

Ricardo looked up as someone pounded on his office door. "Yes? What is it?" he demanded, irritated by the interruption. He had enough on his mind without any further aggravation.

"There's a messenger here from the country, Señor Salazar. He insists that he must speak with you. He says it's urgent," the clerk from the outer office explained.

"All right, send him in," Ricardo replied, wondering what could have happened in the country that could merit such importance. Francesca was hidden away with her baby, and there were plenty of hired hands on the place to keep her safe just in case that fool of a husband of hers decided to try something.

The door opened and Juan, one of his most trusted workers, rushed in looking frantic.

"Señor Ricardo . . . we don't know what happened!" the man cried in great distress.

"What happened about what?" he asked, suddenly nervous as he observed the other man's upset.

"She's gone!"

"Who's gone?" Ricardo was rising to his feet now as he realized that something terrible had happened.

"Doña Francesca!"

"What?"

"Teresa was with her until late last night, and then

264

this morning, when Doña Francesca didn't come for breakfast, Teresa went to check on her . . ."

"And?" Ricardo's hands were clenched at his sides.

"And she was gone! The baby, too! They both disappeared during the night!"

"Did anyone hear anything? Any screams or any fighting?"

"No, señor, it was quiet all night. All we found was this . . ." Juan handed his boss the note that had been left in the center of Francesca's bed.

Salazar—
I have Francesca and the baby. I'll be in touch
with Carlanta regarding an exchange. I'll trade
Francesca and the baby for Tebeau and Favre.
                                        MacKenzie

Ricardo stared in horror at the note. MacKenzie had taken Francesca hostage! And he wanted to make an exchange!

"Thank you, Juan. You may go now. I appreciate your coming to me so quickly."

"Sí, señor. Is there anything else you want me to do?"

"No. Not now. Tell the others that I will be handling this from here in town."

"I will."

Ricardo waited until Juan had gone, then hurried from his office to find Armando.

Armando had just been in an important meeting with the captain-general during which he'd bragged about how he was going to have the information they needed about Lopez and his plans for an invasion very soon. The captain-general had been impressed and had complimented him on what a good job he was doing controlling the revolutionaries. When Armando returned to his office and found Ricardo waiting in his office for him, he was curious.

"Is there a problem, Ricardo?" he asked as he came in and sat down behind his desk. He was feeling particularly confident and very proud.

"Here, read this!" Salazar thrust the note at him and waited to see his reaction.

Armando's face turned red as he read Slater's taunting message. "I can't believe his nerve! He wants to swap Francesca and her baby for Tebeau and Favre?!"

"What are you going to do?"

"I'll never give them up! Never!" he vowed. He had to stay in the good graces of the captain-general. He couldn't lose face like this.

"But he has Francesca . . . and the baby . . ." Ricardo insisted.

"The baby . . ." he spat. "You mean MacKenzie's bastard! I don't care about the brat."

"But Francesca . . ."

Armando thought of Francesca and of how much he desired her, and he knew he would have to take some action that would get her back. At the same time, though, he did not have any intention of giving up the hostages he so valued. "Don't worry, my friend. We'll do something, but I'll be damned if I'll turn over the spies."

"But what can we do?"

"First, we can sweep the areas where there have been known rebel activities."

"We've done all that before and never found a thing!" Ricardo protested, not wanting to waste time.

"I'm not making any deals with MacKenzie until we've tried everything else," he seethed.

"All right, all right, but be quick about it!"

"I'll get Francesca back and I'll keep the two agents!" Armando's gaze was lethal as he regarded the older man. He was angry enough that his plans were going awry. He didn't need this old fool telling him his business. "MacKenzie won't escape again. He's no cat. He doesn't have nine lives."

"What have you heard from your man in the rebel camp itself?"

"Nothing yet." He wasn't pleased to relate the news, but the nameless, faceless man who'd given him the information on MacKenzie the first time had made no effort to contact him now that the troublesome American had returned.

"What do you want me to do?"

"Just keep me informed should you hear from MacKenzie again. Until then, I'll follow up every lead I can think of. One way or the other, we're going to get Francesca and the baby back and keep the agents. I won't let MacKenzie defeat me again." Armando's blood was boiling with the thought that the damned agent had outwitted him another time. He vowed then and there that it was going to be the last time MacKenzie eluded him.

Chapter Nineteen

"Where on the coast is it safest for a ship to pick us up without being detected?" Slater asked as he and Martinez sat together in Martinez's hut that evening finalizing their plans.

"The Bay of Cabañas would be good," Martinez suggested.

"What's the earliest day you could have a ship pick us up there?" Slater asked.

"One week."

"Good. We'll arrange for the exchange to take place one week from tomorrow at the bay. That way, the minute Tebeau and Favre are released, we can get them on board and set sail."

"It's as good as done. I'll send the necessary messages first thing in the morning. What time do you want to rendezvous with the ship?"

"Why don't we set the meeting with Carlanta for high noon? He won't be able to pull many tricks in broad daylight."

"I'll take care of it. What about your letter to

Carlanta? When do you want it delivered?"

"Have it taken to his house in town tomorrow after he's left for his office. I need to send one to Rafe, too, to let him know what's going on."

The men agreed on their plan of action, and Slater quickly penned the letter to his enemy. He did not tell Carlanta the location for the exchange right then, but promised to notify him of the exact time and place the day before the trade was to occur. He didn't want to give him the chance to set up an ambush of some kind. Slater was glad when the messenger left with the letter. He was definitely looking forward to the upcoming confrontation.

It was long after sundown when Slater made his way back to his own hut. Estevan had been replaced by Carlos, and when Slater approached, he dismissed him for the night.

The flap was down over the doorway, and Slater brushed it aside as he entered the hut. The lamp had not been lighted, and so Slater stood just inside, holding back the material so he could get a look around by the light from the low-burning campfire outside.

When his eyes had adjusted to the gloom, Slater saw Francesca. Despite all his logic that told him he despised her for all that she'd done, he found himself mesmerized by the sight of her sleeping. He couldn't move away. He could only stand and stare.

Francesca was lying halfway on her stomach, with her face turned away from him. In the semidarkness, he could just barely make out the sweet curve of her body and the lush, thickness of her ebony hair as it tumbled, untethered about her, but it was a sensual enough image to strike the very breath from his body.

Deeply buried memories of holding Francesca in his arms while she slept, escaped from the jail of his mind to entice him. It had been so long ago, and yet it seemed like only yesterday when they had lain together, limbs entwined, loving and laughing. She had fit perfectly in his arms. It had been almost as if God had made them for one another. He recalled how wonderful it had been to fill her hot sweetness with the strength of his love, and how she had always given back to him just as much as she had taken.

Without realizing what he was doing, Slater moved closer to the bed. A part of him wanted to touch her, wanted to hold her, wanted to love her. As he reached the bedside, though, it happened. He caught sight of the infant slumbering at her side on the bed between her and the wall, and it brought him up short, striking all the foolish, idiotic, romantic notions from his head. She'd had a baby now . . . Carlanta's baby . . . Carlanta's baby . . .

His anger was reborn, and he was glad. He needed it to keep himself from being distracted. He needed to concentrate on what Strecker wanted him to do, not on the sordid memories of the time when he'd been living a lie.

Disgusted with himself, Slater moved away from the bed and dropped down on one of the less than comfortable chairs. As he braced his feet up on the other chair, Slater told himself that it was better he slept this way for as small as the hut was, there was no way Francesca would be able to sneak past him during the course of the night.

Slater slept fitfully, and it was no wonder. Every

time he was just about to fall into a deep sleep, he'd shift positions and almost land on the floor. By dawn, he was even more exhausted, and unable to find comfort, he quit the hut in complete agitation, leaving Francesca slumbering on peacefully with her baby.

Some of the rebels were already up and had made a pot of coffee. Slater helped himself to a mug of the strong, black brew as he stood before the bright, blazing campfire. Judging from the night just past, he knew the next week was going to be long and hellish if he didn't get some rest. Slater glanced over at Anna's hut. The temptation to sleep in her hut was great, but he knew better than to put himself in that position. Raking a hand through his hair, he stretched his cramped muscles and tried to come fully awake, but it was a useless endeavor. His body was moving, but his mind was numb with weariness.

Anna emerged from her hut a short time later, looking completely rested. She had gone to bed at sundown the night before and had slept a full twelve hours without interruption. Spotting Slater standing by the fire, she went to join him. She thought he looked awfully tired, and she wondered if he looked that way because of what had happened between him and Francesca last night. The green-eyed monster raised its ugly head as she imagined Slater in Francesca's embrace.

"Good morning, Slater," she greeted him, ignoring the pain in her heart over her vivid, graphic imaginings.

"Anna," he returned, pouring her a mug of coffee and handing it to her. "Did you sleep well?"

"Yes, all night. How about you?"

"I tried to in one of the chairs, and it didn't work well," Slater confessed, the dark circles under his eyes giving credence to his words.

"Well, I'm up now, and you can have my hut all to yourself if you want. Why don't you go lie down there for a while? I'll make sure that no one disturbs you."

It was an offer he couldn't refuse. "Thanks. I think I will. Can you get someone to watch the hut for me?"

"Sure. I'll watch it for you."

"Thanks. Come get me when Martinez starts moving."

"I will. Get some rest," she encouraged, cheered by the news that he hadn't slept in the same bed with Francesca.

Several hours passed before Michael came awake and, in the process, woke his mother. Francesca had lain awake long into the evening, nervously expecting Slater to return at any minute. When she'd finally dozed off, she had slept deeply and dreamlessly. It startled her now to wake up and find that it was already broad daylight and that the camp was astir. She glanced quickly about the hut, but could detect no sign that Slater had been there at all. Though she knew she shouldn't care, she couldn't help but wonder where Slater had spent the night.

Michael's impatient cry drew Francesca's attention back to her first priority. With no clean diapers for him and nothing left of the food she'd been given the night before, she knew she was going to have to ask for help. Picking up her very damp son, she lifted the doorflap and stepped outside only to have Anna suddenly appear, blocking her path.

"Do you need something, Francesca?"

Again, she was forced to ask Anna for help, and it irked her. But she was desperate for the baby's sake. "Yes, please. I brought some diapers with me for Michael, but I've used them all already. I'll need something I can make into a diaper, and I'll need some milk, if there's any more left."

"I'll see what I can find for you," Anna replied. "Wait inside." When Francesca had gone back in, Anna asked one of the men to watch the hut for her while she went in search of the things needed for the baby.

It took Anna a few minutes, but she finally got everything together that Francesca wanted. She was on her way to take them to her when she saw that Martinez was up and moving about the camp. Knowing that Slater wanted to see him, she went to get him up.

As tired as he was, Slater had fallen asleep quickly in the solitude of Anna's hut. Since he was expecting her to come for him, though, she had no difficulty waking him. He got up easily, and they emerged from the cabin looking very comfortable together.

Francesca happened to be standing just within the doorway of her own hut watching for Anna's return, when she saw them come outside. It was obvious to her that Anna had just roused him from bed, and she went cold inside, feeling almost as if some vital part of her had died. She immediately assumed the worst—that they had spent the night together in bed in that hut.

Francesca couldn't bear to face the other woman right then. She felt certain that Anna would be gloating over winning Slater's love, and she withdrew back inside.

When Anna finally brought her the things she'd needed, Francesca said only a curt "thank you," then turned and busied herself with Michael. After Anna left, her mind began searching for a way to escape this place . . . and Slater.

Francesca came up with an idea she thought would work perfectly. She waited eagerly for Slater to come to her again so she could make arrangements to go to the stream to wash out the baby's things. Her plan was simple. She would pretend to be doing the wash, then make a break for it the minute no one was looking. All she had to do was to make sure that there was a horse nearby. Francesca knew she would never be able to move fast enough on foot to make it to freedom carrying the baby. Her plot was reduced to ashes shortly after it was hatched, though, when Anna came for her with the news that she could go to the stream, but that the baby would have to remain behind.

"I'm going to keep the baby here with me, while Estevan takes you down to do the wash," Anna informed her.

Foiled before she even had the chance to try, Francesca decided to look around the area while she was at the stream in the hopes that she could figure out another way to escape. As long as she had a breath in her body, she was determined to get away from Slater.

The sun was setting and as it did, Marita's bedroom grew even darker. Marita didn't notice, however. She was sitting on her bed, staring off into space as she'd done for most of the last nearly forty-eight hours. She was wondering for about the millionth time how in the world she'd gotten herself into such a mess. A knock at her bedroom door disturbed her troubled thoughts.

"Come in," Marita called out, glad for the interruption and eager for some companionship. Since her uncle and her mother had discovered her absence that night and had left her room in anger and disappointment, she had spoken to neither one of them. Cut off from all communication and any knowledge of what was happening, she'd had only the few servants who'd brought her her meals and baths for company. She was thrilled when the bedroom door opened and her mother appeared. "Mother . . ."

"Hello, Marita." Rosa came into the room and closed the door behind her. Her expression was serious as she faced her daughter.

Marita looked pâle and worried. They faced each other without speaking for a moment until Marita finally broke the mood.

"I was wondering if you were ever going to talk to me again."

"I had nothing to say until today."

"Mother . . . I . . ." Marita almost blurted out that

she was sorry, but she stopped herself. She would never regret helping the rebels. Her only regret was that she'd gotten caught and had made up that stupid lie . . . and it had been a stupid lie. To this day, she had no idea why she'd dragged Rafael into this.

"Your uncle has handled everything as he said he would. Your wedding to Rafael will take place tomorrow at 11 A.M."

"My wedding?! What are you talking about?!" Marita stared at her mother in horror.

"Armando has spoken with Rafael and the priest. It has all been arranged."

"I don't believe this. Rafael agreed to marry me?" Marita couldn't believe that this was really happening.

"It is done," Rosa said firmly.

"Tomorrow?" She shook her head in confusion, closing her eyes to the shame of it all. Why had Rafael agreed to the wedding when everything she'd said had been a lie? Rafael probably hated her right now, and she didn't blame him. Marita wondered how she was ever going to face him in the morning.

"Yes. That's why I'm here to see if my wedding gown fits you," she told her. She opened the door one more time, and several of the maids came bustling inside carrying the beautiful ivory silk and lace dress Rosa had worn so proudly all those years ago.

All of her life Marita had dreamed of having a beautiful wedding and of marrying a tall, dark, handsome man who loved her above all others. Part of her dream was coming true. She was getting a tall, dark, handsome man, but instead of a love match, she was getting a forced union that she was sure would result in hatred and mistrust.

"Mother . . . ," Marita pleaded, "isn't there some other way?"

"No, Marita. You saw to that."

"But . . ."

"We will speak of it no more. This should be a happy time, and right now the only important thing is to make sure the gown fits. I also want to help you lay out your things for in the morning."

"Yes, Mother," Marita agreed, realizing there was no way out of the tempest she'd created with her lies.

Armando returned home late that afternoon to find Slater's note awaiting him. The demand Slater made was much what Armando had expected. He cast the letter aside in disgust as he imagined the American celebrating what he perceived as his impending victory. Armando, however, was determined that the exchange would never take place. He was going to defeat MacKenzie, one way or the other.

Striding to his liquor cabinet, Armando poured himself a stiff drink. First things first. He'd done all he could for right now in terms of trying to locate Francesca. For the immediate future, he would concern himself solely with his niece's wedding to Rafael. Once the marriage had taken place, he would once again turn his full attention to Slater Mac-Kenzie and making sure the hated American got just what he deserved.

Rafe sat alone at his dining room table, savoring

an after dinner drink. His mood was pensive as he considered that after tomorrow, he would be a married man.

Rafe had always known that one day he would have to take a bride, and as he considered it, he realized that Marita was certainly the fairest of the fair. From her background to her inheritance, she appeared the perfect bride for him. He was certain that the many in society who had always gloried in his romantic escapades would take great delight in his "downfall." He was sure, too, that they would be counting the months after their marriage on their fingers and watching Marita's figure for signs of a coming child. It was going to please Rafe greatly to watch their faces when Marita remained slim and attractive months after the wedding. He was determined to make sure that only the most immediate of family members knew of the reason for the quickness of the ceremony.

The circumstances of his upcoming nuptials continued to annoy Rafe, though. He was resentful at having been manipulated this way, even though deep down inside, he knew that if he hadn't been half-intrigued with the idea of wedding Marita, he would never have agreed to it in the first place. Rafe was not a man who could be forced to do anything he didn't want to do. Had it been any woman but Marita, he would have gladly met his fate on the dueling field rather than face a lifetime shackled to a female he didn't want. For a very short while he'd seriously contemplated keeping it a marriage in name only, but whenever he thought of his future bride, his blood warmed. Besides, if they were legally married, why not enjoy it? Only the memory of all the lies she'd told to her uncle and mother that had gotten them in this situation in the first place kept him from really looking forward to the following night.

As he downed the last of his liquor, Rafe wondered how difficult it was going to be for him to continue his work with the rebels. He had just received Slater's note, informing him of the success of his plan and the upcoming exchange he was arranging. Rafe smiled to himself as he thought of the turmoil Carlanta and Salazar had to be facing right then. He knew it was essential he get back to the encampment within the week for he wanted to help if he could. The difficulty was, though, that Marita was not a stupid woman. He hoped he'd be able to get away from her during this next week for several days without too much trouble or too many questions. He certainly didn't want to put any of his friends in danger by arousing his bride's curiosity. He couldn't afford to have Carlanta become suspicious of him in any way. Rafe knew he would have to be very careful.

Again, Slater delayed as long as he could before retiring. The campfires had burned down, and the moon hung low on the distant, starry horizon. The prospect of trying to sleep in the hard chair again was a painful one, but Slater stubbornly refused to go elsewhere for rest. Girding himself, he entered the hut and took up his dreaded position. He deliberately turned his back on the sight of his sleeping wife and her baby. His legs propped up on the opposite chair,

Slater folded his arms across his chest and finally drifted off some time after midnight.

At first Slater wasn't sure what it was that woke him, but he came awake with a start and sat up abruptly. It surprised him to find that he'd fallen asleep at all for he hadn't thought it possible in the uncomfortable position. He stared around himself trying to figure out what had disturbed his rest.

"No . . . no . . . ," Francesca cried in low tones.

The soft, distressed sounds of Francesca's voice in the darkness of the hut caused Slater to turn toward her quickly. Only then did he realize that she was talking in her sleep and that that must have been what had disturbed him. She sounded so upset in her dream that he knew he should probably waken her, but he held back. He didn't want to touch her while she was sleeping, let alone try to comfort her if she'd been having a nightmare. While he was sitting there, debating with himself about what to do, Francesca called out again.

"Armando . . . Oh, Armando . . ."

Slater surged to his feet nearly toppling the chair as he did so, and he stormed silently from the hut. He couldn't believe it! *His wife was calling the other man's name in her sleep!* The thought sickened him even as it left him in a helpless rage.

Several of the rebels were still sitting around the low-burning campfire, drinking from a single bottle of native rum, and Slater went to join them.

"Have some?" one of the men asked, thrusting the bottle toward him.

"Gracias." Slater took the bottle gladly and swigged deeply of the potent liquor. The raw rum burned all the way down to his stomach, and Slater almost wished it had the power to burn away all the feelings he still had for Francesca. Maybe then, when his heart and soul were in ashes, the sound of her calling another man's name wouldn't hurt him as it just had.

Dropping down beside the others, Slater took one more big swallow then offered them the bottle back. They remained there before the campfire for another hour, drinking the straight rum and talking of their plans for the revolution. Slowly, one by one the men moved off to bed down for the night until Slater was left alone with the remnants of the liquor.

Still unable to bring himself to return to the torture of the hut, Slater stayed where he was. With each succeeding drink of rum, his anger and jealousy flamed higher. Francesca was still his wife!

The more he drank, the more Slater remembered. The more he remembered, the more he found he wanted to go back into the hut and make love to Francesca until she cried out to him that Armando had never meant anything to her, that she had loved him and him alone! He wanted to forcefully drive all thoughts of Carlanta from her mind.

Francesca had been having nightmares ever since she'd first fallen asleep. In vision after vision, she was running from something or someone, trying to escape. Brambles tore at her clothes and hair. Hands reached for her trying to stop her and drag her down. She kept running, searching for a safe place, for a haven where she could hide.

In the torment of her dream, though, there was no safety or escape. Out of nowhere, suddenly, Armando loomed before her, blocking her path, his expression hard and ugly. She called his name, thinking he was there to help, but instead of helping her, he, too, grabbed at her. His smile was leering as he tried to snare her and trap her in his arms. Francesca whirled away, looking back, trying to see where she'd come from, but swirling fog obscured the way. She felt lost and helpless with no way to save herself.

In her dream, Francesca suddenly realized how terribly alone she was. She broke out in a cold sweat and began to tremble. She felt devastated by the emptiness that possessed her. Wasn't there someone, somewhere, who could help her? Wasn't there someone, somewhere, who cared?

Jarred from her sleep by the power of the emotions that wracked her, Francesca's heart was pounding in a fierce rhythm. Her eyes flew open, and she stared up into the darkness of the night-shrouded cabin, telling herself it had only been a dream . . . a stupid dream. Her eyes widened in amazement, though, and she went completely still when she saw Slater standing above her, gazing down at her.

Chapter Twenty

The rum Slater had drunk had robbed him of all rationality. He was running on pure, raw emotion as he stood over the bed, staring down at Francesca. His emotions were telling him with gut-wrenching intensity that she was his wife and he wanted her.

"Slater . . . ," Francesca whispered his name as she stared up at him in wonder, and it came out as a husky, velvet caress. Was Slater the one she'd been searching so desperately for in her dream? Was he the one who was going to save her? Misted as her mind was by the tendrils of sleep that still claimed her, the past was forgotten. Of their own volition, her arms lifted to Slater in an age-old sensual offering.

Slater didn't answer. He couldn't. A part of him was dying with the need to hold her and love her. The fury he felt over her involvement with Armando didn't lessen the driving, devouring hunger he had for her. Without disturbing the sleeping child, Slater bent toward Francesca and swept her up in his arms. His mouth sought hers in a hot, searing brand that proclaimed his dominance. He turned away from the bed and moved across the room, carrying her easily.

Francesca realized distantly that she was glad they wouldn't be disturbing Michael, but with that foggy memory of her son came the horrified reality of what was happening. She was allowing Slater to kiss her!

Francesca began to struggle, pushing at his chest in an effort to dislodge herself, but her efforts were ineffectual. Slater was not about to let her go. Tonight, in the heat of his drunken desire, he was going to have her. He had waited for so long . . . wanted her for so long . . . Slater ignored her attempts to be free. Instead, he deepened the kiss, parting her lips with his questing tongue and meeting hers in a dark, passionate duel of love.

Francesca knew she should resist. She knew she should continue to fight him. This was the man who'd deserted her when she was pregnant with Michael. This was the man who hadn't even looked at his own son since they'd been together. When the kiss broke off for a second, she protested, "Slater . . . no . . . !"

"You're mine, Francesca," Slater growled fiercely, refusing to listen. This was Francesca. She was alive. She was in his arms. He didn't have to live without her anymore. She was here, with him, now. The months of agony were over. His heart ached. His very soul cried out for union with her.

Slater's mouth found hers again with a fevered intensity that shocked them both. He groaned almost painfully as he crushed her to him. He had no idea where they were or why they were there, and more importantly, he didn't care. Slater only knew that he had to have her. He knelt and lowered them both to the ground.

Suddenly, all the bitterness Francesca harbored toward Slater was gone as his lips plied hers with intoxicating fervor. She wanted him . . . She always had and she always would. His kiss and touch had haunted her for all the months he'd been gone. She knew it was wrong to give in this way, but she didn't care. She needed to be in his arms. She needed his love.

Caught up in the ecstasy of Slater's passion, Francesca could only surrender. She clung to him as if he and he alone could save her from some terrible fate. All that mattered was that they get close—body to body, heart to heart. They were together, at long last. The dirt floor was hard beneath them, but neither noticed. They were cresting on a rising tide of rapture.

Where before Slater's hands had held her pinioned, now they caressed her. With the most delicate of touches, he stripped away the simple daygown she wore, baring her slender body to his questing lips and hands. Slater had always known how to pleasure her, and he had dreamed of loving her so often since they were parted nothing had been forgotten. With exquisite care, he sought out those most sensitive of places. He wanted only to arouse her, to take her to the heights of excitement and to hear her call *his* name as she reached the peak of fulfillment. He needed her to realize that he was the one bringing her that joy, that he was the one holding her and loving her.

Trailing hot, burning kisses down her throat,

Slater moved ever lower to the swelling mounds of her breasts. His lips found the taut crests and as he drew one in his mouth to suckle it, Francesca moaned and arched to his touch. Her hands tightened on his shoulders and her nails dug into his back.

Slater drew back from his sensual ministrations just long enough to strip off his own shirt. He quickly lay back down with Francesca and pulled her tightly against him. He needed to feel the coolness of her bared breasts against him. Holding her close, Slater kissed her once again, his mouth slanting across hers in a brazen demand.

Silent tears were tracing down Francesca's cheeks, and she didn't know why. She only knew that she had longed for Slater to hold her and love her for such a long time that she couldn't bear the splendor of it any longer. She wanted to be one with him. She wanted to hold him within the heat of her body, to be gloved together not knowing where one began and the other ended.

Slater shifted away slightly to rid himself of his pants, and yet Francesca held to him, not wanting to be separated even that much. When he came back to her, his body was a hot flame, searing her with his possession. She couldn't prevent the whimper of excitement that escaped her. The fire of her passion matched his. Every inch of her burned with desire for this man and this man only.

Francesca wrapped her legs around Slater's waist, drawing him to her, but Slater wasn't ready to possess her just yet. With deliberate, slow caresses, he explored her hips and thighs until she began to move restlessly beneath him. She was nearly out of her mind as she strained to get nearer and nearer to the hardness of him. She felt empty inside and only Slater could fill her.

"Tell me, Francesca . . . Tell me you want me . . . ," Slater breathed in her ear as he continued his maddening play.

"I want you . . . ," she confessed hoarsely, embarrassed, and she tried to pull him down for a kiss. She didn't want to talk. She wanted to love.

"Say my name, Francesca!" he commanded almost angrily. "Say it!"

"Slater . . . Slater, I want you . . ." Francesca could no more have refused to answer at that moment than she could have given up breathing.

It was all Slater needed. He had won. Lifting her hips, he positioned himself before the portals of her love and thrust forward, claiming her as his own.

It was as if they had never been apart. They were one. Their bodies melded and blended. One surged forward and the other moved to take all that was given and to give back more in return.

Francesca moved ceaselessly, writhing in ecstasy as Slater plumbed the depths of her womanhood. She gloried in his possession. She celebrated his desire. Her hands explored the solid ridges of his muscle-corded arms and shoulders, then moved lower down his back, past his trim waist to clasp his hard-driving hips and guide his rhythm.

Deep in the womanly core of her, the soul-stirring beginnings of love's sweetest reward blossomed. Francesca matched Slater's movements, straining ever nearer until in a cataclysmic burst of beauty, her climax was upon her with a pulsing, throbbing intensity that left her gasping his name in a soft, desperate cry.

"Slater . . . !"

Slater felt her body convulse beneath him, and, knowing he'd given her passion's gift, he allowed his own desire full rein. Unable to deny himself a moment longer, he abandoned himself to the intoxicating thrill of perfect union with her.

They surged upward together, wrapped in each other's arms, seeking the bliss they knew could be theirs. Like a shooting star, their desire rocketed skyward. Then, at the height of its path, it flashed in a brilliant, shimmering shower of sparkling delight and was gone.

They drifted back. Their breathing was labored, their bodies sweat-slicked from the heat of their spent passion. They lay locked together, unable and unwilling to move.

Across the room on the bed, Michael stirred. Finding his mother gone from his side, he let out a sleepy, lonely cry for her.

Even the intimacy of Francesca's and Slater's position, could not keep reality at bay. The sound of Michael's soft cry penetrated the haze of sensual contentment that had held Francesca in its grip. Her son's loneliness shattered the protective shell she'd erected around herself, and all that she'd denied for that short period of time came roaring back with vicious vindictiveness.

Francesca couldn't believe what she'd done. She had given herself to Slater! Willingly! How could she have, after everything he'd done to her?! Had she lost her mind? Her humiliation ran deep. She'd surrendered to the man who'd caused her so much grief and pain. Was she such a weak-willed wanton, that he only had to touch her and she would lay down for him? Francesca cursed the need she had for him, the need that defied all reason and control.

The flush of love that had stained her cheeks moments before paled. Now that her passion was gone and she realized just where she was lying, she wondered how she could have been so foolish as to lose complete control that way. He had taken her right there on the dirt floor and she'd revelled in it. . . .

Francesca remembered his words from earlier that day—that she would be whatever he wanted her to be and do whatever he wanted her to do. She knew now with devastation that he'd been right. Garnering what little strength she had, Francesca tried to slip away from Slater.

"Let me go," Francesca finally said in a cold voice when her attempt was thwarted. "My son needs me."

Still under the powerful influence of the very potent rum, Slater had been thinking only of how wonderful it had been to love Francesca again. But when she spoke and he heard the cold remoteness in her tone, he knew he'd only been fooling himself. Francesca might have admitted in the throes of her passion that she'd wanted him, but there had been no love in their mating. It had been lust. They had come together because they'd desired each other. That was all. And that had been all that had drawn them together in the first place.

"Ah, yes, the perfect mother . . . ," Slater mocked as he rose up on his elbows above her.

He wasn't moving quickly enough for Francesca. She needed to get away from him, to hide her shame. "Get off me, Slater. You got what you wanted, now leave me alone."

"That wasn't what you were saying a few minutes ago." He moved suggestively against her.

Francesca knew he was right, and she flushed hotly at his words. She was glad for the cover of night that hid it from him. She renewed her effort to get out from beneath his pinning weight.

"I have to see to my baby . . . ," she insisted, not allowing herself to think about the male force of him still filling her and the press of his hair-roughened chest against her sensitive breasts.

Michael cried out again, and the sound of the baby's wail reminded Slater of Francesca's betrayal. A shaft of pain lanced through his heart.

Suddenly, without another word, Slater rolled away from Francesca, setting her free. He was angry with her, but more so with himself for having allowed his lust for her to overcome his good sense. Slater dressed quickly, then he quit the hut. Making his way to the campfire, he sat down again and reached for the nearly empty bottle of rum. With relish, he finished off the last of it.

Francesca was so surprised by the suddenness of Slater's departure that she lay unmoving, staring after him. Her emotions were a mixture of pain and confusion. Finally forcing herself to move, she struggled back into her clothes. Her hands were shaking as she reached for her son, and she held him close to rock him back to sleep. All the while she cradled him near, though, her thoughts were on his father and the agony his heartlessness caused. Francesca vowed to herself as she sat there in the darkness with her sleeping child in her arms that somehow, someway, she was going to escape this place—and Slater.

After a hectic, wild morning of endless activity, Marita found herself alone for a moment. She stood in the middle of her bedroom, staring at her own reflection in the full-length mirror.

The woman in the mirror who returned Marita's regard was stunning. Her dark hair was piled up atop her head in a sophisticated style that emphasized her classic features. She wore a high-necked, long-sleeved white wedding dress, and it graced her slim figure to perfection. The bouquet of fragrant island blossoms she carried enhanced the dreamlike beauty of her. To the casual observer, she was the vision of what a bride should be. But Marita knew the truth. Marita knew she might appear the lovely bride, but she was just what the mirror showed—an image. Her heart was encased in ice. Her soul was frozen with the fear of what her impetuous actions and lies had wrought.

"Marita? Are you ready to leave?" Rosa came hurrying into the room carrying her daughter's veil and stopped in the doorway. "My darling, you are beautiful . . ."

Marita managed a small smile. "I'm sure I must look just like you did when you married Papa, since this is your gown."

Rosa smiled softly at the memory of her dead hus-

291

band, and tears filled her eyes. "He would have been so proud of you . . ."

Marita dropped her eyes from her mother's. She felt deeply ashamed at the thought of her father and her current predicament. She doubted seriously that he would have been proud of her right now. "Is it time to go?" She changed the subject.

"Yes, Armando's waiting downstairs and the carriage has already been brought around front."

"I guess I'm ready, then, except for the veil."

"I have it right here. Let me help you with it." Rosa went to her and turned her so she was facing the mirror. Then standing behind her, she arranged the pearl-encrusted, white lace veil carefully on her head. With loving care, she adjusted the folds of frothy material about her face and shoulders and then stood back to admire her. "Rafael will be pleased, you can be sure of that," she told her with confidence.

Marita knew a moment of panic at the mention of Rafael. She was trapping the poor man into marriage! He was going to hate her forever! Frantically, Marita considered running away. Surely any life would be better than one married to a man who despised you! "Mother . . . I . . ."

Rosa saw the fear in her eyes and took her daughter's cold hands in hers. "You are about to become a married woman, Marita."

"Isn't there some other way?" she asked miserably.

"No, my darling. I'm afraid not. Now, we must go. Rafael will be waiting for you, and you wouldn't want to upset him today of all days. I'm sure he's eager to see his bride."

Marita almost told her mother that she was pretty

sure Rafael wasn't looking forward to seeing her at all and that he would probably rejoice if she never showed up, but she didn't. She felt certain that this was the beginning of a disastrous end to her young life. Rafael was the most sought-after bachelor in Havana, and she was forcing him into holy wedlock. Marita was sure his mood was anything but eager about their upcoming nuptials. She gulped down her protests, knowing that it would be useless to argue, and she followed her mother downstairs.

"Rafael, it is good to see you—especially today," Father Morales, the heavyset, silver-haired priest who was going to perform the ceremony, greeted him warmly when he arrived at the church. Father Morales had known the Ramirez family for many years, and he was pleased that Rafael was finally going to settle down, even if it was under such 'pressing' circumstances.

Rafe smiled widely at the friendly padre. "You've waited many years for this moment, haven't you?"

"Far too many," he agreed. "You should have married long ago."

"Ah, but I hadn't found the right woman yet."

"And now you have."

"I am here, am I not?" he replied with a grin.

"Good, good." He patted him on the back with approval. "Come with me. There are documents to sign. We can take care of that now, so you won't be troubled later."

They disappeared into the back of church to take care of the business of the marriage.

The Carlanta carriage drew up before the church and Armando descended first, then turned to help his sister and niece down. Keeping a woman on each arm, he escorted them up the steps and inside. Armando left Marita and Rosa in the vestibule and went to locate the priest. He feared for a moment that Ramirez hadn't shown up, but when he found them in the sacristy, his fears were quickly relieved. After the necessary documents were finalized, Armando went to bring Marita and Rosa forward to the altar for the ceremony.

"Are you ready, Marita? Rafael is waiting."

Marita couldn't answer. She could only nod. Rosa quickly adjusted the veil once more and allowed her brother to move on ahead of her with Marita.

Because of the circumstances surrounding the marriage, all had agreed that it was to be a solemn affair, bare of the trappings of the usual society weddings. Marita didn't mind. As tense as she was right then, the quicker they got this whole thing over with, the better. She started up the aisle on her uncle's arm, and she knew it was a good thing he was there with her for she was more than tempted to bolt and run.

The church was a huge, cavernous structure. Sunlight shone through the stained glass windows richly illuminating the interior in a multitude of vibrant colors. Glowing candles lit up the altar, and the heavy scent of incense hung in the air.

Marita felt very small and insignificant as she approached the altar where Rafael and Father Morales waited. The sound of their footsteps echoed eerily around them, and they passed pew after empty pew as they moved ever forward. She offered up a silent, fervent prayer that Rafael, and God, too, would forgive her for the deceit that had caused this whole debacle.

Rafe heard the sound of their steps and turned to watch Marita draw near. He had not expected to feel much of anything today except annoyance, but when he caught sight of Marita coming his way, he found himself spellbound. She was beautiful, and he couldn't bring himself to look away. Gowned in white satin and lace, Marita was the walking, breathing vision of what every man dreamed his bride should be on their wedding day. Rafe stood beside the priest, stunned by the power of the emotions that besieged him.

"Who gives this woman in matrimony?" Father Morales asked.

"I do," Armando replied proudly as he handed her over to Rafe.

Rafe had to tear his gaze away from Marita in order to turn his attention to the priest so the ceremony could begin, and it was not an easy thing to do. He wanted to gaze at Marita in wonder. He wanted to study the perfection of her beauty and commit to memory everything about this moment. It took an effort, but he managed to keep his features schooled into a serious expression that didn't give away any of his surprise over the way he was feeling.

Marita was terrified. Rafael looked so angry to her, his expression seemed so stony and unfeeling that she truly believed she might be better off living in the streets than spending the rest of her life facing his wrath. In spite of the fear that filled her, though, she couldn't help but admire what a handsome figure of a man Rafael really was. He was wearing a dark suit made of the finest cloth, an embroidered silver vest and white shirt and cravat. He looked rakish and devastatingly attractive, and Marita understood without a doubt why so many women had tried to snare him for their own.

Marita's guilt over having won Rafael by illicit means assailed her. She wanted to offer Rafael a conciliatory smile, but couldn't muster one. Instead, she kept her expression as calm as she could behind the filmy protection of the veil and prayed desperately that this would all be over soon.

"Let us begin . . . ," Father Moralez intoned.

Chapter Twenty-One

The flickering candlelight combined with the moving intensity of Father Morales voice left Marita mesmerized. Her world seemed bathed in a golden glow. She could feel the heat of Rafael's presence at her side and when he responded to the priest's questions, the deep, melodic sound of his voice sent shivers of awareness through her whole body. When Father Morales asked her to respond, she was so gripped by the tumultuous force of her emotions that her answers were barely above a whisper. The priest then directed Rafael to take her hand in his, and Marita trembled as his big, warm hand closed over her small, cold one.

"You may place the ring on her finger," Father Morales instructed, and he waited as Rafael reached into his coat pocket for the ring and then slid it onto her finger.

Marita almost gasped out loud at the sight of the beautiful emerald-studded gold wedding band. She had never seen anything more lovely.

"I now pronounce you man and wife. What God has joined together, let no man put asunder," the priest concluded.

Marita was trembling. It was over. It was done. She was Señora Ramirez for now and for all eternity. Rafael's brand was on her finger.

"Rafael, you may kiss your bride."

Marita swallowed nervously as she faced Rafael. Her eyes grew round and fearful in anticipation as he lifted the gauzy veil. Their eyes met, his dark-eyed gaze probing hers for a fleeting moment before he drew her into his arms and kissed her thoroughly. She gasped at the sensations that swept through her. Then, as quickly as it began, the kiss was over; and Rafael was stepping back away from her, seemingly unmoved by the embrace. Marita watched in dull surprise as he very calmly accepted the congratulations of the priest and of her uncle and mother. He seemed ever the man-about-town, always completely in control.

"Shall we go?" Rafael, ever courteous, turned to Marita and held out his hand to her. When she placed her hand in his, he noticed again how chilled her hand was, and he smiled down at her mockingly as he drew her to his side. "Nervous, my love?"

Marita glanced up at him quickly, trying to read his expression, but to no avail. "Yes," she finally replied, unsettled. She had expected anything from Rafael, but this gentlemanly act of congeniality he was putting on.

"I have arranged a special celebration dinner for you at my home," Armando announced proudly as

298

they were starting from the church. "We shall go there next."

Though inwardly Rafael bristled at Carlanta's assumption that they would abide by his wishes, he went along. "That was very thoughtful of you, Armando."

"Yes, thank you, Uncle Armando," Marita managed.

"It's my pleasure, Marita. It isn't every day that I gain a nephew as special as Rafael," Armando boasted with a big smile, more than satisfied with the way things had turned out.

"Indeed, we're both very happy for you," Rosa added. She was beaming with delight over the nuptials for she had long thought Rafael would be the perfect husband for Marita. "I hope you'll both be very happy together, in spite of this rather unorthodox beginning."

"I'm sure we will," Rafe told her easily, still not giving Marita any hint of his true opinion of what had transpired.

Rafe's continued pleasant demeanor was making Marita even more nervous. She wished they could be alone for a while so she could find out what he really thought. Instead, she realized in misery, they were going to be surrounded by people for the rest of the day. She found the prospect tedious, not to mention wearisome.

They stepped outside into the bright noonday sun to find the carriage awaiting them. The driver opened the door as Rafe escorted Marita down the few steps to the sidewalk. He turned to help her into the carriage, his big hands closing on her tiny waist as he lifted her effortlessly into the shady interior.

For the breath of a moment, their bodies brushed together as Rafe lifted her up, and in that second their eyes met and locked. Marita saw a flash of some intense emotion in his eyes. Before she could fully understand what it was, it was gone, hidden behind a polite, yet slightly mocking smile. He let go of her, and she moved back onto the seat, and the moment was lost forever. Rafe waited while Armando helped Rosa ascend and then the two men climbed in to join them.

As the carriage started up, Armando inquired, "Have you made plans for a honeymoon?"

"Not as yet," Rafe informed him. "I have some important business I must see to first. Once that's out of the way, I'll be able to take a week or so off without the threat of interruption. I thought a trip to the coast might be nice. Somewhere quiet and peaceful where Marita and I can go and spend some time alone."

"Sounds wonderful," Rosa sighed romantically, thinking things were going to turn out just beautifully for her daughter.

Marita, however, found herself watching the friendly interplay between her uncle and her new husband. She wondered just how close they really were, what this important business of Rafe's was, and if it had anything to do with spying on the rebels.

Anna had emerged from her hut that morning to find Slater already up and about. She'd offered him the use of her hut again, believing that he'd spent

300

another miserable night trying to sleep in the chair, but he'd turned her down flat. She'd reserved comment on his bloodshot eyes and surly disposition, but her heart had ached for him.

They spent the early morning hours meeting with Martinez, laying out the plans for the trade. Slater wanted to be certain that everything would be perfectly timed. He wanted to make sure they would be prepared, in case Carlanta tried any tricks. At Martinez's suggestion, Slater and Anna decided to ride to the bay area to check out the lay of the land themselves, and they left the camp together at mid-morning.

Estevan had watched their activities from afar, his jealousy flaming. MacKenzie was a married man and his wife was right here in camp; yet, the American made no effort to distance himself from Anna. It angered Estevan that he thought nothing of hurting her this way. Frustrated, he wondered if he would ever have a chance with her.

Francesca was frustrated and furious as she sat just outside the hut in the morning sun playing with Michael under the watchful eye of the man named Estevan who was guarding them. Though she told herself she didn't care about Slater, that she hated him and wished he'd never come back, she hadn't been able to stop herself from surreptitiously watching him as he moved about the camp with Anna.

It infuriated Francesca that Slater and Anna seemed comfortable together and talked easily together. He seemed so solicitous of the other woman and so attentive to her every word. Francesca could never remember a time when their relationship had been that close, and they had been man and wife!

When Anna and Slater rode out of camp, Slater never once glanced in her direction. Francesca watched them go and felt strangely devastated, though she didn't know why.

Hours passed. The morning aged to afternoon, and still they did not return. Though she tried not to think about it, Francesca's thoughts ran wild. She had seen Slater come out of Anna's hut that first morning she'd been his prisoner, and she'd known he'd spent the night with Anna. Francesca wondered where they had gone now and what they were doing. Was Slater making mad, passionate love to Anna as he had to her the night before?

The possibility was a bitter one for Francesca, and she kept watch in earnest now, looking for a way to slip from camp without being caught. She had to escape from Slater's captivity before sundown. She couldn't risk another night with Slater, especially after he'd passed the entire day with Anna. Last night had been degrading enough. She had disgraced herself, and she couldn't suffer through another night like that, knowing he was coming to her from the other woman's arms.

It was late in the afternoon when Slater and Anna finally made it back. The trip to the bay had been well worth it, for Slater now knew the best location for the exchange to be made. As they rode into the encampment, black storm clouds were gathering on the horizon, and the faint sound of thunder rumbled threateningly across the land.

"I wasn't sure we'd make it back before the storm broke," Anna told Slater as they dismounted.

"It was close," he agreed. "You go on, I'll take care of your horse for you."

Anna was pleased by his thoughtfulness, and she touched his arm in appreciation and gave him a quick kiss on the cheek. "Thanks."

Estevan had had it. He had been victimized continually by his own overactive imagination all day, and the sight of Anna gazing up at Slater adoringly and then kissing him pushed him over the edge. Estevan's iron-willed self-control vanished and all thoughts of guarding Francesca and the baby disappeared. Estevan stalked across the clearing to where Slater was tending their horses. Slater did not see him coming.

"Just what the hell do you think you're doing, MacKenzie?" Estevan snarled as he grabbed Slater by the shoulder and spun him around.

Slater was caught off-guard and was shocked by his actions. His instincts told him to swing at the other man, but he managed to stop himself. Estevan was little more than a boy.

"What the hell is your problem, Estevan?" Slater asked, confused. He couldn't imagine what was wrong.

"You're my problem, American! You come in here and try to run things your own way with no thought to what you're doing. All you care about is what you're after . . . what you want!" Estevan charged, his temper hot.

"Look, I don't know what you're talking about." Slater saw the anger in his eyes and realized there was more going on here than just his concern about him being an outsider. He tried to be conciliatory.

"I'll tell you what I'm talking about! I'm talking about Anna!"

"Anna?" Now Slater understood. "Estevan, Anna and I have known each for a long time. She's a very special friend to me, but nothing more."

"Ha!" he scoffed in disbelief. "I've watched you together, and I've seen . . ."

"You've seen nothing. We're friends," he insisted firmly.

"I see the way she looks at you! She loves you!"

"There's nothing between us."

Slater's continued refusal to admit his involvement with Anna, infuriated Estevan even more. Estevan believed he was just using her, and that made him lose complete control. He swung at Slater, putting all his frustration into that blow.

Slater was irritated by the younger man's hot-headed ways, and he was ready for him. He blocked his swing, then slapped him upside the head as he shoved him away.

"Slow down, boy. There's nothing to fight about."

"Why you . . ." Estevan was enraged at being so easily manhandled and by what he considered to be Slater's taunts. He threw himself bodily at his foe, tackling him. Together, they grappled on the ground, each trying to land punishing blows as they struggled for superiority. Around them the wind picked up, swirling the dust and blinding them with vicious gusts as they continued to fight.

Francesca had not seen Slater and Anna return. She just happened to hear something that sounded like a fight going on outside and moved to the doorway of her hut just in time to hear Estevan say something about Anna and then take the first swing at Slater. She watched, startled, as they soon were brawling in the dirt. She was shocked to see them actually fighting, but she was humiliated to know that it was Anna they were fighting over.

Francesca stood for a moment frozen by the misery of it. Her concern soon faded, though, when she realized that there was no longer anyone guarding the hut. The other rebels were being drawn to watch the fighting, and she was being given her chance! This was the opportunity she needed to get away!

Lightning cracked nearby causing Francesca to jump nervously. She'd always hated thunderstorms, but today she said a prayer of thanks to God for it, for she knew the storm was her salvation. Running to get Michael, she wrapped him tightly in a blanket and quietly left what had been her prison.

Step by step she edged toward the place where the horses were tied. Her heart was in her throat as she crept off. She felt certain that at any minute she would be discovered. When lightning jolted through the sky again, this time striking closer to the encampment and creating even more of a diversion, Francesca knew she had to make a run for it. No one even noticed as she darted for the horses for they were too caught up in watching Slater and Estevan battle it out.

Slater finally managed to throw the younger man off of him. He got back to his feet and stood over him. "Get away from me, Estevan," he threatened, not wanting to take the fight any further. "I don't want to hurt you."

"You stay away from Anna!" Estevan came back at

him, the taste of blood in his mouth. Though he was dizzy from Slater's powerful blows, he wouldn't quit where Anna was concerned. He wanted to keep fighting. He wanted to show this man, and Anna, that he was his equal, but Carlos grabbed him and held him back. "You've got no right to her."

"I've told you that there's nothing going on between me and Anna, and I don't lie." Slater glared him down.

He returned his glare as he got slowly to his feet. He wiped the blood from his mouth with the back of his arm after he shook off his friend's protective hold.

Carlos, recognizing that these two men needed to speak privately, encouraged the others who'd been watching to leave. When they'd moved off, seeking to get out of the coming storm, Slater spoke again.

"Have you talked to Anna?"

"No. What's the point? You're the one she wants."

"It'll never be," he told him plainly. "It's up to you if things are to work out between you and Anna. It has nothing to do with me. Does she even know how you feel?"

The two adversaries stood facing each other as lightning split the ever-darkening sky once more. With the crashing thunder that followed, the rain began to fall, pelting the men and the earth with near violent intensity.

Slowly, as the heat of his anger was cooled by the storm, Estevan began to see the truth. It wasn't Slater's fault that he didn't have Anna's love. It was his own. He would have to take charge of his own destiny.

Another crash of thunder and lightning shook

them, and they both looked up, surprised by nature's force. It was in that moment that they saw Francesca as she galloped from the camp on horseback.

Francesca didn't look around or worry about being discovered as she put her heels to the horse. She focused solely on keeping her seat and getting out of there as quickly as she could. It was a struggle for her to ride while holding Michael, but somehow she managed. The rain was pouring now, but Francesca hung on for dear life as they charged onward in their desperate bid for freedom.

"She's leaving! She's riding out!" Estevan suddenly shouted.

Slater grabbed the reins of the horse he'd been about ready to unsaddle and gave chase, while Estevan soon followed.

Now that she'd made the break, Francesca was frantic. She had a headstart, but she wasn't familiar with the trails and she wasn't sure exactly which way to go. The rain was beating down on her mercilessly, soaking her to her skin, and she could hear Michael's pitiful wails as she clutched him tightly under one arm. She was forced to slow down when the path became slippery with mud, and that made her even more nervous. All she wanted to do was to escape from Slater.

Slater was livid as he charged full-speed after Francesca. It was bad enough that his jaw was aching and his knuckles were sore from his fight with Estevan over Anna, but now this was too much. He'd stayed away from Francesca because he didn't trust his temper around her after the night just past. She had been responsive when he'd touched her, and he'd possessed her body completely. The concern she showed for Carlanta's son proved to him, however, that her heart still belonged to Armando, and he could never forgive her for that.

Slater glanced up through the blinding rain, and, ahead in the distance, he caught a glimpse of Francesca as she maneuvered her way down the slick trail. He urged his mount to a quicker pace for he knew that around the next turn the path leveled out, and he didn't want to give her that advantage.

Estevan was giving chase too. He knew he should have been guarding Francesca instead of fighting with Slater, and he felt responsible for her escape. Though he was still behind Slater, he stayed with him. Slater could easily have continued the fight, instead of trying to talk it out with him. He had said Anna was just his friend, and Estevan wondered if he could believe it.

Francesca cast a backward glance as she took the next turn in the path, and she saw Slater riding headlong in her direction at breakneck speed. "Oh, God . . . please, help me!" she cried into the storm. "Help me . . ."

Her pleas went unheard, though, as Slater's horse gained on hers with every powerful stride. She turned her horse, charging off the trail and riding like the wind toward a wooded area nearby. She thought she might possibly be able to evade him with the help of the trees, but Slater caught up to her as she was just about to enter the woods. Grabbing her bridle, he forced her horse to a stop.

"Damn you, Slater! Damn you!! Why don't you just let us go?" she screamed at him, nearly hysterical from her failed attempt.

Slater was so angry, he swung down off his horse and dragged her bodily down from hers. Though she fought and kicked at him, he held her without flinching. When Estevan rode up, Slater grabbed the baby from her.

"Do you need any help?" Estevan asked, reining in beside them.

"Here," Slater said brusquely, handing the baby to Estevan. "Take the baby back to camp."

"No! You can't take my baby!" she cried.

"I can do anything I want to do, Francesca," he bit out. "Get going, Estevan."

"All right." Estevan took the crying infant from Slater, then turned his mount around and began the wet, miserable ride back to camp.

Francesca was beyond control. She fought Slater with all her strength, wanting to hit him, wanting to hurt him. Her blow caught him on the side of the face that was already aching from Estevan, and he grabbed her wrists in a viselike grip to stop her.

"I've had all I can stand from you, Francesca," he seethed. He realized now as he thought about it that during the entire ride from the camp, he'd been worried that her horse would fall and she would be hurt. That he still cared for her infuriated him. He didn't understand how he could after all that had happened.

"Then let me go!"

"Oh, I'll be letting you go, all right, but not until I'm ready. You're a commodity to me, Francesca. Nothing more. You're something to be used until I have no further need for you."

"I hate you, Slater!" Francesca was wet and cold and beyond logical thought.

"You didn't hate me last night! You liked the way I used you then," he snarled, fed up. She had taken vows to be his wife, then had betrayed him with his enemy, and she had the gall to say she hated him?

Francesca tried to wrench herself away from him. She didn't want to be reminded of last night. She just wanted to escape. "Let me go! I don't want anything to do with you! I hate you! You're a no-good, lying . . ."

Lightning split the black, roiling clouds, and thunder reverberated through the land, drowning out her words. The rain fell in a steady, drenching downpower that left not an inch of their bodies dry.

Slater dragged Francesca into his arms and crushed to his chest. "I love the way you hate me, Francesca . . . Maybe I should see just how much I can enjoy you during these next few days before I give you back to your lover. I'm sure Armando won't care if you're unfaithful to him with me, since we've shared you before . . ."

He gripped her chin in one hand and forced her head up. Then with his emerald eyes boring fiercely into hers, he lowered his mouth to take hers in shameless domination.

"No!" Francesca was not about to give in today. She bit his lip and drew blood.

Slater pulled back to look down at her, but did not stop his assault on her senses. One hand found her breast as he pulled her hips tightly against his. Still, the rain continued. Slater pressed intimately against her as he sought out the sensitive chords of her throat.

He trailed arousing kisses along the line of her neck, even though she was pushing with all her might against his broad shoulders.

"No . . . no . . . Please, no!" Francesca wasn't sure if she was crying out to Slater or to herself as heat began to pulse through her body. She didn't want Slater. She hated him. . . . And yet . . .

Francesca's protests meant nothing to him. He lifted her, then lay her down upon the soft, wet bed of grass. The rain sluiced off them as they lay together. Slater kept Francesca in his embrace as he kissed her once again. He knew he was risking the danger that she might attack him, but he chanced that she wouldn't. Instead of kissing her forcefully, he softened the assault, teasing her with soft, tantalizing kisses meant to entice.

Francesca wanted to fight, to resist, to ignore the hunger rampaging through her betraying body, but she couldn't. This was Slater, and she realized as she lay with him in the midst of the soggy field that she still loved him. She lifted her hands to frame his face as she refused to let him end the kiss. Her mouth met his, showing him how much she wanted him, telling him without words how much she cared.

Slater could not believe the change in her, yet he gloried in it. They stripped away their offending garments, baring themselves to the elements and to the elemental attraction that brought them together. Rain slicked their bodies. Each caress was silk.

They didn't notice the lessening of the lightning for they were caught up in their own electrifying excitement. The fading thunder didn't bother them for now they only heard the thundering of their own hearts. They came together, their bodies fusing in love's devotion.

The rain continued to fall, but more gently now as the lovers searched for their elysian ecstasy. Each touch, each kiss led to another more deep, more enduring. They explored one another with abandon, wantonly seeking to please. When at last the rapture they'd pursued conquered them, they clung together as the tempest of their loving swept over them.

Slater didn't know what to say when the blissful beauty of the moment had faded. He shifted away from Francesca and stood up to dress.

Francesca, too, was dumbstruck by the power of what had passed between them. She needed time to think. She needed time to get herself together again. She had confessed to herself that she loved him, but she knew he didn't love her. He was using her now, as he'd used her then, and she didn't know what to do.

When Slater offered her his hand to help her up, Francesca took it, but she refused to look up at him or make eye contact with him. She was afraid she would see that same old mocking expression on his face, and she knew she wouldn't be able to stand it right now. She dressed in silence, then mounted when he told her to, and said nothing as he led her horse behind him back to the encampment.

By the time they reached the rebel hideout, the rain had completely stopped and the sun was once again breaking through the cloud cover. Estevan saw them coming and went forth to meet them, carrying the baby.

"Your son's a strong boy, MacKenzie," Estevan told him, holding a now dry Michael up for Slater to see. "He survived that ride without any trouble."

Slater started to deny any claim to Michael's parenthood when the baby lifted his head and looked him straight in the eye.

"He even looks like you . . . ," the younger man was saying.

Estevan's remark faded into nothingness as Slater gazed openly upon his own offspring for the very first time. He tensed, then blanched as he stared into a pair of emerald eyes so like his own. There could be no mistaking the resemblance. Francesca's child was a MacKenzie. Slater stood frozen in his place. She had borne his baby and had never told him. She had tried to hide the child from him all this time. Hatred more intense than anything he'd ever known possessed him.

His voice was deathly quiet as he took the baby from Estevan, "Take her back to the hut and restrain her. See to it that there are no more escape attempts."

"Slater . . . wait no . . . ," Francesca began.

"Gag her, too. I don't want to see her or hear her again, do you understand?"

"Yes . . ." Estevan hurried to do as he was told.

"Slater, I want my baby . . . What are you going to do with Michael? Give him to me!" she cried, fear clutching at her heart.

Michael? She'd named him Michael? His expression was stern as he ordered. "Now, Estevan."

Slater knew there was nothing more to be said between them. Her silence regarding Michael's birth had said it all.

Chapter Twenty-Two

As she paced the master bedroom clad only in the silken negligee her mother had told her she had to have for her wedding night, Marita realized that there were scores of women who would have traded places with her in a minute. They would have told her to shut up, lay back, relax, and enjoy herself. She was Señora Rafael Ramirez now and this was her wedding night. But Marita knew it wasn't that easy. They were not a loving couple, and this was not a love match. She was almost positive that Rafael despised her.

Marita felt uncertain as she considered finally facing her new husband alone. She wished with all her heart that she hadn't gotten them into this mess, but now that they were married, she hoped they could make the best of it. She stopped her pacing to glance nervously around, wondering how much longer she would have to wait before Rafael came to bed.

Suddenly, Marita could stand the worry no more. She was not a woman who let situations rule her. She ruled them, and the only way to handle this was to take the bull—Rafael—by the horns. She would go to him and try to make him understand that she had never intended to trap him this way and that they could work something out to make the whole thing more acceptable to them.

Rafael had given the servants the night off and the house was dark and deserted as Marita left the bedroom. She started down the wide front staircase to find that only a single room was lighted below—Rafael's study. She moved silently on her bare feet to the partially open study door. Marita considered knocking, but quickly dismissed it. If she was going to confront him, she didn't want to give him any advantage. Squaring her shoulders, she lifted her chin in what she knew was her most elegant pose, and walked right on into his study.

Marita stopped just inside the door to stare at her husband. For a second it seemed to her as if she were seeing him for the very first time, and in a way she was. They had never been alone together in such intimate circumstances before, and she felt a very real attraction to Rafael as he stood across the room before the casement window, still unaware of her presence. He looked roguish and maybe even a little dangerous right then, and Marita's pulse quickened as she continued to stare at him without speaking. Rafael had discarded the suit jacket, vest and cravat he'd worn all day, and had unbuttoned his shirt now to relax. The broad expanse of his strong chest was bared for her to see, and she couldn't look away. She realized distractedly that he would have made a very good pirate had he wanted to be one. Giving herself a mental shake, Marita knew she had to say something.

It was his wedding night, and Rafe was in the grip of a strange mood as he lingered overlong in his study. He knew any other man would have beaten a path to the bedroom long ago. He was married to Marita Valequez, now, and she was waiting for him to come to her upstairs, for heaven's sake! But somehow, he wasn't quite ready yet. He had other things to consider.

Rafe was a bit confused. He knew he should still be angry with Marita for the lies that had landed them in this situation, but somehow anger wasn't what he was feeling. Curiosity was more the thing.

Having just spent the day with her, Rafe had found Marita's behavior raised many questions in his mind. It seemed to him that if she had set out to trap him into marriage, she would have been acting very sure of herself today. Instead, she'd been exceedingly quiet during the whole ordeal. That puzzled him, and he wondered if there was more to this than he had been told so far. He still made no sense of her spending the night with another man and then naming him the culprit.

For the first time ever, Rafe was pleased about his reputation as a ladies' man. Tonight, it would serve him well. He would hide behind it and use it. He would play the part of the trapped devil-may-care bachelor to the hilt and see what happened. He had just made that decision, when Marita's voice cut through the quiet of the study.

"Rafael?"

"Marita?" Rafe glanced up quickly, surprised by the interruption. He'd been lost so deep in thought that he hadn't heard her come into the room. She stood before him now with her hair down loose around her shoulders, wearing only a shimmering, white silk dressing gown that clung to every feminine curve like a caress.

"Rafael . . . ," she began again, forcing her gaze upward from his chest to meet his. "We haven't had a moment of privacy all day long, and I wanted to talk to you about something important."

"Yes?"

"Look, I know you were forced into marriage with me to protect my honor and . . . ," she began.

"Yes, I was," he interrupted. "And I'd like to know why, Marita. Why, out of all the men in the world, did you tell your uncle that I was the one you were with? We both know we weren't together that night."

Marita had been afraid he might ask this question. She looked a bit guilty as she shrugged. "I had to give them a name they'd believe, and yours was the first one I could think of."

Rafe bristled at her attitude and her answer, but before he could say anything else she went on.

"But I want you to know that I understand if you're angry with me about all this and that it's all right if you want to have separate bedrooms. This can be a marriage in name only if you like," she offered, then hurried on. "And then after a suitable time when my mother and my uncle have calmed down, we could maybe get an annulment." There, she'd said it, and she hoped madly that he'd agree to her plan.

Rafe couldn't believe what he was hearing. She wanted a marriage in name only and would then

317

agree to an annulment? Her suggestion only deepened his suspicions about her motive in trapping him. Had her uncle been behind this? Had he been set up for another purpose other than what he'd originally thought?

"Oh, no, my dear, this won't be a marriage in name only." Rafe gave a soft, derisive laugh as he crossed the room toward her. "You stood before the priest with me and exchanged holy vows, Marita. I took those vows very seriously. You're my wife, and you'll be my wife in all ways."

Marita felt as if she were being stalked by a very hungry predator as he drew near. When he stopped before her, she stiffened. Rafe smiled slightly as he bent toward her. He lifted both hands to tangle them in her hair on either side of her face and then he tilted her face up to his. He gazed down at her, and for a moment something in her expression touched him deeply. He wasn't sure what it was . . . an innocence, maybe? Or a flickering shadow of fear in her eyes? Unable to deny the power that drove him, Rafe lowered his mouth to hers with slow, sensual deliberation.

Marita hadn't been sure what to expect, but it certainly hadn't been this. She'd thought offering him a way out of the marriage would please him, and she was shocked that he wanted theirs to be a real marriage. She tried to resist his kiss, but the moment his lips met hers something happened.

Ecstasy.

Marita's breath caught in her throat, and she stood poised and immobile before him, enthralled by that ever-so-gentle, simple touch of his lips on hers.

When they had kissed before, it had been exciting and arousing, but it had been nothing like this. Though his touch was light, she found herself quaking from the force of it.

"Rafael . . ." Marita moaned his name as his mouth left hers to explore the shell of her earlobe. The intimacy of that caress sent shivers through her. Instinctively, she thrust herself against his chest, wanting to be closer to him. Her arms found their way around his neck and she threw her head back to allow him free access to her throat.

Rafael was still in complete control, and he intended fully to teach her a lesson. He wondered if she was really that affected by his kiss. The truth would be out soon, he knew. If she had been with another man, she would know what to expect. Boldly, he caressed her breast through the silken material, and she went rigid in his arms.

"No . . . don't . . . ," Marita said, troubled by the riotous feelings that were rushing through her.

"But, love, we're married. It's all right . . ." If she wanted to play the virgin, he would accommodate.

Marita lifted her head, and as she gazed up at him, Rafe could see the bewilderment in her eyes. He wasn't sure that she was really playacting, but there was that innocence mirrored there again along with a look of uncertainty and maybe even a little fear.

"It's all very simple, Marita. Man and woman were meant to come together . . . ," he explained in low, seductive tones as his hands skimmed over her in a calming caress.

"I know," she whispered, being lulled into a sense of security by his gentle touch.

319

"You do?" Rafe asked quickly, drawing back a little.

"Well, Mother and I talked about this . . ."

"You did?"

"Years ago . . ."

"And what did you decide?" He let his hands skim nearer to the bottoms of her breasts, teasing without touching, just to see how she'd react.

"That it would be something very nice . . . ," Marita answered, tensing a little in anticipation of a bolder caress and finding herself disappointed when he didn't actually touch her breast.

"And is it?" Rafe pressed a soft kiss to the corner of her mouth, becoming more convinced by the minute that she was untouched and unschooled in the ways of love.

A shiver frissoned down her spine at that sweet caress, her eyes drifted shut as she answered only, "Um . . ."

The complete guilenessness of her words and actions touched Rafael's heart as he had never been touched before. In that instant the instructor became the student.

"Marita . . . ," he groaned her name as his lips sought hers in a blazing possession that transcended all that had gone before.

Crushing her to him, Rafe bent just slightly and lifted her into his arms without breaking off the kiss. He strode from the study and took the steps two at a time in his sudden eagerness to have her.

One lamp burned low in the bedroom as he entered carrying his bride, and he was glad, for he wanted to see her as they made love. He wanted to watch her expression as he came to her for the first time and made her his in every way. With great care, he lay her upon the bed and then followed her down. His body molded against her, and she inhaled sharply at the sensation of having him pressed so tightly to her.

Marita didn't understand how she could be so excited and frightened at the same time. This was Rafael . . . her husband. She knew it was as it should be, but the newness of it all scared her—the feel of his thrusting thighs boldly between her own, the heat of his burning kisses, the rapture of his touch.

"Rafael . . . ," she said his name softly, but all the confusion she was feeling was in her tone.

Rafe heard it, and slowed the runaway pace of their lovemaking. Damn, but he wanted her! She was like a nectar of the gods, one taste and you would die for more. . . .

"I'm sorry, love. I know I'm going too fast for you, but you're so lovely . . ." He kissed her slowly, drawing her into the flame of his own desire. With one hand, he slipped the negligee down off her shoulder, then followed its path with hot, exploring kisses.

Marita had no idea what he was going to do next, but she was loving every minute of it. She wondered if her own touch would have such power over him, and she reached out tentatively to caress his back and shoulders. When he gave a low growl of pleasure, her confidence increased in knowing she could give him as much joy as he was giving her. Marita began to explore him as he was her, working on the last few buttons of his shirt to completely unfasten it, then slipping her hands inside to touch his bare flesh.

"Marita . . ." Rafe shuddered as her hands skimmed over his bared chest and shoulders. Suddenly, he couldn't wait to be free of the tangled shirt. He shrugged out of it as quickly as he could, and he thrilled to her touch as she continued to caress him.

His own hands skimmed over her silken limbs, arousing, teasing, evoking sensual responses in her that she'd never dreamed herself capable of. Her desire was building. She ached to have him near.

Rafe, too, was feeling her desperation to get close. He slipped from her arms and left her, to finish undressing.

"Rafael?" Marita was bereft when Rafe moved away. She didn't understand at first, but then when he started to shed his pants, she understood. She watched, her eyes rounding as he began to unbuckle his belt and rid himself of the restraint of the last of his clothing.

When she spoke his name, Rafe glanced up at her. What he saw in her expression stopped him. There was no doubt in his mind that she was truly unversed in the ways of men, and he knew he didn't want to shock her.

"Rafael . . ." Marita lifted her arms to him and welcomed him back to her.

He went to her without a word, but first he helped her discard the negligee so he could see every inch of her lovely body. She was shy about her nakedness, covering her breasts with her hands as best she could, while she bent one knee to shield the essence of her from his avid gaze, but his next words erased her fears.

"It's all right, love. You're beautiful to look at, and

I promise I won't hurt you."

Marita's gaze locked with Rafe's and she saw there the truth of his words. Slowly, she lowered her knee and drew her hands away to give him his first view of her nude body.

"Ah, God, Marita, you're gorgeous . . . You're everything a man could want . . ."

He came to her then, his mouth finding hers in a treasuring exchange as he pressed himself forward to sheath himself deeply within her. For a moment, there was pain and she tensed against it, but Rafe kissed her tenderly.

"Easy, love . . . easy . . ." The proof of her virginity was met and done away with, and he claimed her as his wife and lover.

They were one, joined as man and woman were meant to be, glorying in their differences and celebrating their unity.

Rafe began his rhythm. Though at first it was foreign to Marita, his hands at her hips began to guide her, and she quickly came to understand the ways of loving. They soared upward together, straining for that pinnacle of rapture and sharing it in a soul-shattering moment of complete bliss.

Where Marita had thought his first kiss ecstasy, it had been nothing compared to the full beauty of his lovemaking. They lay together, holding each other as their breathing slowed.

"Are you all right?" Rafe questioned, afraid that he might have hurt her. Experienced though he was, he had never made love to an innocent before, and he was a little unsure of himself.

"I'm fine, Rafael . . ." Marita sighed, running a

hand over his hairy chest. Her mother's description of 'nice' left a lot to be desired. 'Nice' didn't even come close to describing what had just taken place here with Rafael.

"I'm glad." He pressed a soft kiss to her temple.

Exhausted by the activities of the day and feeling completely content, Marita rested her head on her husband's shoulder and drifted off into a deep sleep.

Rafe held her close, enjoying the moment of intimacy. He had never known such excitement. Marita was everything he'd ever dreamed of in a woman . . . she was responsive and exciting and beautiful. . . .

With his listing of her fine points, though, reality intruded, conjuring up the one thing he hadn't wanted to think about. While Marita was all those wonderful things, she was also Carlanta's niece.

It was a sobering thought as Rafe lay there with her in his arms. He stared down at her profile in repose. She hadn't been happy earlier in the day, and the terrible thought struck him that Carlanta might have manipulated this entire situation.

Rafe's mind began to race. Could Carlanta have become suspicious of his connection with the rebels and decided to force him into a marriage with Marita so she could spy on him? Certainly, Carlanta had been adamant about keeping him from speaking with Marita before the wedding. Was that because she was opposed to the union and he was forcing her to go through with it? It was an ugly thought, and it left Rafe feeling cold inside, but he knew he couldn't ignore the possibility. He glanced down at his beautiful bride and knew he would have to be very careful.

Slater looked up from where he sat by the campfire as Anna returned from her hut. "How is he?" he asked, his voice flat and emotionless.

"Sleeping . . . finally," Anna told him. "He misses his mother."

"He'll get used to it," Slater returned curtly. "He's a MacKenzie. He'll do all right."

"He's just a baby, Slater."

"He's my son, and I'll raise him as I see fit." His tone brooked no argument.

"What do you plan to do?" Anna dropped down beside him on the ground.

"I'm taking him with me when I leave. He's my child, and he belongs with me."

"What about Francesca?" She was shocked by his plan.

"What about her?" Slater asked with callous indifference. "She's made it clear that she wants nothing more to do with me, and that's fine with me. I lived without her before, I can do it again. As far as Michael goes, a boy should be with his father."

"How will you care for him?" she questioned.

"I'll manage. I always have." He sounded bitter.

"Slater . . ." Anna reached out to touch his arm. "I'll come with you and help you with the baby—if you want me to."

Slater searched her eyes and saw in her gaze that the love she felt for him had never lessened. It hurt him

325

that he couldn't return the same feelings. "What about your life here? What about the revolution?"

"There is nothing here to hold me," she said sadly.

"There's young Estevan . . ." He broached the subject he'd not mentioned before.

"Estevan?" This surprised her.

"He cares about you, Anna."

"Estevan is nice enough, I suppose, but I don't feel anything about him one way or the other. You know how I feel, Slater."

"I know, Anna, and I wish things could be different, but they aren't."

"It doesn't matter. If you want me to come with you and help care for Michael, I will come."

"Is this what you'd really want to do? Spend your life raising another woman's child?"

"Michael is your child, too, Slater."

"If you want to come with me, you can."

"I will."

He fell quiet for a minute before saying, "I can't believe I didn't suspect anything before, and I can't believe that she never tried to tell me about him. I automatically assumed the baby was Carlanta's, and she never said a word to convince me otherwise."

"Would you have believed her if she had? And really, Slater, would you have cared?"

Her queries were pointed and painful, forcing Slater to examine his conscience. He realized reluctantly that even if Francesca had told him Michael was his son, he would have doubted her word. Any trust that had existed between them was shattered, gone forever. There was nothing left of the love he'd thought was theirs except the child, and since Slater

326

planned never to get involved with another woman again, he would take Michael with him.

"I don't care about Francesca anymore, Anna. I want you to make sure she's kept in that hut, restrained and gagged, at all times. I don't want to see her again until the time of the exchange."

"I'll take care of it."

"I'll check with Martinez and find out if you and Michael can board the boat early on the morning of the trade. That way, I won't have anything to worry about except making sure Tebeau and Favre get on board."

"We'll arrange something. What if Francesca doesn't want to let her baby go? What if she causes trouble?"

"What can she do? Michael's my son. She lost any claim she had to him when she started sleeping with Carlanta."

The conversation ended then on that caustic note. Anna moved off, leaving Slater alone. Though she'd gotten no pledge of love or devotion from him, she was certain her future with him showed promise. Since he now harbored no feelings for Francesca, except bad ones, she hoped she might still have a remote chance with him. She would travel to Louisiana with him and care for his child, and maybe some day things would change.

Once Anna had gone, Slater got to his feet and went into the hut to check on Michael. His mood was troubled, and his thoughts were running deep as he stood there in the darkness staring down at his sleeping son. It was all still too new for him to completely grasp it. This was his child. This baby had been born from his seed. This boy was a MacKenzie. . . .

Slater studied Michael, committing to memory the sight of him lying there looking so innocent and so precious. Michael made a soft sound in his sleep, almost a forlorn little whimper of loneliness, and something stirred within the hardness of Slater's heart. He reached out gently to touch his son's soft cheek and then one of his little hands, and he was surprised when Michael's tiny fist gripped his finger.

Slater went still. He found he was unable to move as he gazed down at that small hand holding so tightly to his one single finger. A fierce need to protect this child surged through him as father and son bonded without words. He remained where he was for some time, watching and guarding, and Slater learned for the first time the power of a father's love for his own.

In the darkness of the stifling hut, Francesca lay upon the bed, her wrists tied behind her back, her ankles bound, a gag stuffed tightly in her mouth. She wished she were dead. She had nothing left to live for, nothing to care for, no reason to go on. Slater had taken her baby, and now she had nothing left.

Francesca didn't understand Slater's anger over Michael. Her father had told him of his birth and he'd refused to acknowledge them. Now, suddenly he was furious. It made no sense.

Francesca wanted to ask Slater why he cared now

after all this time, but gagged and bound as she was, she would never get the chance. She'd overheard the guard talking that it was only a few more days until the exchange was made. She didn't know who or what they were exchanging her for, and she didn't care. All she wanted was to get her baby back. As much as she'd complained about the hut, she would have preferred eternity with Michael in the miserable, little windowless hut, than a lifetime of riches living in the most sumptuous mansion without him. Michael meant the world to her. Michael was her life. She couldn't just let him go with Slater. She just couldn't. . . .

Chapter Twenty-Three

It was mid-morning and Ricardo sat in the carriage beside Armando as they rode through the busy streets of Havana, his expression grim. "What do you mean you haven't learned anything yet? This is my daughter we're talking about! Francesca's been missing for days!"

"No harm will come to her. MacKenzie knows better."

"I'm glad you trust him," Ricardo spat out sarcastically. "I don't."

"I never said I trusted him. I just know that he wants those agents, and he's not about to let anything happen to Francesca. She's the means to getting what he wants."

All of Armando's logic still didn't make Ricardo feel any better. "I thought MacKenzie was a dead man? I thought you were going to see that he was taken care of?"

Armando would have gladly throttled the older man right then. He was deathly tired of being reminded of how many times the American had eluded him. "When we are notified of the exact location for the exchange, I will make my final plan."

"Final for you or final for MacKenzie?" he challenged. "The captain-general is not at all pleased with the rumors that are abounding over General Lopez."

"I will take care of it!" Armando snapped.

"I hope so, for both of our sakes."

Armando sat there quietly seething. He did not take criticism well, and Ricardo's comments stirred his ire. If he didn't want Francesca so badly, he might have considered doing away with this man who was a continual thorn in his side.

"What is this I hear about your niece and Rafael Ramirez? Is it true that they were married yesterday?" Ricardo changed the subject, knowing he'd pushed Armando as far as he dared on the subject of MacKenzie for the moment.

"Ah, so the word is out, is it?" He smiled. "Yes, it's quite an advantageous match, although Rosa and I were a bit distressed by the rush of it all."

"It happens in the best of families. Don't concern yourself too much. Ramirez is a good sort, though he's always run a little wild. It's long past time his ways caught up with him."

"Marita's always been the headstrong sort, too."

"Then, I would think they'll do well together."

"Very well, considering the money involved."

Ricardo gave a low laugh. "Almost as well as you and Francesca, when the time finally comes."

"Indeed."

*　　*　　*

Across town in the privacy of his study, Rafe was debating with himself exactly what he should do. He'd wanted to go back to the rebel camp to see how things were going with Slater. According to the note he'd received, the trade for the agents was to take place in three more days, and he wished he could be there and help out in some way.

Rafe scowled blackly. A week ago he could have left for the encampment at any time and not have worried about answering to anyone. But now, his actions and any traveling he did would have to be carefully planned to avoid giving Marita any reason to be suspicious.

Marita . . . The thought of her came gently to him, and his expression changed without him even being aware of it. The serious frown faded to a look of pure enchantment. She'd been so wonderful last night. . . . A rush of heat shot through him as he remembered their long hours of explosive loving. She had napped after their first joining, but later she'd awakened and they'd spent the balance of the night learning more about how to please each other.

Rafe had never experienced anything like it before, and he wondered if it would continue, or if it had been a one time thing. Marita had been practically insatiable. The more he'd taught her, the more she'd seemed to enjoy it. Her shyness with him had melted away, and by dawn she was clinging to him in her passion, encouraging him to take her again. He'd gladly obliged, though it had left him weak and happily exhausted from the pleasure of it all. Rafe was beginning to think that perhaps this marriage wasn't an altogether bad idea, and he was certainly glad he'd insisted on his husbandly rights.

At the sound of a soft knock at the closed study door, Rafe's thoughts were torn away from his memories of the night just passed. He looked up, as he called out, "Come in."

Marita was nervous. There was no other way to describe it as she turned the doorknob and started inside the study to speak with Rafe. Last night had been—well, a revelation to her. She'd never imagined making love to Rafael could be so marvelous. She'd been a positive wanton in his arms, glorying in his touch and kiss. But when she'd awakened and found that Rafe had already gone, she'd been worried. She wondered if she'd done something to displease or anger him. Marita had dressed quickly and hurried downstairs to confront him. She had to know if he hated her for last night or if it had been as special for him as it had been for her.

Marita swallowed, wet her lips nervously and entered the study. "Good morning . . . ," she managed softly when she found herself facing her handsome husband across the width of the room. She had thought him good-looking before last night, but now, today, she found him absolutely heart-stopping.

Rafe gazed at her, thinking her the most gorgeous woman in the whole, wide world. "Are you so sure?" he asked with a slight smile. He was referring to the time for it was well past noon.

Marita's nerves were already on edge, and, unsure of herself as she was, at Rafe's comment, her hopeful expression fell. Tears stung her eyes for she thought he was mocking and belittling what had taken place between them.

Rafe saw the change in her and almost panicked. He didn't know why she suddenly looked so sad and lost, but he knew he had to make it right. He came from behind his desk and took her by the arms and turned her to him. "Marita? What's wrong?"

"I . . . I thought last night was special . . . I thought maybe . . ."

"Darling, last night was special," he insisted tenderly.

"But you said . . ."

"It's long past noon, love. It's not morning anymore. That's what I meant. Nothing else." He took her in his arms and kissed her deeply.

"Oh, Rafe . . . ," she sighed, all her doubts swept away by the power of his love. She looped her arms about his neck, pressing against him, wanting to taste again the sweetness of him.

Without ending the kiss, Rafe reached out to push the study door shut so they could have some privacy. Then, lifting her by the waist, he moved to his desk.

"What are you going to do?" she asked, her eyes widening in surprise at his ploy.

"You'll see."

With one arm, he swept the desktop clear and then sat her down on the edge of it.

"Spread your legs a little, sweet," he encouraged.

When she did as he'd directed, he stepped between them and drew her forward so that she was sitting on the desk and he was standing before her. It was a very intimate position, and she looked up at him a little nervously.

"Rafael . . . What are you doing?" her question was a husky whisper.

"You'll see," he teased lovingly. He undid the buttons of her bodice and freed the fullness of her breasts to his gaze and to his caresses.

It seemed so decadent that she was shocked as well as excited by his daring. "But it's daylight . . . ," she protested.

"I know, I can see you better," he told her, bending to press hot kisses on her bared flesh.

At the touch of his lips on her burgeoning breasts, Marita cried out his name in a passionate gasp. "Rafael!"

Rafe couldn't help himself. He had to have her. He needed to be deep inside of her. As he continued to lave kisses upon her bosom, he slipped one hand beneath her skirts to seek the hot, wet center of her need.

"You can't . . . we mustn't . . ." Marita was panting, scandalized but unable to deny the passion his touch and kiss aroused.

"We can and we must. You're my wife," Rafe's voice was deep with feeling. He could wait no longer then. Brushing her skirts out of the way, he freed himself from restraint and then pulled Marita toward him, linking her legs about his hips. They came together in a perfect blend, hardness piercing softness, and he immediately began to move.

"Rafe . . . Oh, Rafe, hold me . . . ," Marita cried.

He lifted her up so he was holding her full weight,

then turned and braced himself against the edge of the desk as he thrust hungrily into her depths. Marita held tightly to him as his mouth once against found her breast. The ecstasy of his rhythm and the hot caress of his mouth was more than she could bear. She surged against him as her climax wracked her, sobbing his name over and over again. The joy of knowing she wanted him as much as he wanted her sent Rafe's desire spiraling out of control. His own excitement burst upon him, and he clutched her to him, never wanting to let her go, never wanting this to end.

Love weakened, Rafe remained unmoving, his breathing ragged. When finally the world righted itself, he slowly let Marita's legs down, but still he held her close. He almost whispered to her that he loved her, but managed to stop himself. He couldn't love her. Not when she was probably spying on him for her uncle.

Marita couldn't believe what had just happened, and she wondered if all married couples were this way. When Rafe would have finally released her, she gazed up at him, and, framing his face with her hands, she drew him down to her for a kiss.

"Good afternoon, Rafael," she purred in the throaty voice.

"It is definitely a good afternoon," he agreed, amazed at the spontaneous combustion that took place whenever they touched each other. No other woman had ever affected him this way. It was a bit unnerving, but he figured with an inward smile, he could learn to live with it.

"I was coming to see you to see if you'd like to get

something to eat with me . . ."

"Is that all?" Rafe asked as he bent to press a single kiss on the pert crest of her breast.

"Well, I was hungry, and I thought you might be needing some sustenance to restore your strength. I can see I was wrong about that." Her head dropped and she drew a slow ecstatic breath as he trailed his lips over the succulent mound across her collarbone to the sensitive hollow at the base of her throat.

"No . . . no, there's nothing I'd like more than to dine with you . . ."

"Nothing?" she teased as he moved to kiss her once again.

"I can think of one other thing, but perhaps we really should eat first . . ." Rafe slowly rebuttoned the bodice of her demure daygown, then stepped back to adjust his own clothing and her skirts.

"Does anyone ever come in here without knocking?" Marita asked, her expression almost impish as she realized just how carried away they'd been.

"Occasionally, but I do keep a pistol in my desk drawer, love, and from now on, if anyone dares come through that door unannounced while we're so occupied, I'll shoot first and ask questions later."

She was smiling as they headed for the dining room.

The next two days passed in a dreamy haze for Marita. Marriage to Rafael was turning out to be a joyous adventure. He was a delightful companion and a magnificent lover, and to her amazement she found herself falling deeply in love with him in spite of the fears she had that he was the spy. There had been several times when she'd felt so close to him that she'd been tempted to ask him straight out about his involvement with the rebels, but she'd held back.

On the morning of the third day after the wedding, Rafael went out to a business meeting, and rather than stay home alone, Marita decided to drop by her mother's for a visit to let her know how much she was enjoying married life. When she arrived at her mother's house, though, she was told that her mother had been invited to Armando's to join him for the midday meal. Eager to see them both, Marita had her driver take her on to her uncle's.

It was just before noon when Marita's carriage drew up at Armando's house. The driver helped her down, and she went up the walk to the door.

The maid welcomed her happily. "Come in, Señora Marita, it is good to see you again."

"Thank you. Are my mother and Uncle Armando here?"

"Señor Armando is at home, but he's meeting with someone in his study right now. Your mother is not here yet, but she is due to join him for lunch at any time now. Would you like to wait in the front sitting room?"

"That would be wonderful, gracias."

After the maid had left her alone, Marita decided to try to find out just who her uncle was talking with and why. Once she was certain there was no one around to see her, she crossed the hall and stood outside the study door to listen. They had obviously been talking for a while, but she heard enough to worry her.

Armando gave an evil chuckle. "We will give the appearance of following MacKenzie's directive

338

regarding the trade, and the rebels won't realize what's happening until too late. I will meet you at the old Alvarez warehouse at midnight, Manuel, and then . . ."

Just as she was about to hear the most important part, her mother started up the front walk, and Marita had to rush back into the sitting room and pretend that nothing had happened. Her heart was racing and she had a terrible sense of forboding. Something was going to happen very soon! She wondered if her uncle was talking about the missing agents. Had the rebels found a way to make a trade for them? She had to notify Pedro right away, but she feared he might not be back from his visit to his cousin's yet. What was she going to do? How in the world was she going to get away from Rafael to get word to the rebels? Her worries were interrupted as her mother came bustling into the room.

"Marita, darling!" Rosa hurried to hug her. "You look wonderful. Obviously married life is agreeing with you . . ."

"Very much so, Mother."

It was much later that night that Marita's fervent prayer that God show her a way to get a message to Pedro was answered. She and Rafael were lying in bed together, their passion for one another temporarily sated, when he announced, regretfully it seemed, he was going to have to go out of town for a few days.

"When do you have to go?" Marita asked, trying to sound disappointed.

"I'll leave first thing in the morning, and I'll come back to you just as soon as I can."

"I'll miss, you know," Marita pouted prettily as she turned in his arms to lie across his chest and gaze down at him. As he kissed her sweetly, though, she couldn't help but wonder if Rafael's unexpected trip had anything to do with her uncle's villainous plan against the rebels. Marita knew she couldn't waste time worrying about that too much. In truth, she was just relieved that he was leaving so she could do what she had to do.

After a night of love, Rafael rode out the following morning for the rebel encampment, a tired, but happy man. Marita had not questioned his need to go, and his suspicions about her were easing. Perhaps she really had just told the lie to Armando because she wanted to marry him. He knew he would never harbor a bad thought about that again.

Marita waved good-bye to her husband until he was out of sight, then rushed upstairs to dress. She informed the servants that she was going to run an errand and would be back shortly. She directed the driver to take her to Pedro's house, but when she arrived, to her dismay she discovered he had not yet returned. Frustrated, but knowing things could have been worse—Rafe could have been in town—she returned home and began to plan her escape to the rebel camp.

Rafe arrived at the encampment near mid-day, and he eagerly sought out Slater. Though only a few days had passed, a lot had happened, and he wanted to fill him in on everything.

"Rafe! I didn't know you'd be coming back!" Slater came out of Anna's hut to welcome him.

"I got your note and I was worried. I take it things have gone all right so far?"

"Everything went perfectly. I managed to catch Francesca alone and I brought her up here to the camp. Rafe . . . ," he paused as he wondered the best way to tell his friend that he was a father.

"What is it?" Rafe could tell he was concerned about something.

"There's a lot you don't know . . . Hell, there's a lot I didn't know until just a few days ago. Come on in Anna's hut, and we'll have a drink and I'll tell you what I found out."

"I've got a few interesting things to tell you, too," he added dryly, wondering how his friend was going to react to the news that he was now wedded to Carlanta's niece. The sight of the baby playing on the bed surprised Rafe, and he commented, "I thought no children were allowed in the camp?"

"He's mine, Rafe. This is my son, Michael."

Slater said it so tersely, that Rafe knew something was very wrong.

"Your son?" He was stunned.

"Francesca had my baby, and she never let me know." His disgust was obvious.

"Where's Francesca now?"

"We're keeping her safely locked away in another hut."

"Have you talked to her about this? Did she explain any of it to you?"

"What is there to explain? She's always been her

341

father's and Carlanta's pawn. She went along with whatever they wanted." His words were bitter.

"Surely they wouldn't have wanted her to keep your baby, though."

Slater shrugged. "Maybe they didn't care what she did as long as I was out of the way."

"What do you intend to do about it?"

"I'll go through with the exchange. Francesca will be returned unharmed to her father and her lover as planned. But the baby goes back home with me."

Rafe understood the fierceness of his convictions, but he wondered if Francesca, or any mother for that matter, would let her own child go so easily. "Do you think she'll just let you take her baby from her without a fight?"

"He's my baby, too." Slater picked up Michael and cradled him close. He then lifted his glittering gaze to his friend. "If she tries to fight me, she'll lose. She can go back to Carlanta. Hell, I'll even give her a divorce, so she can do whatever she wants. I'm certainly never going to marry again. But she can't have my son. Michael's mine."

Rafe could see the resemblance between father and son. Distractedly, he wondered what a child born to Marita and him would look like. He gave himself a mental shake, forcing such thoughts from his mind so he could concentrate. "There's something I have to tell you . . . ," he ventured.

"Oh? What? Has Strecker been in touch or have you heard something in town that will help us?"

"Not exactly," he hedged, not quite sure how this news was going to sound.

"Then what is it?"

"I got married this week."

"You what?" Slater stared at him in surprise.

"I married Marita Valequez several days ago."

"Marita? Carlanta's niece?"

"Yes."

"But why? I know you were seeing her, but what happened?"

Rafe quickly explained all that had gone on, and Slater listened closely, his expression serious.

"Do you think you were set up? Could Carlanta have been behind it all?"

"The thought has occurred to me," he admitted regretfully.

"You'll have to be careful."

"I know. I told Marita that this was a business trip and that I wouldn't be back until tomorrow."

"She believed you?"

"She had no reason not to. I want to stay and help you with the trade in any way I can."

"The best thing you could do is to get as far away from this as you can. Go back home on schedule. You wouldn't want to risk someone seeing you with us at the rendezvous site," Slater advised. "The rebels need leaders like you. What you're doing in town is more important than any help you could give us tomorrow."

Though he longed to be involved, Rafe reluctantly agreed that Slater was right. "When do you leave?"

"Tonight at sundown. Anna and Michael are to be safely boarded on the ship ahead of time. Then the rest of us will get to the exchange point early so we can make sure Carlanta doesn't try to set up some kind of an ambush."

"And what about Francesca?"

"What about her?" Slater was cold. "She'll be turned back over unharmed, and she can resume her life with Carlanta."

"Are you sure you can just let her go this way? Are all the feelings you had for her really gone?" He remembered far too clearly how deeply Slater had loved this woman just a short time before.

"Any love I thought I felt for her was destroyed the moment I found out the truth. She betrayed me and our vows. She bore my child and would have kept him from me forever. The woman I thought Francesca was, never existed, I was a fool . . . a damned fool. But I'm not anymore."

Chapter Twenty-Four

Disguised as La Fantasma, Marita raced the distance to the rebel camp. Her heart was in her throat as she tried to get there in time to let them know about her uncle's rendezvous set for midnight that night with the man named Manuel. Though her horse was near the point of exhaustion, she pushed even onward, finally reaching the narrow trail that led the last mile to the camp just after dark.

Carlos had been keeping watch, and he stopped her only briefly. "Ah, La Fantasma . . . It's good to see you again."

"Thank you, Carlos. Is Estevan or Martinez in camp? I must speak to them at once."

"Estevan remained behind. Ride on in."

"Remained behind?" Fear struck at her.

"Yes, the others have already ridden out to prepare for the exchange."

Dear God! It was already happening! Was she too late to help them?

"Do you know which hut is Estevan's?"

"Yes."

She put her heels to her mount's sides and galloped the rest of the way into the encampment, reining in sharply before Estevan's abode. The camp was practically deserted. Dismounting, she hurried to the doorway.

"Estevan! I must talk to you at once!"

"Marita?" Estevan heard her call and came rushing outside. He gave her a quick, welcoming hug. "How are you?"

"Estevan, there's no time . . . ," she told him nervously.

"Why? What's happened?"

"Tell me about this exchange."

Estevan filled her in on the details.

"Then we've got to hurry!"

"Hurry? Where?"

"There's going to be trouble of some kind. I overheard my uncle talking to a man named Manuel. He's meeting him at the Alvarez warehouse tonight at midnight. They've got something planned for the time that the trade's supposed to be made. If we hurry, we can still get to the warehouse before they leave! We can stop them before it's too late!"

"I'll get us fresh horses, and we'll go!"

When Martinez had directed him to remain behind, Estevan had been angered, but he'd done as he'd been told. Now, though, he knew he finally had the chance he'd long dreamed of—the chance to redeem himself in his own eyes for his betrayal of MacKenzie the year before. His traitorous action had haunted Estevan day and night since he'd found out what had happened to MacKenzie, and he'd hoped and prayed for an opportunity to make up for it somehow. This looked to be his chance. He would not fail the revolution or MacKenzie again. He brought the horses around, then knowing they were going to need them, he grabbed his own rifle and an extra one for Marita.

As Estevan and Marita rode away at top speed, neither was aware that they'd been observed from the moment of her arrival.

Rafe stood just inside the door of the hut he was using staring after them, and as he did, his heart turned to stone. Marita had been the one he'd seen dressed as a boy in camp that night! No wonder Estevan hadn't given him a straight answer when he'd asked about her identity, they loved each other. He'd just seen the way they'd embraced.

Rafe swore violently under his breath as jealousy seared him. He shook his head slowly, berating himself for his lack of judgment. He had almost thought that he'd fallen in love with her! His handsome face turned to a mask of carved granite as he realized how thoroughly he'd been duped.

Marita had been playing him for a fool the whole time. She'd probably been thrilled when he'd told her he was going out of town, so she could plot her intrigue with her uncle! She was probably using her considerable charms, too, to entice young Estevan to work with her against the revolutionaries.

Pain ran deeply through him, but Rafe knew he had no choice. He had to stop them before anything happened to Slater and the others. Rushing to saddle his own mount, he headed out of camp in pursuit of Estevan and Marita. He spurred his horse to a gallop and charged after the two spies with murder on his mind.

The area where the old Alvarez warehouse was located was dark and deserted. Estevan and Marita slowed their horses to a walk as they approached. They were tired, but gave no thought to rest. Lives depended on their success.

Estevan slowed to a stop a block away from the warehouse. "Marita . . . what do you think?"

"I don't know. It looks so empty . . ."

"You wait here. I'll go check," he ordered, meaning to scout around the building to see if there was any sign of Carlanta or Manuel.

"No. You need me with you. There's no telling what's really going on or how many men are in there with my uncle."

"But what if we run into him? We can't let him know you're working with us!"

"Give me your bandana," she directed, and when he did, she tied it across the lower half of her face as a bandit would. "Now I'm ready. Let's go."

They dismounted and, after tying their horses there out of sight, they took their weapons and approached the warehouse cautiously. At first, there seemed no sign of life anywhere, but then as they moved around the corner light shone from one window. Exchanging a nervous look, they made their way carefully toward it. They moved silently. Estevan went first and managed to get a look inside.

"My God! Tebeau and Favre are in there!" he whispered as he grabbed Marita's arm and dragged her back around the corner out of sight where no one could hear them.

"Both of them? I can't believe it! What luck! I thought they were keeping them separated . . ."

"Who cares? We've found them. Now we can free them!"

"What about my uncle?"

"I didn't see him, just the Americans with two armed guards watching over them," Estevan told her excitedly.

"And there's no sign of Armando or Manuel. They were supposed to meet here at midnight . . ."

"Hold it right there, you two. Turn around, and you—take off the mask." Rafe's deadly, hushed order chilled then where they stood. He had just heard the tail end of their conversation, and it sounded like Estevan and Marita were there to meet with Carlanta themselves.

Both Marita and Estevan did as they were told and then looked up to find Rafe standing nearby, his gun aimed straight at them. They were shocked at being discovered and even more shocked that it was Rafael who'd discovered them.

"Rafe!" Estevan was relieved—for a moment. Then he saw the savage look on the other man's face and knew the icy grip of true fear.

"Rafael? What are you doing here?"

"I might ask you the same question," he sneered. "My precious, innocent bride."

"Bride?" Estevan gave Marita an amazed look.

Marita had no time to explain as Rafe continued.

"I guess she didn't tell you. It is inconvenient to have a husband at times like these, isn't it, my dear?"

"Rafe, you don't know what you're saying."

"I know that I just caught the two of you doing your dirty little work!"

Marita blanched. Her most dreaded nightmare was coming to pass. She had wanted it not to be true, but it was! Rafael was working with her uncle! She didn't know whether to rage at him or break down and cry.

Rafe stared at his wife through a red haze of fury as she stood proudly at Estevan's side. It left him feeling dead inside to know that his worst imaginings had been true. Carlanta was undoubtedly the one who put Marita up to marrying him.

"Wait, Rafe! You don't understand!" Estevan tried to explain.

"I understand plenty. I understand you and my wife are real close, and I understand that you're planning to meet Carlanta here so you can give him information to set MacKenzie up."

Marita stared at him in confusion for a minute. What he was saying made no sense. Why would he be angry with her for working with her uncle, if he was working for him?

"No, you're wrong," Marita spoke up.

"Why don't I believe you? I find you running all over the countryside dressed like a boy and armed to the teeth, and you want me to believe you?" His gun never wavered from where he had it pointed at them.

"Look, Rafe. Marita's working with us, not against us. She and I have been friends since we were children. Our fathers were friends. She's known as La Fantasma among the rebels, and she brings us information whenever she can—*from* her uncle, not *for* her uncle. We've kept her identity a secret, just as

350

we've protected yours."

Rafe lowered his gun as he and Marita stared at each other, their preconceived notions about each other warring with the truth.

"You mean, Rafael's on our side?" Marita asked, stunned.

"Yes, he has been for some time now," Estevan supplied.

"Then you're not the traitor . . . ," she repeated, slowly coming to accept that she'd been so wrong about him. It lightened her spirit more than she could say at that minute, and her heart swelled with love for him.

"You think there's a spy in the camp?" Rafe questioned.

"From what I know, my uncle has a contact among the rebels. He must be with Martinez right now! We have to do something . . . we have to hurry and help them."

Estevan knew he could keep his terrible truth no longer. He had borne it for as long as he could, and he knew it was time. He could only hope they would forgive him.

"Marita . . . I know who the spy is."

"What? Who?" Both Marita and Rafe looked at him quickly.

"If you're looking for the one who betrayed MacKenzie. It was me."

"You?" They were both shocked.

"I'm sorry . . . It was only that one time . . . I never thought for a moment that MacKenzie would be hurt in any way, I just thought Carlanta would throw him out of the country . . ."

Marita could see all the pain and guilt in his features. "Why, Estevan? Why would you do something so vicious when MacKenzie was here to help us with our cause?"

"I was jealous of him, Marita. I love Anna, but she only has eyes for the American. I couldn't stand it, so I sent anonymous word to your uncle about his connections with the American government. I had no idea they would do what they did . . ." He lifted tortured, pleading eyes to her.

"I should shoot you on the spot!" Rafe seethed, knowing the hell Slater had suffered.

"I deserve no less, but if you'll give me the chance, I swear I'll make it up to you and to MacKenzie!"

"How can you make up for the fact that the man's life was practically destroyed?" Rafe demanded hotly.

"I have regretted my actions every day since it happened. I can't change the past, but I can save MacKenzie's life now. Carlanta's up to something, we know that. The two missing Americans are in this warehouse. I just saw them."

"Tebeau and Favre are here?"

"Under guard. Give me the chance to prove myself to you and to the cause. Give me the chance to free the agents and get them to MacKenzie before Carlanta shows up with whatever double cross he's planning," he spoke with such fervor and humility that Rafe was forced to listen.

"Estevan . . ." Marita ached for him. "I have known you since my childhood. I know you are a good man . . . and I trust you with my life." She looked up at her husband, putting a gentle hand on his arm. "Rafael, Estevan made a horrible mistake, and he has begged our forgiveness. We can do no less than forgive him. He is a true patriot. We have nothing to fear from him."

"You trust him, Marita? After what he's told us?" he asked incredulously.

"Love can make people do terrible things as well as wonderful things. I trust Estevan as much as I trust you, Rafael. We must work together, not against each other. Now, let's get the agents freed!"

They debated the best way to surprise them and chose an unlocked window on the far side of the building. Rafe climbed in first, then helped Marita. While they waited for Estevan to enter, Rafe couldn't stop himself from drawing her into his arms and kissing her quickly, but passionately. He stared down at her in the gloom of the dirty old building.

"I want you to stay behind me at all times, Marita. I don't want you at risk."

Her eyes glowed with her love for him. "You have forgotten already. I am La Fantasma."

"You have forgotten that you are my wife. As I recall 'obey' was in the ceremony," he said seriously.

She lifted up on her tiptoes to press her lips to his. "I will be careful, but you must be careful, too. I have no desire to become a widow so soon."

"I'll do my best to make sure we have a long and happy life together." He gave her a crushing hug before letting her go. Estevan was there, sidearm drawn, ready to attack.

They reached the outside of the small office without incident. There was only one door, and they knew they would have to storm it and take the two guards by surprise.

Inside the room, the two hired guns were bored. Though they had only been there an hour, it already looked like it was going to be one long, lonely night. They paid little attention to the two Americans who were bound and gagged and sitting on the floor across the room from them.

"How soon did Manuel say he'd return for these two?" one man asked the other.

"He didn't. He just said they had to ride out to the coast and that they would be back."

"You mean we may end up just sitting here all night?"

"It's easy money, fool," the one guard chided.

"You're right about that. Too bad we can't drink while we're here."

"You know what Carlanta said about drinking. Besides, I heard you only get one chance with him, and I ain't stupid. I'm going to do just what he told me to do."

The other man grunted, having heard the same deadly rumor himself. It wasn't smart to disobey Armando Carlanta's orders.

After telling Marita to stay back, Rafe and Estevan charged the door. The portal shattered on its hinges as they crashed through, guns drawn. The two guards immediately went for their own weapons and were mown down before they could even clear leather.

Tebeau and Favre watched in amazement as, in a matter of only a few seconds, the two men did away with their jailers.

"Rafael . . . are you all right?" Marita was right

there, her own gun at ready, her heart pounding in fearsome excitement.

"I'm fine, love," he answered, putting an arm around her. "Now, we've got to get them out of here fast, just in case someone heard us."

"Who are you?" Tebeau asked, his voice hoarse from lack of use, when Estevan released his gag and untied his hands.

"Names are not important. The only important thing is that we get you to MacKenzie right away."

"Slater came back?" Favre said in surprise as he, too, was freed.

"Yes," Rafe replied. "And he's made arrangements through the rebels for a ship to sail with you on board tomorrow. That's why we've got to hurry."

"Can you make it?" Estevan asked as he helped the two men to their feet.

Their faces were bruised and their movements were stiff and painful from the weeks of abuse they'd been subjected to, but their will to make it never faltered.

"We can make it. Thanks," Favre said ferociously. "Riding to meet Slater will be the easy part. Have you got any extra guns?"

"Here." Marita came forward and handed him hers.

"A woman?" Tebeau and Favre were both shocked to discover that one of their saviors was a female, and a very pretty one at that.

"Women here want their freedom, too," she informed them with pride.

They were hurrying from the building to where the horses were tied, when Rafe stopped Estevan.

"You did well," he complimented him. "Marita

was right about you. You are deserving of our trust.''

Estevan stared at him for a moment, then manage~
a smile. "Thanks. You won't be sorry. I'll make sure
of it."

"I know."

"Listen, considering what Martinez said before, I
think it would be best if you and Marita stay here in
town. I know where the rendezvous point is, and
since there are only three horses . . ."

Rafe knew he was right. First, there was what
Martinez had told him about his being needed in the
city, and secondly, if they rode double they would
exhaust their mounts long before they reached the
bay, and there was no time to get the extra horses
needed. "I know. Take them and go."

They clasped hands, true brothers in their dedication to Cuban freedom.

"Vaya con Dios . . ." Marita bid the three men
good-bye, and she watched from her husband's side
as they rode for the Bay of Cabañas.

For safety's sake, Marita maintained her boyish
disguise as she and Rafe made the trek through the
streets to his home. They moved as quickly and as
quietly as possible, for they didn't want to draw any
notice to their passage. Both were relieved when they
were safely inside.

It was much, much later as Marita lay in Rafael's
arms sated from their wild, unrestrained lovemaking, that they spoke of what had happened.

"The night I first saw you dressed as boy at the
camp . . . That was the night you told Armando we'd

356

been together," he ventured as he caressed her slowly in the afterglow of their love.

"Yes," she confessed in a soft voice. "And that was the night I'd seen you in camp, too."

"But why, Marita? Why did you tell him that you'd been with me?"

"I had told my mother I was ill just to get to go to bed early, so I could sneak out of the house and ride to the camp. She came to check on me, though, and found I was gone. She notified Uncle Armando and he came to the house to be with her."

"He was there when you got back . . ."

"Yes, they were both sitting in my room waiting for me. Trapped as I was, I couldn't think quickly enough. I knew I couldn't tell him I'd been working for the revolution. I had to make up something he'd believe, and since I did care for you and we'd just had lunch that one day . . ."

"You cared for me?"

"Um . . . ," she agreed with a throaty chuckle. "Very much, although I didn't realize how much until tonight."

"How much, Marita? Tell me now," he demanded as he sought her lips in a deeply moving kiss.

"I love you, Rafael, my husband. I love you with all my heart."

He rose over her and smoothed the hair back away from her face as he gazed down at her. "I have never known love so sweet, Marita. I love you, too."

His words so tenderly spoken thrilled her. "I honestly didn't mean to trap you . . ."

"But I'm glad you did . . ." He kissed her again. "If you hadn't, we might never have come together."

"That would have been a tragedy," she sighed as he nuzzled at her throat.

"Indeed."

She slipped her arms around his neck to pull him even closer to her, moving her hips against his in an offer he couldn't refuse. Soon they were caught up in the exquisite rapture of their devotion, and this time their loving and giving was on a different, higher plane. They knew and accepted that they would be one forever, and they knew they would have it no other way. Their fight for freedom would continue, but their battle for love had been fought and won.

Chapter Twenty-Five

The sun was nearing its zenith in the cloudless sky. It was almost noon.

Aboard the good ship Windward, Captain Hall, a tall, dark-haired, bearded man of considerable girth, ordered his vessel be put at anchor just outside the Bay of Cabañas. After having met with Martinez and MacKenzie further up the coast at dawn to take on the woman and the child, the first two of his promised five passengers, Hall had sailed to the bay as Martinez had requested. He had posted lookouts, for his friend had warned him about the danger of the situation, and he waited now for further contact from his friend and comrade in the revolution.

Anna had come aboard the Windward with Michael much earlier that morning. She had taken the baby to the cabin assigned them for he had been crying constantly. When she'd failed to quiet him in the stuffy confines of the stateroom, she'd brought him outside to try to interest him in the activities on the ship. It had pleased her to find that he seemed reasonably content in the sunshine and fresh air, and she was greatly relieved. Anna was having trouble enough trying to keep her mind off of Slater's danger, but if Michael had continued to cry, she was doubtful that she could have maintained her sanity for very much longer.

In the days since Slater had taken his son away from Francesca, the boy had not been happy. Even though Slater had doted on him during his every free minute, it had been easy to tell that Michael missed his mother. Anna hoped Slater was right and that the baby would eventually forget Francesca and adjust to the change in his life. But she wondered if anyone could ever really forget his own mother.

As the noon hour neared, Anna's worries grew more and more oppressive. She knew how barbarous Carlanta could be when he was cornered, and she feared desperately for Slater's life. Anna knew she wouldn't be able to relax until he was safely on board along with the others. She paced the deck in agitation, carrying Michael as she kept her attention focused completely on the bay. Nervously, she watched for some sign of the small craft that would be bringing him to her, but there was still no sign of them anywhere.

"There's some movement on the beach . . . It looks like something might be happening . . . ," one of the lookouts called to her as he watched the activities in the cove through his spyglass.

Anna immediately rushed to his side to borrow the telescope so she could get a better look.

*   *   *

360

"Are you ready?" Armando asked Manuel and Ricardo as they stood together on the top of one of the hills overlooking the cove where MacKenzie had said the trade would occur.

Manuel nodded confidently. "Our men are ready. Their hands are tied loosely in front of them so they look like they're completely restrained, but they can slip out of them in a minute. Their guns are hidden in the back of the waistband of their pants, so no one will know they're armed until it's too late. I've got the burlap sacks ready to put over their heads so MacKenzie won't realize they're not the right men until we've already got him where we want him."

"Good," he gloated. "Ricardo, you know Mac-Kenzie's going to demand to see the men's faces, so when the trouble starts, grab Francesca and get her out of there as quickly as you can. The second you're out of the direct line of fire, all hell is going to break loose."

"It will be my pleasure to see the bastard killed." Ricardo was pleased with the plan. They finally had MacKenzie right where they wanted him.

Francesca was sitting on the ground, her hands tied behind her, her gag still in place. No one had spoken to her since they'd roused her from the hut and dragged her off last night for the cross-country ride, and she was nearly out of her mind with worry about her baby. She hadn't been with Michael since that fateful day when Slater had taken him from her. She missed her son, and realizing how vengefully out of control Slater was, she feared for Michael's safety more than she feared for her own. Her own life was useless without her son. Nothing mattered to her except making sure Michael was safe.

"Well, MacKenzie, it will soon be all over," Martinez remarked as they stood together a short distance away from Francesca.

"The men are all in position?"

"Every one of them. I've got two men guarding the trail, so we can make a quick escape once this is completed, and I've got four more on the hill to cover us. The Windward's in place, and two of the crew are waiting for you with a longboat in the cove. All we have to do is get Tebeau and Favre, and you can be on your way."

Slater nodded his approval. "It feels good not to be slinking off in the dark of night this time."

"You had no choice before. From what Anna's told us you were a walking dead man."

"If she and Nick had been one day later, I wouldn't have been alive for them to rescue me. Carlanta wanted me dead, not just tortured. I hope Tebeau and Favre are in better shape than I was."

Francesca was listening to their conversation, and growing more and more horrified by the minute. When Slater had mentioned sneaking off in the middle of the night, she'd wanted to sneer at him that he was a snake and so he acted like one. But then, as they continued to talk, she slowly came to realize that there was something very wrong here.

Her father had told her that Slater was an agent for the American government, which obviously was true. He'd also told her that they had arrested him and questioned him and then let him go. According to her father Slater had left the country without even asking about her. But now, Slater was saying that he'd been held and tortured and that if Anna hadn't rescued him, he'd be dead.

Someone was lying, either Slater or her father, and despise him though she did, Francesca could see no reason why Slater would lie to this rebel. Still, there was no denying that he had left Cuba without her, had agreed to the divorce, and, until now, he had never made any attempt to contact her. Suddenly, she wanted to talk to him, to ask him questions about what had really gone on that night. There was no chance, though, for at that moment, another man who'd been keeping watch came running up to them.

"They're coming!"

Slater grabbed his rifle and told the rebel leader, "Get her on her horse."

Gagged, Francesca tried to express her need to speak, but Martinez ignored her attempts to communicate as he helped her mount.

"Just sit tight and don't cause any trouble, señora. You'll be back home with your father very soon."

She wanted to scream at him that she didn't want to go anywhere without her baby, but it was useless. She was just a helpless pawn in a very dangerous, very deadly game.

"Thanks," Slater told Martinez as he took up the reins to Francesca's horse and then mounted his own.

Leading her horse behind his, Slater went forth to face down his rivals. He emerged from their hiding place behind the rocks and bushes and rode toward the beach of the cove where the four riders were waiting.

Slater's eyes narrowed suspiciously when he saw that the two agents had been brought in with the bags over their heads. It puzzled him. He let his gaze slide to the two men riding with them. He recognized Francesca's father, then glanced at his companion. Slater was expecting it to be Carlanta, and it wasn't.

For a second, Slater was disappointed that he wouldn't get to see his enemy's face close up when the swap was made. However, when he suddenly realized who the other rider was, he went still in the saddle. A cold, hard knot of hatred formed in the pit of his stomach, replacing any fleeting upset he'd felt over Carlanta. Slater's hands began to shake, and he longed to raise the rifle and open fire without warning. The man riding with Salazar was none other than Manuel.

Slater tightened his grip on the rifle, but did not act. He couldn't. He was not an animal. He was a man, and he didn't want to risk that any others would be hurt . . . Tebeau, Favre . . . and Francesca.

"We're almost there," Estevan encouraged as he looked back over his shoulder toward the two men who were following him.

Tebeau and Favre had talked for the first several hours of their trek from the city to the bay. They had told him everything of any significance that had happened during their captivity. While it hadn't been much, some of what they'd remembered was useful, and Estevan knew he would have to relay it to Martinez as soon as he could. The two worn, exhausted agents had fallen silent after a while though, for they'd needed to conserve their strength. They had not been physically strong to begin with after all those weeks of torture, and the ride was a difficult one.

"Are we going to make it in time?" Tebeau asked.

"I think so." He glanced up at the sun to check its position. "It's just about noon now, and I haven't heard any shots yet. When we reach the top of the next hill, we'll be able to see the cove, and we'll know . . ."

Estevan urged his exhausted horse to an even quicker pace, and they made it to the lookout point just as Slater was riding forward to meet Salazar, leading Francesca's horse. Estevan sized up the situation immediately.

"It's an ambush! Those are Carlanta's men!"

The three of them knew exactly what was going to happen, and they knew they had to stop Slater from being shot down in cold blood the minute Francesca was out of the line of fire.

"Let's ride!"

Tebeau and Favre saw that Manuel was one of them, and they wanted their revenge. The strength that had been failing them returned full force as a surge of adrenalin rushed through them.

They dug their heels into the horses' flanks and charged forward, guns drawn and ready.

Slater's expression reflected none of his inner fury as he drew nearer his adversaries. He looked cool and in charge as he stopped his horse about ten feet away. "Hello, Salazar. Manuel, I always hoped we'd run into each other again."

"So have I," the Cuban said with a wide, cruel smile. His black eyes flashed with arrogance and confidence. "I enjoyed our time together."

His words sent the chill of death down Slater's spine.

"You haven't hurt my daughter, have you, MacKenzie?" Ricardo demanded in outrage.

"I return her to you as I found her," he answered coldly, looking away from Manuel.

"Where's the child?"

"Don't worry about the baby. He's fine."

"The deal was Francesca and the baby for the agents," Ricardo insisted.

"I haven't seen the agents yet," Slater returned. "Why don't you take those sacks off their heads so I can make sure they're the right men?"

From above them, Estevan's cry tore through the air surprising not only Slater, but Carlanta and the others as well. "MacKenzie! Watch out! It's a trap!"

Slater was fast. Dropping Francesca's reins, he lifted his rifle and fired. Carlanta's gunmen were ready, too, and they made grab for their guns.

Ricardo yelled at Francesca as he spurred his own mount away from the deadly action. "Francesca! Kick your horse!"

She didn't even have to bother for as the shooting erupted all around, her horse bolted in fright.

Slater managed to get only the one shot off. He had the pleasure of seeing Manuel blown out of his saddle, before the two men pretending to be Tebeau and Favre drew their guns and fired. Gunfire erupted

366

from all around them then, as Martinez and his men, spurred by Estevan's valiant, timely warning and attack, came to Slater's aid.

Slater was thrown from his horse's back as he felt the slug hit his shoulder and burn deep into his flesh. He wanted to keep an eye on Ricardo and Francesca for they were his one connection to the missing agents. He wanted to follow them to Carlanta, but they had already disappeared from sight.

Bullets were still flying. Carlanta's two hired guns kept up a running exchange of fire with Estevan and the men riding with him as they came swooping down the hill.

Tebeau and Favre had been glad to see that Slater had gotten Manuel. If ever a man had deserved to die, it was Manuel. Cruelty had been his pleasure, and he'd enjoyed every minute of the torment he'd inflicted upon his helpless captives. The Americans continued their pursuit of Carlanta's men as Estevan reined in beside Slater.

"Are you all right?" he asked, worried.

"I'll make it. Just go get those bastards and find Carlanta if you can. We've got to free the agents!" he told him, his jaw clenched against the pain.

"Rest easy. Tebeau and Favre are already free. They're the ones riding with me."

Slater looked up at him with respect in spite of his agony. "Good job."

Estevan nodded, then he wheeled his mount around and joined the pursuit of the fleeing gunmen.

Within minutes, Carlanta's hired henchmen had been done away with, and Estevan, Tebeau, and

Favre returned to join the others in the cove. Martinez and his men had fashioned a bandage of sorts to help stop Slater's bleeding, and though his color was ashen and he felt very weak, the knowledge that he'd gotten Manuel made it worthwhile.

"MacKenzie, how bad is it?" Tebeau asked in concern as he swung down from his horse to check on his friend.

"I'll be all right, now that I know you two are free," Slater replied with a weak half-smile.

"Thanks for coming for us," Favre said. "If it hadn't been for you, we'd still be locked up in a dark cellar somewhere counting the days before they tired of their game-playing and finally just killed us.

The three men who had suffered the same fate shared a look of understanding.

"Do you want to go after them?" Estevan asked. "Carlanta got away, so did Salazar and the woman."

"No, not now," Martinez joined in. "We've got to get these three men out to the Windward so she can sail. The Americans have done what they can to help us, now we must help ourselves. The revolution is in our hands. We will take care of Carlanta and Salazar and their likes by throwing out the Spanish."

A cheer went up from the rebels gathered there.

"Slater, will you make sure that word is sent to us as soon as General Lopez makes his decision?"

"I'll see that Strecker knows the urgency of your need."

"Good. We can ask no more than that. My friend, thank you for your help . . . and your courage. I know this hasn't been an easy thing for you to do."

"No, it hasn't," Slater answered slowly. "But I'm

glad I returned." And he was. Slater knew that if he had never come back, he would have gone on mourning a woman who had never really existed and he would never have discovered that he had a son. The miracle of Michael made the torment of it all bearable.

"Travel safely."

"We will." Slater turned to Estevan and drew him slightly away from the others. "Thank you for the warning. I'd have been dead if you hadn't yelled when you did."

"I was glad I could help."

"Where did you find them?"

"Tebeau and Favre will tell you everything that happened once you're on the ship. Ramirez helped, as did La Fantasma. We were very lucky last night."

"You're a good man, Estevan. I'm sorry about the way things are with Anna."

Pain stabbed at the younger man. He knew Anna was on board the Windward waiting for MacKenzie to come to her. "She is a very independent woman. She must make her own choices. I can't force her to love me." He paused, then added, "Would you tell her something for me?"

"Of course."

"Tell her that I will miss her."

"I will."

The two men shook hands and then Slater made his way, a bit unsteadily, toward the waiting boat where Tebeau and Favre were already seated.

"Adios, my friends," Martinez called out.

The rebels watched as they put out to sea. They remained there on the shore following their progress until they'd seen them climb aboard the Windward. Martinez lifted one hand in a gesture of farewell, then turning away from the sea, he headed back toward his camp. He was ready to continue to battle against the evil government troops and to begin planning for the invasion he hoped would come very soon.

Carlanta had watched as the scene had unfolded below, and though he was annoyed that things hadn't gone exactly as he'd hoped, there was still his other plan—the plan that would now prove MacKenzie's downfall. A thin smile curved his mouth as he watched the boat carrying MacKenzie out to the ship that awaited him. He had suspected that the rebels might try something like this, and that was exactly why he'd instructed one of the government ships to stand guard off the point. MacKenzie and the others would just clear the bay area when his own ship would be upon them. Carlanta hoped MacKenzie enjoyed his watery grave.

Turning away from his vantage point, Armando climbed onto his horse's back and went in search of Ricardo and Francesca. He had not told Ricardo about his alternate plan, and he would do so now with relish. Putting his knees to his horse's sides, he started on the road back toward Havana, knowing he would catch up with them somewhere along the way.

Anna had been watching through the telescope when Slater had been wounded. She'd cried out in horror and frustration over her inability to get to him and help him. When at last she saw him rise and speak with the others for a few minutes before getting in the boat for the trip out to the ship, her relief was immense. Still holding Michael, she was waiting for Slater with Captain Hall when he climbed on board.

"Slater, are you all right?" She wanted to throw her arms around him, but she knew better. She could see that he was pale and shaken.

"I'll make it. It was a clean shot. The bullet passed on through," he told her. "The important thing is Tebeau and Favre are with me. We can sail at any time, Captain."

Though he sounded very brave and in control, Anna could tell that he was in great pain. His coloring was gray, and there was a tightness about his mouth that betrayed the effort he was expending to stay upright.

Captain Hall gave the orders to his crew, then turned back to Anna and Slater. "Why don't you go below? I have a doctor on board. I'm sure he'll be able to help."

Slater nodded, then turned to Tebeau and Favre, who'd followed him onto the ship. "Captain, these are my companions who will be making the trip to New Orleans with us."

"Welcome aboard, gentlemen," the captain greeted them warmly. Calling out to his first officer, he instructed, "Take these men to the cabins we've allotted for them below and extend to them every courtesy."

"Yes, sir."

Chapter Twenty-Six

The Windward had just gotten fully under way when the warning shout went up on deck that another ship flying the Spanish flag was bearing down on them. Captain Hall sent word below decks that all passengers were to stay in their cabins and were not to come topside for any reason until he notified them differently.

Hall was not a man who was easily intimidated, and that was one of the reasons why he'd been as successful as he had been in his business dealings. He always expected the worst and prepared for it. Once he was assured that his passengers were all safe, he took charge on deck, ordering full sail so they could make top speed, and also ordering their guns uncovered and brought to bear on the approaching vessel just in case their intentions were less than friendly.

Carlanta's ship, the Halcon, was definitely not sailing toward them with good will in mind. They were under orders to sink any ship found in the Bay of Cabañas area that failed to stop and allow themselves to be boarded. The captain of the Halcon could see that the Windward was not about to slow her passage, so he ordered his own ship brought about and her guns readied, but he was too late. The Windward was ready for them.

Captain Hall got off a round before the Halcon could even bring her weapons to bear. The shot was accurate and took out the other ship's main sail, sending it crashing to the deck and leaving the Halcon virtually dead in the water. A cheer went up from the deck of the Windward, and they made a sleek, fast getaway. Their next stop was New Orleans.

A short time later when things were calm again, Slater stood at the porthole in his cabin staring out at the blue waters of the gulf. The wind had filled the ship's sails, and they were making good headway toward home . . . toward Highland.

Slater's mind filled with thoughts of his earlier passage to Cuba and his reason for coming. He remembered how compelled he'd been to find out the truth about Francesca . . . and now, he had. He drew a ragged breath. Even though he knew the ugliness of everything, he still couldn't forget the passion that exploded between them whenever they touched. The memory was an ache with him, and Slater realized that he was going to have to learn to live with it. Francesca was really out of his life now—forever.

Turning away from the porthole, he flexed his throbbing shoulder to test it. The movement caused him to wince in pain, and in a way, he was glad for the physical agony. It served as a reminder of all that had happened.

Slater went to stand over the bunk and stare down at the angelic form of his sleeping son. He still had trouble completely accepting the child's existence. Michael was so beautiful—and so innocent—and he wanted him to stay that way. He would do whatever he had to keep him away from Francesca.

Francesca... She slipped into his thoughts against his wishes. He never wanted to say her name, hear her voice, or think of her again. She was back with her father and Carlanta where she belonged. She could go on with her life and do whatever she wanted to do. He didn't care one bit as long as she stayed away from Michael. All Slater cared about now was protecting his son.

Slater had already made up his mind that as soon as they got back to Highland and settled in, he was going to initiate a divorce against Francesca. He still had his pride and honor, and he would not permit her to sully his good family name any longer.

As he contemplated the scandal a divorce would involve, Slater found himself wondering why he couldn't have fallen in love with Anna. Anna was beautiful. She was forthright, intelligent, and fair. He cared a great deal about her, but she had never stirred the same fire of feeling within him that Francesca had. Right now, he found that thought very sad.

The fear Anna had felt during the attack was gone,

and she stood now on deck at the rail of the Windward, watching as Cuba faded completely from sight on the horizon. She was leaving her native land, the country she'd fought for for years, and she was venturing to a new, foreign place to begin a new life. A sigh wracked her. She was excited about going to Louisiana with Slater. She'd always just wanted to be with him, and now she was getting her wish.

Anna tried to convince herself that there was a chance she could still win Slater's love—given enough time and patience. But the more logical part of her reminded her clearly of his blunt honesty when he'd agreed to her offer to come along. He'd made no pledge to her other than friendship. Still, as deep as her love for him was, she held on to a fading fragment of hope that one day he might come to care for her.

Ricardo had given chase when Francesca's horse had been spooked by the gunfire, and he'd finally managed to grab her reins and bring the terrified mare under control. Wanting to escape the deadly shootout, he had continued to ride away from the cove, leading her horse behind him. He hadn't stopped until they were quite a distance down the road that led to town. Only then, in the cover of some trees, did he take the time to free his daughter.

"Francesca, darling, I hope you're all right, but I didn't want to stop until I knew we were safe." He could read the terror in her eyes and wanted to reassure her. "We're fine now that we're away from those murderous cutthroats. Thank God, I got you out of there in one piece!"

The moment her hands were untied, Francesca frantically reached up to tear her gag from her mouth. "Papa, we have to go back!" she cried as soon as she could speak.

"Go back? Are you mad?" Ricardo couldn't believe his ears. He stared at her as if he thought she'd lost her mind.

"Slater still has Michael! I've got to get my baby back!" Her dark eyes were haunted with her maddening desperation to have her son with her again.

"Francesca, you can't go rushing back there!" He wouldn't listen.

"If you won't ride with me, I'll go without you!" She tried to grab her reins, but her father got to them first and refused to let go.

"I won't let you ride back into a gunfight. It would be suicide!"

"I don't care! I want my baby! Slater took him away from me days ago and I haven't seen him since." Tears were coursing down her cheeks. "If Slater gets away, I might never see Michael again."

"Calm down, and tell me, was Michael there with you in the cove?"

Francesca drew a strangled breath. "No, I didn't see him."

"Then what would be the point of going back? You don't know for certain that he's there, and you'd only get yourself killed. You wouldn't accomplish anything."

"But my baby . . . ," she agonized.

"I'm sure Michael's all right. MacKenzie is many

things, but I don't believe he'd hurt an infant. I'll get Michael for you, Francesca, but we'll have to do it some other way."

Ricardo had just finished comforting her, when he heard the sound of a horse approaching. They stayed where they were until he could see who it was. When he discovered it was Armando, he rushed out to wave him down.

"I'm glad I found you. I was worried about you! Are you two all right?" Armando asked, glad to finally have caught up with them.

"Francesca's a bit shaken up, but otherwise we're fine. What happened back there?"

"Manuel's dead and so are the other two men I hired. I don't know who that was who warned MacKenzie and ruined everything, but one day I'm going to find out and then I'll see him pay," he vowed.

"Were those the two agents riding with him?"

"Yes, they were freed, although I don't know how. I had them safely hidden out at the old Alvarez warehouse, and no one knew about it except Manuel and me. Manuel must have told someone else and then they talked," he concluded. "The only good thing to come out of this whole ordeal was that MacKenzie was shot," he informed him with particular relish.

"What?" When her horse had bolted in the opposite direction, Francesca had had no opportunity to see what was going on. News of Slater's injury jarred her. To her dismay, she found herself worried about him. "Is he dead?"

Armando and Ricardo thought she was asking because she hated him and wanted to see him dead.

"No, he's not dead," Armando replied almost apologetically.

Francesca's heart sang at the news, and she fought against the perverse feeling of jubilation. She told herself that she shouldn't care that Slater was alive. He had caused her nothing but heartache and pain. Yet, as she tried to convince herself that she despised him, the memory of the conversation she'd overheard between him and the rebel leader returned. Francesca knew she would have to ask her father about that.

"But he soon will be," Armando added with glee.

"How?" Ricardo was curious. He'd thought the afternoon's plot a complete failure except for getting Francesca back.

"I had a ship posted watching the bay just in case MacKenzie tried to make his escape by sea. Their orders are to stop and board any vessel in the area."

"Then they'll be able to find Michael for me." She rejoiced at that possibility, but felt at the same time a fear for Slater she wanted to deny. Her ambivalent feelings toward him left her deeply confused.

"If MacKenzie has him on the ship with them, they most certainly will. Now, let's head back to town as quickly as we can. They'll be bringing word of their success to me there."

Francesca went along readily without any further argument, believing that she would soon be reunited with her son.

After seeing Ricardo and Francesca to their home, Armando continued on to the warehouse to check on the men he'd left in charge there. What he found enraged him and reaffirmed his determination to put an end to the revolutionaries. He reported the men's deaths to the proper authorities, then returned to his home to await news from the ship.

Armando felt confident that everything was going to turn out just the way he wanted it to. MacKenzie and the other two agents were going to be dead, and if they were dead they would never be able to interfere in Cuba's affairs again. He regretted that he hadn't been able to get any information out of them regarding the invasion he suspected was going to occur some time later that summer. The captain-general would not be pleased with his lack of success, but he hoped killing the spies would keep him firmly in his good graces until he could find out more. Armando passed the evening waiting patiently for the good news he was sure would come at any minute.

Francesca was nervous and upset. When they arrived back at their home in the city, she took only enough time to bathe and change into clean clothing, before rushing downstairs to await word of Michael with her father.

Ricardo had directed the servants to prepare them a meal. Though Francesca knew she should eat something, her stomach was in knots and the very idea of eating left her nauseous. She picked at the food before her, taking small bites and forcing herself to swallow.

"Francesca, you're not eating," he pointed out,

concerned about her. He was afraid that MacKenzie might have hurt her in some way. "Are you not feeling well?"

"I'm just scared," she admitted. "I'm worried about Michael. I don't know what I'd do if something happened to him or I never got the chance to see him again."

Her father leaned across the table to pat her hand with fatherly affection. "You will. I'm sure of it. Now, eat a little something to keep up your strength."

She took a few obligatory bites to satisfy him, then broached the subject she couldn't ignore any longer. "Papa, there's something I need to ask you about . . ."

"Yes?"

"When I was with the rebels, I heard Slater talking and something he said troubled me."

"What was it?"

"Slater was saying that he hoped the two agents he was there to rescue weren't in as bad a shape as he'd been when he finally escaped from Armando." She paused, wanting to see the affect of her words on him, but his expression betrayed nothing. "You told me that Slater was questioned and released and left the island without even asking about me."

"That's true."

"But Slater said he had to escape . . . that Armando wanted him dead."

"MacKenzie's lying, Francesca. He was probably trying to make himself sound more important to his rebel friends. Why would you pay any attention to what he says anyway?"

"It just puzzled me. I couldn't imagine that you would lie to me about something so important, but then I could see no reason for Slater to lie to the man he was with."

"He's a spy, Francesca. He has the ability to change himself and his outlook at will to fit the situation. That's what his kind of men do, darling. He can present one face to one group of people and immediately change and become something different for someone else. Look how he took advantage of you . . ." Ricardo deliberately struck at what he knew was a painful place in her heart.

"You're right . . ."

"Not only that, Francesca, but if what he said was true, why then didn't he ever come back for you? Have you forgotten that he made no effort to find you in all those months? Have you forgotten that he agreed to the divorce and wanted nothing to do with his son? He's only taken Michael now for added insurance in his getaway. I'm sure we'll have the boy back soon. MacKenzie made it clear from the start that he had no interest in his child."

Francesca's grip on the napkin in her lap grew white-knuckled, and she knew she just had to get out of the room. "I think I'll go upstairs and rest for a while. Will you call me the minute you hear from Armando?"

"I promise I will."

The night had come and gone, and there had been no word. Growing concerned, but not overly worried, Armando sent a servant to the docks at dawn to see if there was any news of the Halcon. He returned an hour later with no word, leaving Armando puzzled and wondering if his ship had had to give chase. If that were the case, it might be days before he heard anything. The prospect irritated him, but he knew as long as the final outcome was good, he didn't care. He left for his office on schedule and instructed his servants to notify him there of any news regarding the situation.

It was nearly 10 A.M. when word arrived at Armando's office. He sent his assistant scurrying from the room after he'd shown the messenger in.

"Well," Armando began sarcastically, "it took you people long enough to let me know what was going on. Let's have it. Are the bastards dead? Did you sink their ship?"

The man from the Halcon looked decidedly worried. "Señor Carlanta, the news I bring is not what you expect." He gulped nervously. "It has taken me this long to come to you because the Halcon was gravely damaged."

"Damages can be repaired," he disregarded the man's bad news. "What about the American spies?"

"The other ship fired on us first. Their volley took out our sail. We only just arrived in port a short time ago."

Armando slammed his hands down on his desktop as he came to his feet. Leaning foward threateningly, his face red with rage, he demanded, "Are you telling me the damned Americans got away?"

"We were attacking them as you ordered, but they fired first. There was nothing we could do. We couldn't chase them, and they moved out of range before we could return their fire," he finished quickly wanting to get out of his office.

"They're gone . . ."

"Yes, sir."

"Get out of my sight!" he thundered as close to losing control as he'd ever been.

Armando dropped back down in his chair after the messenger had gone and closed the door behind him. He weighed the news of MacKenzie's escape with the other two agents carefully and decided that while he was angry over their getting away, it really didn't matter much. What mattered was that he had Francesca back. Armando was pleased that MacKenzie had taken his own child with him, and he wondered what the other man had thought when he'd realized Francesca had had his baby and had never let him know. It was satisfying to know that at least that much had hurt the American. He might not have been able to kill him, but he'd certainly killed any love he and Francesca had had for each other, and that was enough for him.

Armando knew Francesca was his now. The baby, whose presence had annoyed him greatly, was gone. Armando smiled widely. It hadn't been a happy thought thinking he was going to have to play father to MacKenzie's brat. Now he and Francesca could start their lives together as if her first marriage had never existed. He grimaced inwardly as he realized that there was still the matter of the divorce. Ricardo's lie about obtaining one wouldn't hold up, but he knew they were inventive enough to work around that one some way.

Rising from his desk again, Armando headed from

his office to inform Ricardo of what he'd learned. He knew Francesca wouldn't be pleased to hear that they hadn't found Michael for her, but he felt sure she'd get over him sooner or later. Besides, they could have children of their own once they were married, and she would forget all about MacKenzie's baby.

Francesca came awake with a start. She was lying on the top of the covers of her bed, fully dressed. She gazed around herself, momentarily confused, then the memories of the preceding day returned. Quickly, she got up and after smoothing her hair back, she rushed downstairs.

It upset her that she'd fallen asleep. She'd managed to stay up way past midnight in her effort to be awake when Michael was returned to her, but some time after two in the morning, she must have fallen asleep. Francesca wasn't sure of the hour now, but she knew it was at least midmorning. Worried, she sought out her father to find out if he'd heard anything from Armando. She hurried down the staircase and heard the sounds of voices as she reached the bottom.

"MacKenzie's getting away really works out quite well, though, if you look at the overall scheme of things," Armando was saying. "I frankly am quite glad that we didn't get the baby back. The thought of raising MacKenzie's child as my own sickened me. I despise the man, and I'm glad he took the baby with him."

"I can certainly understand your feelings," Ricardo agreed. "I've never felt any closeness to the boy.

I hated MacKenzie when she married him, and I was only too glad when he left Cuba."

"Things will work out for the best now. We'll tell Francesca that we weren't able to find Michael, but that we'll keep searching for him. She'll trust us, and as time passes, she'll forget all about him. Once we're married and have babies of our own I doubt she'll ever give him another thought," Armando announced with the arrogance and stupidity of a man who knew nothing about the undying strength of a mother's love.

Francesca stood on the steps, her eyes wide with the sudden understanding of what she'd long suspected was Armando's true nature. She could listen to no more, for worry about Michael consumed her. They obviously were never going to help her in her quest to find him. She was going to have to do it by herself.

Rushing back up to her room, Francesca began to throw a few essential things into a small valise. She had no money, but she did have jewelry that was extremely valuable. Putting the gems in her purse, she decided she would stop and sell it on her way to book passage to Louisiana. With any luck, she would get enough money to live on for some time. Francesca knew she would need it for she never intended to return to her father's house. As far as she was concerned, she was on her own now. Somehow, she would get her baby back and make a life for them elsewhere. They would be happy together, she was sure of it.

Chapter Twenty-Seven

It was almost two weeks later when Slater sat in the parlor at Highland, watching in amusement as Michael crawled about, boldly exploring his new home for the first time. He marveled at his son's curiosity and lack of fear as he checked out everything in the room, and he wondered if he'd been that inquisitive as an infant.

Michael was having the time of his life as he searched the parlor from one end to the other, touching everything he could get his hands on. When he reached the small table closest to Slater, Michael pulled himself up so he was standing, and then looked his father straight in the eye.

Emerald gaze met emerald gaze with the force of a collision. It seemed to Slater in that almost unnerving moment that the boy was passing some kind of profound judgment on him and his surroundings. When Michael suddenly laughed and rewarded him with a happy smile, Slater felt his heart constrict with the great love he felt for him. He was glad they were home at last. He was eager for their relationship to develop and grow, and he could hardly wait until the time when they would be running Highland together.

The Windward had arrived in New Orleans the day before. It had been too late in the afternoon to travel to Highland then, so they had spent the night there at one of the best hotels with the intention of making the trip to the plantation the following day.

Slater had left Anna with Michael at the hotel and immediately contacted Strecker to arrange a meeting with him. Joined by Tebeau and Favre, they'd rendezvoused with the intelligence director later that evening to go over everything that had happened in Cuba. Despite Strecker's protests, Slater had left no doubt that his earlier resignation was permanent.

His business in town completed, Slater, Michael, and Anna had made the trip upriver to Highland first thing the next morning. They'd reached the plantation a little past noon and were welcomed back by an ecstatic Raleigh, once he found out that Michael was Slater's very own son. Anna had wanted to freshen up after the trip, so she had gone upstairs to the room Slater had told her would be hers, leaving father and son alone together for the first time in their home.

As Slater gazed down at his son now, he couldn't help but smile. He picked Michael up and held him on his lap, enjoying the feel of his soft, warm body cuddled next to his. He had never known that the love a parent feels for his child could be so powerful, but it was unlike anything he'd ever experienced before. It seemed Michael was a part of him that had always been missing, and that had been now found. Slater wanted to protect him, to watch him grow strong and healthy under the Louisiana sun and to pass on to him all the honor that was his as a MacKenzie of Highland. He kissed his cheek and then set the squirming bundle of energy back down so he could continue with his daring explorations.

Anna stared about the bedroom that was hers, and she was impressed. She had thought that Rafe and the Valequezes were wealthy, but nothing had prepared her for the glory of Slater's home. It was elegant beyond belief. Her room, with its twelve-foot ceilings and ornate, plaster crown molding, was big and airy and richly furnished. It overlooked the gardens on both sides, and she was thrilled with it. She was on her way back downstairs to tell him how beautiful his home was when she heard them in the parlor. She stood in the doorway to watch them together for a little while before speaking. As she watched, Michael pulled himself up to stand by the sofa and then walked along the full length of it before losing his balance and falling down again.

"It won't be long before he'll be walking, you know," Anna said as she came into the room.

"Judging from the way he's moving around I had that feeling, but I know so little about babies his age."

"I don't know a whole lot either, but I'm sure we're going to find out."

"Raleigh will help us. I'm sure he still remembers what a terror I was when I was small. He'll warn us about what to expect."

Anna nodded, thinking of the elderly servant who

had been so kind to her when they'd arrived. "He certainly seemed excited about Michael."

"It's only been me living here since my father died. I'm sure he's going to enjoy having a youngster around again to liven things up."

"I definitely am, Mr. Slater," Raleigh agreed as he appeared in the doorway behind Anna. "I have luncheon ready for you now."

"Thanks, Raleigh," Slater said as he gathered up Michael and followed the servant to the dining room. He was surprised to see the old chair he'd used as a child positioned right next to his own chair at the head of the table. "You found it . . ." He was amazed.

"And the crib, too. We should have the nursery all set up by nap time," he related proudly.

As Raleigh seated Anna, Slater put Michael in his seat and then sat down next to him. The servant had outdone himself in seeing that foods the boy could eat were provided, and Slater was touched by his thoroughness. He was glad he was home, and he hoped the rest of their life together would be as idyllic as this day had been. He ignored the unwelcome fantasy that teased at the corners of his mind of what it would be like if it were Francesca sitting across the table from him, instead of Anna.

Francesca was sitting on the edge of the bed in her stateroom aboard the ship bound for New Orleans. She couldn't believe how simple it had been to make her great escape from her father. She had left him a short, terse note telling him exactly what she thought about his dealings with Armando and informing

389

him that as far as she was concerned she no longer had a father.

After leaving the house by way of the back door, Francesca had stopped only long enough to sell her jewelry and then had gone straight to the docks and booked passage on the next ship leaving for Louisiana. It certainly wasn't the plushest vessel plying the Gulf trade, and they were scheduled to make one other stop along the coast at a town called Mobile before finally docking in New Orleans. Francesca, however, didn't care. All that had been important at the time had been getting out of Havana as quickly as she could before her father could locate her. She couldn't let him stop her. She knew he and Armando would try, but the only thing she cared about was finding Michael again.

Francesca was as tense as she was bored. It would be at least another three days before they reached New Orleans, and then after they docked, she was going to have the problem of trying to find out just where Slater lived. All he'd ever told her about his home was that it was a plantation named Highland and that it was located upriver from the city.

She remembered reluctantly what her father had told her the other night about men like Slater, that their whole lives were based on lies. She found herself wondering if it anything he'd told her while they had been married had been true. Francesca knew she'd find out real soon.

Nick Kane stared at his friend, his expression a mixture of horror and disbelief. "You can't be serious? Your wife was alive the whole time?"

Slater nodded. He had ridden over to his friend's plantation home to let him know he was back from Cuba and to tell him the end of the story about Francesca. "Yes, all the time I was here, mourning her death, she was in Havana—with Carlanta."

"And she had a baby?"

"My baby . . . my son. I have him here with me now."

"How did you get him?"

"Does it matter? He's mine, and I want him with me. His name is Michael."

"Francesca actually named him after your father?" Nick was surprised by this. It didn't quite mesh with everything Slater had been saying about her having just been using him for her own means.

"We had talked about having children once, right after we were first married, and I had told her if I ever had a son I wanted to name him Michael."

"If you really think she never loved you, why do you suppose she would have named him after your father?"

"How the hell am I supposed to know? If I had ever understood any of Francesca's motives none of this would have happened! I'd have been smart enough not to marry her!" Slater retorted hotly, his temper flaring as Nick threw the same question at him that he'd been wrestling himself.

"Where is she now?"

"I have no idea, and I don't care." He stood up and walked to the open window to gaze out at the lush gardens beyond.

"You may not care about her, but I can guarantee

you that she cares about where you are. There isn't a woman alive who's going to let her child be taken away from her without a fight."

Nick voiced a fear that had been troubling Slater.

"She can't have him back. He's mine. I'll give her a divorce, she can marry Carlanta and she can have all the babies she wants. But she's not getting Michael away from me. She'll have to kill me first."

Nick rose and went to put his hand on his friend's shoulder. "Slater, do you really mean it when you say you don't love her anymore?"

"Yes," he answered a bit too quickly for Nick's satisfaction.

"Have those feelings you had for her just disappeared? A month or so ago, you would have given your life for her. Now . . ."

Nick knew what a proud and stubborn man Slater was. Though Slater had declared over and over again that he hated Francesca while they were talking just now, his friend was very aware of the fact that love and hate were often just a breath apart.

"Yes," Slater finally answered flatly. "Listen . . . I'd better go. Give Jordan my best when she wakes up and tell her I'll see her soon."

"I will. She'll be sorry she missed you. You know how much she adores you, but she hasn't been sleeping well lately because of the pregnancy and she needed to rest."

Slater smiled softly at the thought of his friend's wife. "You're a very lucky man, Nick." Then he was gone.

* * *

Francesca had thought the days on the ship would never end, but just when she was about to go completely crazy, they reached New Orleans. She had been at sea a full fourteen days, and she was thrilled to be back on terra firma. She took a room at the St. Louis Hotel, one of the best in town.

"I was wondering if you could help me with something?" Francesca asked the desk clerk as she checked in at the sumptuous hotel.

"Of course, Miss Salazar," he replied after checking the register to see what her name was. "We're always eager to be of help. What is it that you need?"

"I was wondering if you know of a plantation called Highland, owned by the MacKenzie family?"

"Oh, yes, ma'am," the man offered, eager to please this very beautiful woman. "Mr. Slater MacKenzie is a regular guest here whenever he comes to town."

"Could you tell me the best possible way to get to his home? I'm not at all familiar with the area."

By the time Francesca retired to her room, she already knew what she had to do. She had one thing to purchase in the morning, then she would hire a carriage and driver to take her out to Highland and to Michael. Her resolve was unfailing. Her determination was firm. Somehow, tomorrow she would get her son back.

Armando was a man obsessed. He stood on the deck of the ship making for New Orleans, his black eyes glittering with the power of his near maddening fixation. He was going to Louisiana and he was going to find Francesca.

It had been bad enough when the captain-general had reprimanded him for the damages to the Halcon, but when he'd discovered that Francesca had left Havana and had no intention of returning, it had been too much. No one rejected Armando Carlanta—no one.

It had taken a few days of checking, but he'd finally discovered that Francesca had sailed for Louisiana. He didn't know what had transpired between her and MacKenzie in the rebel camp, but if she thought she was going there to be reunited with him, she had another thing coming. He was going to put a stop to it. Francesca was his.

Armando regretted sorely that he'd been unsuccessful in his earlier attempts to rid the world of the likes of Slater MacKenzie. He realized that it had been a mistake to send others to do his job. If he had taken charge in the very beginning, the American would be long dead and none of this would have happened. He was going to New Orleans personally now to rectify that mistake.

Armando thought of Ricardo then, and a sneer curved his mouth. He'd long suspected, but only just realized, what a fool the old man was. Instead of getting angry when Francesca had run away, Ricardo had broken down. It had aggravated Armando tremendously to think that he had so little backbone, and that was precisely why he had not informed him when he'd left Havana in search of Francesca. He didn't need any interference. He would find her and bring her back.

Filled with a grave sense of purpose, Armando looked forward to his arrival in New Orleans with great eagerness. No one would be expecting him—not Francesca and certainly not MacKenzie. This time he was going to win.

Ricardo stood just inside the door of his daughter's bedroom, looking around at all her things, his heart heavy in his chest. It wasn't often that he admitted he'd made a mistake, but Ricardo knew now that he had. It had been many days since he'd found Francesca's note, and in all that time he'd heard nothing more from her. It was almost as if she'd disappeared off the face of the Earth.

When Francesca had eloped with the American against his wishes, Ricardo had been angry. He'd refused contact with her and her new husband, but he'd never stopped loving her. She was his only, precious daughter. This time, however, everything was different. Her note had jolted him. She was gone from his life completely, and knowing how stubborn she was—a trait she'd inherited from him, he knew she'd meant every word of what she'd written in her note. She would never be back.

Sorrow filled him. He moved across her room to stand before the dressing table and in the mirror there he saw the reflection of an old man . . . a miserable, old man. It came as a revelation to him that his life was nearing its end, and without Francesca there really wasn't anything to look forward to. Since his wife's death, she had been his real reason for living.

Ricardo sighed heavily as he reached down to pick up the small oil portrait of his long-dead wife that Francesca kept there on the table. To this day it still pained him to gaze upon his wife's lovely features. He had cared for her so deeply, loved her so much, that when she'd died he'd doubted he would be able to go on without her. He'd done it, though, but only because he'd had his daughter. Now, however, his darling daughter was lost to him, too, and it was all his fault.

A surge of fierce love swept through him, and it almost felt to Ricardo as if his wife had reached out from the grave and touched his heart. He knew then what he had to do. A proud man would have his pride, but he could also end up very lonely. Ricardo realized that it was time he admitted his terrible mistake. Somehow, he would locate Francesca, and he would beg her forgiveness. He only hoped she could find it within herself to give him another chance. He didn't want to lose her. He loved her.

The scenery along the road that led to Highland was beautiful, but Francesca paid no attention. Her whole being was concentrating on the prospect of finding Michael . . . of seeing him and holding him again. Soon, she prayed, she would be with her son. She wanted him so badly that it was almost a physical ache within her.

"We're almost there, ma'am," the driver called down to her as the carriage approached a tree-lined, shell-paved drive that led off to the right. "Highland's right up this road."

At his words, Francesca clutched her purse even more tightly in her two hands. The last thing she'd done before she'd left New Orleans had been to purchase a small handgun. She hadn't used a weapon often, but she knew how it worked and she'd made sure it was loaded before they'd left the city. She wasn't sure what was going to happen when she faced Slater down, but she was prepared to do whatever it took to get Michael back, and she needed to be ready for any alternative. Francesca wanted her son and she wasn't going to leave Louisiana without him. Slater would have to kill her before she'd ever go away and leave him there.

The carriage made the turn into the plantation's drive, and Francesca glanced out the window just in time to get a look at Slater's home. Her eyes widened in appreciation of the beautiful white mansion surrounded by flowering shrubs and big, moss-draped oak trees that had to have been centuries old.

For a moment, Francesca let herself imagine what it would have been like if she and Slater had been happily married and had returned here to build their life together after his business trip to Havana, as he'd first promised all those months ago. She smiled softly as she fancied being the mistress of this wonderful place, and she knew this was the perfect setting for raising a big family.

The carriage hit a bump in the road, and it jarred Francesca back to reality, and she was glad. She didn't need to fantasize about such ridiculous things. There was nothing between her and Slater. Nothing. The only reason she was here was Michael. If it hadn't been for him she would never have come.

As the vehicle slowed and drew to a stop before the front of the house, Francesca felt a shiver of apprehension run through her. She wished she had some great and devious plan for spiriting Michael away, but she didn't. It occurred to her then that Michael might not even be here, but she pushed that possibility away. He had to be. She had to find him. He was her baby.

The driver jumped down and came around to open the door and help Francesca out.

"Wait here for me. With any luck, this won't take long," she ordered, wanting to be able to leave as quickly as she could once she had her son.

"Yes, ma'am. I'll stay right here."

Reassured on that point, Francesca lifted her head high and started up the walk to the wide, shady gallery.

Raleigh had seen the strange carriage coming up the drive and had had no idea who it could be. Slater had ridden out with the overseer that morning, and Anna was upstairs with Michael. Raleigh watched as the beautiful woman got out of the vehicle and started to come up to the door and he grew intrigued, wondering who she was. When she knocked on the door, he immediately opened it.

"Good morning, miss. Can I help you?" he greeted.

"I'm Francesca Salazar." Francesca was running on pure nerve now. She didn't even wait to see if the servant was going to invite her in. Instinct told her he wouldn't. Instead, using her most aristocratic, decisive manner, she brushed right past him and entered the house. "I've come for my son," she announced with regal impatience. "Where is he?"

Raleigh's eyes grew round at her announcement. This was Mr. Slater's wife! He was stunned and quite unsure about what to do next. "I think maybe you should speak with Mr. Slater about that, ma'am."

Francesca was thrilled to know that Slater was there for that meant Michael had to be there, too. She turned burning eyes on Raleigh with a look that refused to be put off. "I have no desire to speak with Slater MacKenzie. I have come for my child."

"Ma'am, why don't you wait in the parlor while I go get him?" Raleigh asked nervously.

"I've waited too long already," she insisted. Without another word, she moved off down the spacious hall glancing in each room as she went.

Raleigh called to one of the other servants and quickly instructed him to go find Slater. He then hurried after the woman who claimed to be Michael's mother and who was so brazenly charging through Highland on her quest.

Francesca finished her quick check of the downstairs and reached for the railing, ready to start up the staircase to the second floor to continue.

"Ma'am, I think it would be best if you take a seat in the parlor and wait for Mr. Slater to come back. Then you can speak with him." Raleigh tried to sound forceful.

"I told you before—"

"I know, but I can't allow you to—"

Before Raleigh could finish his sentence, Francesca acted. Slipping her hand inside her purse, she drew out the small gun and pointed it directly at him. "I don't want to harm anyone or cause any trouble," she told him, "but I've come for Michael and I mean to get him. Now, just tell me where he is and no one will get hurt."

Francesca saw the fear in Raleigh's eyes and hated the thought that she was the cause of it. She didn't want to hurt him in any way. She just had to have her son.

"Ma'am . . . I . . . ," he stumbled over his words, shocked by the sight of the pistol. He looked from the gun barrel to the wild, desperate eyes of the woman holding the gun and then back.

"Raleigh, I saw a carriage out front and I . . . Francesca!" Anna had glanced outside and seeing the vehicle had decided to come downstairs and see who had come for a visit.

Francesca heard her name, and she looked up the stairs to see Anna standing at the top of the steps. Their eyes met, and it seemed as if time stopped for a moment.

"Anna . . . you're here . . ." was all Francesca could say, and her words sounded strangely sad even to herself.

Chapter Twenty-Eight

"What do you want, Francesca? Why did you come here?" Anna demanded, coming down the steps to confront her.

"I came here to get Michael. Where is he?" she returned, still holding the gun on Raleigh.

"That's none of your business," Anna answered not willing to give this woman anything.

"That's where you're wrong, Anna. It is my business!" she seethed. "I'm Michael's mother. I have every right to him!"

"You forfeited any rights to Michael when you betrayed Slater!" she spat the words at her, feeling protective of Slater and Michael. She wouldn't allow this woman the chance to hurt them ever again.

"I betrayed Slater?" Francesca gave a harsh, brittle laugh. "I think you've got that wrong, Anna. Slater's the one who betrayed *me*. He's the one who deserted *me* when I was pregnant. He's the one who left Havana without ever trying to find me! Don't try to tell me anything about betrayal, Anna. I know all about it!"

"You're insane if you think I believe one word of what you said, Francesca. You see, I know the truth! The real truth! You're nothing but a scheming, deceitful, little liar who worked with your father and Carlanta to set Slater up and have him killed!"

"I did not! You don't know what you're talking about!"

"Oh, yes I do know what I'm talking about. I was there, Francesca!"

"Oh, yes, you were always there, weren't you," Francesca said coldly.

"And thank God I was! If I hadn't been, Slater would be dead right now!" Anna snarled. "It was all part of Armando's plan to stop the revolutionaries at any cost, wasn't it? You married Slater to get the information they needed, then when you got it, they were going to kill him so you wouldn't be saddled with a husband you didn't want. Isn't that true? The trouble was, it didn't work, did it?"

"You're wrong!" Francesca insisted, horrified by the scenario Anna was outlining.

"Am I?" Anna scoffed, her eyes flaring with the deep, abiding hatred she felt for this woman. "I was the one who freed Slater from that dark, dank hell on Earth your darling Armando had locked him in. I'm the one who saved him when he'd been beaten and starved for weeks on end. And while Slater was being systematically tortured, you, my precious Francesca, were sleeping with Carlanta!"

"I was not! I've never slept with Armando! I hate the man!"

"I could really tell that the night of the Valequez party," she sneered. "Don't you realize what you did

402

to Slater that night? He'd come back here to find your grave, Francesca, and . . ."

"He what?!" Her expression reflected the true disbelief that gripped her.

"Oh, come on, Francesca," Anna derided. "You know as well as I do that when Armando couldn't break Slater any other way, he told him you were dead just to see if he could get to him that way! Did you enjoy his doing that, Francesca? Did you get a thrill out of knowing that Slater loved you so much that Armando's tale about your 'unfortunate death' nearly broke him when nothing else would?" she challenged in disgust.

"Slater believed that? He thought I was dead?" Francesca was completely in shock. Her hand began to tremble and the gun dipped slightly as her grasp weakened. Her mind was racing and her thoughts were jumbled. She whispered out loud more to herself than to Anna and Raleigh, "What about the divorce? What about his never wanting to see Michael? Were they all lies they made up to trick me?" She lifted her troubled gaze to Anna's as the truth of her revelations finally came together and made complete sense. "My father told me that Slater had been using me. He showed me a note, and he arranged for the divorce that he said Slater agreed to and signed. He said that Slater didn't care about me or Michael and that he didn't want to have anything more to do with either of us."

"Francesca, there was no divorce. Slater loved you more than life itself. He would never have divorced you."

"Then they lied to me . . . They all lied," Fran-

403

cesca whispered, reeling from the pain of her discovery.

The tension that existed between the two women suddenly altered. Their eyes met for the first time in communication as their suspicions about each other slowly began to fade. Anna saw Francesca as a young woman who'd been victimized by men who were hell-bent on controlling her. She realized that Francesca honestly believed everything she'd been saying was the truth.

Francesca looked at Anna, the woman she'd long considered a rival for Slater's affections, and her heart grew heavy. Anna had been there for Slater. She had not. Anna had saved him from almost certain death, while she had doubted him and believed her father's and Armando's endless lies. It was a painful, poignant moment for her to realize how badly she'd failed her husband. Francesca was choked by emotion as she slowly lowered the gun and set it on the steps.

"I didn't know, Anna. I didn't know any of it. They told me so many terrible things about Slater. I can't believe I trusted them . . ."

For so many months, Anna had despised Francesca. She had hated her with a passion for the terrible things she'd thought she'd done to Slater, but now, seeing the real woman, she finally understood.

"Tell me, Francesca, do you still love him?" Anna ventured as she came down the rest of the stairs to stand before her.

For a moment, their gazes locked. Francesca thought of her time at the rebel camp with Slater, of their passionate lovemaking and of the aching emptiness she felt without him, and she knew the answer.

There was no time for her to admit it, for at that very moment, Slater came charging in through the front door. Having been summoned from his work with news that there was trouble at the house, his expression was thunderous, his manner threatening as he came inside. He stopped cold and stared at Francesca, his eyes hard and icy upon her.

"What the hell are you doing here?" Slater demanded.

"I . . . I came for Michael," she offered lamely, still trying to come to grips with all that she'd just learned. She gazed upon her husband and saw the mistrust in his emerald eyes. Love and tenderness used to glow there, but at least now, thanks to Anna, Francesca understood why the change had come about. So much damage had been done to their love. She wondered if there was any hope that she could save it. She wanted to. Oh, how she wanted to. It was all clear to her now.

"Michael is not going anywhere with you, Francesca. Get out of my house," he ordered brutally. "You're not welcome here."

Anna stared at them. She recalled how upset she'd been over Slater marrying Francesca all those months ago, but now she really knew just how much they truly loved each other, and she knew it was important that they not forfeit that love because of other people's interference.

"Slater . . ." Anna spoke up in a gentle but firm tone.

"What?" He gave her a cursory glance.

"I think you need to listen to Francesca. You two have a lot to talk about."

"There is nothing she could possibly have to say that would interest me in the least," he spit out, just wanting her gone, out of his sight. He didn't want to remember her standing there in the foyer at Highland. He just wanted her out of his life forever.

"Slater, I . . . ," Francesca began, but he wouldn't listen.

"Go back where you belong. Go back to Armando in Havana, or is he waiting outside in the carriage for you?"

Before Francesca could say anything, Anna spoke up again, and this time she was even more insistent. "Slater, I want you to listen to her. She is your wife and the mother of your child."

Her attitude surprised him for he knew there was no love lost between Anna and Francesca. He looked over at her, then turned his narrowed, suspicious gaze back to his wife. "What is it that's so important?"

Francesca cringed inwardly at the hardness of his tone. She knew this was the moment that would determine her future. She had to convince Slater that they'd both been the victims of a terrible, devastating game. She had to let him know that she'd had no part in any of the awful things that had happened to him and that she'd never meant for him to be hurt. She had to make him believe that after all the time that had passed and all the hatred and suspicion that existed between them she really loved him and had never stopped. But would he listen?

She took a cautious step toward him, her hands spread a little in supplication, her smile sweet and sad. Her dark eyes were shimmering with unshed tears, and her voice was filled with emotion as she implored, "Slater, we've both been played for fools. But there's no reason to let it go on now that the full truth is out . . ."

"What exactly is this 'full truth' you're talking about?" he asked skeptically. Though Francesca looked like an angel coming toward him, Slater refused to allow himself to soften. He kept his expression harsh and unyielding in spite of Anna's urgings.

"I think it would be best, if Raleigh and I leave and give you some privacy," Anna interjected quietly, and the two of them made a strategic exit, disappearing into the back of the house.

When they were completely alone, Francesca decided that she'd come this far, she might as well go the rest of the way. She would just be completely forthright with him and pray for the best. Her gaze sought his out and didn't look away as she told him everything that was in her heart.

"Armando and my father were plotting against us from the very start. You know how much they hated it when we got married . . ." She paused, trying to read something in his eyes, but he still wasn't revealing anything he was feeling. "They set out to divide us and conquer us, and they did—almost. Just a few minutes ago Anna told me what really happened to you after they took you from me that night in our hotel room. Until we talked just now, I'd never known any of it. My father told me that you'd been questioned by the government officials and released."

"Oh, I was questioned all right, but I wasn't released," he provided with little emotion.

"I know, now, but at the time my father said you'd packed up your things and left Havana without ever asking one question about me."

Slater shot her a startled look. "And you believed that?"

"I didn't want to, but he had a note written in your handwriting, saying something about 'any connection with the woman down here was only temporary and should be disregarded.' He told me that you were only using me to get entrance into our society and because I was his daughter."

Slater groaned, remembering the letter very well, and wondering how Salazar and Carlanta had managed to intercept it. "That note wasn't about you. It was about Anna. I knew she cared about me even then, but I also knew there was no future for her and me . . ."

They gazed at each other, the concealing veils of lies and mistrust that had existed between them for so long disappearing before the wonder of the truth. For the first time since that night in the hotel room when their world had been torn apart so violently, they understood . . . and they loved.

Francesca took another tentative step closer. "That night at the hotel, I was going to tell you about the baby. That was one of the reasons why I was so upset when you arrived late . . . and with Anna. Then after they'd told me you'd left Cuba, I kept hoping you would come back to me. I kept praying that you'd return for me, but you never did. It wasn't until after I'd had Michael that my father brought me the signed divorce papers and told me that you had absolutely no interest in me or your son. I had named him Michael, so you'd know I still cared . . . I was crushed . . . I was heartbroken . . . It was the most terrible time in my life . . .''

Slater lifted one hand to gently wipe away the crystalline tear that traced down her pale cheek. Her skin was as smooth as he'd remembered it and as soft as silk. "I can't believed the web of lies they created just to keep us apart. Carlanta told me you were dead, Francesca,'' his voice was a gruff growl as he struggled with the turbulent emotions that were filling him. "They told me your death was all my fault for being involved with the rebels. Carlanta kept torturing me, trying to get me to talk, but I didn't . . .''

With a soul-wrenching sob, Francesca could stay out of his embrace no longer. She threw herself into Slater's arms and wrapped her arms around his chest, holding him close. He'd suffered so much, and all because of her! The pain in her heart was almost too much for her to bear. She wanted to hold him and love him until she'd erased all the misery and agony he'd suffered. She loved him! Oh, how she loved him!

"Thank God Anna saved you . . . ,'' she whispered in between sobs of sorrow and sobs of joy. "I love you, Slater . . . so much . . .''

Slater's eyes misted with the force of his emotions. He bent to kiss her, their first truly loving embrace in so long. His mouth sought hers in a devastating mating of their souls. They had been apart, but now they were together, and they would never be separated again. . . .

"I love you, Francesca . . . I never stopped . . ." He crushed her against his chest and held her, unable to believe that this could be happening, unable to believe that his dream was coming true.

They stood in the foyer that way, locked in each others arms, rocking together in an intimate embrace that spoke of enduring love and cherished adoration. They were together, reunited, at last.

Anna took the back stairs to the second floor. Having seen Francesca's desperation to have her son back, she knew the greatest gift she could give her right now was Michael.

She was melancholy as she picked the youngster up from his crib and held him close. She could no longer deny the depth of Francesca's and Slater's love. They were meant to be together, and even in her sadness, she felt great joy for him. Loving Slater as she did, she wanted his happiness more than anything. She was glad now that they had found each other again.

"Would you like to see your mama again, Michael?" Anna asked as she smiled down at the almost-toddler.

Michael gurgled in delight and clung tightly to Anna as she carried him from the room. His eyes were bright and he was laughing happily as they walked down the hall toward the front staircase. She paused at the top of the steps to make sure she wouldn't be intruding at the wrong moment, but when she saw them hugging each other, she knew her timing was perfect.

"I think I have someone here you might want to see, Francesca," Anna offered, now making total peace with her.

Francesca looked up, and at the sight of her son, she began to cry in earnest. She left Slater's embrace, though it was a torturous thing for her to do, and raced up the steps to take Michael from Anna. "Thank you . . . Oh, thank you . . ."

Michael immediately recognized his mother and grabbed her for dear life. He didn't understand why she was crying, but he somehow sensed it wasn't because she was hurt. Instinctively, he put his head down on her shoulder and patted her gently, lovingly with his chubby little hands as she held him to her heart.

Francesca lifted her head and her gaze met Anna's. Without thought, Francesca opened her other arm to her, and they embraced.

"Thank you, Anna. Thank you for everything you've done for me."

"I love Slater and Michael, Francesca. You take good care of them."

"I will," she vowed fervently.

Francesca led the way back downstairs to where Slater stood watching them. His heart was near to bursting with the love he felt for his family, and when they reached the bottom step, he opened his arms and they moved into that protective circle. "I'm glad you made me listen, Anna," he managed.

"So am I . . ."

They moved off into the parlor to be together. Michael quickly tired of the endless kisses and hugs his mother was showering on him, and after a few minutes of such unadulterated affection, he squirmed down from her lap and was off, eagerly exploring again the secrets of the room.

"He's a whirlwind, Francesca. You're certainly going to have your hands full when he finally does start walking," Anna laughed as she watched Michael at play.

"I know, but it doesn't matter. I've missed him so badly, he could swing from the chandelier right now, and I'd still love it," she sighed, still not fully believing the beauty of the moment.

"Don't give him any ideas!" Slater laughed as he charged from his seat on the sofa next to Francesca to snatch a vase of flowers out of Michael's way just as he made a greedy grab for it.

They visited for a little while there in the parlor, but Anna could sense that Slater and Francesca's moods were restrained and still unsure. It was then she realized what she had to do.

"I'll be leaving Highland in the morning, Slater," she announced.

Slater was completely taken aback. "But why?"

She gave him a gentle smile. "Before Francesca came, I could help you. But now there's no need."

"We have plenty of room."

"I know, but you're a family now. You don't need me."

"We'll always need and want your friendship, Anna," Francesca said earnestly, and her heart sang when Slater took her hand and squeezed it.

"I feel the same way about you, but I must leave. I'll go back and see if Martinez can use my help again."

"Be careful, Anna," Slater cautioned. He knew things were going to get a lot worse in Cuba before they got better.

"I will." She left the room, telling them she had to pack, but really just to give them the privacy she knew they so badly needed.

Slater and Francesca sat close together on the sofa as they kept one eye on their wayward offspring. A slight noise at the door drew their attention, and they looked up to see Raleigh standing there, looking a bit uncertain.

"Is everything all right, Mr. Slater?" he asked.

"Everything's wonderful, Raleigh. This is Francesca, my wife. Francesca, this is Raleigh. He runs Highland for me."

Francesca blushed prettily as she smiled at him. "We met before, but I was a little forceful in my introduction."

"The gun?" Slater asked, having seen it in the foyer.

"The gun," she confirmed, a little embarrassed.

"Will you be staying, ma'am?" he inquired, hoping the answer was yes. Having heard the discussion in the foyer earlier, he now knew the whole tragic story of their love and had already decided that things couldn't have worked out better. She was definitely the right woman for Slater. Few others would have had the nerve to do what she had done, but her courage and stubborn refusal to accept the loss of her child proved that she was more than his match. Raleigh knew they would be perfect together.

Francesca and Slater looked at each other and smiled tenderly. "She'll be staying, Raleigh. Forever."

"Then I suppose it would be best if I send your hired driver and carriage back to town?"

"Oh . . . in all the excitement I forgot all about him," Francesca replied, blushing a little.

"Pay him whatever he asks, Raleigh, and send him on his way. His services are no longer needed."

"Yes, sir," he beamed, pleased that things had turned out so nicely. Highland had long needed a new mistress.

Chapter Twenty-Nine

It was nearly dusk and the heavenly scent of flowers perfumed the evening breeze as Slater and Francesca strolled the gardens of Highland, hand-in-hand. The day had been warm, but the night promised to be cool. The birds were singing their twilight song, ushering in the welcome hours of darkness and adding to the serene beauty of the moment.

"You'll never know how often I dreamed of this . . . being here, at your home with you," Francesca confessed to Slater. Her expresson was enraptured as she gazed up at him.

"Highland's your home now," Slater told her, the love he was feeling for her filling him with great joy. She was here with him now, and nothing would ever come between them again. He paused there on the garden path to enfold her in his embrace. "There was a time not too long ago when I didn't think I was going to be able to go on. My life was empty without you. I had nothing . . . I was so lonely . . ."

Francesca wrapped her arms around him and rested her head against his chest. The steady rhythm of his heartbeat reassured her and comforted her. "Michael and I are here now. You'll never be alone again."

"I know," he sighed, looking down at her reverently. "It's difficult to believe that things could change so completely in such a short period of time, but I'll be eternally thankful that they did. I love you, Francesca."

"Kiss me, Slater . . . ," she whispered, and he was more than willing to oblige.

There in the peace of the day's end, they held each other. His mouth claimed hers, and he savored her kiss. It was an enthralling exchange, not meant to arouse, but as much as they wanted each other there could be no denying the flare of desire that ignited with just that touch of their lips.

Francesca tightened her arms around Slater, loving the solidness of him. Tonight, they would be together again as they were meant to be. Tonight, they would make love.

Memories of their heated encounters at the rebel camp made Francesca realize that in spite of all the deceptions and lies that had been forced upon them, they'd been unable to deny the primitive, elemental need they had for one another. Their bodies had known all along what their emotions had tried to deny. They were one.

Slater broke off the kiss when the desire building within him threatened to get out of hand. "I think we'd better go in now . . . ," he told her huskily, his gaze passion-darkened.

"Do we have to?" she sighed, not wanting to be out of his arms for even a minute.

"Yes, unless you want me to take you right here in the garden . . . ," he threatened with a hungry smile.

"As I recall, a little thing like being outdoors didn't stop you the last time," she teased with a throaty chuckle.

Slater looked a little guilty as he remembered their encounter in the rain. "I was out of control that night. But tonight, I want to be in complete command. This will be our first time together here at Highland, and I want it to be special for us."

"It will be."

They wandered back toward the house, their anticipation building as they realized they had the entire night and the rest of their lives before them.

Anna was downstairs waiting for them when they reentered the mansion. Dinner was ready, and they shared the meal together, celebrating their reunion and saying farewell at the same time.

When at last it was time to retire, Anna excused herself and went up first, leaving Slater and Francesca to linger below and enjoy an intimate after-dinner drink. There were no words spoken when the time came for them to go upstairs. Slater just stood and offered her his hand, and Francesca put hers in his and allowed him to draw her to her feet. They shared one single, powerful kiss standing there in the parlor before making their way toward the staircase.

"I'd better check on Michael for a minute first," Francesca said as they reached the top of the stairs.

The servants had outdone themselves putting the

nursery together in such short order. They had even furnished a rocking chair for Francesca to use whenever Michael had a restless night.

Francesca and Slater slipped into his room to find him sound asleep in Slater's old crib. It was a tender moment. They stood with their arms around each other's waists, gazing down at the baby they'd created out of nothing more than their love.

Slater had never known an emotion so fulfilling as the one that swelled through him now. It was a mixture of pride, devotion, and ultimate gentleness. He knew as he stood there that he would give his life, if need be, to keep his wife and his son safe from harm.

A short time later, they left Michael's room to seek out the haven of their own bedroom. They moved slowly to make the pleasure of the moment last longer.

"Do you want some time alone?" Slater asked courteously.

"No. I've been away from you too much already," Francesca told him with a smile. "I just wish I had something special to wear for you tonight . . ."

"I kind of like the idea that you don't . . . ," he growled sensuously, moving closer to nuzzle at her neck.

"Oh, really?" Francesca gave a husky laugh as she turned a little and offered him better access to her throat.

"In fact," Slater continued, "since you didn't bring many clothes with you, I was just thinking that instead of buying you a new wardrobe, I might just keep you locked up here in our room here without

as she clung mindlessly to her husband. Slater triumphed in knowing that he'd satisfied her, and when she finally lay quiescent beneath his hands, he smiled tenderly at her.

"You're beautiful . . ."

"You make me feel beautiful," she sighed softly. "Love me now, Slater . . . Please, love me now."

No longer wanting to deny his own need, Slater fit himself to Francesca. Their bodies joined and he marvelled at the sensation as he moved to fill her. The heat of her body gloved him, holding him tightly within her. The feeling was exquisite as he began to move, unable to resist the driving urge to possess her completely. They surged together in a tempest of need, sharing their love and giving fully to each other. Slater reached his pinnacle quickly, and he, too, knew the glory that had been Francesca's just moments before.

When the intoxicating abandonment of their joining had passed, they held each other tightly. A peace born of contentment filled them. They knew nothing could be more wonderful than their being together again in full love and understanding.

They fell asleep that way, still one in body, and the long hours of darkness claimed the land.

It was late, but Armando didn't care. He left the ship as quickly as he could after it docked in New Orleans. He hadn't slept for days and he didn't intend to start now. There was much he had to do.

Francesca awoke with a start. It was pitch black in

421

the room. Darkness surrounded her, pressing in on all sides, threatening and dangerous.

Francesca lay still trying to understand why she'd come awake. She realized quickly that it hadn't been Slater who'd disturbed her rest. He was slumbering peacefully at her side and had one arm around her waist. Francesca trembled and was stricken by the sudden, deathly fear that there was something evil out there in the night that meant to steal her happiness from her.

Thinking of Michael, Francesca knew she had to look in on him. Slipping from beneath the weight of Slater's arm, she donned her husband's discarded shirt, then left the bedroom to make her way quietly to her son. She crept to the cribside, and some of the tension and worry she was feeling eased when she found him sleeping contentedly in his crib. She watched him for a moment, making certain he was safe, then started back to Slater.

While Francesca had been gone from their bedroom, Slater had stirred in his sleep and reached for her. When he'd discovered she wasn't there, he was jarred fully awake. He was sitting up, meaning to go look for her, when she returned.

"You had me worried . . . ," Slater said as soon as he saw her. "Where did you go?"

"Just to check on Michael . . . ," she replied evasively, not wanting to tell him about her fears. the longer she was awake, the less real they seemed, and yet. . . .

"Was he all right?" he asked, moving the covers aside in invitation for her to rejoin him.

"Yes, he was fine."

Francesca threw off the shirt and climbed in beside Slater. She went willingly into his arms, snuggling up next to him. It distressed her, though, that even the warmth and strength of his nearness couldn't banish her premonition that trouble was coming. She shivered in spite of her determination not to.

"What is it?"

"Nothing . . ." She clung to him, trembling.

"Francesca, talk to me, sweetheart. Tell me what's bothering you," Slater urged gently.

She buried her face against his shoulder as she spoke, not wanting to face the nebulous fear openly. "Everything is so perfect, Slater . . ."

"I know. Isn't it wonderful?" He kissed her temple as he held her protectively.

"It's too perfect . . . ," she protested, unable to put what it was she was feeling clearly into words.

"Too perfect? I don't understand . . ."

"Neither do I," Francesca responded, pulling away slightly to make eye contact with him. "It's just a feeling that came over me a little while ago when I woke up . . . Like something awful is going to happen . . ."

"Francesca, darling, don't worry. We're together now . . ." He gathered her to him, kissing her deeply, wanting to wipe all her fears from her mind. "As long as you're with me, nothing will happen. I promise."

But even as he made that vow to her, Francesca couldn't help but remember that terrible night in Havana. She tried to push the memory from her and finally succeeded when Slater's hand sought the softness of her breast. She moaned softly at his touch, eager for more, eager to know his love again.

Slater moved to her, wanting to erase from her mind any shadows of terror that threatened to mar her happiness. With ardent, provocative caresses, he stirred her passion until neither of them were thinking about anything but their loving union. They came together in a blaze of glory, the firestorm of their desire exploding into splendor and then fading into a golden glow of contentment. Drifting back to quietude, they rested, their passions sated, their needs met. The fear that had gripped Francesca was forgotten in the bliss of their love. Sleep claimed them.

Francesca awoke first the next next morning. The sun was clear of the horizon and she could hear the faint, but unmistakable sound of Michael fussing in the next bedroom.

"Where are you going?" Slater asked as she left the bed.

"Michael's up . . ." She pulled on his shirt again and hurried to get their son. After kissing Michael good morning and changing his diaper, she brought him back into bed with them.

They lay there, enjoying the peace of being together. Finally, though, Slater knew he had to get up. Francesca watched him with hungry eyes as he started to dress.

"I thought we were going to stay here, locked in your room for all eternity?" she asked, giving him an impish smile.

"Don't tempt me. It wouldn't take much to get me back in bed with you right now after last night." Slater thought she looked absolutely breathtaking this morning sitting there in the middle of his bed, clad only in his shirt, holding Michael. Her dark hair was down around her shoulders and there was a soft flush to her lovely complexion. It was a memory he would carry in his heart forever—a mental portrait of mother and son.

"So what's stopping you?"

"Anna's leaving this morning. We really ought to go tell her good-bye."

"Well, if you insist . . ."

He moved to the bedside and kissed her gently. "I do. Would you like a bath this morning?"

"Oh, yes, please," she replied happily.

"I'll send one of the maids to help you."

Anna was already downstairs when Slater and Francesca descended, leaving Michael under the watchful eye of his new nanny. They went in to breakfast together, knowing this would be their last visit for a long time.

"Are you sure you want to go back?" Slater asked, concerned.

"Francesca's here with you now. Things are as they were meant to be," Anna told him with a real smile.

"What are you going to do?" Francesca asked.

"What I have always done," she replied. "I'll work for the revolution. One day, the Spanish will be forced to leave and our country will be free."

"I wish you well, Anna," Francesca said slowly, knowing that the changes she wanted would make Cuba a better place.

"Thank you."

When the meal was done, Francesca went to get Michael. Anna gave him a kiss before starting from the house. Francesca said good-bye to Anna inside and then left Slater and Anna alone to say their own farewells. Raleigh had already seen her luggage loaded into a carriage for the trip to the city, and Slater walked her outside to the vehicle.

"Do you want me to travel with you?" Slater offered.

"No. There's no need. You stay here with Francesca. You shouldn't be apart anymore." She gazed up at Slater, and though she'd vowed to herself she wouldn't get emotional, she couldn't hold back the tears. They had been through so much together, and she loved him so dearly.

"Anna . . . ," he said her name softly as he saw her tears, and he took her in his arms to hug her. "Thank you for everything . . ."

."I'm glad you're happy, Slater." She stood on tiptoes to press one kiss to his lips, then tore herself away from him, fearful that if she didn't move then, she never would.

The driver helped her into the carriage, then climbed into his seat.

Anna and Slater regarded each other through the window.

"Take care of yourself, Slater . . . ," she said in an emotion-choked voice.

"You, too, Anna, and if you ever need me . . ."

She nodded tightly as the carriage lurched to a roll.

Slater lifted one hand in farewell, and he watched until they had driven out of sight. When he turned back to the house, he found Francesca standing on the gallery with Michael in her arms, watching him.

"I love you, Slater," Francesca said as he came up the steps to her.

"I love you, too." He put his arms around the both of them, and they walked back inside.

Anna wiped her tears as the carriage turned onto the main road and started toward New Orleans. She was going home.

Anna glanced back just once, catching a glimpse of Highland through the trees, then turned back to face her future. Yesterday, she had confronted the truth that she would never have Slater's love. The pain still burned in her heart, but she accepted it. Having loved him all this time, it wasn't easy to do, but she told herself that if she couldn't have Slater, at least now she knew the kind of man she was looking for.

Anna's thoughts turned to Cuba and the rebels. She decided she would devote herself to the revolution once again, and perhaps some day she would find the same happiness Slater and Francesca shared. She hoped so.

Chapter Thirty

Armando took a room in a less than prestigious hotel and paid the rent on it for several days in advance. He paced the dingy room in the darkness waiting for dawn so he could go after Francesca. She was going to be his or she was going to die with her lover. Right now, as crazed as he was with his anger, it didn't really matter much to him.

As soon as morning arrived, Armando left the hotel and moved around town asking a few pertinent questions here and there, but never enough to arouse anyone's interest. Without a lot of trouble, he found out the location of the MacKenzie plantation. That done, he rented a horse at the stable, and armed with rifle and handgun, he rode out of New Orleans with murder on his mind.

After Anna had gone, Slater rode out with the overseer again to take care of plantation business. Francesca remained behind, and Raleigh took the opportunity to show her around and familiarize her with the workings of the house so she could assume her role as mistress of Highland. The hours passed quickly as she learned the intricacies of running a large plantation home, and she was surprised when Slater returned for the mid-day meal.

"We'll be having company tonight, love," he told her as they ate the light luncheon together.

"Company? Who?" She was surprised.

"My best friend, Dominic Kane, and his wife, Jordan. You might have heard me mention him before. Nick's the one who came down to Cuba and helped Anna rescue me from Carlanta."

"I'll have to make sure I thank him. When are they arriving?"

"I stopped over at their place while I was out, and I invited them for dinner. Be sure to tell Raleigh so he can let cook know to take care of everything."

"I will."

Blonde-haired Jordan Kane looked very beautiful and very pregnant as she sat beside her husband in the carriage as they made the drive from their home to Slater's early that evening. Her expression was animated as she anticipated the dinner to come.

"This is all so exciting, Nick! I'm so happy for Slater! I can't wait to meet Francesca!" Nick had explained to her all that Slater had told him earlier that day about what had happened between him and Francesca, and she was thrilled that things had turned out so well for them.

"Neither can I," Nick agreed. "The change in

Slater is unbelievable. When we talked the other day he was very bitter about everything that had happened, but this morning when he came by he was just like he used to be. Francesca must be one very special woman."

"So Francesca followed Slater here to get her baby back and that's when they finally talked it out?"

"Yes. After Anna heard Francesca's version of what she thought was the truth, she forced Slater to listen to her."

"I bet that was difficult for him . . . You know how proud he is," Jordan remarked thoughtfully.

"None of that matters now that they both know what happened, and they're happily together."

"You're right," she agreed as the carriage pulled into the Highland drive.

Francesca was nervous as she waited in the parlor for their guests to arrive. She'd never met any of Slater's friends before, and she wondered if they would like her or not. Her selection of gowns had been limited, and so she was wearing a simple but tasteful daygown she hoped would pass.

"Do I look good enough?" she asked Slater as he joined her.

"You look beautiful," Slater assured her as he crossed the room. He knew she was a little nervous about meeting Nick and Jordan, and without another word, he drew her to him and kissed her deeply. "Does that convince you?"

"I'm not sure." She gave him a pensive look, though her eyes were twinkling with mischief.

"Maybe you should try to convince me one more time, just to be certain . . ."

Slater did and when he released her they were both panting.

"Do you think they'd understand if we were late coming down to dinner?" he asked, his eyes upon her with passion's intent as he started to undo the buttons at the bodice of her gown. He had a sudden driving need to caress those silken orbs, hidden now from his view.

"I don't know . . . ," Francesca answered, gasping a little in delight as he slid one hand inside her gown to touch her breast. "They're your friends . . ." The daring thought that they could rush upstairs and make love quickly before their company showed up excited her.

"Francesca . . . you feel so good to me . . . ," Slater growled. He was about to further part the concealing fabric when the sound of the carriage pulling up outside stopped him. "Damn!" he muttered his frustration. "That must be them . . ."

He sounded so annoyed that Francesca just had to tease. "I thought you were glad they were coming over?"

"I am," he sighed. "I just wish they could have been late for once."

He hurried to rebutton her dress and then pressed a quick kiss on her lips. There was a pleasant flush to her cheeks now, and her dark eyes were aglow.

"You look like a woman in love," Slater commented as he slipped an arm about her waist and they walked toward the foyer together.

"That's because I am," Francesca answered softly.

She adored him and it showed in her expression.

Slater opened the door and they started outside to greet Nick and Jordan. Safe at Slater's side, Francesca watched as a tall, dark-haired, good-looking man climbed out of the carriage and then turned to help his wife down. She was surprised to see that the other woman, a beautiful blonde, was very much pregnant.

As they approached each other, Slater made the introductions as quickly as he could, wanting to get them over with. "Francesca, this is Jordan and this is Nick."

One look at Francesca was enough for Nick to know why his friend had fallen in love and why he had mourned her so greatly when he'd thought she was dead. Francesca was ravishing. Ever the gentleman, Nick took Francesca's hand and kissed it, while Slater and Jordan shared a hug.

"I'm glad I finally got to meet you. You're every bit as beautiful as Slater claimed you were."

She colored prettily, pleased by his compliment. "Thank you."

Francesca turned to Jordan then. Though she was warmed by Nick's gallantry, she was still feeling a bit unsure about this woman who was obviously so close to Slater. The moment their eyes met, though, Francesca knew they were going to get along fabulously. There was no guile in Jordan Kane's clear green-eyed gaze, only openness, honesty, and complete acceptance.

"Hello, Francesca . . . welcome to Louisiana," Jordan spoke first giving her a bright smile as she reached out to take her hand. She liked her immediately. "I can't tell you how thrilled we are that you're here."

"You are?" This surprised her.

"Oh, yes. You and I have a lot to talk about . . . ," Jordan confided as she drew her away from Slater.

"Jordan . . ." Slater said her name like a mock threat, but she only flashed him a quick grin.

"You wanted something, Slater, dear?"

"Don't believe a word she says, Francesca. The woman is incorrigible," Slater cautioned good-naturedly.

"I think I like her already," Francesca said over her shoulder as she and Jordan walked ahead of them to enter the house. "How soon is your baby due? Slater didn't tell me you were expecting."

"Men!" she said with an exasperated laugh, resting a hand lovingly on the swollen mound of her stomach. "They never talk about the important things, do they? It shouldn't be too much longer."

"Are you excited?"

"Very. This is our first. Slater told us you have a son . . ."

"Yes, Michael," she beamed, thinking of her baby tucked away safely upstairs with his nanny so they could have an evening of adult companionship. "He's getting close to a year old now."

"Is he downstairs?"

"No, but I can go get him if you'd like?"

"I'd love it."

"I was hoping you would say that. As active as Michael is, we thought dinner might be more peaceful if we kept him up in his room with his nanny, but I miss him already."

"Could you bring him down now? I love babies, and I know I'll especially love yours and Slater's."

"I'll go get him . . ."

Within minutes she was back downstairs with her bright-eyed son in her arms.

"Oh, he's so handsome!" Jordan exclaimed, meeting her at the bottom of the steps. "He looks just like Slater! May I hold him?"

"Of course." Francesca handed him over and was pleased to see that he took to her right away.

"Slater, you must be very proud," Jordan said, glancing over at him.

"I am. I'm very blessed." His answer was heartfelt.

Even Nick was enchanted by the squirming bundle of energy. He and Jordan shared an intimate, knowing look as they imagined holding their own child in their arms.

The men went into the study to talk business for a minute, allowing the women to visit as only women do. Francesca and Jordan wandered into the parlor with Michael and settled in to talk and get to know one another. Jordan found her initial reaction to Francesca had been right. She was a genuinely lovely woman both inside and out. She thought Slater had chosen very well.

"You know," she said confidentially, "Slater was a terror when he thought you were dead."

"He was?" This touched her heart deeply.

"He was inconsolable. He mourned you always. When I think of all those months and how much he suffered . . ." Jordan patted Francesca's hand reassuringly. "He's a wonderful man. Nothing's made us happier than your being together again. Slater's family and so are you now."

"Thank you, Jordan. I love him so much . . . I'm so glad all the misunderstandings are behind us now."

"They certainly are. You've nothing but happiness ahead, I'm sure of it," Jordan told her confidently.

They were called in to dinner then, and Francesca took Michael back upstairs to his room so they could relax for a while. Cook served up her most elegant fare, and it was enjoyed by all. By the time the evening ended and Nick and Jordan were ready to head home, Francesca felt she had known them for ages.

"You must come to our home next," Jordan insisted as they walked out to the carriage. "I'm afraid I won't be able to get around too much longer."

"I'd love it. Thank you."

The two women embraced and a bond of friendship was forged that would last a lifetime.

Francesca stood on the gallery watching their carriage drive off. Slater came to her side and put his arm around her.

"Did you have a good time?"

"I had a wonderful time. Your friends are good people."

"I'm glad you like them. Nick and Jordan mean the world to me."

They smiled at each other and then turned to go back inside. It was late and they were both more than ready to retire. Though Slater had controlled the desire he had for his lovely wife all evening, now that they were finally alone, he could hardly wait to get her into bed.

"I'd better check on Michael first," Francesca told him as they started down the hall toward their bedroom.

"I'll come with you," Slater offered, and they entered the nursery together very quietly for they didn't want to wake him.

Everything was fine. Michael was sleeping soundly. Once they were certain he was all right, they left the room.

Their mood was happy and loving as they stepped out in the hall. The excitement that had stirred within them earlier that evening was now growing feverish. They could hardly wait to throw off their clothes and make love. Slater stopped just outside the door to kiss Francesca.

"I love you," he told her in a low voice, not wanting to disturb Michael.

Francesca smiled up at him dreamily and was about to speak when Carlanta's well-remembered, hateful voice cut through their reverie.

"Very touching, but it's going to be your last."

They both looked up to see Carlanta standing there in the shadows at the end of the hall holding a gun on them.

"Armando!" she whispered in terror as all her terrible fears from the night before came crashing in on her.

"Carlanta . . . ," Slater snarled, facing the man who'd nearly ruined his life. He took a step toward him as he pushed Francesca behind him to protect her.

Armando ignored Slater for the moment, directing his comments to Francesca. "Did you think I wouldn't come after you? Did you think I would just let you walk out on me?"

"Leave my wife out of this, Carlanta," Slater

seethed. "This is between me and you."

"You're a dead man, MacKenzie . . ." Armando's voice was filled with sadistic pleasure.

Slater heard it, remembered it, and realized there was no time for anything but action. He would not let this man toy with him ever again. He knew it was better to die fighting than to stand and be shot down in cold blood. Slater launched himself boldly at Armando, shouting at Francesca to run.

For a moment Francesca was frozen, but the sound of Armando's gun going off jolted her to action. She ran for their bedroom, remembering that Raleigh had put the gun she'd brought with her in a drawer in their dresser.

Slater's attack surprised Armando, and he fired wildly. The bullet went wild, smashing into the ceiling as the force of Slater's assault knocked Armando backward into the wall. The gun flew from his grip and landed some distance away from them. They locked in mortal combat. Both men knew that one of them would be dead when the fight ended.

Powerful blows were thrown. Armando was filled with the driving need to see Slater dead. He fought brutally with all his might. This man had humiliated him time and time again by escaping his best laid plans for his death. This time there would be no escape for him.

Slater was filled with bloodlust. This was the man who'd tortured him. This was the man who'd torn his life apart. He would not stop until he'd paid for what he'd done. Driven as he was, Slater barely felt the other man's punches. He was going to win this time. He could not lose.

Francesca was desperate as she raced into the master bedroom and frantically began to search for the gun. She could hear Michael wailing in his own room, but she knew she couldn't worry about him right now. She had to help Slater. This time she wouldn't fail him. Throwing open drawer after drawer, she dug madly through the neatly folded clothing there until her hand closed over the cold metal of the gun.

Clutching the weapon in a firm grip, Francesca turned, ready to defend her own. She could hear the crashing of the men still fighting in the hall, and she rushed back out holding the gun in both hands ready to shoot Armando. The men were grappling on the floor, though, and she had no chance for a shot right away. She waited for her chance, her hands shaking, her whole body tense.

Slater was a wild man. His training had prepared him for this, and he would not quit. He pinned Armando beneath him and pounded him with repeated, vicious punches until the other man's face was a bloody pulp, and still he didn't quit. Only when the Cuban finally went limp beneath him, did he stop. Slater crouched over him, waiting for him to move, wanting one more chance to attack.

He looked like a savage beast of the jungle, and the raw, unleashed power frightened Francesca. She'd never seen him like this before.

"Slater . . . ," she cried his name in terror, not recognizing him for a moment.

Her cry, plus the sound of the servants as they came running through the house below to see what the trouble was, brought Slater back to reality . . . to sanity. He stood up, staring down at the unconscious man in complete disgust. As much as he wanted him dead, he would leave that to the authorities.

Slater turned his back on Armando and walked to Francesca to hold her. She went into his embrace, sobbing in relief and joy. She still held the gun, but she let her hand drop to her side as she kissed her husband. They clung together that way until the sounds of Michael's continued crying penetrated their thoughts.

"We'd better see to Michael . . ." They gazed at each other in understanding.

Armando had come around. He was still a man obsessed. Seeing Francesca in the arms of the man he hated was too much. As crippled up as he was from Slater's thrashing, Armando went for his gun where it was lying a few feet from him.

"Slater! Look out!" Raleigh had just reached the top of the steps as he saw the stranger reaching for the gun on the floor.

Slater and Francesca turned in unison to see Armando about to swing his gun around toward them. Slater grabbed the gun from her hand and fired.

Armando stared at them, his expression filled with loathing, then he looked down at his own chest and his expression changed to a look of utter disbelief.

"You . . . you . . ." He wanted to revile them, he wanted to spew his hatred at them, but death claimed him quickly and he collapsed back on the floor.

Slater was unable to move until Francesca took his arm and pulled him to her.

"It's over. Now, it's really over . . . ," she said to

him, drawing him back from the darkness and ugliness of what he'd been forced to do into the light of her love.

"Get him out of here, Raleigh," Slater ordered tersely. "Send for the authorities."

Francesca wrapped her arms around Slater and held him to her heart. He held himself stiffly, the gun still in his hand, for a long moment before finally allowing himself to relax. He hugged her close, his chest heaving with emotion. Michael's cry came to them again, and they went into his room.

Red-faced and angry at having been ignored so long, their son stood in his crib glaring at them as they crossed the room to pick him up. Only when he was enfolded in his parents' loving embrace did his crying stop. He gave a small, contented gurgle as he clung to them both. He rested his head on his mother's shoulder as they stood together in the middle of his room, their arms around each other.

Michael didn't know what had happened, and he didn't care. All that mattered was that he felt safe and loved. He was home with his mother and father. He was happy. They were family.

Francesca's eyes met Slater's as they shared the peace they were feeling. In his gaze, she saw the promise of his deepest devotion and everlasting love, and she knew from this moment on their lives would be perfect.

Epilogue

Late August

Marita had been watching and waiting for Rafael to return all morning. The news that had reached them concerning the invasion attempt by General Lopez had been sketchy at best, and they had both been worried about their friends in the rebel camp. Unable to just sit and wait for word to come to him, Rafael had gone out to see what he could learn. Marita stood by the window in the front sitting room now, keeping vigil and hoping the news he brought her when he returned would be good.

It was mid-afternoon before Rafe finally rode up to the house. Marita raced to the foyer to meet him.

"How did it go? What did you learn?" she asked nervously the minute he came inside.

"The news is not good," Rafe replied grimly. Though he'd only heard the government's side of what had happened, it had been enough. He'd seen the grisly proof firsthand.

"What is it?"

"Lopez's invasion failed. He was captured and executed." Rafe chose not to tell her that he'd seen the dead body of the garroted general.

"What of the rebels? What of Pedro, Estevan, and the rest?" She clutched at his arm.

"Rumor has it that they escaped into the hills, but no one really knows. I'm sorry, Marita. I wish I could tell you more." He hugged her, wanting to reassure her about their friends, but realizing he really couldn't offer her anything substantial.

"What are we going to do?"

"There's nothing we can do. I'll get word off immediately to Strecker to let him know. Then we'll just have to sit and wait and pray that we hear something from Anna or Martinez."

They walked slowly back into the sitting room, their moods dark and troubled.

Slater entered his study to find Adrian Strecker there waiting for him. He hadn't seen or corresponded with the man since that first night back from Cuba, and he wondered suspiciously why he was there.

"What do you want, Adrian?" Slater asked without preamble, ready to turn him down on the spot if he'd come to ask his help. He was a family man now. He had no desire to get mixed up in any government business ever again.

"First, let me offer my congratulations on how things worked out for you. I understand you and Francesca are very happy now."

"Yes, we are, but how did you know?"

Adrian smiled. "I have my ways."

"I'm sure you do."

His gaze was solemn as he faced Slater. "I have news from Cuba, and it's not good.

"What happened?" He went still as he thought of Anna and Rafe and the others.

"General Lopez's invasion failed. He was captured along with some of his men, and then he was publicly garroted in Havana."

Slater paled at this news. "What about our contacts there? How are Rafe and Anna?"

"Ramirez is fine and in no danger."

"And Anna?" he pressed.

"We've heard nothing. There hasn't been any word from her or from Martinez."

"Can't you send someone in to check?" Slater demanded.

"You know how these things work. If they're all right, they'll let us know just as soon as they can. We just have to wait."

Slater realized he was right, but it didn't make it any easier. "Thanks for riding out to tell me."

"You're welcome." They shook hands. "I'll send word the minute I hear anything else."

"I'd appreciate it. Anna's very special to us."

When Strecker had gone, Slater debated telling Francesca what had happened. He finally decided not to say anything to her until later that night. They were going to Nick and Jordan's to see their new son, Charles, and he didn't want to ruin the outing.

"Papa?" Michael said his name as he came toddling into his study a few minutes later.

Slater picked him up and gave him a big hug. But even as he tried to distract himself with his son, thoughts of Anna haunted him and he wondered if he'd done the right thing in letting her go back when he could have insisted she stay with them and be safe.

The trip to the Kanes' plantation, Riverwood, was pleasant enough. Slater and Francesca congratulated Nick and Jordan profusely on their beautiful baby, finding the new Kane heir to be almost as handsome as their own offspring.

Finally, late that night when they were lying comfortably together in bed, their hearts, souls, and bodies entwined, Francesca broached the subject of his strange mood.

"Is something bothering you? You've seemed distant all day," she asked, kissing his cheek softly as she did so.

It always surprised him that she could read his moods so well, though after all this time he realized it shouldn't. "I've had something on my mind . . ."

"Do you want to talk about it?" Francesca offered.

"I think it's something you'd want to know."

"What?"

"General Lopez invaded Cuba a few weeks ago."

"What happened?" Her eyes rounded at the news.

"His attempt to stir up a full-fledged revolt failed. He was killed and so were most of his men."

"What about Anna?" As Francesca voiced her concern about the young woman, she couldn't stop herself from wondering about her father too.

"No one knows yet."

"How long will we have to wait before we hear something?"

"I don't know, and that's what's been troubling me all night. If I'd forced her to stay here with us, she'd be fine right now."

Francesca understood what he was feeling, but she called him on it. "Now, you and I both know that Anna would have stayed if she'd wanted to. She's a very strong-willed woman. She wanted to go back to Cuba, and no one could have stopped her."

Slater considered her words and knew she was right. He pulled her close and kissed her. "Thanks."

"You're welcome."

They kissed again, and their worries were swept away by the tide of their desire.

It was almost two full weeks before the messenger rode up to Highland. Raleigh answered his knock.

"I have a letter here for Mr. Slater MacKenzie," the man announced.

"I'll give it to him," Raleigh offered.

"No, sir, I have to hand deliver it."

"All right. He's here in the study." He led the way to where Slater was busy at work on the plantation's books. "There's a gentleman here with a message for you."

"Yes?"

"It's from Mr. Strecker, sir." He handed the envelope to Slater, and Raleigh showed him out.

Slater ripped the letter open and quickly scanned the contents.

Slater—
Word has come that most of the rebels from the

camp made it into the hills and were not captured. Anna is safe.

Strecker

There was also another small note inside, and this one was from Anna.

Slater and Francesca—
Estevan and I made it into the country. We are safe and happy. Slater, you were right.

Love,
Anna

He smiled to himself, pleased that she'd given the young man a chance.

"Slater?"

He looked up to see Francesca standing in the doorway holding Michael and looking very worried.

"Is it news about Anna?" she asked, trying to read his expression.

"Yes," he answered, smiling broadly as he went to her. "And she's fine."

"Thank God!" Francesca replied as she put Michael down and went into his arms.

They embraced, happy and relieved to know Anna was safe.

"She's with Estevan now, and from the way things sound, I think they're getting along quite well."

"I'm glad. She deserves her happiness."

"We've certainly found ours, haven't we?" Slater asked as he kissed her tenderly.

"I never dreamed I could be this happy." She lifted her glowing eyes to gaze up at him lovingly. "I love you, Slater. You and Michael are my whole world."

"As you are mine."

"I couldn't live without you, you know."

Slater held her near as he promised, "You'll never have to."

They both looked down at Michael as he played beside them on the floor, their expressions mirroring the deep love they felt for him. He happened to look up at them at the very same time, and he gave a happy laugh as he smiled at them in beautiful, perfect innocence. Their life at Highland was wonderful, and they knew it could only get better.

In Havana, Ricardo sat at his desk, a frown creasing his brow as he tried to decide what to do. He'd finally discovered where Francesca had gone, and now after all these months and all that had happened, he knew it was time. He could delay no longer. With an unsteady hand and humble heart, he picked up his pen and began to write:

My dearest Francesca . . .